Expanded Praise for *Artist, Lo*

"Cleverly imaginative and riveting from beginning to end, Sheila Sharpe's thoroughly engaging story delivers the reader into the taut, mysterious world of the master art forger Nick McCoy. Fleshed out smartly with engaging characters both lovable and despicable, the ingenious plot is a catch-me-if-you-can story with multiple twists, the tale at once suspenseful, inventive, humorous and disturbing. You'll find yourself accelerating towards a riveting, unexpected finale, one crafted by a skilled writer very much at the top of her game."

—Chuck Weikert, author of *Coral Reef Curiosities*

"With razor-sharp psychological insight and an insider's look at the often-brutal machinations of the art world, author Sheila Sharpe reveals a world where nothing is as it seems and where questioning authenticity—be it of a work of art or a person—can come with deadly consequences. *Artist, Lover, Forger, Thief,* with its surprising twists and turns follows the story of therapist Kate O'Dade and her most intriguing client, infamous forger Nick McCoy. It's a thrilling ride from Southern California on the brink of fire season to London with its storied history of famous forgers where Kate and Nick will fight for their lives in this ruthless world of avarice and deception."

—Lisa Fugard, author of *Skinner's Drift*, a NY Times Notable Book and *21 Days to Awaken the Writer Within*

"Sheila Sharpe's beautifully written art crime novel takes us on a twist-filled, heart-pounding ride through the dark underworld of art forgery, theft, and murder. With her background in art and psychology, she expertly imbues her art forger and therapist protagonists with uncommon depth and nuance, giving them an unforgettable villain to combat. Her clinically honed grasp of the complexities of being human provides us with a multi-layered story and uniquely authentic characters who elicit our sympathy, outrage, and fear, sometimes all on the same page."

—Allan E. Mallinger, M.D., Psychiatrist, author (with Jeannette DeWyze) of *Too Perfect: When Being in Control Gets Out of Control*

"Fasten your seat belt as you dive into the fascinating and complicated world of Nick McCoy, a respected art conservator who is also an undercover art forger on the precipice of being caught. Part psychological thriller and part love story, Sheila Sharpe takes us into the high stakes world of art forgery and weaves a tale of intrigue, revenge, and murder. A fast-paced and captivating page turner that reverberates with psychological and social relevance."

—Susan Pohlman, author of *Halfway to Each Other* and *A Time to Seek*

"An entertaining read revealing the underbelly of the art world. Complex layers are pulled back as the characters are propelled toward an unexpected conclusion with well-executed twists in their stories."

—Linda Moore, author of award-winning novel, *Five Days in Bogotá*

Artist, Lover, Forger, Thief

Artist, Lover, Forger, Thief

A KATE O'DADE ART CRIME NOVEL

SHEILA SHARPE

Redwood Publishing

Copyright © 2025 Sheila Sharpe

All rights reserved. No part of this publication may be reproduced, distributed, or transmitted in any form or by any means, including photocopying, recording, or other electronic or mechanical methods, without the prior written permission of the publisher, except as permitted by US copyright law.

Published by
Redwood Publishing, LLC (Orange County, CA)
www.redwooddigitalpublishing.com

ISBN: 978-1-966333-95-1 (hardcover)
ISBN: 978-1-966333-14-2 (paperback)
ISBN: 978-1-966333-15-9 (e-book)
Library of Congress Control Number: 2025903272

Cover Design: Michelle Manley, GraphiqueDesigns
Cover Image: *The Open Window* by Henri Matisse (public domain work as of 1/1/2025)
Interior Formatting: Jose Pepito

To see the paintings referenced in this book, please visit: **SheilaSharpe.com/copy-of-art-2**

For Michael and Colin

Illusion is the first of all pleasures.
—VOLTAIRE

*One sees what one wants to see.
It is false, and that falsity is the
foundation of art.*
—EDGAR DEGAS

Art is what you can get away with.
—ANDY WARHOL

PART I

SAN DIEGO, CALIFORNIA

CHAPTER 1

A bad forgery's the ultimate insult.
—John Grant—

San Diego, Tuesday, October 9, 2018

When Nick McCoy spotted the nude reclining on the red divan across the spacious gallery, his heartbeat quickened. As he moved closer to the propped-up painting, his excitement fizzled.

"Ninety-five million for this babe?" Steele asked.

Nick glanced from the nude displayed on the easel to his wealthiest client. Squat, with a lumpy bald head and shrewd pinpoint eyes, Dixon Steele was the worst kind of crook—a hedge fund billionaire. As his art adviser, Nick was tempted to stick the old vulture with the mediocre forgery, but that might endanger his larger scheme.

"Is she worth it?" Steele asked.

"Not if you want a Modigliani. Your babe is a fake."

"How can you tell?"

"The low price is a flag, plus Modigliani nudes are rare. One recently sold for a hundred and fifty-seven million. Then there's the artistry, the feeling. Does she turn you on?"

"I'm sixty-eight, young man. Takes more than a plastic babe to move my flesh."

"Plastic—there's your answer. Modigliani was a sensualist. You can feel that in every line, color, and texture of his paintings. This is no Modigliani. It's the plodding work of that phony Hungarian count."

Steele turned the bogus nude toward the wall, then strutted around the gallery, inspecting the gems in his priceless collection. The ass flaunted his ugliness like a weapon; he seemed to get off on repulsing people. Nick found this in-your-face behavior intriguing. It was easy to picture Steele as a boy scaring other kids with his Godzilla act. Nick could have used this attitude to face down his boyhood tormentors. Instead—to his shame—he ran from them and hid in museums until he was old and strong enough to fight back.

He touched his right cheek. Thanks to plastic surgery, the hideous burn scars were gone. All that was visible was a slight discoloration and tightness near his right ear. Some considered him handsome now in an exotic sort of way, but the face he saw in the mirror still looked foreign to him—his black thicket of hair and reddish-brown complexion resulting from Spanish, Black, and Celtic blood. And his old self-image as a freak still haunted him.

Nick shifted his attention to the luminous masterpieces hanging on the canvas-colored walls. He focused on one of Degas's elegant ballerina paintings. The dramatic lighting and glittering swirl of pastels washed over him, lifting him out of his dark thoughts. He appreciated the moments of silence in Steele's soundproof and well-protected gallery. Few would guess that a multibillion-dollar collection was hidden inside a dilapidated barn on a large estate in the elite community of Rancho Santa Fe.

Steele lumbered across his sight line, and Nick got a whiff of his pine-scented aftershave that momentarily overpowered the familiar odors of new varnish and weed.

The collector stopped before his most prized painting, *The Blue Room* by Picasso. Nick sidled up to him and admired the naked beauty giving herself a sponge bath in her shades-of-blue bedroom. She reminded him of Raquel, Steele's wife and his lover. The mere image of his fleshy mitts touching her delicate skin sickened him. He regretted his inability to return Raquel's love, but she would be better off with a man who could give her a normal life. If he could risk loving a woman, it would be his brilliant former therapist who'd made his life-long grief almost bearable.

"Hey Pablo, you're still the cock of the walk." Steele gave the work a thumbs up and kept it up while passing Van Gogh's *Sunflowers*. Then he sneered at the next painting, jabbing his thumb down. "This one's weak. Let's get rid of it."

"Weak? You're looking at one of Monet's famous water lily pond paintings."

"It's too airy-fairy, and there's too much pink. No lovely lilies allowed in the Man's Lair." He thumped his chest. "Listen, my boy, I want to feel young. I need bold, virile paintings around me—injections of vitality. I have a young wife to service."

Nick knew the Monet was a better-than-average fake, and if marketed, could raise questions and put him in the spotlight. So far, he'd managed to elude the authorities after decades of maneuvering and had finally gotten into an influential position as Steele's adviser. He owed Raquel for helping him secure the art conservator job at the Steele Museum, paving the way for his current role as Steele's principal consultant on all his art purchases, trades, and sales. At last, he was in the perfect position to avenge his family, but he had to complete his last scam and vanish before the FBI or Scotland Yard caught up with him. *Don't blow it now!*

Steele usually listened to his advice, but he was fickle and rash and required canny handling. "The Monet is one of your most valuable paintings," Nick said. "Prices are still rising on the water lily series. Might be wise to hang onto it for a while."

"Yeah, I hear you. Let's dump the Braque. I'm done with brown Cubist shit."

Nick stifled a sigh. He was used to Steele playing favorites and suddenly turning on a formerly loved treasure like a petulant child. "This still life looks a bit muddy because it's the only painting I haven't restored in this gallery. Let me clean off the surface grime, then we'll see how you feel."

Steele grunted his assent, lifted the Braque off the wall, and handed it to Nick. "Are you almost done with Cézanne's *Card Players* and Matisse's *Joy of Life* sketch? I've been missing them. They're my family, you know, the only ones I can count on. People never fail to disappoint and screw you over. Am I a cynic or what?"

"I'd say you're a realist, Mr. Steele. I can fix the flaws in paintings but not in people."

"Hey, Nick, you're like a son to me. It's time you called me Dix." He gave Nick's shoulder a heavy-handed squeeze.

A feeling of power surged through Nick. Finally, all his work to win Steele's trust and affection was paying off. He flashed back on Steele's role in the fire that had destroyed his home, his face, and massacred his family. He counted the days until he could break the killer's heart as his had been broken. Remembering his father's courage at the horrific end gave him the strength to put his life on the line.

"If all goes well, uh, Dix, I might be able to get the Braque, the Cézanne, and the Matisse back here in the next few days. The cleaning won't take very long."

"Good. Then the whole family will be together again, all dolled up." Steele grinned, showing off his stump-like teeth.

Steele's childish expression of affection for his paintings unnerved Nick. True love of great art was a strong but unwanted bond he shared with this infantile old man who, at times, seemed a most unlikely nemesis.

"I'll be out the next few nights and a lot of the days," Steele said.

"No problem. I've got the entry codes." Nick cleared his throat, then rolled out the lie. "I'll also need to be gone for a while after completing this job. I've got out-of-town business."

Steele scowled. "That's very inconvenient. What if I need to decide fast on a deal? You'd have to be here to evaluate the works in question."

"Consult my mate, the British art historian at UC San Diego. I'll alert him. He knows the market and has a great eye—almost as good as mine."

"I like your modesty, Nick, my boy." Steele chuckled.

Nick gave him the art historian's card, wrapped up the Braque, and headed for the gallery's rear exit, leaving Dix to spend quality time with his family of masterpieces.

Nick was surprised and annoyed to find the inner steel door unlocked and the outer wooden door open. He never forgot to lock up or guard his back. Other than Steele, Raquel, and himself, only Steele's rotten son, Simon, knew the code.

Nick locked the doors and strode from the cool, sheltered gallery into the dicey world of bright light, dark shadows, and October's hot Santa Ana winds. He picked up his pace. The wind dried up his skin and everything green outside. Wildfires were due to strike. His sensitive radar picked up a more imminent threat. He scanned the surrounding pines and eucalyptus trees, his vigilant eyes alert to any movement in the dappled light. He turned the corner and spotted Simon's red Maserati parked on the gravel beside his dusty SUV. The bloody twit was leaning against Nick's car door, watching him through mirrored sunglasses. Nick preferred Steele's ugly mug to his son's sly-eyed prettiness.

"I heard you in the gallery with Pops," Simon said as Nick approached him. "You really know how to work the old goat, don't you? He swallows any bull you feed him."

"You forgot to lock the doors after eavesdropping. Move aside."

"Make me." He rubbed his puny ass on the car door.

"What do you want, Simon?"

"I want you to leave."

"You're in luck; I am leaving."

Simon kicked the gravel. "Shit, I mean for good."

"Why? You don't give a rat's ass about the art collection."

"It's my inheritance, and I don't want a slick Brit screwing with it. You've conned Dad. He thinks you walk on water, but you don't fool me."

"Likewise." *Shut your face*, he told himself, but he'd had it with this spoiled parasite. "Does Papa know his son uses his allowance to deal drugs and make sadistic porn flicks?"

Simon glared at him through slitted eyes. "Tattle on me and I tell on you. You're screwing his latest slutty wife."

"That's a lie."

"I have proof from a private eye. If you don't disappear, I'll show the PI's report to Pops. There's an obscene shot of you and Raquel shagging at Rosarito Beach."

Fury narrowed Nick's eyes. "You'd like that, wouldn't you, shocking your old man into a heart attack?"

Simon shrugged, smirking.

Nick suspected the cold-hearted bastard's greed included wanting his father dead. Simon no longer had to compete for the inheritance with his mother—Dix's second trophy wife—or his older brother. Nick recalled they had died in a convenient-for-Simon car crash three years ago.

Simon strolled to his car, folded into the low-slung seat, and turned his mirrored glasses on Nick. "Take the slut and get out of San Diego, and I'll bury the report. You have ten days to find another place to squat. Otherwise, I squeal, and you'll be the one who stops Pop's ticker." Simon showed his pointy, little-boy teeth, another part of him that hadn't matured to his thirty-something age. "But if the old cuckold survives, he'll make sure you both croak in the worst possible way. You're screwed, asshole." Giggling, Simon gunned the motor.

Turning his back on the punk's squealing wheels, Nick loaded the Braque into the back of his SUV and then slammed the door, a rush of adrenaline spurring him to run. Old man Steele incited Nick's hatred and contempt, but his psychopathic son scared the piss out of him.

No way could he trust Simon's deal. Most likely, he had less than ten days to pull off an intricate revenge scheme and get out of here alive. He could almost hear the clock ticking.

CHAPTER 2

Good artists copy. Great artists steal.

—Pablo Picasso—

Wednesday, October 10

The next afternoon, Nick opened the door of his conservation laboratory at the Steele Museum and there she was—the woman he desired and feared more than anyone. Since Kate O'Dade's phone call yesterday, he'd been on edge, wondering why she'd made this appointment with him. It was about a painting, she'd said. He hoped there was more to it.

"Good to see you, Kate." Her soft hand in his quickened his pulse. "It's been a while."

"About three years," she said, smiling warmly while adjusting the package under her arm.

Time hadn't diminished her English-rose good looks, with her flawless complexion that required no makeup. Nick could easily imagine the willowy figure hidden beneath her baggy pantsuit. A mass of unruly auburn hair set off her emerald-green eyes, and he could feel those luminous eyes reading his expression and body language. Her lips twitched, forming the hint of a smile. Was she sensing the rush of attraction heating his blood? Christ, he didn't need this complication right now. He couldn't allow himself to be sidetracked. He was on the clock with a critical job to do.

"Thanks for taking the time to meet with Allegra and me," Kate said.

Her melodious voice still captivated him as it had during his ten months of psychotherapy with her.

He bridled at the thought of Allegra, his pain-in-the-ass British intern and a slapdash restorer. She was only reliable in aggravating the hell out of him. So far, his posh accent had her believing he was another upper-class toff, but one slip—a wrong word or intonation—and she'd know he came from London's East End. Allegra was late as usual. He hoped she wouldn't show.

No such luck. He saw her sashaying through the door in a red miniskirt, making her usual breathless "look at me" entrance, black hair flying as she stabbed the floor with her spike heels.

He led the two women down a wide hall with paintings from the last two hundred years stacked against the walls—all the scarred, cracked faces crying out for his healing touch. The corridor opened into a bright central workspace, the hot sun shining through three tall windows. He stopped at the central worktable, and Kate placed the package on the surface.

"Last night, something extraordinary happened. Someone left this picture on my doorstep with a thank you card and no signature." Kate began unwrapping the large sheet of brown paper and the protective bubble wrap to reveal the small two-foot by twenty-inch painting. "I assumed it was a copy of one of my favorite Matisse paintings, but the work looked so genuine that Allegra and I started to have doubts. If the picture is an original, it would have been stolen from a collector or a museum. Allegra suggested getting your opinion and said you're a Matisse expert and the best conservator in the West. That's why I called you." Kate's gaze connected with his, both aware that she already knew these facts, knew him better than anyone, having listened to his secrets for all those intense hours of therapy.

He helped her pull off the wrappings, and a kaleidoscope of vivid colors radiated from the painting's surface, lighting up their three faces.

Holy shit! This can't be!

He felt a sudden dizziness and sweat beaded on his brow and under his arms. "It's Matisse's masterpiece, *La Fenêtre Ouverte* (*The Open Window*). The pulsing colors exhilarated him—the red and gold French shutters flung open against walls of turquoise and rose, the view of blue and orange sailboats tilting on pink waves. The sky in brushstrokes of white, blue, and purple, the whole scene radiating light, air, and *joie de vivre*.

Nick was puzzled. Copies, however expert, usually did not turn him on this way. Since an unknown person had left this *Open Window* on Kate's doorstep, he couldn't believe it was genuine, as the original painting was worth multimillions. *Who and why would someone anonymously give away this brilliant masterpiece?* If Matisse hadn't painted this, his doppelganger must have wielded the brush. Sometimes, neither the real artist nor the forger could distinguish which painting was the original. Even Picasso once failed to distinguish his work from an expert forgery. As the story goes, he even signed it, saying it was as good as his.

"No wonder you have doubts," Nick said, standing between the two women.

"Thanks for not laughing at me," Kate said, and his heart skipped a beat. What an idiot. He'd quit therapy with her because he couldn't go on being a pathetic cliché—the poor-sod patient in love with his psychologist.

"Any idea who left this on your porch?" He sidestepped closer to Kate and away from Allegra, who inevitably crowded him.

"I assume it's from someone who knows I'm an amateur landscape painter and perhaps also knows I'm a Matisse fan—most likely a friend or a grateful client connected with the art world. I've made a list of those art friends and clients, and I plan to contact them. The whole thing is baffling and intriguing, also quite exciting," Kate's green eyes shone.

"The gift-giver could be a nut job," Nick said, "like someone with an obsession about you. Doesn't that worry you?"

"Not yet." Kate regarded the Matisse less dreamily. "But maybe I should be worried."

"Could be a gift from a secret admirer." Allegra giggled, bumping Nick's arm.

"Fat chance," Kate said. "I'm an invisible, middle-aged widow down on her luck."

Nick wanted to shake her. He never understood Kate's inexplicable need to portray herself as a sexless wallflower. From reports of her husband's death, he figured she'd been a widow for about ten months. By now, she might be open to going out with other men. Him, for instance? *Nah.* Aside from her caring therapist act, he doubted she had ever seen him as anything but an intriguing curiosity. Moot point, anyway. He'd be gone soon.

"Can you tell whether it's genuine?" Kate asked.

"Usually, but experts can often make mistakes."

"This must be a copy," Allegra said. "If somebody sold it as the original, then it's a forgery. Right, Nick?"

He nodded.

"Why would anyone give away the original?" Allegra asked. "Besides, isn't the original at the National Gallery of Art in Washington, DC? I called the gallery this morning to check and am waiting for a callback. I *do* hope we're not wasting your time."

Allegra leaned into him, and Nick quickly maneuvered away from her. This insatiable woman was always touching or grabbing some part of him. He sensed something twisted underneath her flirtatious behavior. He'd thought about calling her out for harassment—a turning of the tables—but he couldn't risk the scrutiny and her likely drama queen reaction. He'd been a fool to accept her as his intern from the Tate in London six months ago, but he'd owed the head of conservation there a favor.

"Even if Washington, DC's National Gallery has the painting, it might not be the original," he said. "The Met did a recent study and found an alarming number of fakes and misattributions in museums. Nearly 40 percent. Numerous experts had vetted these works as originals."

"I hope my picture is a fake," Kate said. "I'd hate to have to turn it over to the FBI art crime team."

Blocking out thoughts of the FBI, Nick turned the painting facedown. The back looked surprisingly familiar, but so had the front. He was getting a bad feeling about the origins of this work, to say nothing of the disturbing mystery of who gave it to Kate.

"Let's start with the basics," he said. "Note the mottled brown color of the canvas. This means it's old, possibly old enough to date back to 1905, and the fabric's simple tabby weave is consistent with the cheap materials used by Matisse at that time. But these facts prove nothing. The clever forger knows he must use only a canvas and paints from the time period of the artist he plans to imitate."

"If this were the original," Allegra said, "wouldn't we see stamps or seals on the canvas back or the stretcher bars, indicating previous owners and where the painting was exhibited?"

"Probably, but this painting has been relined," Nick said. "See the two layers where the canvas is tacked over the stretcher bars?" He lifted the top layer slightly. "Over time, canvases start to sag or buckle or get damaged. Conservators correct the problems by gluing another canvas onto the back of the old one, and they often replace the original old stretcher bars."

"What about the frame? Is it the right age?" Kate asked.

Nick turned the picture face up and ran his hand down the plain pine wood. "No, it's an inexpensive, contemporary frame." Putting a cheap frame on this first-rate work struck Nick as odd and foolish, particularly if the artist intended the painting to pass as the original.

"So, do I have this right?" Kate interrupted his thoughts. "If an old painting has an age-appropriate frame and stretcher bars, has been relined, or has the right stamps on the back, could we be more certain that it's genuine?"

"Not really," he said. "Clever forgers find or make age-appropriate frames and stretcher bars. Then they use relining to hide the fact that there are no historical markings on the back of their work, or they go to the trouble of forging or finding old stamps and seals to put on the back."

"Seems like the expert forger has to do a ton of work," Kate said.

"Indeed." Nick flashed a knowing smile. "Often a lot more than the original artist does."

"How much would the genuine Matisse be worth today?" Allegra's breath felt hot on his neck, and the scent of her herbal mouthwash stung his nasal passages.

"Well over a hundred million."

"Wow, that's higher than I expected," Kate said.

"The painting's historical importance ups its value," he said. "It was in the first exhibition of *Les Fauves—The Wild Beasts*—in Paris. Matisse and his gang broke all the rules."

"Ah, yes," Kate said. "They brought the world kicking and screaming into a new era of modern art. Assuming this is a copy, what would it go for?"

Nick cleared his throat. "The work is so skillfully done. Even if it is a copy, it should command a hefty sum. Let's look at the brushwork."

Nick reached across Kate, pulled the long arm of a lamp toward them, and positioned the light to shine down on the Matisse. With the lamp turned on, the hot colors blazed more brightly, seeming to give off heat in the cavernous studio. Kate slipped out of her linen suit jacket. Nick rolled up his sleeves, hyperaware of her arousing proximity.

"See the short, horizontal brushstrokes that make up the water under the sailboats?" He pointed to the midsection. "These brushstrokes match Matisse's style in his *Fauve* period. But I also see a few uncharacteristic brushstrokes, and some of the colors are slightly off."

"Show me," Kate said.

He slid the painting toward her. She leaned forward as he explained what he saw as the give-away signs. "See these strokes of pink water under the sailboats? They're too tentative, too wimpy for Papa Matisse. And the lines of purple in the sky, the hue is slightly too reddish. The same goes for the orange of the sailboat masts." As his finger traced the lines, he inhaled the musky odor of her sweat and felt her excitement. Great art was a powerful aphrodisiac, especially for art lovers like her. His gaze slipped down to her breasts, taut nipples pressing against the thin silk of her blouse.

"Are there other clues?" she asked.

"The signature," he said, his throat thick. He pointed to the bottom right corner. "There's not quite enough slope or dash in the printing of Henri."

"What an amazing eye you have."

Her praise heated his insides better than whiskey.

"Will you do pigment, X-ray, and infrared analyses?" Allegra asked.

He hesitated. "Not necessary. I can see the painting isn't a genuine Matisse."

Allegra answered her vibrating phone, listened, then said, "You still have Matisse's *La Fenêtre Ouverte*. That's all I wanted to know. *Merci,* Jean-Claude." She beamed at Nick. "The National Gallery's head European Art curator just confirmed your opinion."

Nick grunted and said to Kate, "In any case, what you have here is an impressive work. This *Open Window* is an almost perfect copy."

CHAPTER 3

When I discover who I am, I'll be free.
—Ralph Ellison—

Wednesday, October 10

After her meeting with Nick at the Steele Museum, Kate headed north on the I-5 en route to her home in Del Mar. The exit to La Jolla was coming up, and she decided to make a stop there to visit Gerard Devereaux, an old friend who'd been her father's best buddy in the Vietnam War. When she considered the possible people who might have given her the Matisse, he was at the top of her list. He now owned the only serious art gallery in this wealthy resort town. He knew she loved Matisse—and *The Open Window* in particular—and he probably knew Nick McCoy. She chided herself for still feeling stirred up from her encounter with him.

Zipping down Torrey Pines Road in her toy-sized Mini Cooper, she turned right onto Prospect in downtown La Jolla. Specialty boutiques, art galleries, and eateries—some with views of La Jolla Cove—lined the street. She found a parking spot near the Devereaux Gallery next door to The Spot, a popular pub grub tavern.

The wrapped Matisse secured under her arm, she pushed through the gallery's opaque glass doors and ran into a dapper, dark-haired man.

"So sorry," she quickly stepped back.

He gave a slight bow. "No damage done," said the suave gent with a tony British accent and a pencil mustache. He reminded Kate of David Niven, her mother's favorite actor.

Gerard's resonant baritone boomed across the gallery. "Hey, Kate, good to see you." He strode toward her, grinning. A former Hollywood stuntman, Gerard looked less like an upscale art dealer than a fit, late middle-aged bodybuilder in a black T-shirt and jeans.

Gerard introduced her to the British gent. "She's my favorite local landscape painter who shrinks heads as a psychologist on the side." He turned to her. "Meet the art critic Dr. Miles Hartwright, who also teaches art history at UCSD and collects Post-Impressionist art."

Her eyes lit up. "My favorite period. What artists do you have?"

"No one famous," Miles said. "I'm the champion of the ignored, the forgotten, the out-of-vogue, or never in vogue, but not always the lesser talents of our last era of Modern Art."

"You're stuck in the outmoded past, my friend. The present is Performance and Conceptual Art." Gerard swept his muscular arm toward the work currently on display.

"Bollocks," Miles said. "Contemporary art *sucks*, to use one of your *au courant* words. The problem is that artists aren't taught to paint, so they photograph and make movies of themselves doing profound things, like looking in the mirror and counting calories."

"Cheap shot." Gerard winked at her. "Miles often stops by to mock my latest contemporary show. Then he feeds me lunch at The Spot to soften the blow of his review for the campus rag."

"Let's see what Dr. O'Dade thinks of your latest exhibition." Miles gestured toward the display beginning a few feet from where they stood.

As Gerard handed her a catalog, Kate placed her package on the reception desk. Then she strolled toward the show, reading the title on the far wall of the rectangular space:

Who is it that can tell me who I am?

Awkward phrasing in that title. Pictured on the back of the catalog, the artist, Tanya Boon, looked out with a vacant stare as if she were waiting for her features to form. She credited Shakespeare for her show's title. Kate winced. It was a quote from *King Lear*. How cheeky of her to criticize the great bard's prose.

Kate moved to the artist's first photo, titled *Masks*. It pictured a woman lying in bed, her face a featureless blank. She was reaching toward the rows of masks hanging on the wall next to her. Each one exhibited a different expression—a smiley face, a sad sack, and a mask with an angry red mouth. Kate thought of waking up in the morning, struggling with how to face the day. What mask would best conceal her current brooding state?

Next to this photo, she faced a triptych titled *Mirror, Mirror*. Tanya appeared as a black, brown, and white-skinned woman. The three faces were partially concealed behind handheld mirrors. "Who's the fairest of them all?" Kate murmured, wondering if Tanya was saying all races are equally fair or that she didn't know what color skin she preferred.

Kate moved on to an eight-foot-tall image of Tanya naked, portrayed in a succession of overlapping, fragmented shots as though she was moving down from the top of a staircase. The work reminded her of *Nude Descending a Staircase* by Marcel Duchamp, the granddaddy of Conceptual Art. But, unlike Duchamp's painting, this nude arrived at the bottom of the stairs transformed into an androgenous-looking young man. The title—*Transitioning*—could mean the artist was in transition from female to male, was revealing her wish to be male, or was just expressing her thoughts about the fluidity of gender.

She scanned the remaining photographs, all elaborating on the identity theme. In Tanya's last photograph, she was leaning over a coffin, screaming in the caption floating above, "Is that me?"

"So, what's your diagnosis, Dr. O'Dade?" Miles asked as Kate rejoined them. "Would you say Ms. Boon has a serious identity problem?"

"Who doesn't?" Gerard asked. "That's her point—her concept—and it's relevant, especially these days. Right, Kate?"

She nodded. "Identity issues are certainly more prevalent and out in the open now. It seems that Boon is trying to show us the pain and confusion they can cause."

"The work has no nuance, no subtlety," Miles said. "I've been bashed over the head."

"Subtlety is not the American way," Gerard said. "In your face is exactly—"

"Mind if I interrupt?" Kate asked.

"Ah, like an American, you mean?" Miles teased.

"Precisely." Kate grinned. "I'd like to show you something special." She walked to the reception desk and pointed to the package. "Inside is the work of an old-fashioned painter whose strength is pure, unadulterated joy. But first, I'd like to ask you, Gerard, if you happened to give me any surprise gifts lately, like leaving a painting on my doorstep?"

"Are you kidding?" Gerard asked. "Too risky. Someone could steal or damage the work. Is this the surprise gift?" He gestured toward the package.

She nodded, then carefully pulled off the wrapping. The painting's brilliant colors lit up the room, a welcome contrast to Tanya's conceptual angst.

"My God. Matisse! *The Open Window*," Miles said.

"This must be a copy," Gerard said.

Miles looked at Kate, incredulous. "You say some unknown person gave this to you?"

"Yes, it was on my doorstep with a thank you card."

"From someone you know?" he asked.

"Seems like it must be," she said.

"That's astonishing and quite peculiar," Miles said.

She nodded. "Do you agree it's a copy?"

"I don't know." After studying the back of the painting first, as Nick had done, Miles sniffed the canvas and stretcher bars. Then he turned it over and gazed at the front, seeming to scour every square inch of the work. Finally, he stepped back, his brow furrowed.

"Without any tests or provenance for a proper assessment, I'd say this painting is either the original or a superb forgery. It gives me goosebumps."

"Why do you say forgery instead of a superb copy?" she asked.

"Because it's signed with the artist's name, indicating it's intended to pass as the original," Miles said. "Copyists don't sign their work with the artist's name. That's illegal. The copyist signs the back of the canvas with his or her name, but forgers do sign the artist's name if the painter usually signed his or her work."

She frowned. Nick hadn't mentioned this distinction. "What do you suggest I do?"

"Get it into a safe art storage place," Miles replied. "The painting could be quite valuable, even if it is a forgery. Your mysterious gift-giver worries me. He or she might want such a fine work back or possibly wants to hide it somewhere temporarily for unknown reasons."

"That's creepy." Kate shuddered. "This reminds me of that fourth of July, nine years ago, when Dixon Steele sent Simon to ask Gerard to authenticate Johannes Vermeer's masterpiece, *The Concert*. Remember that surprise, Gerard?"

"Shock was more like it. I'll never forget it."

"*The Concert*? You can't be serious," Miles said. "That masterpiece has never been recovered since the Isabella Gardner Museum theft almost thirty years ago."

"Well, we think it might have resurfaced here in 2009," Gerard said. "I only had a brief time to examine it before I locked it in my vault for the night. Unfortunately, it was stolen from the vault before I could get to it the next morning, and no one's reported seeing it since."

"Christ, man. I'm on pins and needles. Did you think it was authentic?"

Gerard hesitated. "Based on my first impression, I'd say it was an authentic Vermeer."

"So would I," Kate said. "It gave me tingles all over just like this Matisse does."

Miles laughed. "Well, that's the best test, isn't it?"

"Yeah, but there is one artist who can produce such tingles with his forgeries," Gerard said.

"Ah yes, the one Scotland Yard has code-named Phantom," Miles said. "Imagine if you'd hung on to that Vermeer, I'd guess it would be worth over three hundred million today."

"But anyone possessing *The Concert* would be at great risk," Gerard said. "The whole art and criminal underworld covet that painting. The Devil and Death would be right at his heels."

Kate looked at *The Open Window*. "Surely, I don't have to worry about that with the Matisse."

"Don't bet on it. A hundred-million-dollar Matisse abandoned on a lady's front porch would bring out the hungry art wolves in packs."

"Jesus, Gerard, you're scaring me. So, what do I do now?"

"Get all the scientific tests done right away so you know what you're dealing with," Miles said. "There's a first-rate authenticator in town, the conservator at the Steele Museum. His name's Nick McCoy, a colleague of mine. He'll know what to do about this bombshell."

Since Nick hadn't mentioned the distinction between a copy and a forgery, Kate was reluctant to tell Miles about that consultation. Nick had spoken of the imperfect signature, but then he'd called the Matisse "a nearly perfect copy" instead of a forgery—a mistake he was unlikely to make. Had he intended to mislead her?

CHAPTER 4

Creativity takes courage.
—HENRI MATISSE—

Thursday Afternoon, October 11

In his East Village loft on the south border of Balboa Park, Nick looked from his portrait of Raquel to the half-clothed, in-the-flesh woman modeling for him. His vision started to blur, then queasiness hit. Like a slow poison, Simon's threat was debilitating him, depriving him of the focus and energy he needed to survive. With an uncertain eight days to pull off their scheme and leave town, Nick had struggled to focus on getting Steele's last two paintings cleaned and restored. But he'd had enough of Steele and his sleazy son pushing him around. Screw them. He needed to do his own work if he was ever to become a genuine artist instead of a forger.

Nick felt cramped in his tiny bedroom. But, since a reclining nude required a bed, he couldn't use his large, adjacent studio for this portrait. Raquel lay propped up on several pillows, her arms and body partially concealed by a sapphire-blue dressing gown. With her classical features, translucent skin, and graceful limbs, she resembled a dark-haired Aphrodite. Her beauty could trigger any man's lust, including his own.

Through the window behind Raquel, he could see the park's greenery shimmering in the sunlight. A reluctance to leave San Diego crept up on him. He liked Balboa Park and his loft, and the location was ideal. To the north, he could walk to four fine museums on winding trails through the park, and to the south, it was just a few blocks to the Steele Museum on the border of the Gaslamp Quarter. But he didn't like San Diego's dry heat this time of year, the Santa Anas, and the threat of fires. He longed for London in October—the cool crispness, the misty rain, the lush greens, and the vibrant autumn hues.

What would keep him here? Only Kate and his wish to win his ideal woman. He also yearned to have real friends and to focus on making good, original paintings. Futile wishes for a dedicated outsider who could only fake belonging.

He turned to the oblong canvas on the easel in front of him. He'd captured Raquel's unique features and unearthly beauty, but the overall result depressed him. The work was highly skilled but with no flash of originality or depth of expression.

Take some risks with the damn brush for a change. Nick looked at his favorite Manet quote on the wall to his right. "Every new painting is like throwing myself into the water without knowing how to swim."

Be bold, be brave, like Édouard Manet, Nick chanted to himself, like a mantra. *Jump in the bloody water!* Nick could hear the jazz classic *Kind of Blue* playing on the stereo in his studio. Miles Davis on the trumpet courageously dove into free-fall with every spontaneous note.

Imitate Miles.

"You frown," Raquel said. "Because of your painting or the model?" Raquel's French-accented English had a stilted, school-girl quality.

Both, Nick thought. *What the hell was he to do about his loyal partner in crime?*

"I will adjust my pose." Raquel started to move and winced.

"What's wrong?" he asked.

"Napoleon bucked me off again. I wear this robe to cover the bruises. Can you do without my naked body today?"

"With difficulty." He flashed her a flirty grin. "That animal has banged you up before, more than once. If you must ride, isn't it time to get a safer horse?"

"Pointless now. We'll be gone soon." Her tone sharpened. "Have you figured out the exact timing yet, *mon chéri?*"

Long pause. "Well, you know the drill. I have two more of Dixon's paintings to clean and restore. Then I'll be ready to deliver the *coup de grâce*. Since this Sunday is the California Impressionist Exhibition at the museum, I've got to work on that for the next three days. I could be done with all my jobs for Steele in four or five days after that. I'll shoot for completion by next Thursday, the eighteenth. Sooner, if possible."

"*Bon*. I can wait seven or eight days. The waiting is torture. *La Bête* is more of a *terroriste* each day." Raquel's mash-up of French and English usually signaled strong emotion. "I have bad nightmares of that monster trapping me in hell."

"I won't let that happen," Nick said, but her fear of Steele intensified his foreboding. The reality of Raquel staving off that brute, along with Simon's hatred, had been a constant worry. Nick's sinuses ached from the fumes of turpentine and oil paint. The refrigerated air did nothing to ease his tension. At least the air conditioning kept them from sweltering.

Seven days. Nick had to be ready in seven days. Fewer days would be safer.

He stared at his painting. The work looked too slick, the model too beautiful, and the atmosphere was like a sunny California day. Stretching behind Raquel and the bed, the overly detailed background captured the view through the rectangular window. The window framed the rainbow eucalyptus tree—its handsome trunk striated with red, yellow, gold, and green streaks. The crisscross of branches outlined irregular patches of blue sky. Raquel had posed semi-nude, and he'd made the bed appear outside rather than in the bedroom. This conceit was inspired by Manet's *Luncheon on the Grass* (*Le Dejeuner sur L'Herbe*). In his infamous Pre-Impressionist painting, Manet had abandoned the long-held custom of depicting a nude woman as an idealized goddess or Madonna. Instead, he painted an ordinary naked woman picnicking in a forest with two men dressed in black. The scene—shocking in 1863—was outside, but the work had the atmosphere and lighting of an interior studio painting.

Nick sighed through gritted teeth. At least he was mixing, matching, and reversing an illusion instead of just copying or imitating. But Manet's paintings had much more emotional punch and complexity than his effort. And the truth of his current reality was dark and dangerous, not sunny and safe. Raquel was not a goddess or Madonna but a brave, embattled woman at risk of losing her sanity. Nick thought of himself as a dedicated conservator and artist, but he was also an unreliable lover plotting a diabolical crime.

Manet, the maestro of black and dashing brushstrokes, would say the painting called for more darks and contrast, more reality. Nick glanced up at Van Gogh's inspiring words emblazoned in sunflower yellow on a plaque affixed at the top of his easel. "If you hear a voice within you say 'you cannot paint,' then by all means paint, and that voice will be silenced."

His mentors spurring him on, Nick squeezed out coils of black, a mound of white, and dabs of ultramarine paint and began mixing various shades of gray on his palette.

"Do you think we should go to London?" Raquel asked.

Raquel seemed to assume they would leave San Diego simultaneously, and he was quite sure she thought they would stay together as a couple. He hadn't found a good way to challenge this fantasy. For both practical and emotional reasons, Nick was in no position to commit to anyone. He did cherish Raquel. Her looks had captivated him as did anything or anyone of exceptional beauty. Her presence in his life could temporarily ease the psychic pain brought on by his freakish self-image. He felt a strong affection for her, but he knew it would never become an enduring passion. Perhaps her less loveable traits were too much like his own—secretive, devious, damaged, and full of rage.

"I've given our plan a lot of thought," Nick replied. Then, loading his brush with a gray mix, he began painting over the tree's scattered green leaves and the patches of blue sky. "After we take down Dixon, we should be prepared for the crime to be discovered quickly. I will probably be a suspect. We can't leave town at the same time, or you will also be suspected."

Raquel nodded. "I'll leave sooner, before the last act."

"Yes, that's best. I can complete the plan without you here. Then I'll follow you as soon as possible." Nick thought of all the difficult work Raquel had put into their revenge scheme, a plan they had developed over time after meeting at an expat event two years ago. He recalled the early days of their affair and the discovery that both had come to San Diego to wreak revenge on Dixon Steele. A strong bond soon developed between them, and they began plotting ways to get closer to Steele. Raquel had the most challenging role—seducing and marrying a man she loathed.

"You've had a very tough job, Raquel, much harder than mine. You deserve to get out of your hellish existence with Steele as soon as possible."

Her pale face flushed with pleasure. "I am done with being the dumb trophy wife in awe of a rich thug. I want a better job, much better."

Nick chuckled. "You sound like a budding Yankee feminist."

"*Merci.*" She smiled. "I can't wait to leave. Living with Dixon after the crime terrifies me. He will be insane and need a scapegoat. That will be me. I need a good excuse to be gone."

"You have one," Nick said. "Remember we talked about using your sister in Paris? She could be ill, or there's the birth of a child, your first niece. You must go there. Then, when the time is right, I'll meet you in Paris, or you'll come to where I am," he fabricated.

"Will that be London?"

"Possibly, because I know it so well."

"*Bon,* I adore London."

Nick did not respond, letting her believe they would meet up somewhere. He wanted to forget all that could go wrong right now and withdrew into reworking his painting, always an effective escape. The formerly blue sky was now an ominous slate gray showing through a sparse number of bare branches. Outside, the sky had clouded over as if in response to his mood.

"I must be here for the exhibition," Raquel continued. "I'll arrange to leave the country as soon as possible afterward."

"That works," Nick said.

Raquel sat up and faced him, giving him a grim look. "It scares me to leave without you. What if something bad happens to you? What if we never find each other again?"

A distinct possibility, Nick thought, *but not the worst one*. "Keep in mind that I don't usually screw up or get caught. Phantom, as you know, is an old hand at disappearing. But you must stay away from Simon. He's toxic and explosive."

"*Merde*, I always avoid Simon. We detest each other."

He hadn't told her about Simon's threat and hoped the scumbag would not go so far as to threaten her directly. Her fear of Dixon was more than enough for her to manage.

Nick had to be prepared to leave at any time. Simon was as unpredictable as a viper full of venom and could blab their secret tomorrow. He would most likely wait to expose their affair until their crime had been discovered. At that point, Nick would look guilty as hell. He had to find a way to turn the tables and implicate the treacherous twit. The image of Simon's sly smile made the gorge rise in Nick's throat. He quickly gulped some water from the bottle on his cart.

Nick turned back to his painting, glad it was something he could fix right now. The background with the tree's newly blackened bark and branches that allowed only thin lines of muted rainbow colors to show through gave the tree an abstract, haunting quality—stark against the backdrop of a brooding sky. The picture was no longer pretty or pleasing, except for Raquel's silky skin and goddess-like beauty. She needed to look less perfect, more mysterious.

"Raquel, take off your dressing gown."

"*Pourquoi?* I have bruises. I look ugly."

"You could never be ugly to me, *ma belle.* Let me see."

"*Merde*, you cannot make me look ugly in the painting," she cried as she stripped off the robe. Mottled bluish-purple bruises discolored her right arm, side, hip, and thigh.

Nick was shocked. "My God, Raquel. You've got to get rid of that horse."

She said nothing and looked at him with pain-filled eyes, her lips fixed in an enigmatic half-smile. The meaning eluded Nick, but his sudden discomfort and her body language told him she was hiding something significant from him. His muscles tensed. *What would she not tell him at this critical point in time?* His eyes surveyed her lean, damaged body. She had clearly lost weight and wore more makeup than usual. Why? To conceal the discoloration under her eyes? Was she ill? He had suspected she might have an eating disorder. Then he noticed her larger breasts and the roundness of her belly. *Holy shit, she can't be pregnant!*

CHAPTER 5

*You wanna fly, you got to give up the
shit that weighs you down.*

—Toni Morrison—

Thursday Evening, October 11

After dinner, Kate sat on the stool in her converted garage studio and gazed at the Matisse propped up on the easel, not quite believing this gorgeous painting was hers. Even though Nick had judged it to be a copy and Miles thought it a possible forgery, the painting felt genuine to her. Its vitality made everything else in the studio—the madras-covered daybed, the art show posters, and her old watercolor landscapes—look drab. It seemed a shame to lock up this blast of sunshine in a dark storage unit. She'd do more investigating first. If she found out the picture was a copy from a friend or client, she wouldn't need to lock it up.

Considering Miles's and Nick's suspicion of the gift-giver, Kate couldn't think of anyone who would give her such a treasure out of an obsessive fixation or some other weird agenda. Still, there were a few things that puzzled her, including Nick's failure to mention the meaning of the artist's signature. Unless this omission was an oversight, it either meant he knew the painting was a forgery or was the original. *Could he still be a fraud and a liar despite all those months of therapy?* The thought was almost too depressing to contemplate.

Kate pulled out her short list of people who might have given her this gift. The many artists on her list reminded her of what a vibrant, friendly art community existed in San Diego. She eliminated the friends and clients who didn't know she was a Matisse fan and those who could or would not consider spending a chunk of money on her. Five names left. Two were former clients: one was a San Diego art dealer, and the other a wealthy collector of primitive art. None of the three women friends, who were also avid amateur painters, seemed likely to be the gift-giver. She also wondered about the significance of the timing of the gift. She assumed it was a supportive gesture intended to ease the pain of her empty nest, given her husband's recent death and her son's departure to Berkeley for his first year of college. Perhaps the giver had remained anonymous, fearing she would refuse such an extravagant present.

Kate picked up her phone from her worktable and sent similar texts to each person, asking if they had left an anonymous gift for her yesterday. She stressed the importance of knowing this generous person's identity and promised confidentiality.

Shifting her attention to *The Open Window*, the picture transported her to a magical world of color, light, and freedom. Making joyous pictures like this had helped Matisse get through his many black depressions.

Matisse's dark moods reminded Kate of David's death and her chronic stress about paying the bills—including Sam's college expenses. Kate had once loved her confident, devil-may-care husband, but she deeply resented his reckless climbing accident in Yosemite. Now, she was saddled with a mountain of debt from his impulsive investments. Despite his shortcomings, his optimism in the face of bad news had often helped to brighten her mood. She was glad Sam had his upbeat temperament. She missed her son's quick humor and can-do attitude, and he'd been a huge help in taking care of their rental property.

Kate reached for her cell to call Sam, but her call went to his voicemail.

"It's me, your favorite mom. Just thinking about you. Give me a call when the spirit moves you." She hoped her casual, upbeat tone concealed her maternal neediness.

The stuffy studio reeked of oil paint and turpentine. Kate opened the door to a blast of hot wind. The dry Santa Anas from the desert irritated her eyes and made brittle parchment of her skin. She turned to her latest painting on the center worktable. This work was not one of her usual seascapes. She had intended it to resemble a Guy Rose Impressionist landscape without being a copy—copies being easier to detect as forgeries. The picture was a novice forger's pastiche that contained familiar but rearranged elements of Rose's work, rendered with his characteristic brushstrokes. Kate frowned at the surface of her painting's duck pond. The water lacked shimmer, and her brushwork was a lame imitation of the master's. *What would Nick think?* What if he knew how his saintly therapist was attempting to augment her income? That shocking discovery would certainly send her tumbling headfirst off his pedestal.

Kate started mixing a new batch of blue-green paint as she focused her thoughts on how to solve her serious money problems without resorting to forgery. She knew she was fortunate to be able to stay in high-priced Del Mar. Her generous landlady had accepted Kate's offer to landscape and renovate the dilapidated cottage in exchange for a low rent. Having learned to get by on a shoestring after her father died and her mother became too ill to work, Kate could do and fix just about anything a household might need. Her favorite task was working on her Japanese-style entry garden, which, to her, was like making a three-dimensional landscape painting. Her clients loved walking through this Zen-like space while hearing the soothing tinkle of the bamboo fountain.

She considered increasing the time devoted to her practice from four days to five, plus working on Saturdays. But the income from a few more therapy clients wouldn't be nearly enough to cover her expenses and the humongous debt she had been left with. Also, a full-time practice would leave her with hardly any time to do her artwork and take care of the property. Painting was food for her soul, essential to her well-being. Doing this nourishing, often uplifting work made it possible for her to take good care of others.

Sensing a fleeting movement outside the window across from her, Kate glanced up. She stared at the empty glass but saw only the reflection of her pale face with its frame of messy auburn hair. Her cell pinged, alerting her to a text. She hoped one of the five suspects had responded. One had. The text was from Mel, the wealthy primitive art collector.

> *Sorry, Kate, it wasn't me. If I were to give you a gift, it would be an aboriginal wood carving—a bird—for your collection. And I wouldn't give it anonymously. OCD still under control. Maybe you deserve a bird for that. Hope to see you at the Impressionists exhibition. Mel*

Her cell signaled a call coming in, and she answered to Allegra's annoying greeting, "Hey, poppet." Even though she was much younger, Allegra acted as if Kate was her naïve little sister. "Tell me, what did you think of my boss?"

Kate flashed back on Nick's polished performance. "McCoy sure knows his stuff. His analysis was fascinating." However, she'd sensed something off about it. He'd sounded too cocksure, which to her meant he was lying.

Allegra said in her breathy voice, "But don't you think he's hot?"

"No, he seemed rather aloof to me," Kate responded. Fortunately, Allegra didn't know that Nick was once her client, and Kate never broke confidentiality.

"Oh, my sweet poppet. You don't know this kind of bloke like I do. He's one of those proper British types, smoldering with passion underneath. Just wait. I'll get him to show his true colors soon." Allegra giggled.

Kate swiped at the lock of hair flopping in her eyes. This focus on Nick unnerved her. She bridled at Allegra's snooty act, even though her friend's confident go-after-what-you-want attitude had attracted her. She swallowed her annoyance when she thought back on what a good friend Allegra had been to her after David died. She brought dinners and books and checked in on her regularly.

She thanked Allegra for arranging the consultation with Nick and ended the call. Now Kate was left alone to contemplate her own stirred-up attraction to the "proper" British bloke.

When David was alive, she'd usually been able to suppress her erotic responses to Nick's presence, but lately, he often appeared in her thoughts and dreams. Underneath his restrained, polished manner, she sensed a caged wildness, exhibited only in his out-of-control black hair. During one therapy session, she'd had the off-color fantasy of plunging her hands into that curly black mass and becoming just as wild and out of control. At first appalled, she later wrote off this aberration as a result of overwork and professional stress. But now she considered it a sign of her unacknowledged marital unhappiness and feeling trapped.

Nick McCoy had been a compelling and mysterious presence from the beginning. First, his Scottish name didn't match his Mediterranean good looks. He called himself a "Black Scots mongrel," but the cultured British speech didn't sound the least bit like a mongrel. He also did not look like a straitlaced art conservator. It was three years ago, during their second therapy session, that he revealed his hidden persona. She recalled the disturbing scene in vivid detail.

CHAPTER 6

The more identities a man has, the more they express the person they conceal.

—John le Carré—

Three Years Earlier

"The problem is I can't do my own work," Nick said in his second therapy session. "Whenever I try, the blank canvas taunts me, and I freeze."

"Have you any idea what blocks you? What you might be afraid of?" Kate asked.

The light nearly went out of his vigilant, black eyes. "You need a strong sense of who you are to make original paintings, and I'm a collection of masks with no real face behind them."

This sounded like a poignant description of an identity disorder. "Tell me about your masks."

Long silence. "Does what I say here remain between us?"

"Absolutely, with two exceptions. I'm obliged to break confidentiality if you seriously threaten to harm yourself or someone else."

He glanced around her earth-toned office and then out the window at the Japanese maple's red autumn leaves flickering in the breeze. Shifting his gaze back to her, his deep voice broke the silence between them.

"I suppose there's no point in my being here if I don't come clean." He eyed her warily. "Please assure me that what I say next will not leave this room."

"Keeping secrets is part of my job."

"After hearing this one, you might not want to take my case."

The back of her neck tingled. This intriguing man could be a serial killer or a pedophile. "You might decide not to work with me."

"Doubtful," he said. "I've done my homework and talked to several professionals about your credentials and expertise. You come highly recommended as a therapist who also has an art background. I need a therapist who knows about painting and the art underworld."

Kate nodded, impressed with his motivation. "Let's see how it goes, shall we?"

"I'd rather keep stalling."

She half-smiled, his self-mocking candor appealing.

He moistened his lips. "First, you need to know I have another trade besides art conservation." Pause. "It's not what you would call respectable." He stopped, seeming at a loss.

"Just spit it out."

"A grand idea." He gave her a wonky smile. "The FBI and Scotland Yard have been after me. So far, I've managed to elude them. My code name is Phantom, and art forgery is my trade."

His sharp eyes tracked every nuance of her reaction. Kate held a professional, neutral expression, but her heart was kicking up hell in her chest.

"Go on," she said.

"You see, conservation work in museums provides the ideal cover for making forgeries. While working in a museum laboratory on off hours, I can copy the paintings I restore or use one as a model to make a pastiche that can then be sold as a newly discovered work."

"Clever," she said. "But how does forging help you with doing your own work?"

"Unfortunately, it doesn't."

"Then why continue it?"

"I can't stop doing it. It's like a drug."

"How so?"

"To paint something as unique as the original, you must become the artist—see through his eyes, feel his mood, move the brush with the same rhythm and speed he does. In his *Fauve* period, Matisse saw the world in clashes of vivid, opposing colors. His strokes were bold, energetic, and often staccato. While channeling Matisse, you feel like cocaine is shooting through your blood. But when you're inside Modigliani's style, everything flows—smooth and subtle—more like a dreamy heroin high, and you float away from yourself." His eyes gleamed.

Fascinating. He was addicted to forging art, as of yet an unknown syndrome.

"Does the high come from the stimulating experience of escaping yourself?" she asked.

"Not entirely. Forging or copying another artist's painting is a way for a loner to feel less alone. When you are painting solo, you don't get the companionship and support that copying the work of someone you really admire provides. Papa Matisse is there with you: his vitality, his brushstrokes, his wisdom, and his heart."

The longing in his tone made her wonder if he'd lost his father at a young age.

"A fine imitation of a great painting is highly skilled artwork," he said. "It's not an original work of art, except in the way you figure out how to make it sing with the master's voice. Voltaire once said, 'Originality is nothing but judicious imitation.'"

She suppressed a smile at his artful, self-serving argument. "So, you've studied philosophy and thought about this a lot. Impressive. Do you also enjoy fooling people, Mr. McCoy?"

"Only those I don't like. Call me Nick, please. I doubt I'm

fooling anyone who doesn't want to be fooled. The buyers are mostly shady dealers, puffed-up curators, or the greedy rich who want a self-serving deal." He cocked his head. "You'd probably call that a cynical attitude."

She raised her brows. "Psychologists call it rationalization."

"I'll buy the 'rational' part," he said with a slow smile.

His cheeky response tickled Kate. "Well, Nick, so what brings you to therapy now?"

Long pause. "Have you seen that TV series, *The Sopranos*?"

"Years ago." She recalled *The Sopranos* very well, especially the storyline of an intelligent female psychiatrist who gets into trouble trying to treat a Mafia boss.

"I have the same issue that drove Tony Soprano into therapy."

Kate waited, but he offered nothing more. "Have you had a recent panic attack, perhaps?"

"Spot on." He beamed as though she was a bright pupil. "So, will you work with me? Do keep in mind that I don't kill or beat up people like the Soprano goons. A gentleman forger is a better class of criminal, don't you think?" He grinned. "I've had two panic attacks recently when I tried to do an original painting. The last time I blacked out in the street and a lorry almost ran me over." His expression turned solemn. "What's your take, Doctor? Is this a Freudian death wish thing?"

A wiseass quip, but his haunted expression revealed a serious core. Her thoughts raced. The man clearly needed help, but no private practice therapist in her right mind would take on a criminal. But Nick wasn't a mafia thug like Tony Soprano, so what was there to fear? At the moment, she didn't see the psychological dangers. What she saw was the case of a lifetime. Uncharted terrain. Nick's depth of insight and unusual ability to articulate his issues excited her—gave her a professional high, like the teacher who discovers an exceptional student or the biologist who finds a new species. She wanted to believe in his determination to give up forging, but she also knew con men were unlikely to change. In addition, there were many unknowns and probable pitfalls in such an unusual case. Tread cautiously, her instincts told her. This exotically attractive guy was a charming con artist. It would be prudent to see him for a third evaluation session before deciding to take him on.

CHAPTER 7

Art is to console those who are broken by life.

—Vincent van Gogh—

Thursday, October 11, 2018

After the consultation with Kate and Allegra, Nick checked the museum's vault, where he stored three of the most valuable paintings from his collection. He stared in horror at the one empty slot. *The Open Window* was missing. Although his paintings were concealed under thick bubble wrap and protected in wooden crates, he should not have stored them here. He'd chosen the museum for storage because of its superior atmospheric control compared to his loft. The air here was maintained at the ideal seventy-degree temperature for preserving paintings. He was a conservator, so taking good care of paintings was his job. He'd thought the museum's vault provided greater security than the storage space in his loft, but he'd made a grave mistake.

Even though he'd sensed that Kate's Matisse might be his, the loss shook him badly. A thief must have stolen the painting and given it to her for some incomprehensible reason. *Who would do that, for fuck's sake, and why?* No one had the code to his private section of the vault. His heart thudded in his chest, his breath coming in shallow gasps, warning of a panic attack. Losing one painting was nothing compared to everything else he'd lost. He slowed his breathing, counting each breath as Kate had taught him to do.

Loss and panic. He recalled these were the subjects of his third therapy session with Kate over three years ago. At that time, he'd also been on edge because Kate had not yet accepted him as a client.

—

"Tell me more about your panic attacks," Kate said. "What were you doing, thinking, and feeling when they started?"

Nick hated admitting this weakness, but the point of coming here was to rid himself of these crippling attacks. She sat across from him, her head cocked, her emerald-green eyes warm and receptive. He tried to recall the preamble to the attacks. Both times he'd been starting to paint on a blank canvas. The second time it happened came back more clearly.

"I was in my studio, squeezing out the colors I planned to use on my palette—red, yellow, and orange—the colors of the glowing sunset I could see from my window. At some point, my hands started shaking. Then my vision blurred, and the colors swirled together on the palette." He paused, feeling a rush of hot rage. His face broke out in a clammy sweat.

She jumped up, suggesting a glass of water, and hurried to the cabinet next to the bathroom. Two primitive wood carvings of birds stood like tall sentinels next to the water pitcher. As she set a full glass on the side table next to his chair, he caught a whiff of her fresh, fragrant scent.

"Thanks," he said, and drank deeply.

"Do you feel an attack coming on?" She sat down.

"No, I'm just overheated," he lied, loosening the kerchief tied around his neck. He cleared his throat. "I was loading my palette knife with red pigment and slashing the color across the canvas. Then suddenly, I froze. I began reliving my panic as a nine-year-old boy when a fire burned down my father's shop and our flat upstairs. I saw the flames flickering in front of my eyes. Then . . ." He stopped, his breathing ragged.

"It sure sounds like a flashback," Kate said. "Slow down your breathing if you can, and think of something calming, like the rhythmic sound of waves breaking."

He listened to the tinkling sounds of the fountain outside and took a long swallow of water. He was aware of Kate watching him closely, her warm gaze and presence calming him.

"Feeling any better?" she asked.

"Fine now, thanks." Sitting straighter in the chair, he tightened and released his stiff muscles. "I recalled how desperate I was to escape these memories, and I ran half-blind out of my loft into the street. That's when I almost got hit by a lorry." Nick rubbed his eyes as though they were still smarting from the smoke. "I can't say why it all came back to me at that time."

She leaned forward. "Maybe the sky that day looked like it was on fire—those flame-like colors—red, orange, yellow."

He nodded. "I'd also heard fire warnings on the car radio, and earlier that day, I saw a few images on the news before I went to sleep."

"Can you tell me more about the real fire?"

He hesitated, reluctant to bring back any more of the horror. "I don't have much recall, just fragments. I was helping my dad in his shop. He sold and restored antiques and paintings. It got late, and I went to sleep on the couch in the back room. The next thing I knew, Dad was shouting and slapping me and the burning couch with a towel. The room was full of smoke, and he pulled me up off the couch. Flames had caught the back of my clothes, so he wrapped me in a blanket and shoved me out the side door, yelling, 'Get on the ground, Nicky! Roll over and over!' I think at this point, I must have tripped and fell, and I blacked out. The next thing, a fireman was carrying me, and I yelled, 'Dad! Dad! Where's my dad?'"

As he relived those terrifying moments, his heart galloping, he worked to focus on a calming image and pictured pink water, blue sailboats, and purple clouds—*The Open Window*.

Kate's soothing voice was reassuring. "You don't need to talk about this anymore."

Parched, he took a few sips of water and continued reporting the facts, struggling to hide his fear. "I was told Dad went upstairs to rescue my mum and my two little sisters. The entire place was a firetrap and burned down in record time. None of my family made it out alive."

Nick heard her sharp intake of breath. "What a horrific tragedy!"

Her strong reaction made his pain more bearable.

"A fireman told me the fire was probably caused by the space heater overheating near a paint-stained rag that caught fire. The blaze must have gotten out of control because Dad had fallen asleep at his worktable." He paused, trying to summon more memories. "Later, when I could think clearly, I started questioning that explanation, but that's a complicated subject for another time."

She nodded. "What happened to you after the fire?"

"Trust me; you really don't want the details. The devil lives there."

"Please, tell me the details. It will help you to discuss them."

He shrugged. "Well, I was in hospital, then I was moved to a burn care facility where I stayed for nearly a year. Luckily, most of my burns were first- and second-degree. Nevertheless, I had to have multiple skin grafts on my back, right arm, neck, and the right side of my face." He touched his cheek out of habit to assure himself that what had been rough, cratered flesh was now almost smooth. "Skin grafts and growth spurts don't go together, as you probably know."

"No, I don't know. Tell me."

"Every time I grew a tad, the previous grafts would tear, and I'd need another surgery."

She winced, her eyes glistening.

"I warned you," he said softly. "The details suck."

"I totally agree. Did you have any relatives left—grandparents, aunts, uncles?"

"My living grandparents were in a nursing home. My nasty aunt and uncle visited once. My friends dropped away quickly. It was only my art teacher from school who visited me often. Fortunately, the staff and doctors at the burn facility were very kind."

"Any counseling?"

"Not the talking sort. Nine-year-old boys don't talk or complain much under the best of circumstances. Besides, you don't want to feel any more pain than you already have. Burns teach you not to cry, to adjust to living in the dark."

"What do you mean?"

"Just imagine how salty tears might feel on facial burns, and heavy breathing tears the scarring. I had a gauze bandage on my eyes for quite a while to catch the leaks."

Her green eyes glistened. "What you've experienced is truly horrendous."

While her empathic response comforted him, it also gave him a powerful feeling. He had her in the palm of his hand. She would not turn him away now. He despised people's pity, but he'd also learned to use it.

"The best therapy came from my art teacher," he said. "She got me to look at art books and guided me back to drawing and painting. I must have drawn every member of the staff and every patient I met dozens of times. It really kept me going."

"That teacher was a godsend," she said. "I remember reading that Matisse started painting in a hospital—he was a boy about the same age as you."

He was surprised she knew this relatively obscure fact. "Yes, Matisse was recovering from appendicitis, and then he fell into a severe depression. I believe he had the condition you now call bipolar. I was also around his age when I started copying his work and the other masters I admired, such as Van Gogh, Manet, and Cézanne. They became like a substitute family for me." He shifted in his seat. Kate staring at his face made him feel overly exposed. He wanted to cover the hideous scars he imagined she might be able to see.

"It looks like your treatments were successful," she said.

"Eventually, they were, but I didn't get plastic surgery until I was twenty. I looked like a freak between the ages of nine and twenty." As her gaze dipped down to his neck, he fingered his neckerchief. "You may wonder why—in this heat—I wear this thing and a long-sleeved shirt. It's to hide the scars plastic surgery didn't fix. People stare otherwise, or else they quickly look through me."

She held his gaze for a few moments, a look of compassion in her eyes. "We just have a few minutes left. Tell me, what happened after you left the hospital?"

"My aunt and uncle acted as my guardians briefly. They were cruel, and I detested them. It was only a matter of time before my abusive uncle buggered me. So, early one morning, I ran away. Things improved when I started living in the National Gallery of Art in London."

Her brows lifted. "You lived in the National Gallery; how was that possible?"

"I had read a grand story about a sister and brother who spent the night at the Met in New York," Nick said. "That gave me the idea. So, I studied the gallery routine and found out when guards made the rounds after the gallery closed. Then I hid in the Baby Room, where mums changed their poopy babies. It had a sink, a toilet cubicle, and a sturdy wooden change table for sleeping. Also, a chair I could sit on to read and draw. When the guard came to check this room for occupants, I left the cubicle door slightly ajar and stood on the toilet seat so my feet wouldn't show. That first night, I remember standing frozen, holding my breath, certain the guard would hear my thundering heart." He paused, savoring the intense interest in her eyes.

"What happened?" She leaned toward him. "Did you get caught?"

"Not by a guard. Six months later, a custodian caught me when I overslept one morning. I remember his distinctive voice waking me up. He imitated the bloke's Scottish lilt: "Top of the morning to you, laddie. Charlie's my name. What's yours?"

She smiled. "He sounds friendly. Did he kick you out?"

Nick chuckled. "Charlie was kindhearted. He was old and ailing, and in danger of losing his job. I offered to work for him for nothing if he'd keep my secret and let me stay in the gallery. I suggested I could pose as his grandson."

"That was resourceful of you. Did Charlie buy it?"

Nick nodded. "He did, especially after I showed him my sketches of paintings and people in the gallery. He loved art and was impressed with my ability. I remember him saying, 'Nick, me lad, you'll be famous and running this joint one day.' He was my first real fan."

"Charlie sounds like a miracle." She broke eye contact and looked down at her notes.

What would she decide? Had he won her over and made her forget he was a con and a crook? Did she even believe his story? It sounded like a made-up fairytale—the damaged wunderkind who found a home with a kindly old janitor in a world-famous museum. Of course, he'd left out some of his less endearing behavior, like stealing food from the gallery kitchen and raiding the lost-and-found for a warm jacket and hat. He'd done much worse, but that was later after Charlie died.

She looked up. "Nick, I'm sure what you've shared with me today wasn't easy. But, despite all you've lost and suffered, you are resilient and resourceful. You are also highly motivated to change and seem to have the capacity for psychological insight—though where you got that gift is a mystery." He felt the warmth of her smile. "I believe therapy can help you if you can tolerate the stress of opening old wounds and digging up your past. So, if you're willing to give this a trial run, let's schedule a regular meeting time." She opened her appointment book.

With Kate's acceptance, he heaved a sigh of relief, followed by a warm rush of triumph.

—

Nick stared at the empty slot in his section of the museum's vault, recalling Kate's warmth and words of acceptance from that critical session over three years ago. These warm recollections eased the pain of his present loss, and he wondered if the stolen Matisse given to Kate was somehow an act of fate, given that it had brought them back together. Maybe in an altered state, he'd left the painting on Kate's doorstep to bring her into his life. But that romantic notion didn't fit since it was Allegra who told Kate to call him about the Matisse.

Sly Allegra. Had she also engineered the theft? If so, how did she get a hold of his code, and why didn't she sell the painting or keep it for herself? She knew the original was worth millions, and a fine copy could pass as the original with some buyers. But to anonymously leave it for Kate? That was not credible, and he couldn't fathom her motive.

As he closed and locked the steel door of the vault, he considered the curators and the museum staff. He'd have to evaluate each one carefully. Steele never went into the museum vault. He always had the staff—including him—fetch and carry the artwork.

He cursed this monkey wrench complicating his plans. Getting out of town and away from Simon was still the priority. This meant he'd have to fix this problem tonight.

CHAPTER 8

The deep necessity of art is the examination of self-deception.
—ROBERT MOTHERWELL—

Thursday Night, October 11

Kate was asleep in her bed when a noise startled her awake. She listened, her heart thumping and the old cottage creaking. Her first thought was that her precious Matisse was in danger. Then she remembered Miles's warning. Maybe the gift-giver had come to take it back. As she jumped out of bed, she glanced at her bedside clock. It was 1:45 a.m.

At the back door, she threw on her jacket, pocketed her stun gun, and grabbed her keys. Flashlight in hand, she moved cautiously through the stand of giant bamboo to her studio. A light flashed in one of the studio's unshaded windows. Quietly, she tried the door and found it unlocked. She opened it slowly, with a strong premonition of who was inside. Across the dark space, someone else's flashlight shone on the storage room's double doors. A tall, shadowy figure was picking the lock.

"Looking for something?" Kate asked as she switched on the overhead lights.

The man in black straightened, then whipped around.

"Hello, Nick." She moved to the end of the worktable, stopped, and pulled out the hidden drawer. "Looking for this?" She placed the Matisse on top of the table. The colors blazed in the coldness between them. "So, you're still a thief?"

"Not as a rule," he said, crossing his arms. "That Matisse is my property."

Mirroring him, she crossed her arms. "If you wanted to keep it, why give it to me?"

"I didn't," he said, flashing his teeth, "but I *am* a secret admirer."

Kate rolled her eyes, "Oh, *please*. Who left it outside my front door?"

He shrugged. "Probably the thief who stole it from me."

"And who was that?"

Another maddening shrug. "How would I know?"

Nick's insolent indifference made her want to scream. She stared at this rogue wearing a black baseball cap and a badass smirk. His charming, cultivated persona had vanished, along with the sensitive artist full of self-loathing and invisible weeping wounds who had moved her so profoundly in therapy sessions.

Reining in her temper, she asked, "When did you paint this?"

"Why does that matter?" He brushed her off.

"It matters to me. You said you'd stopped selling forgeries when you left therapy three years ago."

"This is a copy," he said. "It only becomes a forgery if I try to sell it as the original."

"It's signed." She pointed to the signature. "That suggests you were planning to sell it."

A beat of silence. "I hadn't decided."

She stared at his impenetrable black eyes, looking for a hint of their lost connection. Had it all been lies and evasions? How could she have bought his pretense of a cure? "What a clever con man you are," she said, injured sarcasm in her tone. "You quickly figured out how to woo a therapist, didn't you? Psychic pain, self-revelation, deep insights, and the most compelling of all—a heartrending childhood. Was that *Oliver Twist* story of yours all a crock?"

"No, it was not," he said, his deep voice rising. "You think I made up the fire, living off garbage and scamming in the East End? I'll strip so you can see the scars that plastic surgery didn't fix." He began to unzip his black leather jacket.

Her hand flew up. "Don't."

Kate imagined Nick's scrawny boy's body and face mutilated by scars from a street kid's life and from the fire that burned down his home. *How could she attack this terrible truth?*

Nick moved to the table's edge, standing directly across from her. "Listen well, Kate, you're the only one who knows the truth about me, enough shit to destroy me." He paused, his gaze fixed on hers. "To survive, I've had to keep the upper hand, but I couldn't do that with you. I had to trust you and let you in on the details of my sordid life. That was freeing for a time, but—"

"Were you afraid I'd betray you?"

"That's not why I quit." He looked down.

"Why then?"

But he'd slipped out of reach and was scanning the various materials on the table—the open art books, her notes, drawings, cans of brushes, photographs, and her new painting. Her fear escalated as she watched him, trembling, hardly able to breathe. In seconds, the tables would be turned, and he would know what a sham she was. Only a con artist like Nick could quickly guess her nefarious intentions. He sidestepped around the table's corner, edging closer, a frown on his face. Her heart racing, she moved to her left and around the corner. Through the open window, she heard the wind crackling through dry leaves. The torn branch of a eucalyptus tree thudded on the roof. Inside, the hot air sizzled with tension. Nick took off his hat and ran his hand through his tangled hair, his puzzled gaze lingering on her Guy Rose pastiche.

Kate stopped breathing.

He looked up, shocked, his laser gaze cutting right through her. "You have quite a few photographs of Guy Rose's paintings, along with all these close-up shots of his brushwork. I assume you painted this pastiche?" He pointed to the small oil.

"Yes, I admire Guy Rose," she said haltingly. "I'm trying to learn his technique."

"I'd say you're learning it quite well," he mocked. "You need to clean up the brushwork by the pond, get more sparkle in the water. Dazzling water is a Guy Rose signature, don't you know?" He gave her a patronizing smile.

His bitter disappointment in her stung. She was supposed to be the model of good mental health, unsullied and saintly. How she wished he'd just yell at her and call her a pathetic fraud and phony instead of shaming her with his scornful condescension.

He turned the painting over. "Ah, a suitable old canvas." He looked up, eyeing her with disdain. "Are you planning to sell this as a Rose?"

Pause. "I haven't decided."

He rolled his eyes. "So, now you're a smartass as well as smart." He leaned forward, hands on the table, his voice blasting, "You're a better con than me, Kate. No one has ever fooled me the way you have. All the time I spent in your office spelling out the dirty tricks of my trade, it never occurred to me I was teaching my pure-hearted therapist how to become the next Phantom."

"No! That's not how it was. I never had one thought of copying or making forgeries for the ten months I saw you in therapy. I only wanted to understand and help you."

"Bollocks. Dig deeper, Kate."

She sat on the high stool next to him, hands covering her face. How could she be drawn to a con man and then dabble in the same kind of crime? An unnerving thought broke through the confusion in her head. Maybe she was drawn to him *because* he was a gifted con artist, a superb shapeshifter who could become someone else in a blink. That he could make such brilliant paintings by so convincingly imitating the masters seemed an extraordinary ability. But why did she find his faking expertise so appealing? The answer now rushed to the forefront. Nick resembled her famous father, the great singing actor who could disappear into any role and mesmerize an audience. No one, including his family, could decipher his real character, and they only sensed, under his surface charm, the dark secrets that eventually destroyed him. Onstage, Conner O'Dade had been just as convincing playing heroes as he was playing villains. Because of young Katie's unusual singing talent, her father had driven her relentlessly to become a child singing star. But after he was murdered, nine-year-old Katie lost her bell-like singing voice.

Kate had coped with the trauma of losing her larger-than-life father, her angelic voice, and a glamorous theatrical life by turning inward and to another kind of art. Painting pictures didn't require a beautiful voice, and it freed her from depending on people and the need to examine her feelings. Also, her mentally unstable mother required constant care, and Kate spent much of her time doing chores, fixing things, and being the responsible grown-up. When her artwork would not support them, she went into psychology and became an expert at treating traumatized creative people. Clearly, Nick not only embodied aspects of her father, but she saw him as the bold, confident self she would like to be. He, like her, also wanted to become someone else. Perhaps she harbored the wish that he could free the repressed side of her—the dutiful good girl, the faded flower who'd lost her radiant bloom a long time ago.

She now questioned her "goodness" and devotion to helping people. It seemed the main engine driving these traits was her need to please, first her parents and now everyone. She judged this as a character weakness, although it was a common trait for women of her generation. In the past, it made any self-expressive work in the arts feel self-indulgent and kept her focused on pleasing gallerists and critics instead of developing her own style. Nick wasn't the only one with an identity problem.

She looked up at him. "Okay, Self-Analysis 101. In addition to wanting to help you, maybe the good girl in me secretly longed to be a talented badass like you. Maybe I got off on how cleverly you screwed rich assholes in the fucked-up art world."

He laughed. "That's more like it. What have you sold so far?"

"A fake Maurice Braun landscape."

"Who bought it?"

"The collector Bryce Morton bought it, even after I told him I painted it. He refused to believe me. He was convinced it was an early Braun, an unknown work."

"Brilliant." He grinned. "You screwed a pompous ass in exactly the right way. He could never accuse you of a crime since you'd admitted to painting the picture and didn't pass it off as a Braun. Smart girl. All perfectly legal."

"You taught me well." But, so far, she'd just been flirting with the devil. If she sold her latest painting as a Rose and not under her own name, she'd be a bona fide crook. She couldn't accept that outcome. But how else was she going to earn enough money to meet her obligations?

Kate looked down at the exuberant Matisse, longing to fly out of his window and dive into the warm, pink waves—floating, rocking, freed from all the pressures and anxiety.

When she looked up, Nick was standing close to her. She could feel his body heat and smell his masculine scent.

"Kate, I'm the last person to judge you." He looked her straight in the eyes. "Allegra told me you were in serious debt. I have money, a lot of money. Let me help you."

"No!"

"Kate," he said softly, "I wouldn't bet on my being alive today if not for you. I've been working on original paintings and have little desire to make fakes, all because of your help."

"That's good to hear." She wanted to believe him, but given the severity of his problems, his recovery seemed suspiciously quick for only ten months of therapy.

"Thanks to you, I can feel for others at least some of the time." He gently stroked back the lock of hair flopping in her face. "As for the ability to love a woman, I'm working on it." He kissed her hand and then put his arms around her.

She sat very still, warmed by his body, touched by his words, the blood pulsing through her. His musky, masculine smell soothed and aroused her. Her body ached to melt into his, but she held back, resenting the part of her mind that still worked—the rational voice that said beware, this man is a brilliant con artist with the world's slickest silver tongue.

CHAPTER 9

The ends justify the means.
—NICCOLÒ MACHIAVELLI—

Thursday Evening, October 11

Private Investigator Francisco Flynn stood outside Kate's open studio window, grinding his teeth. The strong, dry wind made his eyes tear and his nose itch. He recalled those exciting days when he and Kate were investigating her father's murder, trading insights and insults, and falling in love. He hadn't contacted her since she'd gone back to her cheating husband for Sam's sake nine years ago. He'd let her go, too proud and wrecked to put up a fight. Probably the biggest mistake of his blunder-prone life. What about now? Did he regret not contacting her after her nitwit of a husband fell off a mountain? Yes and no. Way too risky, he'd decided. The old wound still festered. Shaking that thought, he reminded himself to keep his head in the game and focus on the task at hand.

He'd been watching and listening to McCoy's manipulations and slick seduction.

Raoul, his partner, had reported following McCoy from his loft to Kate's house and had said the dude was dressed all in black like a cat burglar. Given the lateness of the hour, Flynn thought it prudent to be on hand to ensure Kate's safety and to prevent the possible theft of her potentially valuable painting. Knowing McCoy was an art thief as well as a forger, he hoped to catch the crook in the act of breaking the law. Instead, he was stuck outside watching the bastard bully and seduce his latest female mark—Kate, the woman he had loved so fiercely after the debacle of his and her broken marriages.

And he'd hated the intensity of his emotions when his job of following Raquel Steele had led to Kate's home therapy office. Raquel was clearly in treatment with Kate. Hired by Simon Steele to keep tabs on Raquel and her secret lover, Flynn waited in his SUV on the street outside Kate's office, battling the desire to catch a glimpse of his lost love. But now, seeing her slim figure through the studio window, he felt nothing but regret, heartache, and the burning wish to rewrite his life.

He inhaled the sharp scent of parched eucalyptus leaves, longed for a cold beer, and fumed. From the bug he'd placed in Nick's conservation lab at the museum, he'd heard Kate's and Nick's interaction over the Matisse. He'd sensed a past bond had existed between them and could almost feel the heat simmering beneath their formal greetings and polite exchanges.

Listening to McCoy's evaluation of the Matisse, he was bothered to find himself impressed by the limey's intelligent delivery and breadth of knowledge. But he didn't trust the con's bravura snow job. The guy was a gifted scammer, and Flynn knew Kate could be taken in by seductive liars. She'd grown up with two—her devious father and smarmy uncle. But she was a smart shrink. *How could she fall for McCoy's obvious manipulations?* The answer was obvious, he realized. She was lonely, unhappy, and vulnerable. Do-gooder therapist types like her could be suckers for sob stories and hard luck tales. After all, she'd fallen for his.

The studio lights went off, and Flynn heard McCoy and Kate going out the door. He stood rooted outside the window, the harsh wind tearing at his clothes and hair. He wanted to smash McCoy's smug face, but, to his disgust, he was also turned on by their intense attraction.

Flynn took the opportunity to jimmy Kate's pitiful studio lock and bug her studio in case McCoy showed up there again. He'd already bugged Kate's home office. He figured at some point Raquel would tell her therapist about her affair with McCoy and whether they were planning to rob Steele as Simon suspected. Flynn knew that none of his bugging activities were legal, but invasion-of-privacy surveillance was the only way he might burrow inside the Nick-Raquel liaison and find out about their plans to rip off Steele. If the end justified the means, Flynn would break the rules, a mindset that had gotten him booted from the Sheriff's Department after he broke the corrupt captain's jaw.

On the way to his car, he saw McCoy get into his SUV. He did not appear to be carrying the Matisse. Flynn breathed a sigh of relief. *Good for you, Kate, I taught you well.* She still had enough sense to throw out the wolf and keep the painting.

CHAPTER 10

And Then There Were None
—AGATHA CHRISTIE—

Friday, Late Afternoon, October 12

DCI Eddie Cromwell stepped out of an Uber at an ocean-front address in Del Mar. The California sun dazzled his eyes, but his brain was still fogged from the fourteen-hour flight from London. Was this the right place for his team's first meeting? He hadn't met any of the three investigators, though he'd researched and selected all of them. Destiny Hawk, the LAPD Lakota Sioux detective, had alerted him that Nick McCoy was in San Diego and was now the conservator at Dixon Steele's Museum. He stood at the Asian-inspired entry gate and pressed the buzzer. What were coppers doing in this slick, high-end home?

"G'day, mate," a twangy Aussie voice boomed over the intercom.

Inside the interior courtyard, a stout bloke in a bush hat and a dark-skinned beauty came toward him.

"Detective Archie Hasofer, San Diego Police." The Aussie pumped his hand.

Eddie smiled, turning to the striking woman. "You must be Detective Hawk."

"Welcome, Chief Inspector Cromwell." They shook hands. "Please call me Desi."

"And I am Eddie, temporarily on leave as DCI of Scotland Yard's Art and Antiques Unit."

He followed the pair across a Japanese-style bridge arching over a koi pond. The huge black and orange koi looked too big for the modest pond they were thrashing around in. Their extra wide mouths gaped open. He showed an empty hand, "Sorry, mates."

After setting down his travel bag inside the entryway of the house, he followed the two detectives into a spacious living room, then through a sliding glass door and onto a deck. With one hand shielding his eyes against the Pacific Ocean's metallic glare, he took in the vast expanse of glittering water that stretched to a sharp horizon and a blinding neon yellow sun.

"Is this your place?" Eddie asked, eyeing Archie's sunglasses with envy.

"Hell no. I'm house-sitting for a filthy rich mate, guarding the valuables. It's mine for a month." He grinned, sweat gleaming on his good-natured face.

Eddie would not have guessed that this jolly-looking guy was an expert in financial crimes with the San Diego Police Department. Archie took off to the bar inside to fetch Eddie a drink.

The strapping chap standing at the deck railing turned around, revealing the beak nose, carved cheekbones, and mahogany skin of his Apache ancestors. Only his blue eyes and Irish surname suggested he had a white father.

"Lord Cromwell, I presume?" The hunk thrust out his hand, his ice-blue eyes mocking. "Francisco Flynn, Private Investigator."

"Bugger Lord Cromwell." Eddie shook his hand. The cheeky PI had done his homework. "I only pull out that nonsense for special jobs. But Nick McCoy just might be one of those jobs. He's a lad who's half in awe of the peerage."

"You're shitting me," Flynn said. "I'd guess McCoy gets off on shafting the toffs."

"That too." Eddie took his gin and tonic from Archie, now standing at his side. "Both can be true. McCoy's a man of many personas."

Desi sat down at a table covered with platters of appetizers. "Think we can uncover the *real* McCoy?" she asked.

Flynn rolled his eyes at Desi. "I doubt there is a *real* McCoy."

The PI is sharp, Eddie thought, feeling dull in comparison. "I've been after this crook for the past ten years. He's the most successful, elusive art thief and forger I've ever tried to catch."

"Was chasing a phantom really worth ten years of your life?" Flynn asked. "Who the hell cares about a lowlife forger ripping off rich assholes."

"I care!" *You're the asshole* Eddie wanted to say. His Art Squad had gotten little support from the Yard or the public because of such ignorance. "I see you're uninformed about art crime, Mr. Flynn. Most people are, including cops."

"Inform me then and drop the mister." He crossed his arms.

Eddie now regretted including Flynn on the team. While the PI was a first-rate tracker and formerly an effective homicide detective, he'd been fired from the Sheriff's Department for gross disrespect and insubordination. He stepped toward the PI, adrenaline coursing through his bloodstream, wetted his dry mouth, and began.

"Art theft and forgery are much bigger enterprises than you suppose. Early in the 1960s, when paintings were selling for stratospheric prices, organized crime syndicates began using forgeries and stolen art to fund their black-market operations—trafficking in guns, drugs, and cultural artifacts. Funding terrorism came later."

"You'd think the link between art and terrorism would wake people up," Desi said.

"But it hasn't. Blindness persists. Even when a researcher found that certain stolen paintings funded the 9/11 terrorist attack on the World Trade Center. At that time, there was only one art crime detective in New York City. *And then there were none.*" Eddie looked at the three alert faces and knew he had their full attention.

"We seem stuck in Hollywood's old art heist movies," Archie said, "like the one with that bored billionaire—*The Thomas Crown Affair*."

"Right, and McCoy resembles a Hollywood art thief," Eddie said. "In reality, McCoy and his coterie of shady dealers, crooked galleries, criminal collectors, and complicit auction houses are at the top of the list of what's made art crime the third biggest criminal enterprise, right after drugs and guns. Art crime generates six to eight crooked billion per year."

Flynn whistled. "I don't get how thugs can profit that much from art."

"I'll start with the selling of forged or stolen paintings to unscrupulous or unsuspecting dealers and collectors. Then there's using the art for barter or collateral on the black market—for example, trading your stolen Picasso for money, drugs, or guns with members of another crime syndicate. The criminal art world also uses fine art for money laundering and tax evasion. Are you getting the picture?"

"Yep, it's not pretty."

Eddie gave each of the three a hard look. "You all have excellent credentials, but I want a committed team. So, if you doubt the worthiness of this project, please bow out now."

Desi's hand shot up. "I'm all in. Recovering stolen art is my passion. Next to nothing has been done about looters who have stolen Indian art and artifacts for generations." She glanced from Archie to Flynn. "Listen, guys, if we don't make a splash now and catch the big players like McCoy and Steele, we'll never get the proper services and support for dealing with art crime in LA or anywhere." Her voice rose. "The LA Art Theft Detail, the only police art crime unit in the US, is about to be disbanded even though it's very effective."

"What stupidity," Eddie said.

"Doesn't the FBI have an art crime division in LA?" Archie asked.

Desi nodded. "I often work with the two investigators on their team. They get little training, and the available resources are pathetic. The FBI has only twenty-four agents covering art crime in the entire US.

How crazy is that? Me and my partner—Detective Don Hrycyk—plus twenty-four FBI agents are up against one of the planet's biggest, most corrupt, and dirtiest industries."

"How right you are!" Eddie said. "No one gets the connections between pretty pictures and ugly crimes. My art squad of six detectives is on its way to being reduced to a smaller team, soon to be zero, I predict."

This insanity made Eddie want to strike out at the people in power who inevitably failed to see the big picture. But demoralization had taken its toll, and he didn't have the heart to go on much longer. His mission to clean up even one corner of the filthy art world seemed increasingly futile, and his energy and motivation had dipped since his only son had died in a hit-and-run a year ago. Eddie was making undercover efforts to track down his son's killer, ignoring the Yard rules against investigating a crime involving a family member. He still didn't know if it was an accident or a murder. His promise of an early retirement to his ailing wife weighed heavily—this operation had to be Cromwell's last stand.

"Archie, do you still want to be on this team?" Eddie sounded weary.

"I'm a documents expert, and that includes forgeries, but I don't have art crime credentials. I'm good at learning new stuff, and I detest fraud and con men of any kind. Count me in."

A good bloke. With his sweat-stained bush hat and beer-swilling, Archie had the rough-hewn look of a stereotypical "No worries, mate" Aussie. But with his impressive financial crimes record and research expertise, Eddie knew better than to underestimate him.

"I'm in if you can tolerate my easygoing personality," Flynn smirked.

"We'll see." Eddie hoped he could manage this abrasive PI with his vexing authority issues. In his favor, Flynn had natural investigative talent, years of experience, and unusual drive.

Eddie pulled out the chair next to Desi and sat down. "Let's see where we go from here. Flynn, I commend your foresight in bugging McCoy's conservation lab and being on the spot at Dr. O'Dade's studio to record McCoy's late-night theft and seduction attempts. Desi sent me your recordings. Did you see that dramatic scene unfold?"

"Most of it," Flynn said. "I got to Doc Kate's studio a little after she did, and I stood at the window, peeping and recording. Hardly noticed the windstorm ruining my stylish hairdo." He stroked his coal-black ponytail.

Eddie flashed a grin. At least the cheeky lad had a sense of humor. "I gather the loving couple held your attention."

"Not without grinding my teeth. That slick bastard almost succeeded in seducing her."

"Do you believe McCoy really painted Kate's Matisse?"

"It sure sounded like it. But McCoy's a con; he instinctively misleads."

"Good point." Eddie tried to sound genuine. Giving praise had never been encouraged or modeled in Eddie's cold family. It was a struggle for him to get the insipid American pap out of his mouth, but he knew it would be worth the effort. The fact that his father was an English earl, owner of more than one large estate, was not likely to endear him to Yankee cops.

He glanced at Archie. Behind his dark glasses, the Aussie seemed to be making eyes at Desi, whose gaze was fixed on Flynn. Was a lust triangle brewing?

"I assume you've both heard the recordings?" Eddie asked.

They nodded, and Archie sat down next to Desi with his back to the view.

Eddie turned to Flynn. "Tell us what you know from your client Simon Steele, Dixon's son. He hired you to follow Steele's wife, Raquel, right?"

"Yeah, Simon hates McCoy and wants him exposed, disgraced, and blasted out of his money-lined art nest." Flynn rattled the diminishing ice in his water glass and downed a couple of swallows. "When Simon approached me, he suspected three things. One, that this slick Brit was having an affair with his father's third wife, Raquel, a beauty thirty years younger than Steele. Two, that McCoy had wormed his way into his father's affections to get control of his collection and the fortune. And three, Raquel and Nick are in cahoots to rip off Big Daddy. Simon thinks he deserves to inherit the entire collection when Daddy dies."

"What's your take on Simon Steele and his suspicions?" Eddie asked.

"Simon is a good-for-nothing parasite. Spends his time getting high, dealing drugs, and making sadistic porn flicks. He's also smart and sly and can smell a rat because he is one. He was right about McCoy having an affair with the ravishing Raquel, but I didn't buy that McCoy was a crook. Not at first. I knew this wasn't about Simon wanting to protect his dear old dad. It was about getting rid of competitors and securing his inheritance. I didn't want to touch this case—I don't work for sleazebags or mess with adultery if I can help it. I only took on this case because I owed the referral source a big favor, and he called it in."

"Did you find any other evidence against McCoy?" Desi asked.

"I found no criminal record for the adult Nicholas McCoy," Flynn said.

A train rumbled by on the tracks below, blasting its ear-splitting horn and causing the deck to tremble. Eddie got up, went to the railing, and looked down. The train appeared to run right along the edge of the bluffs, sending tremors through the dry, brittle sandstone. He imagined the loosened chunks raining down on the beach below.

"No wonder your mate got the hell out of here," Eddie said. "Let's go inside."

Archie gestured toward the food. "Help yourself. It'll tide you over till tea."

Eddie loaded a stoneware plate with a selection of chips, salsa, olives, and fruit, then retreated into the mercifully dim and cooler living room. He sat across from Desi, a low coffee table between them. Archie sat next to Desi, and Flynn had no choice but to lower his strapping frame onto the cramped loveseat next to Eddie.

Flynn shifted to gain a tad more distance from the British inspector.

Eddie, slouched so close to Flynn's fit body, felt more fatigued and ancient. "This low seat is killing my back." He stood up awkwardly to avoid brushing against Flynn, then pulled a black lacquered chair closer to the table and sat. He picked up his gin and tonic. "Better. A good view of the paintings from here. Puts me in the right mood to talk about art crime."

"I want to hear the evidence you've got against McCoy," Flynn said.

Eddie bit into a dill pickle. "While the incidents do follow a clear pattern, we lack hard evidence. McCoy came to my squad's attention ten years ago when Sotheby's in New York discovered a forgery. But that occurred only because the original painting, a Manet, was found to be in storage at London's National Gallery. Since McCoy worked as a conservator there, he had unlimited access to stored paintings and the necessary supplies and the talent to make a perfect copy—he'd won prizes in painting at the Royal Academy of Arts. So, we suspected him of selling the forgery to the collector who brought it."

"Did the buyer then finger McCoy as the seller?" Flynn asked.

Eddie sighed. "No, McCoy is a pro. He's very clever in covering his tracks, and the art world is notoriously secretive—a godsend for criminals. Also, auction houses, gallerists, collectors, and museums typically don't report thefts and forgeries, as it could hurt their reputations and negatively impact their business. First, the buying and selling of art is wholly unregulated, and no paperwork is required. In this case, the buyer never revealed his identity to Sotheby's. Second, the clever art forger rarely sells directly to a buyer. Crooked dealers usually serve as the go-between."

"After that incident," Eddie continued, "McCoy didn't surface again until he'd moved to the States and was teaching conservation and art history at the Barnes Foundation in Philadelphia. Somebody uncovered one of their Matisse paintings as a forgery after McCoy left. Unfortunately, the Barnes staff did not suspect McCoy, so we couldn't make a dent in their conviction. They thought he walked on water."

"Shit," Flynn said.

"Precisely," Eddie agreed, taking a swallow of gin. "Here's my last and most recent example. It occurred here in California at the Norton Simon Museum in Pasadena, where McCoy worked as a conservator before moving down to San Diego to take the Steele Museum job. Quite a while after McCoy had left Norton Simon, a curator discovered one of their Degas pastels was a forgery. No one even suspected McCoy. They seemed sorrier to have lost him than the Degas."

"Christ, does everyone love McCoy except for sleazy Simon and me?" Flynn asked.

"Not me, mate," Archie said.

"That bloody spook haunts my sleepless nights," Eddie said.

"He's not all bad," Desi said. "From those recordings, I sensed he genuinely cares for Kate."

Flynn grimaced. "And Raquel Steele; does he care deeply for her, too?"

"Hey, the lad's got a big heart," Archie said.

Eddie snorted, rubbed his aching eyes, and straightened. "Back to the problem. We can't nail McCoy with what we have now. We must trick him into showing his hand and catch him in the act of theft or selling a forgery. It would also be helpful to track down his coterie of crooked contacts."

"I bet there's evidence—forged or stolen paintings—in that East Village loft of his," Flynn said. "But it's locked up like a fortress."

"I'm not surprised," Eddie said. "We must get more on McCoy's history before he became known for his triumphs at the Royal Academy of Arts. We do have the potboiler fiction of his first twenty years, which sounds like it was inspired by Charles Dickens. Somehow, this street kid claws his way out of London's East End and climbs to the top of three highly-skilled occupations—art conservation-restoration, sophisticated art theft, and expert art forgery. How did he get there?" His gaze shifted among the three sober-looking investigators.

"Haven't you found out anything else?" Flynn asked.

"Not much. McCoy likely changed his name and appearance at various points, plus he's a consummate actor. He plays the part he senses will win you over. I observed him once being interviewed at the Yard about the forged Manet. Fortunately, he was unable to see me. The bloke came across as a pitch-perfect, erudite toff—you'd think he'd gone to Eton and Oxford. McCoy's a speech virtuoso who can play multiple roles. He'd make a great undercover art crime detective. It's our bad luck that he chose the wrong side."

Eddie swirled the melting ice in his glass, wishing he had an undercover operative like McCoy to catch McCoy the Phantom. "So, how and why did our talented Renaissance man become a crook? We know he worked for the successful but shady dealer Jackson Chase in his youth, but we haven't been able to uncover his identity before he became Nick McCoy at the age of fourteen. We don't know his birth name or why he may have needed to erase his earlier years. What motivations drive this man? Answers to these questions would help us catch him. We must find ways to get closer to him, perhaps become friends or associates."

Flynn stood up and stretched, then went to the bar for a refill.

"Archie," Eddie said. "I'd like you to do another deep background check on our boy and look harder at his sketchy history. See what you can uncover. My lads are on other assignments."

"I'll give it a go," Archie said.

"Desi, you help Flynn with continued surveillance and see if you can find a way to get close to Raquel or Kate, which will put you closer to McCoy."

"Flynn, I'm assuming you'll keep up round-the-clock on all the players?"

"Yep, that's my plan."

"Good," Eddie said. "To catch McCoy in a scam or a theft, we need a better idea of whether he and Raquel are colluding in a plot against Steele as Simon suspects. It would be grand if we could catch the two sods at once. We have a unique opportunity coming up, which is why I'm here now. The Steele Museum has an important exhibition of the California Impressionists opening Sunday evening. It's a unique opportunity to interact directly with most of the players."

"Great." Flynn scowled. "But how do us nobodies get invitations?"

"Fay Martinez, the museum director, owes Desi for past services," Eddie said. "Martinez has been told that we're looking for possible art thieves in disguise who might be attending the show in preparation for a heist. She arranged for Desi to be a server with the catering service. Flynn, you'll be one of the guards."

"Right," Flynn said. "We brown folk make the best help."

Cromwell resisted rolling his eyes. "I will pose as a rich, effete, but shady French art collector. I'm hoping to engineer a sting that will entrap Steele and McCoy. Archie, I'd like you to be my driver for the evening."

"Sure thing, boss, so long as I don't have to look at the art."

CHAPTER 11

A museum is a place where one should lose one's head.
—Renzo Piano—

Sunday Evening, October 14

Archie held the door open as Eddie stepped out of a black limousine in front of the Steele Museum in downtown San Diego. Eddie noticed the museum's pillared, classical façade, which clashed with the surrounding Victorian architecture. A steady stream of people who had been invited to the black-tie opening began queuing up to enter the California Impressionists Exhibition. A small gaggle of mostly local news media stood at the sides of the entry, greeting guests while their cameramen and photographers took pictures of the mayor and other dignitaries.

"Archie," Eddie said, "could you please come back here after you park the car and watch who comes in? Just observe, listen, and take photos of any of our players and those with them. Strike up conversations if you can do so naturally."

"Got it, boss."

"Please call me *sir* or, if you prefer, *Monsieur Le Comte*."

Archie smirked. "Got it, *sir*." He was almost unrecognizable in a rented chauffeur's uniform, a peaked cap replacing his bush hat.

Eddie strode down the walkway to the high, open doors of the entrance. He'd jettisoned his rumpled British don look for the formal attire befitting his role as the rakish French aristocrat and art collector *Le Comte Antoine de Guise*. His formerly gray hair was now a soft black shot with silver, and his pale skin glowed with a deep tan. Sporting a Van Dyke beard, he looked through a pair of contact lenses that colored his gray eyes a dark brown.

At the entry to the reception hall, he stopped at a table where a pretty greeter, holding a checklist, asked for his name. "Good evening, I am *Antoine de Guise*," he said with a French accent. Thanks to Amalie, his French nanny of many years, he spoke Parisian French like a native.

A tall, statuesque brunette in a turquoise sheath stepped up to him, smiling. "Welcome, *Monsieur Le Comte*. I am Fay Martinez, the director of the Steele Museum. We are so pleased you could join us."

"*Enchanté, Madame.*" Eddie kissed her hand. "Please call me Antoine."

"And I am Fay," she smiled. "Come, Antoine, let me show you around." She took his arm, and they strolled into the crowded reception hall.

The director's welcoming manner assured Eddie that Desi had prepared her well for his presence and purpose. Desi had informed him of Fay's desire to help identify anyone posing a threat to the museum's artworks. Fay was also in favor of keeping the undercover operation a secret from others in attendance, including the museum's founder, Dixon Steele, a notorious control freak who would likely interfere and blow up the operation. According to Desi, while Fay knew of Steele's personality flaws, she had no inkling that he was one of the art crooks under investigation.

Desi, who somehow managed to come off convincingly as a server, approached them with flutes of champagne on a tray. Her gaze momentarily connected with Fay's, then with Eddie's. He hardly recognized the detective with her hair pulled back in a bun at the nape of her neck and a pair of large, black-framed glasses obscuring the fine structure of her face. With the addition of pasty makeup dulling the copper glow of her skin, she'd managed to conceal her good looks and appear almost homely. Eddie was impressed with her artistry but could only give her a polite *"Merci, Mademoiselle"* as he picked up one of the flutes.

Sipping the cold bubbly with the elegant Fay on his arm, Eddie scanned the crowd for Steele and McCoy. He spotted neither of his prey, and for a few minutes, he allowed himself to be swept up in the illusion that he was just a special guest at this glamorous event. The spacious reception hall seemed flush with sparkling women in stylish gowns, flashing their jewels and whitened teeth at the self-satisfied gents packed into their black tuxedos.

Through the crowd, Eddie caught glimpses of the distinctive landscapes of some of the most talented women painters of the California Impressions era—Meta Cressey, Alice Klauber, Lucy Bacon, and E. Charlton Fortune. Their colorful landscapes and garden scenes appeared to recall an earlier era on the walls, and—for a moment—Eddie imagined he was inside one of Renoir's vibrant garden party paintings. A few ladies in period dress on the arms of men wearing top hats added to the distinctive *fin de siècle* vibe. Lighting created a glow of candlelight, making even the elderly look young. A blending of pricey perfumes filled the air, along with the uplifting sounds of a string quartet playing Mozart.

As Eddie strolled beyond the central circular bar laden with hors d'oeuvres, he saw a raised stage and a veiled, rectangular object hanging on the back wall. Two black-clad guards flanked the veiled rectangle, signifying its importance and value. On the platform to the left were three chairs and a podium. In front of the stage were rows of chairs.

"I assume that is an artwork?" Eddie pointed to the draped rectangle.

"Indeed." Fay flashed her perfect teeth. "It's our special surprise for the evening. Dixon will unveil the work and donate it to the museum later this evening. He thinks it will spice up the evening in case the guests become bored with our humble California Impressionists."

Eddie wondered how the charming Fay managed to stomach such an arrogant ass. "Do you know the artist?" he asked.

"No. Dixon won't tell anyone. He's quite a showman and wants it to be a total surprise. I'm to go around whispering to everyone about it to build up the suspense." She giggled. "That's hardly necessary, do you think?"

"*Non, pas du tout.* It's obviously a unique artwork behind that lavender veil, and those muscled guards indicate the monetary value. Why a lavender veil? That's unusual."

"So is Dixon," Fay said. "The color is supposed to be a clue to the artist or the painting."

"Ah, like a game show. Is there a prize for getting it right?"

Fay shrugged. "Probably. Dixon likes games."

Eddie assumed Steele had a self-serving motive for this donation. In addition to his own self-aggrandizement, he would get a hefty tax break. He wondered if Steele was brash enough to risk donating a forged painting in front of an audience full of art lovers and experts.

"Have you ever been to the Barnes Foundation in Philadelphia?" Fay asked.

"Yes, indeed," Eddie said. "It's unforgettable, especially if you're an Impressionist-Post-Impressionist fan."

Fay grinned. "Now you're in for a treat."

As she led him through the doorway to the main gallery, Eddie saw Flynn standing guard, a black-clad statue, rigid and expressionless. He'd tucked his distinctive ponytail under a brimmed cap pulled low, cleverly shadowing his striking blue eyes.

Once inside the long, rectangular gallery, Eddie stood, stunned. *Déjà vu*—he thought. He knew Steele Museum had features in common with the original version of the Barnes Foundation, but he hadn't expected such a close replica. At first glance, this room resembled the enchanting interior of the Barnes's main gallery. Unlike the stiff formality of other modern art museums, it had the welcoming atmosphere of a cultured, Italianate country manor. The paintings were displayed in layers—salon-style—in what Barnes called "ensembles," often incorporating complementary objects like an antique chest, an African sculpture, a certain ceramic vessel, and a chair. Like the Barnes, Steele Museum had light wood floors, and the walls were coated in a golden-toned burlap that warmed the atmosphere and brought out the lush colors of the Impressionist paintings.

"What do you think?" Fay asked.

"It's an impressive imitation," Eddie said. "Who is responsible for creating this grand illusion? Clearly, *Monsieur* Steele fancies himself the modern Albert Barnes, but who put this exhibition together?"

"The man most responsible for the paintings' care and the Barnes-like arrangements—the ensembles—is our talented conservator, Nick McCoy, who has worked at Barnes and assisted the curator."

Eddie nodded, aware of McCoy's time at Barnes and his imitative genius. "The only way I can tell I'm not at the Barnes is the actual paintings on display. The artists are talented, but they are not Matisse, Picasso, Monet, Cézanne, or Renoir."

"Or Modigliani, Manet, Pissarro, Degas, or Seurat," Fay chimed in, then threw up her arms, laughing.

Eddie smiled. "I doubt your Mr. Steele will win this competition."

Weaving through the clusters of lively, chattering people, Fay was asked many questions about the veiled painting. What was it? Who was the artist? She told everyone that she didn't know what artwork Steele was donating but that the lavender veil was supposed to be a clue.

The secret surprise seemed to heighten the general euphoria fizzing like champagne bubbles in the room. Fay led Eddie toward the trio peering at a William Wendt landscape and introduced the stubby, bald gent first.

"Ah, *Monsieur* Steele," Eddie said. "I am delighted by your museum, and it is a great pleasure to meet such a distinguished collector." He then launched into a robust but skillful effort to establish his shady connections. "I've done business with a good friend of yours—François Massenet."

"Ha! Rival is more like it." Steele bared his frightful teeth and crushed Eddie's hand. "That bastard thinks he has a better collection than mine. Tell him he'd kill for the Picasso I've got. By the way, this is my wife, Raquel. She's another frog."

Raquel winced at his derogatory term for the French, then gave Eddie a warm smile, "*Monsieur Le Comte, enchantée.*" She was a vision in a white, flowing Grecian gown.

"*Le plaisir est pour moi.*" Eddie kissed her delicate, outstretched hand.

"I'd introduce you to my son, Simon, but he's outside, up to no good I reckon," Steele grinned, clearly pleased at the thought.

"You must meet my adviser, Nick McCoy," Steele said, turning to Nick. "He won't let me make a move without his say-so. He's why my collection beats *Monsieur* 'Le Rat' Massenet's." He chuckled.

Eddie quickly sized up his adversary. Like him, Nick was about six feet tall but with broader shoulders and a more self-assured bearing, which made Eddie feel diminished. The forger's penetrating black eyes seemed to see right through him but gave nothing away. He had long, strong fingers and a confident grip. Eddie felt his confidence slipping. His temples throbbed. *Merde*, this can't be happening. After decades of risking his life and keeping his cool undercover, at last, he stood face to face with the elusive Phantom—his nemesis—only to be weakened by a bloody attack of stage fright.

CHAPTER 12

A painting in a museum probably hears more foolish remarks than anything else in the world.

—Edmond De Goncourt—

Sunday Evening, October 14

Nick watched the count's genial smile freeze on his face, the man's dark eyes widening in surprise or fear. Something had rattled this suave gent. Nick searched his memory but could not recall ever meeting this collector, although the count's name seemed familiar. He noted that the count's dark complexion had the evenness produced by a tanning salon or expertly applied makeup to conceal his age or something else. The count was either quite vain or attempting to disguise his actual appearance.

"I hope you're enjoying the exhibition, *Monsieur Le—*"

"Antoine, please. Titles are a nuisance. The exhibit is most impressive." The stiff, formal-sounding count spoke with a perfect Parisian accent.

"Nick, the paintings look fresh, thanks to your magic," Fay said.

"Good thing Nick brings some class to this lot of second-rate paint pushers." Steele's sweeping gesture took in the room full of luminous paintings.

Fay stood frozen, her lips fixed in an icy smile. The count's nostrils flared in distaste. Nick itched to smack Steele's smug, ugly mug and took in a slow, deep breath. He could make no mistakes. For the next five days, Nick had to stay in Dixon's good graces and arouse no suspicion. But he couldn't let this insult pass.

"Dixon." A friendly smile softened Nick's sharp tone. "It's not like you to crap in your own nest. I believe it was your conception of this exhibition, *your* approval of the selections, and the loan of many of your paintings that were the impetus for this second-rate show, as you call it."

Steele chuckled. "So, you see, I can't put any of my bullshit past Nick McCoy. Okay, slight correction. The entire show is not second-rate, just the obvious Monet imitators, like this asswipe—pardon my French." He pointed to the William Wendt painting on the wall behind him. "Notice the tight-ass version of Monet's brushwork, and why in hell is it called *Cup of Gold* when it boasts a friggin' field of red pansies?"

The count sighed. "*Assurément*, not one of Wendt's best efforts."

Nick sensed that the count, like everyone else, felt obliged to curry Steele's favor. He despised this universal pandering to the spoiled, so often insecure rich like Dixon. The appearance of Allegra in a flashy red dress further soured Nick's mood. She thrust her hand in the count's direction and spoke with an exaggerated posh accent.

"*Monsieur Le Comte*, I am Allegra Castlewhite, Nick McCoy's intern, here from the Tate for the past six months. It's an honor to meet you."

Forcing a tight smile, the count barely touched her red-painted fingertips.

Done with the nobility, Allegra turned to the billionaire collector. "I've been longing to meet you too, Mr. Steele. You are such a celebrity in this town."

"Is that a fact, sweetheart? Nick, where have you been hiding this hot tamale?"

The group froze in shocked silence. Even chatterbox Allegra appeared at a loss. *Typical*, Nick thought. Steele had insulted everyone present, sparing only him. He was still the gorilla's golden boy, though not much longer. He couldn't wait to be gone.

Desi, posing as a Latina server in a pair of black-framed glasses, appeared with a tray of red wine. Raquel signaled her to come to her side and asked, "Is that burgundy the *Maison Louis Latour* Mr. Steele ordered?"

"*Si,* I believe so," the server said.

"I'll taste it to be sure," Raquel said.

Nick moved between Steele and Raquel, picked up a glass from the tray and handed it to her. He watched Raquel take a sip, then she lowered the glass and made a show of rolling the expensive burgundy around in her mouth. Despite the distraction, Nick noticed her drop something too tiny to be seen into the lowered glass.

Raquel nodded to the server. "It's perfect, *gracias*." Then she glided around Nick and handed the glass to Steele. "It's the *Maison Louis Latour* you ordered. *Très bon*."

"About time." Steele sniffed the wine, took a gulp, then smacked his thick lips. "It'll do." He turned his back on Raquel and headed toward the count, who was a few strides away, gazing at one of Dixon's prize paintings.

Raquel whispered something to the server and then flashed a sly smile at Nick. Had she slipped a pill into Dixon's glass? An upper, a downer, poison? *Bloody hell, was she losing it?* He frowned at her. Couldn't she wait just a few more days to skewer the bastard?

Allegra sidled up to Raquel and started chattering. Then, to Nick's disgust, Simon appeared at Raquel's side and demanded that she introduce him to Allegra. Simon flashed Nick a high five, a *fuck you* reminder of his five-day deadline. Allegra flirted with Simon, Raquel shooting him dead with her piercing glare, while Nick itched to tear off the weasel's head.

The Latina server approached Nick as Simon ushered the two women through the crowd.

"*Senora* Steele said to offer you this excellent burgundy." She held out a glass to him, expertly balancing the tray on the palm of her other hand.

"*Gracias.*" Nick took the glass, wondering if Raquel might have also doctored his drink. Then something struck him as odd about the young woman's hand. It was graceful and artistic, unlike a waitress's overused, roughened hands. Hyper-sensitive to color and skin tones as an artist and expert in disguise, Nick also noticed the skin color of her hand was wrong. It was a smooth, coppery color, quite different from the muddy beige paste on her face. He sipped his wine, wondering why a woman with such beautiful skin would wear pasty makeup and then accentuate the homely effect with thick, clunky glasses. Did she need to look unattractive? Or was she deliberately disguising her appearance for a more sinister purpose?

The count had similarly raised Nick's antennae. He eyed the homely server, who should have worn gloves. A novice mistake? He caught the flash of wary intelligence in her eyes. She turned around and quickly slalomed through the crowd, possibly aware that her cover was blown.

A photographer came up to Nick and asked him to take his picture. He sent the young man to photograph Steele and the French count, whom he described as an important visiting collector. Thanking him, the photographer hurried over to the bigger fish, Steele and the count. Nick watched as Dixon leered at the camera. The count frowned and turned his face so the picture would show him only in profile, a maneuver that heightened Nick's suspicions.

A hand touched Nick's arm. He turned, catching a whiff of Fay's lilac scent. She asked if he knew about Dixon's surprise for the evening—the unveiling.

"I noticed the setup, but I don't know the details. What's the art?"

"I don't know," Fay said. "It's a mystery. Dixon's idea of fun."

"Which means it won't be." Agitated, he swallowed a slug of wine. It seemed out of character for Dixon to make such an important decision without consulting him. Had he thought Nick would disapprove? If so, why? Was it possibly something about the choice of the work or the timing? His jaw ached from clenching his teeth. Had Steele become suspicious of him?

As Fay spread the exciting news through the crowd, the quartet started playing an arrangement of Vivaldi's *The Four Seasons*. Nick thought it prudent to find out what Steele and the count were discussing. So, he quietly positioned himself a couple of feet behind the collectors and tuned into their exchange.

"Do you like this work, Antoine?" Steele asked. "The artist, Guy Rose, is internationally famous. He's the only painter in the exhibit to get his work into several Paris salons."

"It's a fine painting," the count said. "What else might you be willing to trade? I've got a rare Modigliani reclining nude, a handsome Pissarro, and a superb early Matisse."

Steele exposed his gruesome teeth. "You're not exactly small-time, are you, Antoine? A Modigliani nude—an original, you say?" He licked his lips. "An odd coincidence. A dirty dealer tried to sell me a fake recently. McCoy quickly spotted the inept hand of Elmyr de Hory."

"Ah, yes, the phony Hungarian count. Modigliani was beyond him. He should have stuck with Cubist Picassos. I'd be delighted to have *Monsieur* McCoy authenticate whatever I offer."

"Did I hear my name mentioned?" Nick moved up to them.

Steele turned to Nick. "You did, indeed. Antoine and I were discussing the possibility of a trade. He has a Modigliani nude—genuine, he says. Where did you get your nude, Antoine?"

"From an Asian collector, an old friend," he said.

"Name?"

"He wishes to remain anonymous," the count said.

Nick knew this statement would translate as "stolen" or "forged" to a crooked collector like Steele. The count likely also dealt in stolen art on the black market, although in what capacity it was not yet clear.

"Wasn't a Modigliani and a Matisse among the five paintings stolen from the Paris Museum of Modern Art about ten years ago?" Steele asked. "Wonder what lucky bastard has those masterpieces now?"

"*Hélas*, not me," the count sighed. "I assure you, I do not deal on the black market."

His staunch denial indicated the opposite to Nick. This French bloke was more cunning and intelligent than Steele. Nick detected no false notes in the count's accent, though he likely wasn't French—not if he was Bulldog Cromwell or one of his team. He scrutinized the count, who appeared to be a highly skilled agent. But this chap had nearly blown his cover with a bad case of nerves upon their first meeting. He'd recovered quickly and smoothly, but Nick doubted a detective of Cromwell's experience and caliber would have lost it like that at the outset.

"But Antoine," Steele's voice intruded, "you *do* deal with François Massenet?"

"*Oui*," the count said, *sotto voce*, "but always with extreme caution."

"Very wise," Steele cackled.

"By the way, Dixon, our good friend Massenet has been after my Modigliani for quite a while, but he hasn't come up with the right offer yet."

Observing the hawk-like gleam in Steele's eyes, Nick admired the timing and artistry of the count's hook.

"Come to my place in the Ranch, and I'll show you what I've got. I smell a deal." Steele licked his worm-like lips, sweat beading on his brow. His unusual, frenetic joviality and rapid speech made Nick think he was hopped up on something.

"Perhaps *Monsieur* McCoy could also join us?" the count asked. "I'd appreciate his observations."

"Smashing idea. You'll join us, Nick, right?" His pasty face flushing red, Steele's loud, good humor grated on Nick's nerves.

He's high as a kite, Nick thought. Raquel must have spiked the gorilla's drink with speed. To what end? The drink-drug combo in a volatile aging man would be—"

"Hey, Nicky-boy, get your ass in gear. You'll join us, right?"

"Delighted." Nick smiled at his shit-faced boss, then at the wily count, certain he was plotting to ensnare *Monsieur Le Phantom* along with *Monsieur Le Rat*.

CHAPTER 13

There is a kind of success that is indistinguishable from panic.

—Edgar Degas—

Sunday Evening, October 14

Kate walked into the main gallery of the Steele Museum and scanned the walls for Maurice Braun's *Field of Gold,* secretly painted by her. Clusters of guests blocked her view as they strolled around the gallery. A roving photographer had several dignitaries turn and smile for a photo. When they moved on, a space cleared, and there it was. Hot damn! Her *Field of Gold* was hanging on the museum wall directly across from her. For a moment, she let herself bask in the thrill of this lie.

Then she saw Gerard Devereaux and dapper Miles Hartwright stop in front of *Field of Gold.* Miles stepped closer to the painting, examining the surface with his authenticator's eyes. Kate almost gagged, her euphoria crashing as the nightmarish reality hit. Her painting would not fool Dr. Hartwright. Surely, he'd see her precious painting was a fake. Fearing she might get sick, Kate turned and hurried back into the reception hall, heading toward the ladies' room. Then a tall, black-clad guard stepped in front of her, blocking her way.

"Excuse me, Miss, but I think you left this on the bar." He held up her purse.

"Dear God, my life's in there. Thank you, thank you!" Kate took the bag and tried to ignore her queasy stomach to give him a grateful smile. She couldn't walk away after he'd saved her from days of misery, and the guard's deep voice struck a familiar chord. "How do you like the show, uh, Frank?" she asked, reading his nametag. Then, looking straight into his brilliant blue eyes, she gasped. She would know those distinctive eyes anywhere. "Flynn! What the hell are you doing here?" Her heart rate spiked, a jumble of conflicted feelings choking her.

Flynn gave her a crooked smile, placed his forefinger on his lips, and whispered, "I'm on an undercover job; please move on quickly and quietly."

For a moment, Kate could not tear her eyes away from his cold stare. She stepped back, murmuring another thank you and turned. She started across the room, the colorful, chattering crowd a nauseating blur. She lived in dread of seeing Flynn again. The swirl of guilt, regret, and longing made her dizzy. Giving Flynn up had been the hardest thing she'd ever done, except for investigating her father's death. She never would have undertaken that treacherous journey without Flynn. What was he doing here? Who was he investigating? As a disturbing suspicion started to form in her mind, she heard a man's voice call, "Hey, Doc."

She turned to see Larry Stanhope, an art dealer and one of the former clients she'd texted about the mystery Matisse. Despite her tension, Kate couldn't help smiling at this generous, pudgy art dealer, who looked endearingly like a penguin in his too-tight tux. She asked how he was doing, recalling his crippling depression after his high society wife had left him.

"Never better. I'm in love." He grinned. "Got your text. Sorry, I didn't leave you that gift, although I'm sure you deserve it."

After they chatted for a couple of minutes, Larry went off with a bejeweled lady client.

Blocking Flynn from her mind, Kate resumed a circuitous journey through the crowd toward her painting. Her bold, curious side wanted to see *Field of Gold* up close, to see how it measured up in an exhibition of talented California painters. She figured this would be the only time a picture she painted would hang in a museum—an accomplishment of sorts. She fought the impulse to run from her shameful secret, but it was about time she faced the dark side of herself.

Kate stopped behind a small group gathered in front of an ensemble of paintings, one of them hers. Standing tall and still, she steeled herself for the space to clear in front of *Field of Gold*. As yet, no one was yelling, "Fake!"

When the gawkers moved on, Kate took slow baby steps until she stood directly in front of the painting, her legs trembling. Her vision blurred as she tried to examine the work objectively. She blinked, took a few deep breaths, and tried again. Then, finally, the small landscape came into focus. It was well-lighted, and the owner had spared no expense on the gilded frame. Degas had called the frame "a painting's pimp." She looked at the joyful picture of a field of yellow flowers and a stand of eucalyptus trees under a blue sky. At a glance, the brushwork and her use of the palate knife closely resembled Braun's, but . . .

"This Braun is yours, isn't it?" a familiar voice whispered. Nick was standing next to her, smiling. "Bravo."

"You think it passes?" she whispered.

"To the majority, it would pass."

"But not to you," she said, deflated.

"Maybe it would if I hadn't known you sold a Braun pastiche to Bryce Morton."

"Okay, but why wouldn't you think it was one of the other Braun pictures owned by Morton?" She stepped to the next ensemble of works, forcing herself to look at the Braun painting *California Hills*. "Damn, this one is way more beautiful than mine."

"It's more romantic, that's all, and the composition and color contrasts are more advanced. But, on the other hand, yours has more grit and is meant to be from Braun's early period."

"Right, when he was still rough around the edges."

"It was a smart move for a beginner, and you captured the most important element—Braun's characteristic golden glow."

She should be pleased. Nick had given her Braun pastiche a good review.

"By the way, you look beautiful," he said, his gaze slowly taking in her new, stylish haircut, subtly made-up face, and black cocktail dress with its daring décolleté.

She smiled, her skin tingling, reminded of how attractive he was; she'd almost succumbed to his advances the other night.

"Just to fill you in," Kate cleared her throat, "I'm making progress on finding out who *did not* give me *The Open Window*. I've eliminated two of my former art dealer clients and a couple of friends who own an art gallery in La Jolla. Do you know Gerard Devereaux?"

"Yes, I've done some conservation work for him," Nick said. "About the Matisse, I think we should be putting our heads together—"

"Pardon me for interrupting." A distinguished-looking gentleman stepped next to them. "When you have a moment, Nick, would you be kind enough to give me some advice?"

Nodding, Nick introduced the count and Kate to each other.

"*Enchantée, Monsieur Le Comte,*" Kate said.

"Ah, you speak French."

"*Oui, un peu.* I lived in Paris for a year."

"*Bon,* I'd welcome your opinion, too. What do you think of these paintings?"

"May I hear your impressions first?" Kate asked.

The count stroked his beard. "It's hard not to like Braun. A deep love of the sunlit California landscape shines through in most of the works I've seen. It's clear Monet influenced him, but he went on to develop his own expressive style."

He's an astute critic, Kate thought, as Nick gave the count his opinion. The men's polished manners and academic discourse reminded Kate of characters from a period drama on *Masterpiece Theatre*. All that cheery bombast sounded rather fake, or did she just have FAKE emblazoned on her brain? She heard the count question the authenticity of *Field of Gold,* and her stomach dropped.

"What bothers you, Antoine? What do you see?" Nick asked.

"It's what I don't see," said the count. "I don't see all the subtle coloration and skilled use of contrasting hues as in this one." He pointed to *California Hills.*

Nick explained that *Field of Gold* was one of Braun's earliest works. Hence, he should expect a less developed eye and hand.

"*Oui, bien sûr.* In any case, I do like it," the count said. "It's a good little painting."

Nick went on to say that Bryce Morton fancied himself to be the premiere collector of Maurice Braun's oeuvre and was unlikely to sell one of his treasures. "However, there's another painter whose work I would recommend more highly than Braun's. Charles Reiffel is considered by many to be the best of the California Impressionists. He's more of an Expressionist really. I'll show you. Follow me."

A close call. *Thank you, Nick.* Kate gradually started to breathe normally again. Her cheeks still burning, she grabbed a cold flute of champagne from a tray passing by and then became aware of the prickly sensation of being watched. Glancing across the gallery, she was surprised to see her friend Allegra and her client Raquel talking intimately together near the door to the reception hall. *Were they friends, or had they just met this evening?* Allegra was a terrible gossip. That she might gossip about her to her client was troubling. More disturbing was the fact that one or the other kept eyeing her and Nick in a rather intense way. Allegra's glances seemed hostile, and there was a sly, foxlike quality to her face from a distance. Aware of Allegra's longtime crush on Nick, Kate moved away from the two men. Sidestepping, her focus on the paintings, she bumped into a young man.

"I'm so sorry. I wasn't looking where I was going."

"You can bump into me any time." His grin was more like a leer.

That leer sent Kate back nine years to when she was stuck with a younger, wild-haired version of Simon Steele in her former La Jolla office waiting room. It was a most unpleasant experience.

"I'll be damned. If it isn't Dr. O'Dade," he said. "It's been a lot of years, and you've become so, so sophisticated." His black, glittery gaze slid down her body as he held out his hand.

"Yes, I remember you, Simon." *Unfortunately.* As she touched his icy fingers, goosebumps rose on the back of her neck.

CHAPTER 14

Lesson in Red

—MARIA HUMMEL—

Sunday Evening, October 14

Raquel was intrigued by Allegra, this bold lady in red who seemed so eager to befriend her. The attention warmed Raquel, as she rarely saw her few friends. How she missed those days of freedom when she was working at André's La Jolla Gallery.

"That's a smashing dress you're wearing," Allegra said. "You look like Aphrodite, you know, the wife of Zeus."

Raquel couldn't help smiling at her childlike expression. "I believe you're thinking of Hera. Aphrodite was his daughter, the goddess of love."

"Oh yes, what a twit I am." Allegra giggled. "I never got on well with Latin and Greek. It must be grand to be married to Dixon, a man almost as powerful as Zeus."

"Grand is not the word I'd use." *Terrifying is more like it.*

"Do tell." Allegra cocked her head.

"Champagne?" The Latina server in glasses presented a tray of flutes.

Raquel thanked her, and Allegra said, "We're starving. Do bring us some of those scrumptious shrimp. They've been taunting me from afar."

Raquel watched the server hurry through the door to the buffet, then she scanned the rotunda, looking for her beast of a husband. She saw him having intense words with Fay Martinez next to the platform. It was getting near the time for the unveiling. He looked agitated and angry; his face flushed. *Bon. The drug is working.*

Allegra leaned toward her, whispering, "Will you let me in on the secret?" She giggled. "What's the painting your husband is unveiling and donating?"

"I don't know. He's kept it secret from *tout le monde*."

"Can you guess?"

"I only know that it's an important work."

Distracted, Allegra glanced across the room at Nick talking to the count.

"Have you heard of that French count?" Allegra asked.

"No," she replied, relieved to be off the subject of her marriage.

"Impressive, isn't he?" Allegra remarked. "I wonder if he's married. I bet he's rich and lives in a chateau with lots of servants, fine wines, and salons full of masterpieces." She sighed. "But Nick McCoy is the man for me. Don't you think he's hot behind that cool, brainy surface of his?"

"*Je ne sais pas.* I don't know." Raquel was amused. She hadn't engaged in foolish girl gossip since her days at *le Lycée* in Paris.

"Do you know the tall redhead standing next to Nick?" Allegra asked.

Raquel raised her eyebrows.

"That's Dr. Kate O'Dade," Allegra said. "She's a psychologist and a good friend of mine. Poor dear lost her husband last year."

Raquel knew all of this. Kate had been her therapist for almost a year.

"Kate never wears make-up or flattering clothes," Allegra chattered on. "And here she is, all dolled up in a sexy dress, and her wild hair is artfully coiffed for a change. What's gotten her back to the land of the living, do you suppose? Dashing Nick McCoy?" She glared at the pair through narrowed eyes and spat out the words, "Well, she can't have him. He's mine."

Raquel bridled at Allegra's assertion of owning her lover. *No one could own Nick. Get her off this subject.* "How do you like working here, at the museum?"

"I adore working for Nick," Allegra said. "Just being in the sphere of his genius is what I live for. No offense intended, but this museum is way beneath him. And me, too, for that matter. He's been a conservator in much grander places—London's National Gallery, for one, and I studied at the Tate. We will be returning to London at some point soon."

Bile came up in Raquel's throat. She was feeling ill, dizzy even. Could Nick be screwing this bitch, this *femme méchante*? Allegra was implying they were already a couple. Through Raquel's blurring vision, Allegra looked like a vampire with her black spiked hair, pointy chin, and blood-red lips.

The server returned with a platter of artfully arranged shrimp, scallops, chunks of lobster, and pots of red cocktail sauce. The room started spinning, and Raquel staggered forward, knocking against the loaded platter. Allegra yelped as the tray tipped, and the pots of red sauce slid off the edge, splattering onto Raquel's white dress.

"*Merde!*" Raquel cried as the red sauce oozed down the front of her white gown. She looked like she'd been shot by a high-powered rifle.

The mortified server spouted apologies in a mix of Spanish and English. Women gasped, and people stopped talking as they moved closer to the drama. A tall, blue-eyed guard appeared at the server's side, grabbed the platter from her, and spoke in her ear.

"Please take Mrs. Steele to the ladies' room or the crew's lounge."

"I'll come with you, Raquel," Allegra murmured, hand over her heart like a martyr.

"No, no, please stay here. I'll be fine," Raquel said.

"Let me get you a drink and some more food," the guard said to Allegra. "This has been distressing for you, too."

"Yes, indeed—such a beautiful dress, ruined!" The gleeful glint in her eyes belied her protestations of distress.

Raquel let the friendly Latina server escort her toward the ladies' room. Then, stopping at the hors d'oeuvres bar, she grabbed a couple of white cloth napkins for Raquel to blot against the red mess on her dress. Fay Martinez stood at the podium on the platform as people began seating themselves in the rows of seats in front of the small stage and the veiled painting.

"Welcome to you all," Fay said over the loudspeakers. "Thank you for joining us for this very special evening. I have a few acknowledgments; then I will turn this over to our founder, who needs no introduction." She smiled at Dixon Steele, seated in one of the chairs onstage. "Most of you know he has an exciting surprise for us this evening." She gestured toward the lavender-veiled artwork. An excited hush came over the crowd.

Raquel stopped at the right side of the platform and whispered to the server, "I really should be on stage with my husband for the unveiling."

"But your dress, *senora*. Shouldn't we go to the ladies' room and clean off what we can?"

"I suppose so. We should be able to hear what's going on from there." No way was Raquel going to miss her chance to show herself as more than a rich thug's dumb trophy wife. With the nice server at her side, she moved briskly down the hallway, the sodden material of her gown clinging to her legs. The sight of her ruined dress would enrage Dixon, and that, mixed with the amphetamine in his system, should wipe out any remaining scraps of fake *politesse*. Visualizing the upcoming scene, Raquel tingled with anticipation.

CHAPTER 15

Give me a museum and I'll fill it.

—Pablo Picasso—

Sunday Evening, October 14

Nick sensed the excitement in the audience as Dixon Steele stepped up to the podium positioned to the left of the veiled artwork. Next to the podium sat Fay Martinez and two empty chairs, one meant for Raquel. When the enthusiastic clapping subsided, Steele raised his hand to the audience in greeting.

"Evening, folks," he said into the microphone. "It's a pleasure to be here in this garden of painterly delights with all of you—the special people who appreciate and support art and my museum."

Dixon could act the part of the magnanimous host, but Nick knew that wouldn't last, given the swine's red, perspiring face and the tic twitching beneath his right eye.

From his seat in the front row, Nick saw Raquel approach the stairs at the right end of the stage. She stopped next to one of the guards, the other guard now positioned at the left end. The clumsy Latina server with graceful hands stood a few feet behind Raquel. She whispered to a tall, strapping guard with distinctive blue eyes—hyper-alert eyes that scanned the audience. When his roving gaze hit Nick's, the guard quickly glanced away. This bloke was not the usual half-asleep museum security guard. Was he another fake? With the count somewhere in the audience, Nick began to feel the cop net tightening around him. What was their game? The hounds chasing the fox? No worries. The fox would outsmart them—he always had.

He turned his attention back to Raquel. The red stains on her white gown were now a watery pink. Her determination was evident in her ramrod posture and the rigid set of her jaw. She was planning to join Dixon for the unveiling despite her ruined dress. Nick's muscles tightened. She was courting trouble, and there was nothing he could do about her or the bloody cops. The tight collar of his dress shirt strangled him, almost cutting off his air. He wanted to rip off the ridiculous bow tie.

"Before I do the honors, that is, strip off the veil, I hope you will humor me and play a little game." Dixon chuckled. "First, I'll give you a couple of clues; then, I'd like you to guess what's behind the veil—either the artist or the work. Both are famous. The winner gets a prize, if there is one." He laughed, showing off his fang-like teeth. He pulled out a handkerchief from his pocket and blotted the sweat on his face and bald head.

"What's the prize?" boomed a male voice.

Nick turned to see Gerard Devereaux sitting in the third row next to Kate.

"That's a surprise, too," Steele smirked, rubbing his pudgy hands together.

The count, sitting on the other side of Kate, gave Nick an amused smile as though they shared a secret loathing of the buffoon onstage. Nick wondered what Kate thought of sophisticated Antoine. She'd seemed quite taken with him.

"So, what are the clues?" asked Miles Hartwright, sitting next to Nick.

"Ah, Dr. Hartwright, I'm surprised an expert of your distinction needs more clues." Steele was into his clumsy, playful act. "Okay, the work is not by an American artist, and the lavender-colored veil could be a clue or a red herring."

Nick sighed. Here comes Tricky Dix.

"Is it an Impressionist painter?" a quavery voice asked.

"Oh, my dear, you ask too much," Steele said.

"Degas?" asked Stanley Goodman, director of the San Diego History Center. "He was keen on lavender."

"Nice try, but the artist is not the poncy prince of pastels." Steele was the only one who laughed at his alliterative insult.

Nick smiled. Steele's true colors were beginning to show.

"Monet," a man's voice rang out. "He did all those lily pond paintings full of lavender, lilac, and pink."

"Yes, and I wish he hadn't." Steele snickered. "This artist might find a lavender veil over his work quite amusing since he tended to avoid that color. Think gritty, not pretty."

"So, the artist was a man?" Kate asked, her low, musical voice heating Nick's blood. Smart lady. She'd caught the buffoon's slips. "Édouard Manet," she said.

"Good guess, but no," Steele said, still in a hyped-up, jolly mood.

Caught up in the game, Nick considered what artist Steele would choose to inflate his standing. Leaning toward Miles, Nick whispered in his ear. "Try Dixon's favorite artist."

"Picasso!" Miles called out.

Steele raised his brows, then waited a couple of beats, scowling. "That is correct, Dr. Hartwright. Can you guess which Picasso? The size may tell you something. Framed, it's twenty-eight inches high by forty-one inches wide."

"Guess it's not *Guernica*," Miles said.

The audience erupted in laughter, knowing *Guernica* was a huge, anti-war mural. Steele looked peeved and asked for other guesses. The audience started buzzing.

Miles said, "Picasso made nearly fifty thousand works, including paintings, drawings, prints, sculpture, and ceramics." He threw up his hands. "I give up."

"Good decision," Steele said, "but you still get a reward. Come on up."

Miles passed the guard at the platform's left end, walked up the three stairs and onto the small stage. He and Steele shook hands, and Fay Martinez congratulated him.

"Since my wife is indisposed and unable to help with the unveiling, you, Dr. Hartwright, will have that honor."

There was a slight creak of floorboards, and then Raquel appeared onstage with her head held high. Nick heard rustling sounds and whispering from the audience behind him. Someone coughed. He took in a deep breath and mentally fastened his seat belt for the rough ride ahead.

"I am not indisposed," Raquel spoke with careful, French-accented diction. "I am here to do my part in the unveiling." She glided up to the podium and faced the audience, the front of her ravaged dress visible to all. The way the damp material clung to the front of her body added a waif-like sex appeal to her ethereal beauty. She gave her husband a sweet smile. "Dr. Hartwright can help—"

"We don't need you, Raquel," Steele hissed, "your gown is a mess—"

"It was an accident," she said. "Please, *mon cher*, I belong here with you." Her lips trembled, her eyes tearing, and Nick had to admire her Sarah Bernhardt-like performance.

"Fay Martinez will take you to the little girl's room," Steele spoke as if to a bothersome child, also implying that Martinez was a mere maid in his service.

Fay looked appalled. To her credit, she did not move from her seat. Nick was torn between urges to chop off the gorilla's head or to cheer on his self-immolation.

Steele jerked around. "*Senora* Martinez, did you not hear me?" his loud tone threatened.

Fay cleared her throat. "I cannot do what you ask, Dixon. It is demeaning."

Nick's respect for Fay Martinez shot up. She had risked her hard-won director's position for Raquel—or denigrated women in general—to put the abominable Steele in his place. *Bravo, Fay!* He hoped the Board would stay loyal to her.

Steele skirted Miles and grabbed Raquel's wrist, his face flushed a reddish puce.

"I will escort you off stage."

"*Non*, I beg of you," she cried. "I wish to do my part as we planned."

He yanked her arm. She yelped, stumbling back. Miles and Fay moved to either side of Steele as the two guards began climbing the stairs. The audience sat in stunned silence. Fay whispered in Steele's ear, and Miles said something unintelligible.

"Holy shit," Nick muttered. This is either a TV melodrama or tasteless Performance Art. He stood up and said with calm authority. "Dixon, our guests are waiting for the unveiling. Let's proceed, shall we?" His matter-of-fact tone conveyed the impression that nothing outrageous was happening onstage and Steele had done nothing disgraceful.

A moment of tense silence. Then Steele let go of Raquel's wrist, wisely taking the out Nick had given him. He strode to one side of the veiled work. Miles and Raquel moved to the other side. Steele nodded, and all three of them pulled at the lavender cloth. It caught on something. Nick could hear Dixon swearing under his breath. People in the audience sat forward, craning their necks, and some stood. Nick heard a high-pitched giggle coming from the back of the crowd. He recognized Simon Steele's hyaena-like laugh. Something foul was about to happen.

Finally, the lavender cloth came unstuck, rippled off, and pooled at the base of the easel.

The audience gasped along with Simon's piercing laugh, followed by a smattering of nervous applause. The domestic scandal onstage was unprecedented, but the unveiled work seemed to be even more of a shock to the audience and Steele. The horrified bully staggered back.

"What the fuck! That is not the work I selected!"

"It's a Picasso, that's for sure," Miles said. *Dora and the Minotaur,* isn't it?"

"Yes," Steele snapped.

Dr. Hartwright turned to the audience. "Picasso thought of himself as a minotaur, and Dora Maar was his mistress-muse at the time, one he seriously abused, unfortunately. There's truth in this portrayal—"

"Shut up, Hartwright." Steele glared at him.

Nick reveled in Steele's fury and humiliation, but his fear for Raquel kept him on high alert. He recognized the drawing. It came from one of Steele's private galleries, featuring Picasso's series of minotaur-maiden scenes. The Dora Maar drawing was the most violent of these, with the rape taking place in a green impressionistic landscape under an ominous, reddish sky. Arched over Dora's contorted, naked body, her head thrown back in swooning submission, the bull-headed minotaur was about to ram his gaping mouth into her genitalia. The beautifully rendered scene detailing a grotesque rape made a powerful impression, but even vulgar Dixon Steele wouldn't have chosen violent pornography for this public unveiling. He cared too much about his reputation. Furthermore, this drawing had a questionable provenance and was either stolen or forged, or both. Nick knew it had once hung at the *Musée Picasso* in Paris.

Steele lunged toward Raquel. "You did this, *putain,* you whore! You switched drawings to bust my balls."

"*Non, non*, I swear it," Raquel pleaded. "I did not know what you selected."

Raquel defended herself with innocent passion, a lovely maiden in her ruined Grecian dress, and Steele embodied the ugly brutishness of the minotaur.

He jabbed his stubby forefinger at her pale face. "You have access to the house and my private galleries."

"So does Simon, his friends, and the help," she said.

Raquel might have switched drawings, or had Simon done it, hoping to implicate Raquel or Nick? Simon's sadistic laughter suggested his guilt. Still, Raquel had proven to be devious, bold, and reckless. This drama could be her own cleverly choreographed revenge. But she would know there would be a terrible price to pay.

He glanced at the audience. Some people were standing, others sitting forward in their seats, necks craned, all wide-eyed and mesmerized by the circus onstage. Then his gaze met Kate's for a moment, and they exchanged brief, knowing smiles.

On stage, Steele grabbed Raquel's arm, his face mottled with rage. "Where's the Picasso drawing I selected? Tell me right now, or I'll—"

"Hold on, Dixon!" Nick shot up. "There's an easy solution to this. You'll take *Dora and the Minotaur* back home, and we'll find the drawing you wish to donate, either here or at your estate. We can start the search this evening or tomorrow, whichever you prefer."

Steele glared at Raquel and dropped her arm. "We'll start now." He picked up *Dora* and stormed off the platform. Nick met him at the bottom of the stairs. Miles escorted Raquel off the other end of the stage.

Fay stepped up to the podium, lines of tension aging her face. She managed a brave smile and said graciously, "That concludes our special program for the evening—truly an audacious, one-of-a-kind display—our first showing of spontaneous Performance Art. Thank you all for coming. Please help yourself to more food and a stiff drink."

She signaled to the quartet, and Handel's jolly *Water Music* rippled through the hall.

CHAPTER 16

When you're out of willpower, you call on stubbornness; that's the trick.

—Henri Matisse—

Sunday Night, October 14

It was near midnight when Eddie returned from the museum's wild festivities. He glanced at the suave *Comte Antoine de Guise* in the mirror of his suite in the Bamboo House, their undercover cop hotel. He guessed he looked convincing enough to fool Steele, but probably not McCoy. This bloke had a built-in radar for detecting fakes, whether people or art. He would have spotted any cracks in the count's disguise and performance. Indeed, those sharp eyes couldn't have missed Eddie's initial attack of nerves. He wondered if this was the first sign that he was getting too old for this game.

Eddie shed his disguise, relieved to be rid of the count, at least temporarily. The fitted straitjacket of a tux ended up in a heap on the floor. For a moment, he luxuriated in feeling unbound and free, then he dutifully picked up the penguin get-up and hung it in the closet, along with his travel clothes. In the bathroom, he carefully removed the false beard, mustache, colored contact lenses, and dark makeup from his face, neck, and hands. His skin would have a day to breathe before he had to put on the disguise again for the meeting with Steele. After donning an old T-shirt and worn sweatpants, he went to the kitchen to eat, drink, and wait for the others.

Archie was already in the kitchen, assaulting the refrigerator. "*Bonne soirée, Monsieur Le Comte*? How's that for French?"

"Painful. Where's the scotch?"

Archie pointed to the decanter on the black marble counter next to the pass-through, then pulled out a beer from the fridge. "Tell me, boss, are museum shows typically such a blast?"

"Hardly," Eddie replied, pouring himself a large shot. "They're usually stiff, staid affairs."

Archie turned on the outdoor lights and opened the shoji screens to the modest dining area. Gazing out from the open screens, Eddie could see the rippling movement of the ocean and hear the constant rumble of waves breaking against the shore. The tangy smell of the sea wafted into the kitchen, which hardly seemed the right word for this elegant space. Most of the appliances were concealed behind maple facades, except for a deep, bowl-like sculpture that served as a stainless-steel sink.

Flynn strode in, carrying two overflowing bags of leftover party food. He put them on the counter next to the Sub-Zero fridge. "Hey, man," he said, looking Eddie up and down, "I couldn't believe that chichi French dude was you."

Eddie gave a slight bow. "*Merci*, I take that as a compliment."

Flynn grabbed a beer from the fridge. "Desi won't be here for a while. She's driving Raquel Steele to a hotel for safety. McCoy is probably still babysitting the Steele asshole."

"Ah, yes, *l'enfant terrible*," Eddie said. "Who do you think substituted the minotaur drawing for the Picasso that Steele intended to donate?"

"Had to be Raquel or Simon. McCoy wouldn't be that stupid," Flynn said.

"I vote for Simon," Archie said, walking in from the deck. "He was all hyped up to see the unveiling, and he laughed hysterically all the way through it. Simon hates Raquel and McCoy. I'm sure he was hoping to implicate them. His trick worked. Steele blamed Raquel."

"Simon's a cunning raptor." Flynn gestured toward the food bags. "Let's eat." He began pulling goodies out of the bag. "I can offer you leftover shellfish and caviar, gluten-free crackers, and a variety of herb bread and dessert tarts. It was torture watching those over-exercised, stringy ladies picking at the food while I stood there awash in saliva."

"What are you grousing about?" Archie asked. "You got to see a grand melodrama with a real-life villain and a minotaur raping a naked lady on a lavender stage."

They all laughed. Eddie felt the built-up tensions draining away as they took their food-laden plates outside and folded themselves into the low-to-the-ground seats. They attacked their food like starving animals, euphoric grunts and sighs filling the air. Finally, Eddie cleared his throat.

"So, what did we accomplish tonight? Archie, you go first. Begin with how you felt in your role."

"Huh? Who cares how I felt?"

Eddie sighed. "A Yard psychologist trained us to debrief in undercover work. Expressing yourself helps prevent stupid mistakes and early burnout."

Flynn rolled his eyes.

Archie looked glum. "The job seemed like a kick at first. The role didn't take much acting. Couldn't see any risk at first either, but I was sorely mistaken, lads."

"What was the problem?" Eddie asked.

"Simon Steele. You can't be with that psycho for long without his poison seeping into you. He bought my crude Aussie act and assumed I was also dumb and gullible. He offered me a joint. Then, for more privacy, we went to the sculpture garden. We got beers at the bar and continued drugging and jawing behind that sculpture of a giant headless woman."

"The Henry Moore," Eddie said.

"Could be." Archie shrugged. "We were bosom buddies by this time, and it was easy to get Simon talking about his cuckolded old man—spewing is more like it. He said McCoy and that scheming bitch Raquel were plotting to steal his inheritance. Billions, he claimed."

"Did he say how?" Flynn asked.

"No, I couldn't get specifics. He just said, 'Nobody fools with Simon. My golden-boy brother tried it. And look what happened to him.' Then he laughed, crazy-like. Gave me the creeps." Archie glanced at Flynn. "What happened to his brother, anyway?"

"About three years ago, he died in a car crash with Simon's mother, Steele's second wife," Flynn said. "It was ruled an accident. Brakes failed along Linea Del Cielo, the road from Del Mar and Solana Beach to Rancho Santa Fe. If you speed around those tight curves and your brakes fail, your car will probably plunge into a deep canyon. A detective at the Sheriff's Department thought Simon might have fixed those brakes, but he couldn't prove it."

"Jesus fucking Christ, the kid's a killer." Archie downed a slug of beer. "Later on, when Simon was flying high, he asked if I'd like in on a lucrative deal. It would be a driving job at night. Big money and no risk. I started asking questions, and he said I'd have to commit to the job before he could give me any more info. 'Think about it,' he said, and he gave me a number to call if I was interested." Archie finished the dregs of his beer. "That's the gist."

Eddie and Flynn stared at Archie in stunned disbelief.

"Brilliant job," Eddie said.

"You missed your calling, buddy," Flynn said. "Right out of the gate, you just about got a confession of murder—a double murder."

"This certainly complicates the landscape," Eddie said as he caught Flynn's eye. Flynn gave a slight nod, their mutual agreement about the next step silently transmitted. It felt strange to be on the same wavelength with Flynn, a man he admired but could not like.

Archie looked back and forth between them. "There's a wolfish gleam in your eye like I'm a tasty piece of raw meat."

"Archie," Eddie said, "we need to know what Simon is up to."

"I'm not a field bloke," Archie said. "I could easily fuck up with a snake like Simon."

"You're a natural, Archie. Just keep playing the dumb Aussie limo driver."

Archie sucked in his breath. "Sorry, boss, no can do. Give me another assignment."

Taken aback, Eddie couldn't recall anyone under his command ever directly refusing an assignment. "What's this about, Archie? Fear of failure?"

"No. Just plain fear. That guy isn't human; he's pure evil and smarter than me."

Eddie didn't have the heart to shame Archie, even though most Aussies and Brits would find it unacceptable to admit fear or say no to a superior. In fact, he admired Archie's openness and honesty, and the Aussie was trustworthy. Unlike Flynn, Archie knew his limits.

"I'll do it," Eddie said. "I'm good at the Aussie accent, and we're about the same height. Furthermore, as you know, I'm a master of disguise," he said straight-faced.

Archie stared at him, stricken. "Shit, boss. I'd rather roast in hell with Simon than have you bail me out."

Eddie held up his hand. "Let's leave this for now. Got anything else to report?"

"Nothing new on McCoy's background," Archie said. "Still working on finding out his original surname and tracking down Jackson Chase, the shady art dealer he worked for as a teen. Right now, it appears that Chase has dropped off the face of the earth, along with his gallery."

"Keep on it," Eddie said. "Your turn, Flynn."

Flynn levered his big body out of the torturous chair and stretched. "Nothing much to report except for babysitting Allegra so Desi could get away alone with Raquel. Want to know how I *felt*, Eddie?"

"You bet."

"Like prey," Flynn said. "Allegra acts coy, but she's a man-eater. She's Simon's female counterpart, like the scorpion that stings her lover to death after mating, then eats him. I overheard some of her catty chat with Raquel. She's fixated on Nick McCoy. Imagines he's madly in love with her. Raquel appeared taken in and looked devastated."

"Keep in contact with Allegra," Eddie said. "She's a great resource and has her predator's eyes on McCoy round-the-clock."

"You want I should sell my body?" Flynn feigned outrage. "When I suggested we get better acquainted, she giggled and said, 'It's always good to have a stallion in the stables.'"

Eddie chuckled. "You need your best men on Raquel's tail and Steele's. She could be in real danger from her husband. She humiliated him brilliantly. He won't let that pass."

"Sorry, but it's impossible to track Steele," Flynn said. "He has a Jaguar he rarely drives, and he mostly uses an elite limo service. He calls them when he needs a driver. I've got a man staking out Steele's estate and a GPS tracking device under Simon's Maserati."

"You've got a tail on McCoy full-time, right?"

"Yeah, a part-time stakeout and a tracking device on his SUV. Got bugs everywhere except McCoy's loft. Should I try to break in there?"

"Hell, no," Eddie said. "If you got caught, we'd be screwed."

"I need a pit break." Flynn strode down the hall to the bathroom.

When Flynn returned, the three detectives went out on the deck and watched the ocean, drinking in companionable silence. Eddie liked the sea much better at night. The ceaseless undulations and rhythmic sound of waves breaking gave him the sensation of being rocked. He felt the bonds of a team developing among them—Flynn, a few degrees less prickly, honest Archie catching on fast, and Desi, the team's queen. Despite this, Eddie did not feel any more at ease. Much less so, in fact. Slick Nick McCoy had buggered him royally.

"So, what did the count achieve?" Flynn asked. "But first, how did he *feel*?"

Eddie balked at revealing himself. "I've played the count before, but this time I had stage fright. Fooling Nick McCoy was the biggest challenge of my undercover career. I wasn't as worried about Steele. I had the feeling McCoy saw right through me. It's possible—"

"Hey," Flynn interrupted. "Desi said almost the same thing. She thinks McCoy made her as a cop. Said she could feel his laser-sharp eyes stripping off her disguise."

"If he saw through me," Eddie said, "he might think it's Steele I'm after. The greedy thug played right into my hands. He's invited me as the count to see his masterpieces and make a deal. That means selling me a stolen painting or exchanging one of his dubious pictures for the count's non-existent Modigliani. If he tries to sell me something from the black market, we'll have him and the evidence to justify a search warrant. I bet he's sitting on stolen works worth billions. He set up the meeting for the day after tomorrow. He also invited McCoy."

"Nice of him," Flynn said. "How do we catch McCoy in this sting?"

Flynn's question and sharp, expectant gaze galled Eddie. The PI's vigor made him feel old and weak. This debilitating effect brought back his encounter with McCoy. He could feel the devil's black eyes lasering right through him, stripping away his disguise and confidence. Eddie's mouth went dry, his heart pulsing in his throat. Just the thought of another bloody face-off with McCoy gave him stage fright. He understood Archie's terror.

"How do we catch a phantom, you ask?" Eddie said to Flynn. "Damned if I know."

CHAPTER 17

*An artist does things naturally, without
effort. Some power guides his hand.
A forger struggles, and if he succeeds, it is a genuine achievement.*

—Patricia Highsmith—

Sunday Night, October 14

Nick jogged up the stairs to his loft, even though he was tired from a long session at the gym honing his martial arts skills—particularly Krav Maga—for instantaneous self-defense. An attack could surprise him at any time. He stopped at the top, catching his breath and a whiff of stale cigarette smoke. A jolt of adrenaline coursed through him.

Someone had gotten in the locked street door. Who? Raquel had the only other key, but she didn't smoke. Simon? He was too lazy. This bloke would need advanced lock-picking skills and a motive. A thief, a cop, or the PI that Simon hired were the likely sods looking to catch him with stolen or forged art. The police were unlikely to risk a search without a warrant, but a PI might. Since last night at the gala, he was sure the cops were watching him. He'd just checked and found a GPS tracker inside the back fender of his SUV. No wonder he hadn't been able to spot a tail. He'd removed the tracker and secured it under a Range Rover parked near the Steele Museum. He smiled at the thought of where the Rover might lead his pursuers. To Mexico, he hoped.

Nick sucked in the polluted air, his mouth watering. Drug-free for eight years, and he'd still kill for a hit of nicotine.

Facing the sign on his door—*Nicholas McCoy: Painting Conservation & Restoration*—he quietly opened the double locks and slipped into the consulting room. Head cocked, listening, he heard only distant street noise and the welcome hum of the AC. Those stalking him would probably never give up. Eddie Cromwell had been the most tenacious, on his tail for at least nine years. Cromwell or one of his team had likely sniffed out his San Diego hideout and alerted his Yankee cohorts to keep an eye on him.

Cromwell hunted and haunted him, keeping him in a state of high alert—a debilitating, never-ending fight or flight syndrome. Nick had never seen Cromwell. Like the best undercover detectives, the sly bastard never showed his God-given face on TV or in the papers and never grabbed the glory for his squad's successes. Commendable? Or it may have been his shrewdness, or maybe his natural face was pug ugly. He couldn't picture Cromwell as being the suave, blade-nosed count.

Inside the central area of his high-ceilinged loft, Nick turned on the overhead lights and scanned the large workspace—the combo of a painter's studio and a chemist's laboratory. Nothing looked out of place. Highly disciplined, Nick kept his workspace clean, tidy, and organized. Conservation and restoration required precision and meticulous work habits. He smelled no traces of cigarette smoke, so he guessed the hall smoker probably didn't get in there. The heady fumes of oil paint, turpentine, linseed oil, varnish, formaldehyde, and other toxic chemicals were likely wrecking his lungs more than fags ever did or would.

He checked every hiding place in his studio, bedroom, and kitchen. Then he strode quickly to the locked door of the storage room where he kept his private clients' valuable paintings along with his copies, pastiches, and a few original works. He unlocked the door and checked the racks. No one had looted his treasure trove yet. Steele's Braque and Cézanne were still there but not the Matisse sketch. Panic seized him.

He turned toward the three occupied easels. Matisse's original oil sketch for his monumental *Joy of Life* (*Le Bonheur de Vivre*) masterpiece was still in its place. How had he forgotten to lock up this jewel? What if a thief or cop had gotten in here? He was getting careless and had made too many mistakes lately. Kate would probably say he wanted to be caught. He studied his charcoal drawing of the Matisse oil sketch. There were many more steps needed to complete this last project for Steele. He had to finish this tonight and get out of town in the next couple of days before Simon broke his meaningless promise and exposed his affair with Raquel.

It felt too warm in the loft, even though it was much hotter outside. Nick checked the air temperature controls on the wall to the left of the studio door—seventy-five degrees Fahrenheit. He lowered the thermostat to seventy for the sake of his paintings. He'd like it cooler, but the paintings' comfort came first—another stab of regret about storing Matisse's *Open Window* at the museum.

Certain at this point that no one was hiding in the loft, he shouted, "Hey, hound dogs, I'm in for the evening alone. Go have a beer." Now he felt somewhat more in control if someone had broken in and illegally bugged his loft.

He crossed the studio, skirted the large central worktable, and looked out of one of the three back windows overlooking Balboa Park. He gazed at the magnificent Moreton Bay fig tree outside the window, thinking of Kate. She looked beautiful last night at the gala and was so warm and receptive. He'd again sensed the frisson of attraction between them. He wondered if she'd be open to something approximating a date. Taking her to dinner might be an excellent way to make amends for breaking into her studio. They still needed to discuss who owned *The Open Window* and who stole the painting and gave it to her. He'd come up with no likely suspects, only a doubtful one with no apparent motive.

Watching the breeze rustle the leaves on the tree, he slipped into a wishful, erotic daydream, allowing himself to feel the sweet ache of arousal. Maybe when he was cured and no longer her client, she'd be open to another kind of relationship with him—a daft thought.

Get to work. Nick had a lot to do before he could pursue anything else.

Before starting the sketch, he looked at his nearly finished painting of Raquel reclining nude on his bed. He stood in a state of disbelief. She was right there in front of him, her bold, impassioned gaze straight at him, her lips parted in an enigmatic half-smile. Her stoic expression and bruised, naked body, lying exposed in his rendering of a harsh, menacing landscape, tore at his heart. The work looked original, like no one else's painting. If he could trust his eyes and judgment, he'd finally done the first crude but distinctive Nicholas McCoy.

He gazed at the new depth he'd accomplished in this portrait. Raquel's beauty shone through, but he was just as aware of her dark side—those secretive, devious tendencies so much like his own. He'd guessed she was withholding something vital from him. Pregnancy was one fear, but she'd denied this when he confronted her, assuring him she was keeping no secrets from him. He didn't believe her, and he doubted that she would totally rely on him. He wouldn't be surprised if she had a backup plan, instinctively aware that he would likely fail her.

He knew Kate was the woman he wanted, but affection, gratitude, and obligation bound him to Raquel. In reality, there could be no future with either of them. How could he subject anyone he cared for to the dangers of partnering with him? He couldn't even imagine his purpose after he completed the mission that had guided his path for the last thirty years. What would he do? Would anything even matter to him?

Bugger it, fuck the future, he didn't have time for moody self-pity. He had to complete his last job for Steele right now.

Nick strode to his bedroom and changed into a T-shirt and paint-stained jeans. Then he grabbed a chocolate bar, nuts, and a Guinness from the refrigerator and returned to the easels. He sat on a stool in front of the Matisse oil sketch he'd cleaned and re-varnished the day before.

The colors now glowed more brightly. Luckily, it hadn't needed any restoration. He was struck by how fresh and more intense the cadmium yellow ground color looked compared to the faded yellow brushwork in the magnificent, large-scale *Joy of Life*. He'd spent a lot of time with that seven-by-eight-foot masterpiece while working as a teacher and conservator at the Barnes Foundation in Philadelphia.

Nick turned to examine his latest charcoal drawing for making a copy of the Matisse oil-on-canvas sketch, propped up on the easel next to the original. He'd cut several pieces of drawing paper to the same size as the sixteen-by-twenty-one-inch Matisse. He compared his sketch with the master's sketch. It looked like the naked lovers and single figures were spaced properly under the canopy of trees. He seemed to have captured the sinuous flow of curving lines demarking the figures and the suggestion of a surrounding forest. But his drawing of the figures was too refined and detailed. "Exactitude is not truth," he could hear Matisse say.

The drawing needed to be more carefree, simple, and loose, like Matisse's. This was especially hard to achieve, given his insides were tied up in a knot. *Do another drawing, then another, yet again, and one more time.* He had to get the right feeling before drawing and painting on the canvas.

He clipped a new page onto the Masonite board, picked up the charcoal from his rolling cart of supplies, took several deep breaths, and started again, imagining himself as Matisse in his light-filled studio in Collioure. The charcoal flowed easier on the paper as he aimed to capture the figures and landscape in fewer lines. After making three more trial sketches, looser and simpler each time, Nick was ready to paint.

He laid his sketch on the large central worktable, picked up the prepared canvas, and put it on the easel next to the oil sketch. Then he squeezed out the desired pigments from tubes of paint—white, black, yellow, green, blue, orange, and red. Nick felt the power in each of these pure pigments. They glowed like precious gems on his palette. Nick had bought these oils in London from an art supply store that sold pigments similar to those used by Matisse. Needing these oils to dry fast, Nick had to mix them with a drying agent and place the finished copy under his ultra-violet light to speed up the drying process. He absolutely had to complete the Steele job in the next couple of days.

Next, he went to his computer station at the left end of the room and selected the right music to inspire him to enter the rhythmic vitality of Matisse's exuberant world. It was an easy choice. *Need a shot of self-confidence? Need courage? Listen to Freddie Mercury.* Nick put on his favorite selection from the 1985 Live Aid Concert in London. It began with Freddie's *Bohemian Rhapsody*, that electrifying blend of opera and rock.

"Hey, bloodhounds," he called out, "hope you like Freddie."

Freddie opened with a series of bold chords on the piano, then out rolled his distinctive voice, starting low in his remarkable four-octave range—"Mama, just killed a man . . ."

Back on his stool, Nick sketched with bold, black lines, keeping his arm and hand moving freely. The *Joy of Life* sketch imprinted in his mind, Freddie's voice reverberating in his ears, he could feel the pulsing music and the master's brushstrokes flow down his fingers through the charcoal and onto the canvas. Matisse and Freddie were with him. He was not alone.

Now for the paint. First, Nick loosely brushed in the figures' skin tones in shades of pink, pale yellow, and white. Next, he loaded a small brush with raw red pigment. Then, using his charcoal under-drawing only as a guide, he roughly outlined the cavorting naked figures in rhythmic red as they made love, danced, and played music in a clearing in the enchanted forest. Now he was inside the painting, transported, euphoric.

He painted the fiery red and orange sky breaking through the green foliage.

Freddie was soaring up the scale; his vocal fireworks spiked with angst.

Last was the ground color. Nick painted the grass in dashes and dabs of yellow and orange, the colors expressing Matisse's joyful emotions at the time. Given that the master suffered from acute bouts of anxiety and depression, Nick wondered if Matisse intentionally manufactured his euphoric moods by painting with bright, exuberant colors. In any case, it worked for Nick.

Taking his time, Nick harmonized the lines and colors, adding accents in various places until all the shapes, hues, and brushstrokes sang together in a joyous chorus. Then he rolled back on his stool and studied the two paintings side by side. Nick could picture how his colors would look when the oil paint dried. Close enough to the original to fool an expert.

"Aaaaaay-o," he sang and shot his fist up into the air. His sketch was a perfect match in color, line, and composition. His copy might even fool Henri. So now Nick joined Freddie, Queen, and the seventy-two thousand people in the Live Aid audience, all soaring upward like birds, belting out *We Are the Champions*.

CHAPTER 18

The job of the artist is always to deepen the mystery.
—Francis Bacon—

Monday, October 15

In her studio, sipping her morning coffee, Kate looked down on her duck pond. The painting was waiting for her to decide its fate. Should she sell it as an early work of Guy Rose or as a Kate O'Dade original? She thought it probably wasn't good enough to pass as a Rose. But suppose it was? Would she sell it as a Rose and become an actual criminal? Even though forgery was not such a bad crime—many called it a victimless crime—she believed it was wrong to defraud people, even misogynists like Bryce Morton. She eased her conscience with the reminder that he'd deceived himself about who painted *Field of Gold* and refused to believe that she, a mere woman, was the artist. True, she had not saved him from himself as her saintly mother would have done. Kate was not a saint, but she was also not much of a sinner, at least not yet. However, she did sense that she was starting to dip more than her toes into treacherous waters.

She wondered if she considered forging less criminal because her father had been a charming, talented fake in many ways, but he'd also been a real hero in the Vietnam War. The back of her neck tingled at the thought of Nick at the exhibition whispering, "Bravo!" about her first fake.

Her cell vibrated on the worktable next to the painting. The number on the screen looked familiar, but it wasn't Raquel's. Thinking it dangerous for Raquel to face Steele's rage after the unveiling debacle, she'd left a message advising her to stay overnight in a hotel. Raquel had not called back, but Kate hoped she'd had the sense to protect herself and would show up for her therapy session tomorrow afternoon.

Kate answered the call, surprised to hear Nick's voice. Wasting no time, he suggested they meet to discuss their mutual concerns about *The Open Window.*

"I know this is late to ask," he said, "but I'd like to take you to dinner tonight. It's the least I can do to make up for breaking into your studio to take your painting."

Kate laughed, high-pitched, nervous. "Ah, so you admit it's *my* painting."

He chuckled. "You have the stronger case, according to the principle that *possession is nine-tenths of the law.* In the 1870s, the McCoys lost their pigs to the Hatfields because the McCoy pigs had wandered onto the Hatfield farm."

"Ah, that's like *The Open Window* wandering onto my doorstep."

"You could make that argument, but—"

"Sounds like I'm the one who should ease the pain of your loss," Kate said, then impulsively added, "Why don't you bring a pizza to my place so we can argue our positions in front of Papa Matisse." She knew meeting alone was risky, but the words kept tumbling out of her mouth. "I like pepperoni and onion. How about you? I'll provide the drinks. It's the least I can do for your rescuing *Field of Gold* from the count's suspicious examination."

"Brilliant," he said, his smooth baritone reverberating in her ear. "We can also compare notes about the identity of your mysterious gift-giver."

"I've yet to hear from my last two suspects." Kate recalled Sam's excited reaction on the phone when he heard about the mysterious Matisse gift. Like Allegra, he guessed it must have been from a secret admirer. Almost immediately, Sam hit on the idiotic idea of Gerard Devereaux, saying he'd always had a crush on her. Kate had pooh-poohed that notion, to which Sam replied, "Jesus, Mom, you're always so dense when it comes to men."

No argument, she thought, tuning back into the latest object of her thick-headedness. "So far, I can't dredge up any more likely possibilities."

"Keep working on it. We'll get somewhere tonight. Two heads are better than one."

Kate sensed he was holding back his side of the investigation, but maybe it was better to wait for an in-person discussion. "By the way," she said, "I think you did an impressive job of heading off a violent incident at the museum's rather unique unveiling. You seem to have a lot of influence with Dixon Steele."

"Yeah, I've saved him a ton of money and embarrassment by stopping him from making bad deals in the art market. He's impulsive and rash, as you may have noticed."

"That's an understatement." Kate flashed on Steele's florid-faced fury. "Did you find the Picasso drawing Steele was planning to donate?"

"Yes, it was quite a clever trick. Steele had bubble-wrapped the selected drawing and put it in the trunk of his Jaguar. Then he took a shower and got dressed for the gala. The drawing was still there when we looked, but a rug already in the trunk had been laid on top of it. Obviously, someone had put the bubble-wrapped minotaur rape drawing on top of the selected one covered by the rug. Both Simon and Raquel rode with Steele to the gala. At the museum, Steele picked up the wrapped drawing on top of the rug, carried it inside, and gave it to one of the staff to prepare for the unveiling.

"Who substituted the minotaur rape drawing? Simon or Raquel?"

"That's still unclear." Kate sensed he knew more than he was saying.

"What Picasso drawing had Steele selected to donate?" Kate asked.

Nick chuckled. "It's called *Girl Helping Minotaur*. In the picture, a half-clothed maiden is offering a wounded, sad-looking minotaur a glass of wine. A lovely drawing and quite touching. The museum crowd would have been delighted with it. In fact, the two of them together would have made a stunning pair and a feast for psychologists."

After they said goodbye, Kate's pulse was racing. *What had she done?* Had she just opened Pandora's box or the door to a thrilling romance? Perhaps both. A few more hours and she'd know. She eyed *The Open Window,* propped on her easel, and gave it a thumbs up.

CHAPTER 19

Need and love [are] as easily mistaken for each other as the real master's painting and a forgery.

—Deb Caletti—

Monday Evening, October 15

Kate opened her front door, and there stood Nick, bright-eyed and smiling—dressed in jeans, a chambray shirt, and a cotton neckerchief. She was momentarily disoriented. Over three and a half years ago, she had greeted this man at the side door to her home therapy office, and now he was at the front door like a guest. He held a box from Bongiorno's New York Pizzeria, emitting savory, spicy food smells. She'd told herself this visit was not a date; it was about the Matisse. However, what to wear for this non-date had driven her crazy for most of the day. She settled on a casual, cream cotton swing top and matching wide-legged pants, all interesting body parts concealed.

"Feels like I'm breaking the rules coming in the front door like this," Nick stood waiting. "Are you going to let me in?"

She eyed the large pizza box. "Well, since you've brought dinner." She smiled and stepped back as he strode inside.

"It's half pepperoni and onion for you and half 'everything on it' for me."

"Perfect," she said, her voice sounding high and girlish. "We'll eat in my office. It's the only air-conditioned room."

"Good, I wouldn't mind a break from this bloody heat."

"And you'll feel right at home." *Remember, I'm in charge*, she wanted to assert. She was surprised at how nervous she felt. She knew this man as his therapist and knew his darkest secrets, but not how to behave on a date with him. There were no conventions for this circumstance, and it felt illicit.

She left him in her office at the end of the hallway and hurried to the kitchen to get the cold white wine and beer. She'd already put plates, glasses, and napkins in her office. When she returned with the chardonnay and beer, she was startled to see Nick sitting in her consulting chair.

"I couldn't resist." He stood and gestured toward one of the client chairs across from him. "Please sit down. I hope you don't mind a little role reversal."

An attack of the jitters said she *did* mind. She didn't like losing the control that being his therapist had provided. She put the wine and beer bottles next to the pizza on the coffee table between them, then sat on the edge of the client's chair, knees pressed together, hands folded on her lap.

"Pardon me for snooping," he said, "but I noticed a photograph of a handsome young man on your desk. He's got your auburn hair and emerald eyes."

She smiled. "That's my son, Sam. I have his picture where clients can't see it. Keeps me company when I'm writing reports. He's a freshman at Berkeley."

"Good choice. How does Sam like it there?" He sounded oddly polite, like they were making small talk at a cocktail party.

"Sam's a social activist," she said. "He's into wiping out racism, white supremacy, and guns. Berkeley is the perfect place for his idealism, but I fear for his safety."

He grunted. "At least he's not into skydiving."

"Something to be thankful for." She recalled the days many years ago when she was a daredevil paraglider. Sam, she realized, was emulating her as well as his rock-climbing father.

Nick poured her a glass of wine. "Here, drink some of this. It'll numb the worry."

She downed a large mouthful, watching Nick open the bottle of IPA, his shapely hands so deft and precise. He served her a wedge of pepperoni pizza and then put a slice of "the works" on his plate. This role reversal of his taking care of her made her feel vulnerable. Still, his kindness also had a nurturing quality that stirred a longing for more—his touch on her fevered skin, her fingers sinking into his lush mane of curly hair, his lips . . . She quickly banished these thoughts, crossed her legs, and drank wine. *Take charge.*

"What are you thinking?" she asked in her neutral therapist's voice.

He chuckled. "First, glad I'm not sitting in the client's hot seat. Second, it's a pleasure to look at you and that extraordinary antique quilt behind you. Two objects of beauty."

Good lord, now he was flirting. *Do not smile.* "My great-grandmother made the quilt. I've loved it all my life. I remember it as the main object of beauty in our rented cottage after we moved to San Diego when I was ten." She recalled that her frantic mother had left almost everything she cared about behind, including anything belonging to her opera star father.

"Where are you from?" he asked.

"New York City," she said.

"So, what was it like growing up in the Big Apple?" Nick took a bite of his pizza, chewed, and washed it down with beer while his gaze fixed on her.

She nibbled at her pizza, aware that he'd taken over her old role. She was more comfortable listening to other people's stories than telling her own. In fact, no one still alive knew about her early life except for Gerard and Elise Devereaux and Francisco Flynn. She wasn't sure it was a good idea to let Nick in on her traumatic past, but she couldn't say anything real about her story without including the dark parts.

She took in a deep breath and began. "I grew up at the Metropolitan Opera. My father was an opera star, a famous bass-baritone at the time. I, too, was a singer then, a child star, but I lost my soprano voice after my father died . . . more precisely, after he was murdered." She stopped, feeling the sweat bead on her brow, her heart racing.

He stared at her as though he couldn't quite take in what she had just revealed.

"I'm sorry," she said. "This was too much for you to hear. Thought I should practice what I preach. God knows, I talked you into sharing your past traumas."

He reached across the table and took her hand. "Please continue if it helps you to talk because I'd like to hear it all."

She took another deep breath. "I was locked in a prop box in the basement of the Met at the time Dad was murdered. I almost died, too, and ended up feeling that I had caused his death. My guilt and grief were so intolerable that I repressed all of what happened that night and a lot of my early childhood as well. I ended up claustrophobic, but I've gotten over most of that."

He looked at her with such compassion, she felt herself melting inside as a stream of warm tears rolled down her face.

"My brave Kate, I had no idea. You had it worse than I did."

"No, I didn't," she said. "You lost your entire family and almost died from those terrible burns."

"True," he said, "but I didn't think I caused their deaths. You were left with the crippling guilt of your dad's death. Burns gradually heal, but I doubt that the guilt of patricide ever does."

She covered his hand with hers and smiled. "Seems like we're having a competition about who had the worst childhood."

He laughed. "You win. Just tell me, was your father's real killer ever found?"

"Yes, but that story is for another time. Did you ever find out how your house burned down?"

He hesitated, averting his eyes. "I'm still working on what happened." He guzzled the last of his beer. "Back to you, did you take up painting after you lost your voice?"

"Yes, that's how I coped with all the losses, much like you did." She reached for the wine bottle, and her hand ran into his. Her fingers were on top of his for a moment. He sat perfectly still, his magnetic gaze holding her motionless. Her heartbeat quickened, a hot flush creeping up her neck. She could feel the heat of his eyes seeing through her clothes to her tingling skin beneath. She pulled her hand away.

"Here, let me." He stood and poured her another glass.

She took a swallow of the cool wine, basking in his focused attention, imagining herself opening like a flower in the sunlight. "You are an excellent listener, Nick. In my experience, most men would rather talk than listen, preferably about themselves."

"Most men didn't need to listen to survive," he said. "As long as they got the parental messages to *succeed* and *make us proud*, other listening skills were not required."

She nodded. "All too true. Are you bitter about that?"

He shrugged. "Probably. I'm a lot more skilled at listening than talking. At first, I found it difficult to carry the talking ball in therapy. But you listened so well and with genuine interest—talking started to feel good. You were the first to really listen to me after I lost my family. The first woman, that is. Charlie was the first man."

"Yes, I remember 'top of the morning' Charlie. He was the Scottish custodian at London's National Gallery. Saved your bacon, didn't he?"

"Yep, and so did you." He held her moist gaze as he loosened the knot on his neckerchief.

"Why don't you take that thing off," she said. "You know, scars don't scare me."

"Are you suggesting I undress?" His eyes glittered.

"Just from your neck up." *What the hell was she doing*? "Maybe we should talk about the Matisse."

"Yes, indeed," he said.

"I'll get the picture. It's in my bedroom. I like falling asleep with it there for company."

She got up and hurried down the hall to her bedroom at the opposite end of the house. She turned on the light and smiled at her fabulous *Open Window*, so much more enchanting than the room's actual window. She had propped the picture up against the bookshelves near the end of the bed where she could look at it while falling asleep. Would she be able to give this treasure back to Nick? After all, he painted it, and someone stole it from him. Would they ever find the thief who gave it to her?

She hadn't heard him following her down the hall, but she felt him behind her now, his breath on her neck. She felt herself respond, wanting this scarred, wild-haired man and a thrilling ride to freedom, whatever that meant.

When Kate turned around, Nick kissed her closed eyes and mouth with such tenderness that she wrapped her arms around him in a fierce embrace. The painting glowed in the soft light on the bed stand, spurring the abandonment of all restraint. He watched in wonder as Kate's smooth, lithe body emerged—like an elegant swan from her loose-fitting clothes. He could hardly believe he was here with the Kate he'd desired for so long. Her silky-white skin beside his brown, battered body reminded him of the cruel boyhood names he was called after the fire—freak, troll, Quasimodo, Frankenstein. Still ashamed of his unsightly scars, Nick turned off the light before whipping off his shirt and pulling her into another long kiss. He explored every part of her with his lips and tongue, her ecstatic sighs spurring him to kiss, lick, and suck those perfect breasts he'd dreamed of for the past three years. She stroked and kissed the cratered moon of his body with a passion and tenderness Nick had never experienced.

As they lay entangled and exhausted in each other's arms, his mind turned to thoughts of what he could do for this remarkable woman who had given him so much.

"Kate, let me fix your financial problems. I can sell the Matisse for millions."

"It's a copy, worth only hundreds of dollars," she said.

"I can sell it as the original to a reclusive Asian collector I know."

"You'd be caught. The real one is at the National Gallery of Art."

"There are ways around such obstacles," he said.

"I can't let you take that risk for me."

With Kate spooned against his back, Nick couldn't recall ever feeling such happiness. Gradually, he drifted off to sleep.

Her cries jolted him awake. He gently shook her trembling body. "Kate, love, it's just a nightmare." As he stroked her hair, she spoke of fleeing from an unknown man chasing her through a dark maze.

"He was after the Matisse. Quick, turn on the light." She sat up as he switched on the lamp. "The painting. Thank God it's still here." She turned toward him, stony-eyed. "You must tell me the truth about the Matisse."

He felt cornered. "Won't this keep until daylight?"

"No. Tell me who stole your painting and how it got to me."

"Sorry, love. I don't know."

"I don't believe you. You're too savvy not to know something." She turned away.

Her sudden withdrawal sent a wave of panic through him. He slipped his arm around her. "Kate, love, can't we just be with our Matisse for a while?"

"*Our* Matisse. So, you're accepting me as a co-owner?"

He pulled her into a tight embrace. "Yes, love, we're together now." *What the hell am I saying?* In the heat of the moment, he'd conveniently forgotten his plan to vanish. Had he been a con man for so long that he now believed his act? If he truly cared for Kate, he couldn't just disappear. But how could he put her at risk and stay with her? A puzzling Matisse quote came into his mind—*In love, the one who runs away is the winner.*

CHAPTER 20

What loneliness is more lonely than distrust?
—George Eliot—

Tuesday, October 16

Kate sat alone in the glassed-in breakfast nook, sipped her morning coffee, and gazed out at the giant bamboo masked in a whitish-gray fog. The questions she had shoved to the back of her mind now leaped to the forefront. Where would her mad attraction to an exciting con artist lead her? Were they destined to become partners in crime? If they each had the power to destroy the other, that could be the outcome. More damning was the trust problem. Nick was incapable of trusting her any more than she could trust him. Lying and deception were his lifelong survival methods. Sadness as thick as the fog enveloped her. She had to end this doomed romance now before it turned ugly.

Nick strode into the kitchen, carrying the painting. He looked so appealing, his eyes bright beneath his thick black hair.

"I've brought our Matisse to keep you happy." He propped the painting up against the window to the right of the table, then he pulled up a chair and sat facing her. Their knees touching, Nick took her hands.

"Your hands are cold." He blew his warm breath on them and kissed her palms.

His tenderness made her weep inside.

"I have a confession to make," he said.

"Don't we have enough dirt on each other already?"

"It's about the Matisse. You wanted the truth."

She nodded, her throat tightening.

"I lied about the painting. I doubt that surprises you, but I can't go on lying to you." He stared at the picture for a long time as though the prospect of truth-telling put him on the edge of a crumbling cliff. Finally, he said, "This is not a copy I painted."

"Oh?" she said, not entirely surprised. "Who did then?"

Slow smile. "Papa Matisse. This is the original."

"What!" She sat upright. "Our *Open Window* is the real deal?" She looked into his shining eyes. "Have you known this all along?"

"I knew it in my gut when I first saw it with you six days ago. But it seemed impossible then. Sometimes even expert authenticators, the actual artist, and the forger can't distinguish a fake. I also thought the genuine painting was locked in my vault at the museum, and it couldn't be the one left on your doorstep in this cheap frame. I didn't know the Matisse was missing from my vault until after you and Allegra left the museum.

"How on earth did the real one end up with me?"

"I strongly suspect someone stole it from the vault and dumped it on you. The motive is unclear, however." He paused, his brow furrowed.

"Spit it out. Who do you suspect?"

"I've ruled out every possible person except Allegra. She has access to the museum's storage rooms, but I don't know how she figured out the code to my vault. I keep my most cherished paintings there, including this Matisse."

"But Allegra makes no sense. Why would she steal the painting, anonymously give it to me, and then arrange for you to evaluate it?"

"Right, Allegra seems to have no apparent motive," he said. "But thinking about her psychology—as you might—I could see her playing a spiteful child's game." He paused. "Were you the one to contact her about your mystery gift?"

"No. Shortly after I found the painting on my doorstep, she dropped in to give me a couple of books. We had a drink, and I showed her the picture."

"She *just happened* to be on the spot? Quite a coincidence."

Kate nodded. "I see your point, but what could be in this for her?"

"To skewer me with the loss of something I love," Nick said.

"But she adores you. She's got the hots for you."

"That's the problem. I've resisted Allegra's charms none too gently. I find her repulsive and never should have accepted her as an intern."

"Ah, so she's a woman scorned, and this is her revenge," Kate said. "Can she really be so conniving and vindictive?"

The memory of a disturbing incident surfaced. "In the watercolor class where I met Allegra, I saw her knock over a container of turpentine onto a talented student's prize-winning painting. Ruined it. I'm pretty sure it wasn't an accident." Kate massaged her throbbing temples. "Christ, where do I fit into this charade?"

"You were the ideal messenger."

"The naïve dupe, you mean." How would Allegra react knowing that her plain-Jane pal was Nick's lover? A screeching hellcat came to mind. "This is not a pretty picture."

"No, but there's an uglier one.'

Kate raised her brows.

"Blackmail," Nick said. "Allegra could suspect me. She knows about the famous British forgers who were also restorers. If she found this *Open Window* in my vault, she would assume it was a copy I intended to sell as the original. Stealing it, then getting you to flash it in my face was her sly, threatening way of saying she wants in on the deal—or she'll screw me and tip off the FBI."

"You think she wants to be your partner in crime, if not in bed?"

"Possibly. A forger at my level makes big money. Her bloody lordship father gambles and is always broke. So, along with her minimal artistic talent, Allegra has no money. She's also unsuited for conservation and restoration work, as she's too impulsive, has low standards, and is allergic to hard work. She might succeed in the petty crime domain."

Either Allegra was a grasping sociopath or Nick was alarmingly paranoid. Both seemed possible. Despite the heat in the room, Kate shivered. She looked at their priceless painting—the prime culprit, a magnificent, wild beast that should be caged in a museum.

"What's your opinion, Doc?" Nick watched her through narrowed eyes. "Am I the crazy one?"

"Let's hope not. You're the psychology expert on this case." Kate looked away from his disturbing gaze. "What's to be done about Allegra if one or both of these vile scenarios are true?"

"True or not, I plan to get rid of her with a good job offer from an important museum, one that owes me a favor. That will be her best chance for a real life."

"Good of you . . . and shrewd," Kate said, steeling herself to ask, "So how did an original Matisse end up with you? Did you steal it?"

He glanced at the painting, stalling, it seemed. "It's a dark, twisted tale, best left for another time." His posture stiffened, and his black eyes turned hard and impenetrable.

His sudden withdrawal shook her. Her head ached, and the heat in the room felt suffocating. Who was this man? What had he done to get this genuine masterpiece? She stopped the questions, the possible answers too disturbing to contemplate.

Concealing her mounting fear, she asked, "What shall we do with the Matisse now?"

"Keep it and enjoy it, or sell it for a fortune." He stood and looked down at her, a crooked half-smile on his face. "Or there's another option." He paused. "You could turn the painting into the FBI Art Crime Team and become a celebrity—the clever psychologist who found an original Matisse and caught Phantom."

The grim set of his mouth and the feral wariness in his eyes told her this was no joke. He was baring his throat to her—his warmth and love were nowhere in sight.

He stood over her, this shadow of a man she no longer knew. He even smelled differently, musky like an animal. Threat hovered in the air. *Did he see her now as another conniving Allegra, or was she the paranoid one?* He was waiting for a reply, his body tensed, poised to strike, it seemed. Her answer—what the hell was it?

So much on the line—her loyalty to Nick as his former therapist and now her lover versus what she believed was right. Was the law more important than a person, more important than her lover's freedom? Wouldn't Matisse want his painting hanging in a museum for all the world to see, not hidden away with two shady, fanatical fans? But she doubted Matisse would want the artist most capable of appreciating his genius locked up. How would Nick react if she chose to turn the painting over to the FBI? She flashed on the devastation, the betrayal, the fury in his eyes. Then he'd vanish, leaving her alone and bitter, the fantasy of a life together dead.

She could feel a scream rising in her throat. Out of the past, her mother's voice—*When in doubt, stall.*

Kate called upon her years of training to keep her response calm and matter-of-fact. "I think we should hold on to it . . . for the time being."

She glanced at the dazzling painting, trying its best to bring joy back into the room.

CHAPTER 21

Vengeance is in my heart, death in my hand.

—Shakespeare—

Tuesday, Early Afternoon, October 16

Raquel hobbled through the walled garden of Kate's home office, swathed in a black hooded wrap, her bruised, bloodshot eyes hidden behind saucer-sized dark glasses. She could let down her guard in this serene place, reminiscent of her small garden in Paris. Rosemary, thyme, and basil scented the air, and the tinkling bamboo fountain calmed her nerves. Raquel stopped at the door, doing her best to summon her strength. She disliked appearing weak in front of her beloved therapist, who was not much older than her thirty-six years. Knowing Kate had witnessed her performance at the unveiling at the museum, Raquel was on edge about how she would react.

She pressed the bell. Kate opened the door, and Raquel limped into the office, pushed back the hood, and took off her dark glasses.

Kate gasped. "My God, what happened?"

Tears welled in Raquel's eyes. "I look a fright, I know."

Kate guided her to the client's chair and brought her a glass of water poured from the pitcher on top of the bookcase. "You must be hurting. Want some Advil?"

"*Non, merci.* I took painkillers."

Kate sat across from her. "Did Dixon do this?"

"*Il est une bête!*" she said, deserting her stilted English. Kate spoke French and had an art background, which had put Raquel at ease from the beginning.

"Was his attack about the unveiling?" Kate asked.

"*Oui,* punishment for humiliating him."

"He humiliated himself," Kate said.

Raquel cracked a bitter smile. "*Mais oui*, Dixon is never to blame."

"Did you get my message about staying at a hotel Friday night?"

"Yes, one of the caterer's employees took me to L'Auberge in Del Mar. Dixon kept calling to apologize. He begged me to come home."

"Dixon apologized?"

"He only wanted to get me back home so he could beat me."

Kate leaned forward. "Dixon is dangerous. I know of a women's shelter where you will be safe. Let me help you."

Raquel nodded, feigning agreement. Kate spoke in detail about how to get a restraining order and even wrote down the name and address of the best women's shelter in San Diego. Raquel knew she wouldn't do any of this. She needed to finish her arrangements to leave Dixon and disguise the purpose of her departure. *What was safe to reveal?* She'd kept her darkest secrets from Kate but felt too frightened and alone to hold them in any longer.

"I sense you're afraid to say what you're feeling," Kate said. "How can I help you with that? I don't judge."

Kate's warmth and receptiveness felt genuine. "My situation is more complicated than you know." She pulled out a Kleenex from the box on her side table. "I have a secret lover. This relationship did not begin as a romance. It began as a mutual passion to destroy Dixon Steele."

"Because of the abuse?"

"No, my lover doesn't know about the abuse. He might abort our plan if he knew, and I want Dixon punished. I came here to work with a French art dealer, but the more important reason was for revenge. Dixon has caused us both terrible grief." She dabbed at her eyes, watching the grim look on Kate's face.

"It's good you're telling me about this. Sounds like this affair has been going on for a while."

"On my side, it is serious," Raquel said. "But I'm not sure about him. I'm afraid he might really want someone else." She stopped and watched her fingers tear at the Kleenex, debating whether to say Nick's name. Until the exhibition, she hadn't realized Kate knew Nick, though that fact should be no surprise given her therapist's connections to the art world. They had chatted at the opening as though they knew each other well. If Kate found out her client and friend were having a secret affair, she might think less of her. And Nick wanted their affair kept secret. She could not betray him. Kate was also a friend of that Allegra bitch, though she had trouble picturing such a friendship. Could she trust anything Allegra had said? The idea Nick would fall for that *femme méchante* seemed absurd.

"Can you say more about your feelings?" Kate asked. "You look so distressed."

Caught in a web of secrets, lies, and violence, Raquel fought to keep her grip on reality. "I am feeling much regret. The early part of our plan worked out easily. We were all in the art world, knew each other, and became friends. Now it is so complicated."

"Dangerous as well. Earlier, you mentioned terrible grief."

She bowed her head. "Forgive me. I've held back the worst of my past." She took a deep breath, wincing in pain. "*Mon père* was a successful art dealer in Paris, but things went wrong. When I was about eight, we ended up in serious financial trouble. Papa had to borrow heavily to keep his business going. He'd inherited a valuable art collection and put up all but one of the paintings as collateral with a financier—Dixon Steele. When Papa couldn't pay his debts on time, Steele refused an extension and seized the paintings."

Memories surfaced. She saw herself as a little girl huddled next to her Papa, one of her small hands enfolded in his protective grip. She remembered counting the empty spaces on the salon walls where the eight beautiful pictures used to hang. And the tears in Papa's eyes as he gazed at the last, most valuable painting—*The Blue Room* by Picasso. That hideous man insisted on taking this most cherished work, along with all the other pictures.

Raquel spoke in whispered snatches. "The horrible failure destroyed Papa's reputation, his business, and his health. He began drinking heavily." She closed her eyes, blocking out images of the next horrific scene. "There was a terrible accident. Papa fell off the platform in front of a train at the Passy Metro and died instantly." She sat frozen. "*Maman* was certain Papa had committed suicide so that we would get his life insurance." She rarely spoke of losing her father, and as the years of buried grief surged up inside her, she burst into sobs, reliving her despair and her depressed, bedridden mother's inability to comfort her. She felt Kate's sympathetic words wrapping her in a warm embrace. Soon she straightened and blotted her face and runny nose.

"That monster still has our Picasso. It hangs in his foul gallery. He will pay for it this time, I swear." She curled her hands into tight fists. Kate's next words seemed to come from a distance.

"Raquel, I understand your grief, rage, and desire for revenge, but we must face the most pressing problem first."

She remained silent. To her, avenging her father was more important than playing it safe, more important than anything.

"Are you and your lover planning to eliminate Dixon?"

"Death would be too easy for him. Dixon must suffer as we have suffered."

"How will you achieve this and not get yourself killed or jailed?"

"I must go." She stood up.

"I'm not okay with you walking out of here into an abusive situation. I don't usually intrude this way but let me take you to the shelter."

She held up her hand. "*Non, non, merci beaucoup.* I will follow your advice. I will go to the shelter tomorrow. I have much to arrange, and Dixon will not be home tonight." Tomorrow she'd leave. That was soon enough.

Kate looked worried. "Call me when you get there or call me if you're having any trouble getting yourself there. This is a difficult thing to do. Do you have a friend you can stay with tonight?"

"Yes, or I will stay in a hotel. You have my word."

CHAPTER 22

The game is afoot.

—SHAKESPEARE & SHERLOCK—

Tuesday Afternoon, October 16

"I've got evidence," Flynn said. He held up a small recorder as he strode toward his three teammates. They were sitting in the front garden of their posh beachfront digs, drinking iced coffee. Flynn was pleased to sit down in an adult-sized chair at an ordinary patio table shaded by a couple of Japanese maples. The air felt moist in this grotto-like garden of ferns, moss, and stones, with a small waterfall trickling down rocks into a koi pond. Archie, Desi, and Eddie eyed him expectantly while the oversized koi were thrashing around and leaping up at the pond's edge, their mouths gaping open demanding food.

"Got nothing for you fellows." Flynn showed his empty palms. To the humans, he said, "Coming up is Raquel Steele's latest therapy session with Doc Kate this afternoon. I gambled it would be worth bugging her office and won. You are about to hear the Nick-Raquel plot against Steele revealed." He hit play on the recorder, and the women's voices came through clearly.

The team was transfixed when Raquel revealed her secret liaison with a man in the art world who also hated Steele and shared her desire for revenge. They already knew that Raquel's lover was McCoy. The only one who didn't seem to suspect the obvious was Kate. Flynn had told the team that he'd found out from bugging Kate's studio and office that she and Nick became lovers last night when he arrived at her place with a pizza. Listening to their falling-in-love talk had been an agony for him.

"These ladies are in deep shit," Archie said.

"It's a deadly triangle, like a mother and daughter sharing a lover," Desi said.

"Why Kate didn't guess that Raquel was banging McCoy makes no sense," Flynn said.

"Lust is blind," Eddie said. "And even intelligent women fall for McCoy. Maybe Kate does suspect, but she couldn't let on in the session."

"Whatever. These women need protecting," Flynn said.

"Indeed," Eddie said, "but the best way to do that is to lock up McCoy and Steele. We have a good plan to expose Steele, and with your constant surveillance of McCoy, he will feel hounded and possibly rattled enough to make a mistake."

The koi thrashed and splashed water out of the pond. A couple rose up, begging for food. Archie threw a fistful of cracker bits at them. They made loud, gulping noises.

"Setting aside the lust melodrama, let's focus on the Nick-Raquel revenge plot against Steele," Eddie said. "Any guesses about what that is?"

"It has something to do with Steele's prized billion-dollar art collection," Flynn said. "That's what he cares about—more, I'd wager, than he cares about any human. So, stealing it would be the most obvious revenge."

"Too risky for McCoy," Eddie said. "He'd be the prime suspect. Did Raquel give anything away about their plot when you were with her?"

"She confided quite a bit," Desi said, "but nothing specifically about Nick and their plot. She told me that she didn't marry Steele for love or money. She despises him and plans to leave him very soon. She loves someone else, but she's afraid this man is in love with another woman.

She thinks that woman is Allegra. But frankly, I don't see McCoy going for a bitch like her. If McCoy loves someone else, I'd guess it's Kate."

"Agreed," Eddie said. "Well done, Desi."

"I like Raquel. I wish we could get her out of the hell she's in."

The koi splashed and squawked for more food. An ugly, whiskered Butterfly Koi with yellow and brown blotches jumped up and almost out of the pond.

"Archie," Flynn snapped. "Can't you put those freaks out of their misery?"

"Food or murder?" Archie reached into a bag of premium koi fish food at his feet, stood, and threw a handful into the pond, then a second handful. The koi went into a wild, thrashing, feeding frenzy.

"Steele's a crook," Desi said, "and he's a big underworld player. Could Nick and Raquel be planning a clever blackmail scheme that would torment and strip Steele of his wealth, including his precious collection?"

"Now that has legs," Eddie said. "Steele did some shady things to secure much of his collection. The lovers could be gathering proof of his crimes. Has anyone seen his collection?"

"According to Simon, Steele only allows select people—usually potential buyers—to see his most valuable paintings," Flynn said. "As the count, you will become one of the chosen few."

"Sounds like an old Bond film," Eddie said. "The one about the arch-villain who has a famous painting hidden in a vault underwater."

"*Dr. No*," Desi said. "The painting was Goya's portrait *The Duke of Wellington,* borrowed from London's National Gallery."

Eddie looked up. "How do you know that? That film is way older than you are."

"It was made in 1962," Desi said. "I love old movies, and I'm an art crime junkie."

"Excellent hobbies." Eddie smiled. "Let's follow the plot of your blackmail idea. Suppose this scam comes off without a hitch, then what?"

"The Hollywood ending." Desi smiled. "Nick and Raquel abscond with the money and the collection. Then, in the next scene, they are toasting each other on an exotic Caribbean beach."

"And poor Kate is left choking in the dust," Flynn said.

"Maybe Nick chooses Kate and ditches loyal Raquel," Archie said.

"Or he dumps both of them," Eddie said. "They've served their purpose, and the infamous Phantom has once again eluded the dim plodders at Scotland Yard, the FBI, and now Detective Hawk—the lone female LAPD art crime detective."

"That ending sucks," Desi said.

"Here's a worse one," Flynn said. "The cold bastard knocks off both women. After all, they know too much and might rat him out anytime."

Eddie rubbed his jaw. He'd never considered that McCoy could be a killer. "Let's move on. We need to review the plan for the count's meeting with Steele tomorrow."

"Any jobs for us?" Archie asked.

"Absolutely," Eddie said. "Archie, you're still the count's driver. And, if you run into Simon, tell him you've thought about his offer and need more details to decide."

Archie grimaced. "Yeah, I can handle that. It'll be daylight, but it seems like we'll be heading blind into a possible three-way shitstorm."

"Right, better bring our wellies. Nothing goes smoothly in undercover work." Eddie turned to Desi. "I'd like you to play the count's art adviser. Flynn, can you handle being the count's bodyguard? You get to wear a wire and carry a gun."

"Whoopee. Why would the *Comte de Guise* need a bodyguard?"

"Because he's a filthy-rich crook just like Dixon Steele, his new best friend."

CHAPTER 23

Outcast, iconoclast, standfast.

—L.M. Browning—

Tuesday Evening, October 16

Flynn took Desi's hand as they walked into Jake's, a restaurant on Del Mar Beach. "This way, we'll look more like a couple than a pair of brown misfits."

Desi smiled at him. "The sea of white faces in here is hard on the eyes."

Flynn resisted the temptation to squeeze her warm fingers. "I picked this popular hangout because it's on the way to Kate's place. Since she and Nick are new lovers, I'm guessing he'll show up tonight."

"Poor Raquel. I hope she dumps him."

The hostess led them through the noisy, crowded bar area. The refrigerated air smelled of spirits and grilling fish. Repetitive thumping sounds began, also known as music, assaulting their senses. Then, as Flynn requested, the hostess seated them outside on the sparsely populated, shaded terrace. They had a dramatic view of the beach from their corner table and saw a few walkers and joggers passing by. A blond waiter appeared, and they ordered drinks and snacks.

After the waiter left, Desi said, "You don't seem exactly keen on our leader."

"To be fair, it's not Cromwell personally I dislike." His hand twitched, his words stilted as though he was on a first date. "Eddie's smart, I'll give him that, and he tries *not* to look down that long, patrician nose of his. Must admit he used his built-in arrogance rather well in playing the count." He paused, reluctant to reveal more of himself. But if he wanted her to open, he'd better lead the way. "The problem is my resentment of the British aristocracy and the upper class. Bunch of pompous, self-serving pricks who screwed the Irish and think working for a living is for lower life forms."

"Talk about resentments," Desi said. "I hate the rich, especially greedy swines like Dixon Steele. I bet my prejudice takes in a lot more people than yours."

"Nope, I've got that one, too." Flynn grinned, starting to relax. "White peacocks give me a belly ache. I'm sure there are good folks in these unfortunate categories, but none of my best friends are rich, white assholes."

Desi laughed, making a throaty, sensual sound. Flynn's gaze slid down her throat, skimmed over her breasts, and down one of her bare arms to the graceful hand resting half-cupped on the table. He wanted to grab that hand and pull her onto his lap. Their drinks arrived, interrupting his fantasy.

Flynn raised his beer. "Here's to a successful hunt and kill."

"Here, here," Desi said. They clinked glasses, and she took a sip of her margarita, glancing at the ocean. "Wow. Look at that stunning sunset. Romantic, isn't it?"

Flynn glanced out at the frothing surf and the vermillion-streaked sky. "Sorry, I'm not into splashy sunsets, and my tribe never was romantic, particularly when stalking prey."

"What do *you* know? You're only *part* Apache," she teased.

"Yeah, yeah, I don't have your creds," Flynn said. "But I mostly grew up on a reservation. You may be pure Lakota, but I don't think you spent much time scratching a living on a broken-down res."

Desi's lips tightened. "What makes you think that?"

"Your self-confidence, cool style, the way you joke around with the white guys."

"There's nothing wrong with your self-confidence, Flynn. You've got a truckload."

He flashed a grin. "Glad I've succeeded in fooling you."

She bit into a salsa-coated chip and regarded him coolly. "You're right about the reservation. But there are worse things than being poor in a close-knit community. It was a treat for me to visit my aunt and cousins on the res. I lived in town with my mother. Sometimes I stayed with my dad for a few days. They lived apart most of my childhood, and I shuffled back and forth between them, cleaning up their messes."

Flynn leaned toward her. "I know something of that. After my dad left us and my mother had a nervous breakdown, I was shunted off to a New Mexico reservation to live with my grandfather."

Desi looked at him, soft-eyed. "How did that go?"

"I ran away nine times. That's how it went."

Their plates of nachos and chicken wings arrived. Flynn bit noisily into a nacho, and his phone vibrated. "Better take this; it's my partner, Raoul. He's tracking McCoy."

"Hey," Raoul said in his ear. "McCoy found the GPS tracker I put on the backside of his SUV bumper. Then the bastard put it under another vehicle. I finally found that car in the airport's long-term parking lot."

"Shit," Flynn said.

"Yeah," Raoul said. "Lost track of the fucker for several hours. He could have been hiding stolen masterpieces or stealing more. I picked him up when he returned to his loft. Now he's driving North on I-5, about to pass the La Jolla exit."

"I'd guess he's going to Doc O'Dade's place or the Steele estate," Flynn said. "Let me know if he takes the Del Mar exit or the one to Rancho Santa Fe." He ended the call and relayed Raoul's report to Desi.

"Can we eat these chicken wings, or should we hightail it to Kate's?" Desi asked.

"If he's coming to see Kate, it'll take about fifteen to twenty minutes. So, we've got time to eat one chicken wing, then we take off with the rest in a doggie bag."

A few minutes after they left Jake's in Flynn's SUV, Desi said, "Hey, this isn't the way to Kate's cottage. We're on the Coast Road, heading back toward our Bamboo cave."

"We're just sightseeing in scenic Del Mar until I hear from Raoul that McCoy is taking the Del Mar exit." If so, Flynn said he wanted to give McCoy another few minutes to get to Kate's place. Then, as they got closer to her cottage, they'd be able to tune in to hear the lovers' voices. "Let's hope they wait to hop in the sack and talk in her studio or office first. Got it?"

"Yep. Want a nacho?"

"Sure. You going to feed me?"

"Open up."

As they both chewed the crispy, cheese-coated chips, Flynn could smell the barbecued chicken, his mouth watering. At a stop sign, he asked for a wing. With no car behind him, he paused to take a couple of bites, and then Desi gave him a napkin to wipe the sauce off his lips and fingers. While she polished off a couple more wings, he turned left on Ninth Street, crossed Camino Del Mar, and drove slowly up the hill.

"So, tell me more about you and your family," Flynn said.

"Well, I was an only child who took care of her unhappy parents," Desi said. "My dad was a dominating, hard-driving, hard-drinking cop, and my mom had serious mental problems. She was bipolar—either soaring on a high or so low down she couldn't get out of bed. But on her highs, she made fantastic jewelry and glass sculptures and taught me the crafts. When I'm not tracking down art crooks, I make jewelry like hers." Desi ate the last chicken wing. "Tell me about your life on the res. Why did you hate it?"

Flynn didn't want to go back to those years of despair. He'd despised his half-breed status so much that he tried to pass as Hispanic and even swore in Spanish. "There's only one good thing I can say about the res. My grandfather taught me discipline for the first time in my life. Every morning at sunrise, a dip in the creek, then a run up the mountain holding water in my mouth."

"You're kidding," Desi said.

"Had to learn to breathe through my nose, didn't I? A warrior always breathes through his nose, never his mouth."

She laughed. "Of course, a warrior's essential skill."

He asked the question most on his mind. "Our job is hard on relationships. Are you in one now?"

"No, and I don't want to be," she said.

"Bad experience?"

"More than one. You?"

"Nothing serious," Flynn said. "I don't do serious anymore." Could Desi hear the regret in his tone?

"Would you call us smart or scared?" she asked.

"Both." Flynn's phone vibrated. Raoul was calling to report that McCoy had just turned off the freeway at the Del Mar exit.

"He's here," Flynn said. "We'd better get to our lovebirds. 'Lustbirds' is more like it. Now that's a smart pair who should be scared out of their skulls."

Twenty minutes later, they were parked on Kate's street, a car length down from her cottage. They had gotten there before Nick and were scrunched way down in their seats, listening to Kate eat crackers over the bug in her studio. Flynn caught the flash of headlights in his mirror.

"Must be Loverboy," he whispered to Desi.

CHAPTER 24

Never love an artist.

—Patricia Highsmith—

Tuesday Night, October 16

In her studio, Kate nibbled on her supper of crackers and cheese and sipped an icy Tom Collins. She checked the time. It was 7:30 p.m. Nick should be here soon. She reviewed Raquel's reactions in their session—her wild stare and fierce tone, her indifference to her own safety, and her hollow agreement to take protective measures. It all pointed to the likelihood of Raquel staying with Steele until she and her lover could punish him in some gruesome way. She debated whether to call Raquel to check on her safety and overnight plans. Would it do any good? Raquel was adept at appearing in synchrony with Kate's advice while playing the opposite tune inside her head. Kate sighed, picked up her cell, and called her heedless client. She got no answer and left a message for Raquel to call her immediately.

In need of a break from her angst, Kate turned to *The Open Window* propped up on her easel. Drawn into Matisse's make-believe world, her worries about Raquel began to recede, but soon, the question of who painted this work began to gnaw at her. Even though Nick had declared the painting an original Matisse, Kate could not be sure of this, as he'd also sounded convincing when he claimed that the Matisse at the museum was a copy. If he'd lied this last time, she couldn't understand why. Even more troubling to her was where and how he'd acquired the painting. Although she didn't much relish hearing the details of his "dark, twisted tale" about how he got the original, she needed to know.

Moving to the side of her worktable, she looked down on her Guy Rose pastiche. If she sold this work as a Rose, she would be no better than her con artist lover. Was she still considering this possibility? Did she need her own reckless thrills now that she'd given up paragliding and tracking a murderer? It seemed she did. Was she scrambling for a bolder, more daring identity? If so, teaming up with Nick was hardly a solution. She'd just be following his lead and trying to heal his wounds, a variation of the same old caretaker role she'd always played—hardly the bold identity makeover she craved.

She heard the door creak open, and Nick appeared, a broad smile brightening his face. Striding toward her, he brought in a blast of hot air and the camphor aroma of eucalyptus trees. He pulled her into a tight embrace. She avoided his kiss, too rattled by the folly of this affair and her nagging concerns about Raquel.

He studied her face. "Is something wrong?"

"Sorry, I'm a little stressed. A client of mine is in bad trouble."

"Want to talk about it?"

"I can't, as you know. Would you like a drink? Some snacks?"

"Sure." He sat on a stool catty-corner to her, his dark skin glazed with sweat. "How about a cold beer, if you have one. This heat is worse than last year. How do you stand it?"

"Cold booze, jumping in the ocean," Kate grinned, handing him a beer from the small fridge, then pushed the tray of snacks toward him.

He chugged the beer. "Ah, that's better. Any more news from your suspects about the Matisse?"

"No." Kate picked up her cell from the table. "I'll send some follow-up texts now." She texted her friends—Allison and Sherry—the same message:

Please get back to me about the mystery gift asap. Thanks. Love ya.

Kate put down her phone and said, "I don't know about you, but I'm having doubts about Allegra. She is spiteful and out for herself, but I'm not sure she has the smarts or the daring to pull off a complicated theft and revenge plot."

Nick grunted. "I hear you, but she's the only game in town at the moment."

Sipping her drink, Kate resumed worrying about Raquel and glanced at Nick.

"Clue me in about Dixon Steele. How dangerous is he?"

His face hardened. "Don't get me started on that lowlife. He's capable of the vilest kind of treachery. You saw his true colors onstage. He'll do anything to get what he wants—I mean anything." His black eyes blazed with a murderous hatred.

Kate's breath stopped. She'd seen the same rage in Raquel's eyes, and the awful truth finally dawned on her. How had she failed to think of Nick when Raquel mentioned that she, her lover, and Steele were all connected in the small San Diego art world? *How stupid she'd been! What blindness! Of course, she didn't want to see this painful possibility.* Hiding her shock and fury, Kate downed a slug of Tom Collins. The louse had shared more of himself with Raquel than with her. Raquel's bruised face flashed in Kate's mind. If she lost Nick to her trusted therapist, the double betrayal could devastate such a sensitive client.

"Tell me, Nick." Her voice was icy calm. "How well do you know Steele's wife?"

Pause. "Enough to say hello to at art events."

She fixed him with a hard stare. "I think you know her a lot better than that."

"What are you—?"

"Don't say anything unless you can refrain from lying." The anger choking her throat made it hard to speak.

He gulped the remainder of his beer. "Let's talk on the beach. I think your studio could be bugged."

"Bugged?" *Is he paranoid as well?* "I'm not going anywhere with you unless you swear off lying."

He held up his hand. "You have my word."

CHAPTER 25

Arise, black vengeance, from thy hollow cell!
—Shakespeare—

Tuesday Night, October 16

Nick eyed Kate's rigid profile. How to tell her the truth but not the whole truth? As he followed her onto a sandstone outcrop, he inhaled the tangy smell of the sea and glanced at the waves frothing a brilliant white against the shore. He turned and looked down at the empty, moonlit beach, then up fifteen feet to the top of the bluffs. In the distance, he saw a couple—arms linked—walking slowly toward them along the trail above. He could make out a tall, dark-haired man in black and a shorter woman. Just a couple out walking on a pleasant evening. No one to worry about.

He leaped onto the packed sand and turned, facing Kate. Stepping down, she started speed-walking ahead of him.

When he grabbed her arm, she stopped.

"Okay, I had an affair with Raquel Steele," he said, "but I was pulling out of it even before I knew you cared for me. I'm devoted to Raquel, but I've never been in love with her. Our mutual hatred of Steele brought us together. Didn't she tell you about it? I assume she's the troubled client you mentioned."

Kate just stared at him. "You bastard. We're caught in the worst possible triangle."

"I had no idea. Raquel never told me she was seeing a therapist."

Kate said nothing. Nick strode by her side, limbs stiff with tension, hoping her anger would gradually subside. But it seemed a long time before the hard line of her lips began to soften.

"That damage is done," she said. "It appears nobody's to blame. I'm trying to eat my anger, but it tastes bad, and I see the risk of taking too many clients from our town's small art world. Let's move on for the moment." She glanced at him. "What rotten thing did Steele do to you?"

Nick's pace slowed. "I'd rather not get into it."

"You have to, *dammit*! Grow up."

"What for?" Nick snapped.

"Because I require it."

He sucked in a deep breath, eyeing this unfamiliar hard-ass. "Remember the fire that destroyed my home when I was a kid? It was not an accident. It took me many years to find out that Steele was responsible. He hired two goons to set our house on fire to kill my father." Nick fell silent, his body aching with the remembered pain. He strode down to the water's edge and let the cold surf wash over his sandaled feet.

Kate took off her sandals and joined him.

He splashed water on his arms and the back of his neck. "When I'd been burned to a bloody crisp, I almost died. I prayed to die and should have died with the rest of my family. But I kept breathing and stayed alive for only one reason—revenge."

Kate was silent for a moment. "I can't buy that, Nick. You wouldn't have come for therapy if getting revenge was your only reason to live."

"A therapist would think that." He shook his fist at the moon, thundering, "Come to me, you gutless cocksucker."

"So why did Steele want your father dead?"

Nick thanked the stars for the warm tone back in Kate's voice.

"It's no good talking about this." He stepped back from the surf.

"Talking has helped before, as you know."

Nick shrugged, his skin prickling but not from the heat. It was the familiar sensation of being watched. Looking toward the bluffs, he could see a narrow trail zigzagging from the top down to the beach. He thought he glimpsed a flash of movement about two-thirds down the cliff. *Was someone there?* Rationally, he didn't believe anyone would follow him here. Why bother watching him while walking with a woman on the beach in the dark? No stolen or forged paintings to incriminate him nearby. *Forget the bloody cops.*

Kate's insistent voice. "Nick, listen. For me to consider sticking with you, I need to know about all the bad stuff that's happened to you, the parts of your past you held back in therapy."

"That's blackmail."

"Right." She took his hand. "Let's sit on that rock."

Once seated, the bluffs rising behind them, Nick began in a halting monotone. "My father was an antiques dealer. He also restored and copied paintings for extra money to support me, my two sisters, and my mother. He was training me in the business. It took years for me to uncover what happened." He stopped and stared at the frothing surf, reluctant to continue.

"Go on." Kate squeezed his hand. "I'm listening."

"Steele had hired my dad to make copies of five masterpieces supposedly to decorate his new home in London. He gave him detailed photographs of these works. It turned out that Steele had used Dad's copies to replace the original paintings when he or his accomplice stole the masterpieces from a filthy-rich collector." Nick's mouth was so dry that it was hard to speak.

"Unlike me, my father was a good man, but if his copies were exposed as fakes, he could have been accused of forgery and would have lost everything. I don't know how Steele got my dad to sign these copies with the artists' names. That should have tipped Dad off to Steele's criminal intentions. I believe he must have confronted Steele, and shortly after that, Steele hired a couple of thugs to set the fire." The old horror and fury rose up inside him. "Dad's copies were so good that no collector or museum has discovered them."

"Jesus, Nick, why didn't you tell me any of this before?"

"I came to therapy to cure my panic attacks, not to give up avenging my family. I also had boyish fantasies of winning you over—that is, when I became a stable, whole, irresistible grown-up. If I'd let you see the monster inside me, you'd have run for the hills."

"Well, I'm not running now. I know all about raging monsters inside."

You should be running. Nick couldn't understand why she would stay with a mess like him.

"Are you certain Steele had your family killed?" she asked.

"My father, yes. I don't know if he meant to wipe out the rest of us. I have no actual proof of what happened. By the time I could investigate, the people who probably knew something were dead. I recall a couple of the paintings Dad copied for Steele, and I want to puke every time I see the original works—Van Gogh's *Sunflowers* and Cézanne's *Card Players*—hanging in Steele's lair. Also, I saw Dixon's ugly mug in Dad's shop once. I thought he was the bogeyman."

Kate gasped, "Oh my God, I just realized Raquel's alone with that monster! From what you just told me, Steele's not just abusive, he's a stone-cold killer. I have to break confidentiality. Steele is physically abusive and viciously beat Raquel last night. I urged her to go to a women's shelter after our session, but I doubt she did that."

"Holy shit!" Nick took off at a sprint, Kate running behind him.

—

"Sorry, Desi," Flynn said. "I had to push you down behind the rocks. McCoy was turning around and would have seen us on the path."

Desi lay face down with Flynn perched on top of her, supporting his weight on his forearms. He quite liked her firm, warm body under his. "Am I crushing you?"

"No . . . but I'm choking on sand."

He rolled off of her and stood.

Coughing, Desi got up and brushed the sand off her blouse and pants.

"Could you hear anything after we moved down the path?" Desi asked.

"Not much," Flynn said. "Even though the wind had died down, the breaking waves muffled their words. We better get moving. We can't risk losing them."

Flynn started up the path with Desi following. "I heard fragments when we were near the beach. It sounded like McCoy was yelling, 'That's blackmail!' Then he said something about Steele killing his family—"

"I heard the word 'revenge,'" Desi said, "and Kate yelling, 'She's alone with that monster!'"

"We didn't learn much that's new," Flynn said.

"Well, we learned that Nick thinks Steele killed his family, and that's why he wants revenge," Desi said. "We heard that Raquel is in danger from Steele."

"We already knew that," Flynn said.

Flynn's phone vibrated. Carlos, currently staking out the Steele estate, reported a personal emergency. One of his kids had a bad accident, and he was leaving Rancho Santa Fe and was on his way to Children's Hospital.

"Dammit," Desi said when Flynn reported this.

They ran the rest of the way to Kate's cottage, arriving in time to see the lovers getting into separate cars.

"We've got one car," Desi said. "Who do we follow?"

"Phantom. He's not slipping away from me this time."

CHAPTER 26

Je ne regrette rien.

—Édith Piaf—

Tuesday Night, October 16

Raquel stepped out of an Epsom salt bath, her sore muscles and bruises hurting a lot less. She carefully blotted her tender body dry with a soft towel and slipped into her sapphire blue dressing gown. The cool silk soothed her skin. Her Édith Piaf recording was playing the defiant song she favored the most now. Raquel hummed along with the singer's throaty voice, then took a swallow of her bourbon on the rocks and tossed down a couple of pain pills. She was starting pain control early this evening, preparing for Dixon. In their grim fairy tale of life, he was *La Bête*, and Raquel thought of herself as *La Belle*, the beauty whom the handsome prince would rescue at the end. She took heart by visualizing the packed suitcase in her closet. Before the gala, she'd informed Dixon she'd be leaving for Paris tomorrow for the christening of her sister's new baby, her first niece. Nick knew she would be going soon, but she hadn't yet informed him of the exact date and time. She smiled. Only one more night with *La Bête*.

Studying her discolored face in the vanity mirror of her bathroom, she debated whether to cover the ugly colors of the bruises. Deciding it was better to look her confident best, she put on the heavy make-up she used for concealing injuries, brushed her long, black hair, and spritzed on her *Lancôme* perfume, *La Vie En Rose*. She smiled as she recalled that this was the title of Piaf's most famous song. If Édith could see her own brutal life through rose-colored glasses, so could Raquel. She raised her glass to herself in the mirror, relieved that she had revealed more of the truth to Kate in the letter she had mailed on her way home today. Confessing the truth made her feel cleansed, and she was also pleased with the special gift she'd decided to leave with her beloved therapist.

"Raquel," Dixon's imperious voice boomed from downstairs.

Tight-lipped, she quickly went through the door to her dressing room and opened her safe. Inside, next to her jewelry box, was a slim dagger with an ivory handle in a scabbard threaded with a leather thong. She undid her silk dressing gown and tied the leather thong around her waist, sliding the sheath from her side to her back so the slight bulge wouldn't show at her waist when she retied the gown's belt. She would not endure another beating.

Raquel went down the spiral staircase, crossed the austere living room, and opened the glass doors to the patio. It was dark outside, and Dixon had turned on the deck and pool lights. He was dripping wet and naked, just emerging from the water. His chest, arms, and legs were covered in patches of stringy, gray body hair. He looked like an alien creature rising from the turquoise pool, the evil star in a new version of an old horror movie. Dixon grinned at her, splayed lips showing off his obnoxious teeth. He pointed toward the patio table.

"Those are for you, my beauty."

Dixon's phony good humor immediately put Raquel even more on edge. She glanced at the large bouquet of the ugliest flowers she had ever seen. The cream-white petals spread out in a star shape and toward their centers were dark red, blood-like spots and black hearts. "*Mon Dieu,* what are they?" She hoped her surprise masked her revulsion.

"They're an Asiatic lily called the Black Spider." He was scrubbing his hairy arms and legs with a towel. "Fantastic, aren't they? Flown in from Kauai or some damn place. Cost a fortune."

"But of course." She sat down, her nostrils pinched against the urine-like odor.

"Only one little problem," he cackled, "they're toxic to cats."

She showed no reaction. "I have given up the idea of getting a kitten." She would knife him in the heart if she and Nick didn't have a better plan for his eternal torment.

He padded to the outdoor bar—still nude—and began fixing himself a vodka on ice. His hairy back and saggy butt faced her. It didn't occur to him to cover his repulsive body with a robe or a towel.

"I've sent the help home so we could be alone together before I go out to my poker game at nine. We have a couple of hours. What would you like to do?" He turned, giving her a leer of a smile, his typical turn-off come-on.

Dixon always acted like nothing terrible had happened the day after he flew into a rage and beat her. Yet, she knew he had not forgiven her for his humiliation at the unveiling. He would punish her forever for that unforgivable crime if she hung around.

"I'd just like to rest. I didn't sleep well and had a tiring day."

"Is that so?" he said in a peevish tone. He stumped to his chair and sat down. "What've you been doing that's been *so* fatiguing?"

"Errands, shopping, a couple of appointments."

"Appointments with who?"

Here it was—the familiar, relentless interrogation. Raquel knew it was the preamble to another jealous rage. She should start placating him, but she couldn't bring herself to play their usual sick game.

"With a skin doctor at a La Jolla clinic. I'm having skin problems, haven't you noticed?"

He glared at her, swirling the ice in his drink, the cubes clicking against the glass. That was a provocative thing to say, but she refused to pretend any longer.

"You're lying," he shouted, his face breaking out in red blotches.

She sat rigidly, feeling the comfort of the knife against her back. "I do not lie." She enunciated each word. Had she made a fuss about the flowers and acted more seductive, she might have put off this repetitive scene for a while longer. But she was done with appeasement.

"Where were you?"

She was silent, her replies meaningless.

"Answer me!" He stood and slapped his hand on the flower vase, sending the glass smashing against the table and some Black Spider lilies flying into Raquel's lap. She jumped up. He leaned across the table, the flower mess between them. "Tell me the truth!"

She said nothing, frantically brushing the black-hearted lilies off her dressing gown.

"I'll tell you," another despised voice said.

Both looked up to see Simon standing in the doorway.

"I could hear you fighting from my room." Simon strode onto the patio, wearing a white tennis outfit, even though he didn't play tennis. He stopped and glanced back and forth between them. His malignant gaze lingering on Raquel, he smiled—a triumphant smirk—revealing his needle-sharp teeth. "She was with her lover."

"That is a lie. I was seeing a therapist in Del Mar."

"Some therapy." Simon sneered. "Bet it felt good."

"Who's the scumbag? I'll kill him." Steele tossed the dregs of his drink at Raquel, who stepped back from the flying ice chips.

"Simon is lying," she said. "Don't you get it? Your son wants to get rid of me."

Simon crossed his arms and spread his legs belligerently, intent on destruction. "Her lover is your snake of a consultant, Nick McCoy."

"What? That's impossible," Steele shouted at Simon. "Don't you dare lie to me! You hate Nick because he's a success, and you're a pathetic failure."

"That's exactly right," Raquel said. "Your son is eaten up with jealousy and envy."

Raquel knew Simon didn't have the guts to turn on his father. Instead, she felt the full heat of his hatred and rage aimed straight at her.

"I have proof of their filthy affair," Simon said to his father. "I suspected her infidelity and hired a private detective to follow her. He took a picture of them rutting like pigs on the beach. I'll show it to you. It's in my room. Want me to get it?"

"Raquel!" Steele howled like a wounded animal and moved toward her, his face contorted in rage. "How could you? You're a fucking whore!"

Shrinking back in fear, she lifted the skirt of her gown to run, but Simon stood between her and the door.

"Killing's too good for her, Dad. So, let's do her, you and me, father and son. A nice, family-friendly *ménage à trois*. I'm sure the French whore knows what that is, don't you, sweetheart?"

Steele stopped, staring at Simon, a puzzled look on his face, a signal that he was not yet as depraved as his son. Then his thick lips spread in a lecherous leer. Raquel could see his cock swelling and rising. She stood, fear paralyzing her as the predators moved stealthily toward her. She yanked open her dressing gown and pulled out the dagger.

"Get back!" she screamed, brandishing the blade.

Taken by surprise, the two men stopped, Steele's erection shriveled, and Raquel moved swiftly toward the open sliding door.

Once inside the living room, she turned and closed the slider. Frantic, trembling, her hands slick with sweat, her gown clinging to her legs, she couldn't get the door's lock to work while holding the knife. She saw the beasts charging toward the door. By fiddling with the lock, she had lost her head start. Blood pulsing in her ears, her heart hammering—she could hardly breathe. Terror had made her clumsy and stupid.

Think, think. Which way to go? Up or out the front door? Her mind raced. She couldn't outrun Simon in her flip-flops. Where would she run outside? No one lived within miles, and she couldn't drive her car without keys. She turned right and headed for the stairs. She'd get to her phone, lock herself in the bathroom, and call the police, Nick, and Kate. Raquel heard herself howl like an injured animal. What a fool she'd been to risk coming home. *Why hadn't she listened to her therapist?*

Her chest heaving, legs trembling, she darted across the living room and started running up the stairs. Midway, she tripped on her dressing gown and fell forward. The knife slipped out of her hand. *Merde!* The panting and grunting noises behind her meant *les bête*s were close. She knew they would tear her to pieces—she had to get away. She grabbed the dagger and crawled upward as fast as she could. *Dieu merci,* the stairs were carpeted. She was almost to the top when one of them grabbed the edge of her trailing dressing gown and yanked. Slipping out of it, Raquel continued scrabbling upward naked, her body glazed with sweat. She was getting to her feet to sprint down the hall when Simon leaped on her from behind. She crashed face down on the floor.

"*Non!*" Raquel screamed, her head throbbing in pain. Simon was on top of her.

"Gotcha, bitch," he snarled in her ear. His fetid breath gagged her.

Raquel's hand groped to find the dropped dagger. Fighting for her life, she threw her weight to the side, trying to dislodge Simon, ready to strike a blow. But Dixon, standing in front of her, tramped down on her wrist. A searing pain shot up her arm, and she let go of the knife.

"*Merde, tu merde!*" she cried.

"You asked for it, bitch." He pried the knife from her useless hand.

"*Tu es une bête*. I detest you."

"Let's do her right here." Simon rolled off her and stood up.

Shifting her weight to her good arm and one knee, Raquel tried to rise. Steele pushed her back down, his puny member swelling in front of her eyes. How she loathed him. Hurting her was what it took to get him hard.

"Look at that beautiful ass." Simon slapped her naked butt and stripped off his shorts.

Raquel knew she had very little time left. *Take charge. It's the last act.* She bit down hard on the beast's pathetic manhood, her one last stand before retreating to that safe, detached state that Kate called dissociation. *La Bête's* inhuman screams filled the air as a triumphant Raquel rose up and out of her body.

CHAPTER 27

This is the law: blood spilt upon the ground cries out for more.
—Aeschylus—

Tuesday Night, October 16

Kate headed northeast in her Mini Cooper toward the Steele estate. She called Raquel on her cell, but still no pickup. She left her client a voicemail saying she was on the way to her house in Rancho Santa Fe and to call or text if she could.

Meanwhile, Nick was heading south on I-5 to his studio to collect the materials he needed to complete the plot against Steele. Nick had continued to withhold details of the scheme, but she guessed a part of the plan must include stealing Dixon's most cherished masterpieces. If Raquel was home, Kate would get her out of the Rancho house as soon as she arrived. Nick hoped to come about thirty minutes later and carry out the revenge plot on his own. The aftermath remained unclear.

She called Nick. "Hi, I'm on Linea Del Cielo."

"Good," he said. "You'll probably get to the Steele estate at about nine-twenty. It's unlikely that you'll run into Steele. He'll be leaving for his poker game right about now. Don't worry about Simon. He stays out getting wasted all night. I disabled the alarm system the last time I was there. Dix doesn't use guards and doesn't trust them. Or anyone for that matter."

"Then why trust you?"

"Dix is lonely. Monsters and freaks usually are. A seasoned con can sense what his chosen victim—the mark—wants. So, I've played the ideal son, like the one he lost and longs to have back. Now he thinks I care about him and his blood-soaked art collection."

At the gate to the Steele estate, Kate spoke into the intercom. No answer. She tapped in the code Nick had given her to open the gate and drove through the opening and down a long, winding driveway. She recognized a Henry Moore headless woman and a spider-like Alexander Calder welding among the modern sculptures lit up along the sides of the road.

Kate parked in front of the sleek, mid-century modern mansion and approached the stained-glass front door. She checked her watch. Nine o'clock. After a few deep breaths, her heart drumming, she spoke into the intercom. "Raquel, it's Kate." No answer. She had no key or code to get into the house. She tried the door handle. The door opened. Startled, she hesitated initially, then stepped into a small gallery of drawings. Silence. No alarm went off. Nick, the pro, had prepared well.

"Raquel," she called out, her voice sounding shrill. Still no response.

A short hallway led into the living room. To Kate's right, a wall of oversized glass doors opened to the lighted patio and the swimming pool. Thank God, no bodies were floating in the shimmering turquoise water. The softly lit room gave her the feeling of being inside a giant watercolor, the furnishings washed in multiple shades of gray. On full alert, her body prickling with tension, she took in the vibrant hues of a gorgeous Morris Louis veil painting that covered most of a driftwood-paneled wall. At the far end was a brushed steel and wood circular staircase. Walking toward it, Kate spotted a mass of blue silk on the floor at the bottom of the stairs. Moving closer, she stifled a scream.

Raquel lay crumpled on the floor in a dressing gown, her face covered by her long black hair. Shards of glass littered the terrazzo floor, the smell of alcohol in the air. Trembling, Kate stooped down. *Please, please be alive.* Smoothing back the hair from Raquel's face, Kate noticed the unnatural torque of her slender neck. It looked broken. Raquel's eyes were wide open and glazed. She was lifeless. Kate could not take in this horror. The room tilted and started to spin. Her limbs froze in shock. Finally, she staggered upright on rubbery legs and called Nick.

"I'm horribly sorry, Nick. I have dreadful news." She sucked in air until her lungs hurt. "Raquel is dead. It looks like she fell down the stairs. Or was pushed."

Deathly silence, then Nick's steel-hard voice. "Any signs of a break-in?"

"No. The front door was unlocked, no alarm went off, and the living room was in order. Raquel may have been drinking. There's broken glass and spills of alcohol on the floor."

"Don't touch anything. It could be a setup."

"I'll call the police."

"No, that would royally fuck me, and I need to complete the plan. Raquel would want that. I'll be there soon, but you get the hell out of there. If someone murdered Raquel, the killer could still be hanging around."

She listened to the dead silence around her. If a killer were in the house, he would have revealed himself in some way by now. "There's no one here. I'm staying. I want to help. It's the least I can do for Raquel after failing her so badly." She ended the call before Nick responded.

Kate stepped around Raquel's lifeless body and onto the bottom step. She'd been a fool to let Raquel leave her office this afternoon. She started to shake, her breath coming in shallow gasps. *No time now for shock and grief and guilt.* Her pulse raced. Dizziness forced her to grab the railing. She took in slow breaths. *Inhale. Exhale. Inhale. Be like Nick. Get revenge. Think!* Raquel must have been coming from upstairs, probably from her bedroom. *Climb the frigging stairs. Solve this godawful crime.*

CHAPTER 28

The very serious function of racism is distraction.
It keeps you from doing your work.
—Toni Morrison—

Tuesday Night, October 16

Flynn tailed McCoy, driving south at high speed down the I-5 to his East Village loft. Parking down the block on the opposite side of the street, Flynn watched McCoy run from his car into the warehouse structure that housed his living space and studio.

Seated next to Flynn, Desi asked, "Didn't you say McCoy probably had stolen paintings and forgeries hidden in his loft? We could try confronting him."

Flynn turned, squinting to see her profile in the dark interior. "Surprised you'd even consider that. Even if McCoy opened the door, we don't have a search warrant and no reason to arrest him. Doubt he'd invite us in." He glanced out the side window toward the door to the building. "He's parked in front of the entry like he's coming right back out."

"I think he'd want to go check on Raquel," Desi said.

Flynn shrugged. "Could be he has more in mind. Like a major heist. Nice if we could be the ones to nail him in the act."

"Yeah, it would," Desi said. "You want to be the one, right?"

He flashed a grin. "I always want to win. Haven't you noticed?"

"Seriously? To win is the main reason you're doing this job?"

Flynn stared out the window at the dark, empty street lined with closed shops and one open pub. He cleared his throat. "I could say I'm against art crime for all the reasons you are, and I detest McCoy for being such a successful scam artist." Pause. "Truth is, I'm envious of him in a warped sort of way. He's at the top of his trades—a first-rate conservator, a brilliant forger, and a thief who never gets caught. I used to think I was a brilliant detective, but no one else ever thought so. I lost my job at the Sheriff's Department. I've lost a lot of other things as well—parents, marriage, someone I loved so much it hurt—so yes, I'd like to win this one. That's it. The end."

He could hear her soft breathing and feel the heat of her gaze.

"I appreciate your honesty," she said.

"And you? Why do you want to catch McCoy?"

"Well, I care about winning, too." Her voice sounded husky. "If I could catch a giant fish like McCoy or Steele, or both of those bastards, I'd be famous at the LAPD. I'd have enough clout to add more detectives to the Art Theft Detail. I could be an inspiring model for women of color. I could make my mentor, Don Hryrck, proud of me and also my impossible-to-please father, who's still alive in my head."

"I'd be proud of you, too." Flynn gave her hand a gentle squeeze.

"Before we win this game, we need to tell Eddie what's going on," Desi said.

Flynn sighed. "Eddie's an old, jet-lagged man. He's probably asleep."

"Eddie's a cop," Desi said. "Cops don't get to sleep. Dammit, Flynn, I know you're a loner used to running your own show, but this is a team effort. Eddie's been working on this case for a decade. McCoy is his nemesis. It's not only impolitic but cruel to leave him out now, and it certainly won't help *my* career."

"Yeah, okay. Call Eddie. But we're not losing sight of the limey tonight."

Eddie sounded wide awake when Desi called. She got his blessing to follow McCoy. If McCoy was going to Steele's estate, Eddie and Archie would meet them there in case a heist was going down or some other form of revenge. Desi was to call Eddie when they arrived. He would do the same if they arrived first. In case he needed it, she gave Eddie the code Simon had given Flynn to open the front gate.

As she finished the call, McCoy rushed out of his building wearing a large backpack and carrying two bulky canvas sacks. He moved quickly to the trunk of his SUV, carefully put the bags in the trunk, jumped into the driver's seat, and started the car. He drove back to the I-5, heading toward North County.

Flynn tailed McCoy for about twenty-five minutes, then followed him off the freeway at the exit to Rancho Santa Fe and the Steele estate. With no other cars on this dark, winding tunnel of a road, McCoy drove recklessly, well over the speed limit of thirty-five miles per hour. Flynn, also speeding, stayed far behind but kept close enough to see McCoy's taillights disappearing around the tight curves.

"Slow down," Desi said as Flynn whipped the Explorer around a sudden sharp curve. "You don't have to follow closely. We know where the estate is."

She was right. He'd been too keyed up and afraid of failure to check his impulses. That was a weakness.

Around the next tight turn, Flynn heard the familiar wail of a siren. Glancing in his rearview mirror, he saw the revolving red light speeding up behind him.

"Christ, it's the friggin' sheriff!"

"Pull over," Desi said. "We can get out of this fast. Just cooperate."

He slowed down and drove on until he saw a wider patch of gravel at the side of the road where he could pull over and stop.

"Are you carrying?" Desi asked.

"Yes, in the glove compartment. You?"

"In my bag. No guns, okay? No matter what happens."

From his wallet in the back pocket of his jeans, Flynn took out his driver's license, got his registration and insurance from the glove compartment, then lowered his window.

Sounds of heavy steps on pavement, then the light from a flashlight blinded him.

"Hey, why didn't you stop?" asked a belligerent voice.

"I was looking for a place to stop that wouldn't block the road."

"You were speeding a good fifteen miles over the limit."

"Sorry about that, Deputy."

"Been drinking?"

"I had one beer with dinner quite a while ago."

"That's right," Desi said. "I was with him at Jake's in Del Mar."

The cop shone his light on Desi's face and then back to Flynn's. Before he asked, Flynn handed him the required documents.

The deputy glanced at his license. "Francisco Flynn. That name rings a bell." He shoved the light close to Flynn's face. "You got a record, Flynn, an outstanding warrant?"

"No. Just write up the ticket."

"In a hurry, huh? What business do you have in the Ranch?"

"Friends are expecting us."

"Oh, yeah?" He cackled, skeptical, then lowered his light. The deputy looked dissipated, jowly, and like the kind of loser who gets off on kicking underdogs.

"What's your name?" Flynn was relieved he hadn't come across this asshole before.

"Deputy Bud Cadwell. Wait here." His stout, pear-shaped body swaggered clumsily to the rear of Flynn's Explorer. He wrote down the license plate number and handed the information to his partner sitting in the department car, also an Explorer, though an older, more basic model.

His temper rising, Flynn turned toward Desi. "This bullshit is because we're brown and driving a better vehicle than he is in la-di-da Rancho Santa Fe."

"What else is new?" she asked. "Why don't you tell the deputy who you are, who we are, that we're working a case?"

"That would lead to more harassment and a longer delay. Cadwell might take me in. I'm *persona non grata* at the Sheriff's Department. They fired me, remember? For not following the rules and breaking the captain's jaw."

"Shit," Desi muttered.

CHAPTER 29

Let my heart be still a moment and this mystery explore.

—EDGAR ALLAN POE—

Later Tuesday Night, October 16

Climbing up the stairs in the Steele mansion, Kate avoided touching the banister. If Raquel was murdered, she didn't want her fingerprints mixed up with the killer's prints. The gray runner emitted a faint odor of bourbon. At the top, she turned right toward the open double doors at the end of a wide hall and walked into a spacious master bedroom. She glanced around the walls crowded with mind-blowing modern art and Picasso's unsavory drawing of a satyr.

On Raquel's nightstand was a half-full bottle of bourbon and two containers of drugs. She picked up one of them using a Kleenex. Xanax. Half the thirty tablets were gone, and the refill date was just a few days ago. The second prescription was oxycodone, a powerful painkiller, two weeks' worth, prescribed two days ago. That was a lot. She must have gotten the drugs for pain from Steele's beating. Dear brave Raquel, she'd endured so much suffering. Kate knew this evidence could point to suicide from a deliberate overdose, but she couldn't believe this possibility. Raquel was not suicidal. She was on an all-consuming mission. An accidental fall? Maybe. But Kate suspected an enraged Steele had pushed her down the stairs when painkillers and alcohol made her an easy victim.

A sound came from below. Kate crept to the railing running along the hall and looked down at the living room. She saw Nick squatting next to Raquel's body. Her hand in his, he kissed her cheek with such tenderness that Kate looked away, tears filling her eyes. She felt shaken. Were these tears about Raquel's tragic death or a fear of losing Nick's love to Raquel's memory? Both, probably.

Kate met a devastated Nick at the bottom of the stairs. They held each other tightly, Nick muttering, "Shit, shit, shit, if only we'd gotten here sooner."

"I know, I know." Kate felt another surge of guilt. "Raquel was such a lovable person. Do you think one of her family members murdered her?"

"I'd bet on it," Nick said. "Dixon or Simon, or both, killed her. I can't prove it. I hope the police or the medical examiner can." Nick turned and looked down at Raquel, his hair wild, his eyes glittery-hard. "In any case, I'll settle for rough justice. Let's get started."

On unsteady legs, Kate followed Nick down a long corridor to Simon's room at the end. Nick turned the knob and found the door locked.

He swore and kicked the door.

"What are you looking for here?" Kate's stomach was in knots.

"Dirt on Simon. This could be where he stashes the drugs he deals. I plan to fuck over that scum of the earth." An experienced thief, Nick quickly jimmied the lock and opened the door.

Inside the macabre lair, brutal images of sadomasochistic pornography plastered the black walls. Kate stared at the only artwork, a copy of Munch's *The Scream*. She fought the urge to howl with the frantic skeleton hunched on the bridge under the blood-red clouds. She felt caught inside a psychopath's perverted mind.

While Nick searched Simon's walk-in closet, she told him about finding Raquel's painkillers and tranquilizers in the master bedroom.

She then heard Nick's muffled cry, "Gotcha!" He'd discovered a huge stash of heroin—likely worth a fortune—hidden underneath the loose bottom shelf of a wall unit. "I'll arrange for the cops to find it here."

Outside Simon's private entrance, Nick silently led the way along a winding path to where his SUV was parked next to Steele's barn. He removed a bulky canvas bundle from his trunk and flung it over his shoulder. "What's inside?" she asked.

"A *fuck you* for Steele," he said.

Kate guessed he was carrying tools for removing the paintings from the frames and stretchers, though she didn't know for sure. She'd get the details later.

"Text me if you see anyone." Nick strode to the entry, tapped in a code, and disappeared inside.

Left outside on her own, Kate looked around the surreal nightscape. The wind rustled through the stand of black-limbed eucalyptus trees. In the bright moonlight, their distorted shadows rippled on the stark-white gravel. She felt alone and very vulnerable. The next terror or horror she encountered might send her shrieking into the night. Raquel's white, dead body flashed in her mind. Squeezing her eyes shut, she tried to block out that horrific image. *What was taking so long? What was Nick doing inside?* She began pacing. Whatever the details of his revenge scheme, Kate feared it would wreck his life and any chance of a life together.

Long, tense minutes passed. She was about to pound on the barn door when a grim-faced Nick opened it, carrying the same bulky bundle flung over his shoulder. He laid the bundle down carefully in the rear of the SUV as though it contained precious glass sculptures. Then he closed the trunk.

"Done," he said. "We're out of here."

CHAPTER 30

I would kiss you, had I the courage.

—Édouard Manet—

Tuesday Night, October 16

"Get out of the car, Mr. Flynn," Deputy Cadwell said. "You need to take a sobriety test."

Flynn swore under his breath, got out of the car, and slammed the door. "This is a waste of time, and you know it."

"A bad attitude is a bad idea." He chuckled at his turn of phrase. "See that white line at the edge of the road?" He pointed the light at the line. "Walk that line. Take nine steps, touching your toe to the heel of your other foot."

Flynn swallowed his anger and checked his watch. Nine twenty-five. They were about ten minutes from Steele's estate. He considered refusing, but he couldn't risk this small-town prick checking out his identity and uncovering his lousy reputation at the Sheriff's Department. It would all take more time than cooperating, and he'd lose his temper and fuck up his life again.

Teeth clenched, he followed Cadwell's instructions, part of his mind on counting steps, the other part on counting the wasted minutes. The flashlight aimed at the white line pierced the darkness ahead of Flynn for a short distance. *Stay focused. Stay in control.* His jaw hurt from the constant clenching. On the ninth step, Flynn turned, and the deputy's light hit him in the eyes.

"Now stand on one foot," Cadwell ordered, "and hold the other about six inches off the ground. Start counting from one thousand and one upwards until I tell you to stop."

Flynn glared at the bully and was about to lose it when Desi slipped out of the SUV and strode up to the officer.

"Deputy Cadwell, I am Detective Inspector Destiny Hawk from the LAPD." She showed her badge. "I am on a time-sensitive assignment here, and Mr. Flynn is my local guide. We need to get to our destination without delay. If you must, please call my captain in LA." She handed him his card. "If you can't reach him right now, you can call my colleagues on this international team—Detective Archibald Hasofer of the San Diego Police Department and Chief Inspector Edward Cromwell from Scotland Yard, London. He arrived here a couple of days ago. They are staying in Del Mar, standing by as backup." She handed over both of their cards. Cadwell's bloodless lips were clamped in a bitter line, his jowls quivering. "If you let us go on our way now, I will ask Chief Inspector Cromwell to call your captain to commend you for aiding this investigation. Otherwise, the chief will make quite a different phone call in the morning."

Cadwell's pasty face looked ashen. "Apologies, Inspector uh Hawk. Just doing my job," Cadwell said. "Drive carefully."

As Flynn and Desi got back in the car, Cadwell's car squealed a U-turn and sped off.

"Killer job, DI Hawk." Back on the road, Flynn floored the accelerator, indifferent to driving carefully.

Three minutes later, Flynn yelled, "That's them!" Flynn yelled as two cars blew by them going in the opposite direction. "McCoy in his SUV and Kate in her Mini Cooper. They're hightailing it from Steele's estate. Shit. We just missed them."

"Stop somewhere," Desi said.

Flynn pulled onto a patch of gravel at the side of the road and slammed on the brakes.

"We need to follow McCoy," Flynn said. "He could have a trunk full of stolen paintings, and we'd have him."

"Raquel wasn't with either of them," Desi said. "Something went wrong. We need to check on her."

"Then we'll lose McCoy. He'll stash the paintings somewhere we'll never find."

"You're just guessing he has the loot. Raquel's life is more important than loot."

"Detective Hawk, recovering stolen art is your job, not rescuing victims of spousal abuse."

"Don't you *dare* tell me my job. You were fired from the job." Desi's voice heated up. "You're just a rogue private eye, a peeping tom."

He squeezed the steering wheel to keep from lashing out. "Let's shelve this and get back to it later. Will you accept Eddie's direction?"

"Yes, he *is* my superior."

When Eddie answered his call, Flynn described the circumstances and their disagreement about the next move. Then he put the call on speakerphone so Desi could hear Eddie's response.

"We're on Linea Del Cielo now," Eddie said. "We should run into McCoy soon. It makes sense for us to follow him. You and Desi go to the estate and check on Raquel and the collection. If all is well and the couple is at home, say you got an anonymous call about a break-in and possible harm to Mrs. Steele. If no one is home, quickly check out what you can, especially Steele's gallery."

Flynn said, "Just so we're clear, are you saying punch in the code and enter the premises?"

"Isn't that what cops here do when a crime is suspected?" Eddie signed off.

Flynn glanced at Desi. "Happy now?"

"I'm thankful we have a sensible, respectful leader."

Flynn started the engine and peeled out of the gravel onto the road to Steele's estate. They rode in tense silence. His anger had turned into a dull ache in his gut and the familiar sense of failure and loss. He'd never get it right with women and would lose his personal war. Nick McCoy was smarter than he was.

The modern sculptures along the driveway to Steele's place looked even more like alien creatures lit up at night. The sprawling black metal thing resembled a giant octopus. He stopped the car outside the gate. Since Desi had police credentials, she got out of the car, pushed the button for the intercom, and waited. No reply. After the third try with no response, she punched in the security code, and the gate slid open. After she was back in the car, Flynn drove to the front of the house and parked the car in the horseshoe drive. At the front door, Desi asked about an alarm system. He said it was often disabled because Simon always forgot to turn it off when he came home late. The door was slightly ajar.

"Something's wrong." He pushed the door open.

They padded through the entry gallery. Partway across the dimly lit living room, the turquoise pool glowing through the glass doors, Desi stopped abruptly with a sharp intake of breath.

She pointed. "What's that?"

Flynn strode to the crumpled mass of blue silk, squatted, and brushed back the dark hair from Raquel Steele's chalky dead face.

Desi gasped. "Jesus, no! We're too late."

"She's been dead for at least a couple of hours. Rigor is beginning to set in. We couldn't have gotten here in time."

Desi stood, stiff as a statue, unable to get closer to the body. "Poor Raquel. She didn't deserve to die like this. Was she murdered?"

"Her neck's broken, maybe other bones, too. It looks like she fell down the stairs or someone pushed her. I smell alcohol, and there's broken glass on the floor. Suggests she'd been drinking and might have lost her balance and fallen. Or this could just be a setup to make us think she fell accidentally. What's your take?"

"I'd guess she was pushed," Desi said. "We know her husband was abusing her, and he felt she humiliated him badly at the unveiling. If it's murder, McCoy couldn't have done it."

"Why not?" Flynn said.

"Time of death. Raquel was dead before McCoy and Kate arrived here," Desi said. "We've got to decide whether or not to inform the Sheriff's Department about the death and wait for them to show up."

"I say not," Flynn said. "If we expose ourselves to the sheriff's gang, we inform them of our undercover investigation. That will blow up our efforts and set the investigation way back. Then there's the load of crap my involvement will bring down on me."

"I'm calling Eddie," Desi said. When he answered, she laid out the situation.

"Do not contact the sheriff," Eddie said. "Undercover work means that no other department can know about our investigation unless it becomes essential. We'll report Raquel's death anonymously after you leave. Take pictures of all the art you see, check out the gallery, then get the hell out of there. Do not yield to the temptation to investigate Raquel's death. That is not our job. Got it?"

"Yes, sir," Desi said. "Are you on McCoy's tail?"

"We lost the bugger temporarily, hoping to catch him at his loft. Keep me informed."

Flynn swore under his breath. "I knew he'd slip away. Let's move. The Steele scumbags could show up any time."

Desi started photographing the art in the entryway. Flynn took several photos of Raquel's body and the surrounding scene. Upstairs, he hurried to record whatever looked like art on the walls in the hall and master suite. Flynn also took pictures in Steele's study of the photographs showing the old crook on yachts with various dictators, like Putin, and other notorious celebrities. Two framed photos on a bookshelf caught his attention. One was of a much younger Steele with his arm around a handsome, blond boy, most likely Samuel, the son who died in the car crash. The tender expression on Steele's face surprised Flynn. Could this vicious asshole be capable of fatherly love?

The other framed photo was of Steele's deceased second wife, a blonde beauty. Sitting on a lawn between her two young sons, she was smiling and hugging the adorable Samuel. Dark, pinch-faced Simon sat apart, dead eyes aimed straight ahead, his hand pulling up clumps of grass. Flynn couldn't fathom why Steele would display this chilling photograph. It was a clear depiction of family pathology that featured his budding psychopath of a son. He wondered if Steele suspected Simon of murdering his wife and Samuel. Was this photo intended to serve as a reminder to him or a cruel means of tormenting Simon with the insinuation: *I know your secret!*

A few minutes later, he met Desi downstairs. "Let's check out the gallery."

Flynn drove around to the back of the estate where Steele's gallery of masterpieces was obscured from the house.

"Lucky you missed the horror of Simon's room," Desi said. "The only way I could stand it was to take photos of all the sadomasochistic filth on the walls."

He could not open the steel-lined door without the code. Using the light on his phone, he examined the ground outside, the churned-up gravel indicating a lot of vehicle traffic.

In the Explorer, Desi said, "So we don't know if the lovebirds came here."

"I'd guess they did. McCoy knows the code to get into the barn. He and Kate probably cleaned out the important paintings."

"At least Raquel didn't die knowing about Nick's new partner in crime."

On Linea Del Cielo, he glanced at Desi, who sat ramrod straight in the dark interior of his SUV. Their temporary civility had given way to the silent tension from the earlier unresolved conflict.

Flynn made the first move. "I suppose you think I should apologize first?"

"Well, you shot the first arrow," she said.

"I was just pointing out the realities of your—"

"Come off it, Flynn—"

"Yeah, yeah. I see how you could take what I said as a put-down. I do that without knowing I'm doing it. Sorry, I'm not very sensitive."

"You got that right. You put down everyone, Flynn, not just me."

Her words felt like bees buzzing in his ears, a preamble to the final sting.

"You think you're better and smarter than anyone," she added.

He felt the sharp stab of truth. "It looks like that, I know, but, as you know, looks can be deceiving. I went with a therapist for quite a while. She said my problem was low self-esteem."

"Well, it doesn't show, I can assure you," she said.

"That's the whole point of acting like an asshole. Then no one can see the pathetic mess underneath." He said this self-mockingly, but the admission stripped away his armor. "I apologize again, Desi, but do you think my slim arrow deserved the club you used on me? Calling me a rogue peeping tom—"

"No. It was overkill. It came from a lot of bad treatment from men, starting with dear old Dad. I apologize." She smiled. "You're a brilliant detective, Francisco Flynn, the world's greatest."

"Thanks. And you are amazing, Detective Hawk. You'll be running the LAPD one day." He flashed her a grin, a soft warmth infusing his usual hard-boiled persona.

CHAPTER 31

"Tis some visitor," I muttered, "tapping at my chamber door."
—Edgar Allan Poe—

Sunday, October 21

Kate set her travel bag and briefcase by the front door. She grabbed her raincoat from the closet, tossed it on top of her bag, and checked her watch. It was 8:15 a.m.; her Lyft to the San Diego airport would arrive in the next forty-five minutes. The four days following Raquel's death had been long and hard. Nick would be hiding out somewhere in London, having left town soon after they had rushed off the Steele estate in separate cars.

Nick had sworn her to secrecy and offered her plane fare to London. "Take the 10:55 a.m. flight on Saturday," he'd said. She would get to London on Sunday mid-afternoon with a stop in Dallas and a connecting flight. "I'll reserve a room in your name at the Leonardo Hotel," he'd told her. "I may or may not be able to meet you there that evening. If I don't show up Sunday night, meet me at the National Café at the National Gallery of Art the next morning at eleven." To be certain no one could trace his movements, Nick had warned against any interim telephone contact. He would be dumping his iPhone. They did not discuss a future plan or the fate of Steele's paintings. That was put on hold until they met in London.

Besieged with flashbacks, nightmares, and exhaustion, she tried to focus on taking one step at a time. She'd canceled her appointments the days after Raquel's death and for the next couple of weeks, pleading a family emergency. That seemed a better excuse than exposing her post-traumatic stress and plans to rendezvous with an international criminal in London.

Lying to Sam in their conversation last night had been difficult. She made up the story of going to London to give a presentation on treating trauma in people who've committed crimes. The only actual untruth was the implication that the talk would be in front of an audience. In one corner of her mind, she still thought of Nick as her trauma patient. She added that she would also take a few extra days to see London and the museums. Sam had seemed happy to hear his boring mom was doing something fun and exciting for a change.

On her way to the kitchen for a water bottle, Kate heard the front doorbell chime. The unexpected intrusion jangled her nerves. It was too early for the Lyft, and the driver didn't come to the door anyway. Retracing her steps, she glanced out the narrow side window next to the door and saw a patrician, silver-haired man standing next to a striking, dark-skinned woman with shiny black hair. Her stomach turned. *Who were these strangers? The police? How could they know about her connection to Raquel or Nick?* She'd better face this now and opened the door, managing a strained, polite expression.

"Good morning, Dr. O'Dade," said the gent in a tony British accent reminiscent of Nick's. "I am Detective Chief Inspector Cromwell of Scotland Yard, and this is my colleague, Detective Destiny Hawk of the LAPD." They each showed a badge. "May we come in briefly? We need to speak with you."

Her belly full of dread, she ushered them inside. "I have very little time."

Cromwell immediately noticed the suitcase with a raincoat thrown over the top. "I deduce you are going on a trip?" he asked with a genial smile.

She scrambled for a response. "Yes, to visit my son at UC Berkeley. He's a freshman and having some trouble adjusting." She was saying too much, the sure sign of an amateur liar. "My Lyft is due to arrive shortly. Please come this way."

She led them down a short hall and into her office. She immediately felt calmer as she stepped into her private practice space and donned her Dr. O'Dade persona. Cromwell scanned the room—the worn leather furniture, the Navajo rug on the hardwood floor, her grandmother's wedding quilt. His gaze settled for a couple of moments on her watercolor of a serene beach scene.

"This is a charming office," Detective Hawk said, "and the fountain outside has such a soothing effect."

"Thank you. Please sit down." Kate wondered if their game was the typical good cop, bad cop—the woman detective assigned to put her at ease. She motioned to the two client chairs across from hers. Sitting in her consulting chair, she adopted her usual take-charge role.

"How can I help you?"

"I believe you knew Raquel Steele," Cromwell said, a touch of warmth in his intelligent gray eyes. "In case you don't already know, I'm sorry to tell you she died Tuesday night."

Kate clamped down on the welling up of her grief. "Yes, I know. I read about her tragic accident in the *Union-Tribune*."

"It must have been a shock," Cromwell said gently. "I believe you were her therapist."

She was taken aback. "How did you know that?"

"One of our detectives followed her here more than once," Cromwell said.

"Why, for God's sake? Raquel was hardly a criminal."

A sound of tapping came from the rooftop above them. It was most insistent and oddly uniform, almost machine-like.

"What's that strange tapping sound?" Cromwell scoured the open-beamed ceiling.

"Oh, that's just Mr. Crow," Kate said. "He visits for a while most days, tapping a fallen pinecone against the roof tiles to get out the pine nuts to eat. Creeped me out at first. I thought it was Poe's raven."

"Ah, yes." Cromwell smiled. *"Tap-tap-tapping at my chamber door— Only this, and nothing more."*

"Quoth the Raven, 'Nevermore,'" Kate said, imitating his deep voice as though bantering with a friend. If she wanted to impress Cromwell with her cool wit under pressure, she might have succeeded. There was an appreciative sparkle in his eyes, and Kate was warming to this smooth-talking Sherlock.

Cromwell cleared his throat. "Getting back to your question. One of our detectives followed Mrs. Steele because of her connection with Nick McCoy. I believe you know Mr. McCoy as well." He raised his steel-colored brows.

She regarded him warily, feeling his sharp gaze focused on her facial expression. "What's this about? Are you investigating Raquel's death? Was it not an accident?" She hoped her disingenuous act was convincing.

"We are not the official investigators," said Detective Hawk. "Since the Steele estate is in North County, the Sheriff's Department has jurisdiction over the case. The sheriff considers Mrs. Steele's fatal fall a suspicious death. We won't know the cause of death until the autopsy and toxicology reports are completed. Unfortunately, toxicology reports can take a long time."

Kate held a neutral expression. "What does Nick McCoy have to do with this?"

"We think you might know where he is," Cromwell said. "And whether he had anything to do with Raquel Steele's death. We are also interested in McCoy as a suspect connected with certain art crimes."

"Why would I know about this McCoy?" Kate asked.

"Come now, Dr. O'Dade," Cromwell said. "You know Nick McCoy very well. You were also his therapist. We've kept track of McCoy for a long time."

She sighed. "Inspector Cromwell, you must know I can't reveal information about a current or former client because of the confidentiality rule."

"We understand," Hawk said, "but we were hoping you could tell us something that might help us to find the truth."

She thought for a few moments. "If Raquel's death turns out to be a murder, I think her husband would be the most likely suspect. I recently observed him physically and verbally abusing Raquel in public. I believe his heartbroken display is an act for the media."

"Thank you," Hawk said. "Anything helpful you can say about Nick McCoy?"

She glanced at the inspector and saw a rational man who might give Nick a break if it was in his squad's best interest.

Looking back at Hawk, she said, "In my opinion, he would not kill Raquel or anyone. He has no history of violence."

"Do you know where he is now?" Cromwell asked.

"No. But, even if I did, I couldn't tell you." She looked down at her iPhone. "My Lyft driver is only a few blocks away. He'll be here in a couple of minutes."

The detectives stood. "Thank you for speaking so candidly with us," Cromwell said. "As a forewarning, the Sheriff's Department might want to interview you as Mrs. Steele's therapist, particularly to explore the possibility of suicide."

Unless Cromwell shared information gained from his team's surveillance, the Sheriff's Department would have no way of knowing she'd been Raquel's therapist. Raquel wanted her treatment to be kept secret from her husband and had always paid in cash. She never sent bills to her home in the Ranch. So, Steele likely didn't know of her existence, and she wanted to keep it that way.

"Suicide is not a possibility in my professional opinion," Kate said. "If you must, please pass that along to your colleagues and anything else I've told you about her. I wouldn't be able to tell them anything more."

"We will not share details of our investigation with the Sheriff's Department or with the San Diego Police, which is the jurisdiction where McCoy lives or did live. We cannot risk leaks about what our team is planning and doing."

As the detectives headed out the door, she said, "If you want to nail a serious international art criminal, I suggest you leave Nick McCoy alone and investigate Dixon Steele."

Cromwell turned. "Rest assured, we are including Mr. Steele in our inquiries. If I may, a word of advice to you, Dr. O'Dade. Stay away from Nick McCoy. The art underworld is a very dangerous place."

She watched them stride through the gate, waited a couple of minutes, then grabbed her bags and raincoat. She locked the front door and gate and hurried down her driveway to her Lyft waiting at the end. While the driver put her suitcase in the trunk, she grabbed her mail from the mailbox and stuffed it into her briefcase. She got in the car, her heart thumping, her breath coming in shallow gasps—the early signs of a panic attack.

Slow your breathing.

"Are you all right, ma'am?" the driver glanced at Kate over his shoulder.

"Fine, thanks. Just get me to the airport before I change my mind."

CHAPTER 32

Every man has his personal devil waiting for him somewhere.
—John le Carré—

Sunday Morning, October 21

Eddie was sitting inside their rental car with Desi as they watched Kate's Lyft drive off.

"Surely, she's not flying to Berkeley to see her son," Desi said.

"Unlikely," Eddie said. "I'd wager she's off to meet Nick McCoy."

"Where?"

"London's my best guess," Eddie said. "That's his home. He knows the terrain there better than anywhere else. Things have gotten too hot for him here." Eddie phoned Archie and asked him to check the San Diego and Los Angeles airports in the unlikely event Nick McCoy flew to London in the past four days using this name. "Also, find out if Dr. Kate O'Dade scheduled a mid-morning flight to London. If so, check the times of the subsequent flights to London from both airports starting tomorrow. Hold off on making a reservation for me."

A short time later, Archie reported that Kate booked a 10:55 a.m. American flight that connects to a British Airways flight in Dallas, arriving in London on Sunday at 2:35 p.m. He also said, "There's a direct flight to London tomorrow on British Air, leaving at 9:15 p.m. from LA."

On the drive back to the Bamboo House, Eddie called Detective

Parish, an old friend at Scotland Yard. As a big favor, he asked him to spot Dr. Kate O'Dade when she arrived at Heathrow on British Airways, Saturday at 2:35 p.m. "She's forty-three, short auburn hair, green eyes, about five-nine, thin, attractive." Then he instructed Parish to follow her to wherever she was staying and keep up surveillance until he got there, probably around six on Sunday. "Watch for the man she might be meeting and get his picture," he added.

At the Bamboo House, the four detectives met outside on the deck. Standing next to Flynn, Eddie leaned on the railing and sipped his coffee, relieved to see the ocean shrouded in fog. The air felt cooler and moist for a change and didn't desiccate his skin.

"Nice morning," he said. "Reminds me of home."

"Homesick?" Flynn asked.

Eddie shrugged. "I prefer the mystery of fog to the blatancy of sun."

He turned around and faced Archie and Desi, who were sitting at the table drinking hot coffee, a basket of chocolate croissants in front of them. "Let's go over what we know and how we should carry on. It's been a traffic jam of activity this week." He felt his face sag with fatigue.

"You going to London?" Archie asked.

"Probably. As you know, Steele put off meeting with the count because of Raquel's death. He's now invited the count to meet at his gallery this afternoon at four to discuss a deal. Miles Hartwright, the art historian, will also be there to act as Steele's adviser since McCoy is not available."

"For God's sake, his wife just died," Desi said. "How could he be pursuing art deals?"

"Art is more important to Steele than wives, dead or alive," Eddie said. "Our plan is already in place, though it won't include McCoy. You know your roles. Archie is my driver, Desi my art adviser, Flynn my bodyguard, and the count will play it by ear. We'll leave at 3:15 p.m." He swallowed a mouthful of lukewarm coffee.

"Here's another update. After the meeting Desi and I had with

Kate earlier, we found out she was flying to London this morning; we assumed to meet McCoy." He moved to the table and poured hot coffee into his mug. "Archie, have you found out anything more about McCoy?"

"No one named Nick McCoy has appeared on any flights to London in the last four days," Archie said. "I've checked his and Kate's mobile activity, and there's nothing between them. No answer on McCoy's cell and no record of any calls since Tuesday night."

"He's probably chucked his iPhone and gotten a burner," Flynn said. "He hasn't returned to his loft since leaving the Steele estate Tuesday night."

Eddie nodded. "Where did that slippery sod go, and why? Not to Kate's place. Did he abscond with any of Steele's masterpieces?"

"He put two bulky canvas bags and a large backpack into his trunk," Desi said. "It suggests he'd prepared to leave town or change his living place that night. I doubt he'd risk taking stolen or forged masterpieces through airport security. They could still be in his loft—"

"They are not in the loft." Flynn squinted at Eddie. "I have a confession to make. Raoul and I broke in and searched McCoy's loft last night."

Eddie's brows flew up. "You did *what*?"

"I broke the rules," Flynn said, not in the least contrite. "I had to do it behind your back; I knew you wouldn't approve."

"You're damned right, smartass. You broke the law and put our operation at risk."

"We left no evidence of a break-in," Flynn said. "It was the quickest way to determine what McCoy had done and whether he'd moved on. The sheriff won't get a warrant to search the loft unless the autopsy and toxicology reports suggest Raquel was murdered and McCoy becomes a suspect."

"Archie, Desi, did you know about Flynn's break-in?" Eddie asked.

Archie quickly shook his head, but Desi averted her eyes and was slow to follow.

She probably knew, Eddie thought. He emitted what sounded like a sigh, then looked out to sea. He was so angry he wanted to bloody Flynn's handsome face. Instead, he counted and took deep breaths as the police psychologist had taught him to do. Then he turned toward the big thorn in his side. "You are a valuable player, Flynn, but if you ever go behind my back again or put the operation at risk, you're off the team. Understood?"

"Understood."

"Since the deed is done, what did you find?"

"In McCoy's studio, five works in the storage area were marked as jobs for private clients. We found no paintings resembling masterpieces. His workspace was neat and well-organized. We couldn't tell if he'd taken any of his supplies. We found no money, wallet, or passport stashed anywhere."

"He's flown," Eddie said. "Depending on what happens with Steele, I have a tentative plan to leave for London tomorrow night. Since I don't have an available team at Scotland Yard right now, Desi is working on getting permission from her department to accompany me. Flynn, you and Archie—"

"I'm going, too," Flynn said.

"What?" Eddie asked.

"To London. I still have enough money left from Simon's advance to cover expenses."

Eddie had no stomach for any more of Flynn's defiance. Holding his temper in check, he said, "You're needed here. You and Archie are to track down where McCoy might have hidden or sent Steele's paintings."

"Archie can do that work by himself," Flynn said. "My Apache grandfather trained me as a tracker since I was a kid. I'm an expert at tracking humans and animals. I've no training or experience in tracing stolen art."

"You don't know London," Eddie said.

"Not yet," Flynn replied. "Do you, Desi?"

"Never been there." Her nervous gaze darted between the two men.

"We Indians learn fast." Flynn licked his lips. "I have to go to nail McCoy."

No one spoke. All eyes were on Eddie. Flynn felt diminished by exposing how much he cared. Eddie crossed his arms and stared down at the planks of the deck, the waves making their usual racket slapping the shore. He didn't want the hassle of Flynn, and he didn't want to worry about how the pain in the ass would defy him next. He glanced up and caught Flynn staring at Desi with a look of naked appeal.

Desi cleared her throat. "Eddie, there's something to be said for a tag team of three in London. McCoy is an expert at spotting tails. Flynn and I can pass as a couple. That makes us look less suspicious than if one of us is hanging around in his vicinity. We could change who's following McCoy more often with three of us, which would give us a better chance of staying under his superior radar."

Eddie regarded Desi with tight-lipped admiration. He assumed she wanted Flynn in London for reasons besides his tracking skills.

Archie said, "I'll be able to find out if McCoy has stored or sent paintings elsewhere on my own. Also, I can work with the sheriff's office. I have a pal there who will give me the skinny on their investigation. Flynn is *persona non grata* with the sheriff. He won't be able to work with that outfit or be useful to me." He cracked a sly grin at Flynn. "I can also follow up on Simon's job offer. Flynn can't help with that either."

"That'll do, Archie," Eddie said. "Do you know if Steele and Simon have an alibi for the time of Raquel's death?"

"A weak and weird one," Archie said. "The coroner estimated that Raquel died somewhere between six and eight, Tuesday evening. Steele supposedly had an accident shortly before six, and Simon drove him to the hospital in the Jaguar, which had no tracking device on it. But they didn't get to Thornton Hospital until 6:45 p.m. and said they didn't get home until after midnight."

"Verified by the hospital?" Flynn asked. "What kind of accident?"

"The arrival at 6:45 p.m. and departure at 11:30 p.m. have been verified," Archie said. "Steele claimed he had a serious injury and that Raquel's stallion bit him."

Flynn rolled his eyes. "Bit him where?"

"Uh . . . his privates," Archie said.

"You mean his bloody cock?" Eddie asked in his toniest British accent.

"Precisely." Archie grinned, and they all burst out laughing.

"She bit his foul, floppy member, then they murdered her," Flynn said.

Desi gagged. "You're sick, Flynn, but it fits. The tox report should reveal the facts. I hope Steele chokes on that cock and bull story of his."

"Cock and minotaur, you mean," Flynn said. "Surely the culprit was one of Picasso's bull-headed beasts from Dirty Dix's collection."

More laughter. Eddie felt he was back at Oxford, chugging pints in Turf Tavern.

"Alright, enough smutty black humor," he said. "Archie, has Steele reported any of his paintings missing?"

"Not yet. He was likely the first to steal some of the missing masterpieces."

"Right," Eddie said. "You're getting the gist of this racket. It'll be interesting to see what Steele shows us today. I'm sure McCoy wounded him in a devastating way."

Flynn nodded. "Maybe McCoy's the one who bit off Steele's willy."

"Here! Here!" Archie lifted his coffee mug. Desi giggled.

Eddie groaned. "Flynn, what the hell am I going to do with you?"

"I'd be more use to you in London than here," Flynn said.

Flynn would be a bloody chore in London, but the bloke was clever, bold, and got things done—and kept them laughing. Eddie scanned the three mutinous faces. "I see I'm outnumbered. You've made some powerful friends, Mr. Flynn." He studied the PI's usual poker face and saw a new vulnerability in his eyes. "Okay, you're on the London team on one condition."

"Yeah, what's that?"

"I'm the boss. That means you do as I say. No rogue behavior."

"Deal," Flynn said, and three of them laughed.

CHAPTER 33

My old heart is cracked; it's cracked.

—Shakespeare—

Sunday Afternoon, October 21

"Miles Hartwright," he said into the intercom at the gate to Dixon Steele's estate.

"Ah, Dr. Hartwright, right on time," Steele said. "After I buzz you in, follow the driveway around the house and park in the lot at the back entrance to the barn. That's my gallery."

The buzzer sounded, and the gate slid open. Miles hopped into his car and drove slowly down the driveway. He was curious to see Steele's collection but dreaded dealing with the volatile bully. Miles was to authenticate Steele's masterpieces for the French collector, *Le Comte Antoine de Guise*, arriving later this afternoon. Steele also wanted advice on which of his masterpieces would be a good trade for the count's Modigliani nude. A "good trade" meant in Steele's financial favor.

Miles arrived at the back of a dilapidated barn and parked. Once out of his car, he headed for the entrance a few feet away just as Steele opened a massive, weathered door.

"Good man, you can follow directions." Steele looked up at the much taller Hartwright, dressed in ironed jeans and a linen shirt. "You look like David Niven, especially with that outdated pencil mustache and stage posture. Gotta British poker up your ass as well?"

"Absolutely, and a stiff upper lip," Miles crooked a smile. "You're quite fond of insulting people, aren't you, Mr. Steele?"

He laughed, a harsh, ragged sound. "Good observation."

Steele looked haggard in the bright light. Bags hung under his pebble eyes, and his flabby flesh had a grayish tinge. Moving inside and down a well-lit hall, Steele lumbered stiffly in flip-flops, his bowed legs widespread as if he had crotch rot or was imitating a gorilla's gait. He looked ludicrous in his baggy cargo shorts and a flashy turquoise shirt, the blousy floral print depicting green fronds and red poppies. It was hardly the outfit for a man in mourning.

"I am sorry for your loss," Miles forced out.

"Enough said. I'm trying to forget that grisly business." Steele stopped in front of an open door on the right. "Take a look in this gallery." He gestured for Miles to go inside. "This is where my minotaur drawing came from, the one you so astutely recognized at the unveiling."

Miles scanned the small gallery filled with Picasso drawings and prints of minotaurs ravishing or caressing half-clothed maidens.

"Remarkable," Miles said. These drawings, although shocking, had been rendered with such sensitivity. They seemed to come from a great, warped talent, struggling to manage opposing forces—a desperate longing for women and a violent hatred and fear of them. "I heard the museum crowd is quite pleased with the replacement for *Dora and the Minotaur*."

"Yep, *Girl Helping Minotaur* was quite a hit. My first wife selected it. But I've got no use for a sad, helpless-looking minotaur with a silly girl in control. Glad to be rid of it."

"All is forgiven then?" Miles asked.

Steele shrugged. "Fay Martinez won't ever forgive me. She said I insulted womankind and treated her like a Mexican maid. But it doesn't matter. She's gone back to licking my ass. She wants to keep her job and get more goodies from me." He winked.

"Ah," Miles said, thankful he wasn't in a supplicant position *vis-à-vis* this scumbag. He wondered how much it had cost Dixon to keep the papers and TV stations from reporting on his shocking behavior at the unveiling. While there were no news stories of the event, nothing could stop word-of-mouth gossip that had gone viral, especially with Raquel's recent death.

"Onward to my gallery of stars," Steele urged, resuming his shambling gait.

Passing a couple of smaller galleries, Steele pointed out that one contained some rare Japanese woodblock prints and still another had a stellar collection of modern sculpture. The gallery of stars was a modern, rectangular space with cream-colored walls and a maple floor. Down the center of the gallery stretched a long, two-sided black leather couch for the comfortable viewing of the paintings on opposite sides of the gallery. Miles's pulse raced as he scanned the walls, bursting with vibrant color and the extraordinary artistry of the greatest Post-Impressionist painters.

Soon, however, his excitement soured. He liked and admired Nick McCoy, but he wanted to wring his neck right now. Almost instantly, Miles suspected that two of the masterpieces were stolen and one was a forgery. *Did Steele know that, or had he been duped?* Miles would have to deliver the bad news.

"Wow," Miles said, trying to sound impressed.

"I see you approve, Professor." Steele showed off his stumpy, yellow teeth. Miles had made his day. "First, take a closer look at these six paintings." He gestured toward the wall across from the doorway. I believe they are my most valuable masterpieces."

Miles started with Picasso's haunting *Blue Room*, one of the most likable of the artist's Blue Period. A lithe, naked girl was giving herself a sponge bath while standing in a circular, pan-like receptacle in the middle of her bedroom. It was painted in shades of blue, with red and orange accents. The last Miles had heard, this painting resided in the Phillips Collection in Washington, DC. Had the museum sold it to Steele, or had it been stolen? Or could this be a forgery? Surely Nick would not have overlooked a stolen or forged Picasso.

"This Picasso is marvelous. Where did you get it?"

"From a fellow collector," Steele said without hesitation. "Had to pay a chunk of change for it, but you know how it is. I fell in love." Miles watched in amazement as Steele stood transfixed by his beloved painting, his hard, pitiless eyes turned soft, and a sloppy smile made him look almost human.

"Who was the collector?" Miles fished. "Does he have any other Picassos from this period for sale?"

"Sorry, I can't reveal his name. Most of us want privacy in these transactions."

I bet you do, Miles thought. *What better way to avoid taxes and the discovery of stolen or forged works.* Miles's gaze fixed on Picasso's signature. Something bothered him about it.

He moved down to Monet's familiar *Japanese Footbridge and the Water Lily Pool, Giverny*. He knew three of these existed—one at the National Gallery in London. However, he sensed that this one came from the hand of the famous British forger, Tom Keating. Miles was looking for the proof of a Keating when Steele remarked that he could let this one go in a trade easily. It was "too pretty," he said.

Van Gogh's *Sunflowers* came next. Again, Miles saw nothing suspicious at first glance except that Steele owned one. He knew there were eleven sunflower paintings but only five major works. He was familiar with the *Sunflowers* at London's National Gallery, and this rendition looked similar. Another was at the Van Gogh Museum in Amsterdam, and he was fairly certain the other three famous *Sunflowers* resided in Philadelphia, Munich, and Tokyo.

"I suppose you won't tell me where you acquired this beauty?" Miles asked.

Steele chuckled. "A Japanese collector, that's all I'll say. Another arm and leg went to that greedy bastard."

If Steele's was the Tokyo version, Miles knew that its authenticity had been the subject of a prolonged and heated debate. *Could the Japanese have dumped a possible fake on Steele?*

"These paintings all seem to sparkle with life and color," Miles said. "Have they recently been cleaned?"

"Yep, cleaned and restored. Nick McCoy is a master of his craft."

"Agreed." Miles was now examining *The Card Players* by Cézanne. There were a series of five *Card Player* paintings, all somewhat different. Four of these paintings were in famous museums, and only one was in an undisclosed private collection. Steele's collection? Miles was uneasy. Something struck him as false about this painting. *Ah, yes, the shadow.*

"It would be hard for me to part with this one," Steele said.

The next two exuberant Matisse paintings were favorites of Miles's. *The Open Window* looked remarkably vivid and captivating, as did the small *Joy of Life* oil sketch hanging next to it. He knew Kate O'Dade had a superlative copy of *The Open Window. Was this another copy?* Forgery was the appropriate description, not copy, since the artist had signed the work. According to Kate, the National Gallery of Art in Washington, DC, said they had the original. *Who knows*? Copious forgeries proudly hung in many of the great museums.

He studied the painting in front of him, scanning for an anomaly—something added, out of place, or missing. Miles had written an article about Matisse's series of window paintings and therefore knew *this Open Window* painting very well. The brushwork was pure Matisse, but then he spotted the misstep.

He moved over to the *Joy of Life* oil sketch. He'd seen it at the San Francisco Museum of Modern Art a few years ago. *Had it changed hands or been stolen?* He didn't recall hearing about a theft. His gaze scoured the surface. The rhythmic colors and brushwork, the harmonized figures and landscape, the vibrant and fresh ambiance—all signaled this was a genuine Matisse. It made you feel like dancing and singing. He touched the bottom corner of the work and felt suspiciously soft paint. He asked Steele for some alcohol and a clean cloth to conduct an important test to determine authenticity.

"Why do you need to test anything?" Steele asked.

"You hired me to evaluate these paintings for your negotiations with *Comte Antoine de Guise*. So that is what I am doing."

Scowling, Steele left the room and soon returned with a white cloth and a small bottle of spirits. Miles took the items and poured a little alcohol onto the fabric. Then, standing in front of the Matisse oil sketch, he explained that what he was about to do would not harm the painting. Miles proceeded to gently rub the moistened cloth on a bottom corner. Looking at it, he then saw the evidence.

Miles took a deep breath and said, "Look at this, Mr. Steele." He held out the cloth for Steele to see. "Do you notice the faint traces of red paint?"

Steele bowed his head, squinting. "Yeah, so what?"

Miles scratched his brain, looking for a way to make the truth less devastating and humiliating. At best, he would be the despised messenger. At worst, he would be silenced. But he couldn't permit himself to become one of the many "experts" who took bribes from a collector or a dealer to authenticate a fake.

Another deep inhale, his gut cramping. "This means, Mr. Steele, that the oil paint is not dry," he said, clearing his throat. "And that means this gorgeous painting is not a genuine Matisse. Someone painted this oil sketch recently. Matisse painted the original in 1905."

Steele glared at his beautiful *Joy of Life* sketch. "What the fuck, Hartwright? Did some lowlife hire you to break my balls?"

"You're the only one who hired me to do this job."

"What you say can't be true, or Nick McCoy would have known. He can spot a fake a mile off."

Steele hadn't made the obvious connection yet. Let him get there on his own. *Jesus, Nick, what the hell are you doing?*

"Sometimes even the best authenticators make mistakes. These are brilliant forgeries."

"*These!*" Steele bellowed. "What the hell do you mean?"

"I regret to say you've got more than one forgery here."

"That's impossible. You're lying," Steele roared, his grayish flesh erupting in red blotches. "Prove it, you pissant fraud!"

Usually unflappable, Miles strained to conceal his urge to bloody this bully's repulsive face. "I will prove it if you agree not to interrupt my report with further insults or childish displays of temper. If you'd prefer, I can hold off on what I have to say until your friend, the count, arrives. Surely, he'd want to hear my report before considering a purchase or a trade."

Steele glared at him, hatred in his inkblot eyes. "Say it straight, Professor. No art babble."

Miles turned to face *The Open Window*. "The painting in this work is superb. It looks like Matisse's style in his *Fauve* period and would fool many experts. What exposes this as a fake are the masts on the boats. Do you see these five red-orange masts?"

"Yeah," Steele said.

"In the original, this one here in the middle," Miles pointed, "it is green, not red."

"What?" Steele shouted. "What kind of forger would make such a stupid mistake?"

"I doubt it's a mistake. Some forgers are wiseass tricksters like the British forger Tom Keating. They put oddities in their works or leave out something that's supposed to be there. It comes from a need to distinguish their work somehow, or it's a way to say *Fuck You* to the art establishment that rejected their original work. Shall we proceed to the next one or—"

"There's another fake?" Steele asked, terror in his eyes.

"Yes, the one next door—Cézanne's *Card Players*."

"That can't be!"

Miles thought he'd seen all five versions of *The Card Players*, but this one was slightly different from the ones he remembered. "Look closely at the painting. Tell me what you see."

Miles stepped out of the way, and Steele stepped forward and described the three working-class men sitting directly across from each other playing cards and another guy standing in the background watching them.

"See anything odd about the guy standing?"

He squinted. "Can't say I do."

"How about this?" Miles pointed to a faint shadow cast by the standing man.

Steele squinted at this segment of the painting. "I see a sort of shadow. So what?" He looked at Miles.

"Have you noticed it before?" Miles raised his brows.

"Not sure I took any special note of it. Why?"

"That shadow means the painting is a forgery. The original painting has no shadow. It's the forger's signature, I believe. He wanted it to be noticed at some point." Miles flashed on the notorious forger code-named Phantom, who was thought to be British.

"Another Fuck You?" Steele snapped, his bald head gleaming with sweat. "You're killing me, Hartwright. Are you done yet?"

"No, I'm afraid not." Miles moved to the next painting. "Van Gogh's *Sunflowers* looks genuine, but I haven't scrutinized it. However, I can't give it a clean bill of health because the provenance isn't convincing enough. It's doubtful any Japanese would sell a Van Gogh, even one of debatable authenticity. Japanese art lovers worship Van Gogh. Shall I do the dry paint test?"

"Don't you dare touch it. What else?"

"The Monet," Miles said. They moved over and stood in front of *The Water Lily Pond*. "This is a Tom Keating forgery. Look at the Japanese bridge over the pond. In the original, four vertical supports are holding up the front handrail. In this version, you can see there are five." Miles pointed to each one. "This addition tells us suckers it's a forgery." He paused, then began walking toward the Picasso. "I'm very sorry to say there's—"

"No! No!" Steele looked terrified. "Not the Picasso!"

Miles quickly stopped to face the Picasso, with Steele breathing heavily beside him. "This is beautiful work, but look at Picasso's signature, bottom left corner," Miles instructed. "The original *Blue Room* shows a bold black line under his name. Do you see that line here?"

Steele let out the high-pitched howl of a mortally injured animal. He was sweating profusely, clenching his fists, then clapping his meaty hands over his blotchy face.

"You've had a shock, Mr. Steele. Why don't you sit down? I'll get you some water. Perhaps you have something stronger."

"Shut the fuck up! This is my worst nightmare. My family's been abducted, fakes put in their places. Who could tear out my guts like this?"

There was only one forger who could've done this, one painter who had the necessary skill. "The work is so brilliant; I think it's the forger who is code-named Phantom," Miles said.

Steele started shuffling up and down the gallery, a stunned look on his face, the horrific truth settling in. He finally stopped in front of Miles, acute grief and rage in his eyes.

"Nick McCoy is the only one who could have done this. He's the only one with the opportunity and the skill. I just can't believe it." Another howl filled the room, his darting eyes now leaking tears. "How could he do this to me? I thought of him as my son. For fuck's sake, why? Why?" Croaking sobs came from his throat, his tear-streaked face cradled in his hands.

For a moment or two, Miles felt sorry for the wretched animal. "Maybe McCoy wanted the genuine masterpieces," he suggested, though Miles thought there was more to this than a clever theft and substitution. Too much effort was involved and, to a trained eye, too many clues to the forgeries. This forger wanted his work discovered, and a devastating scam of this kind seemed like retribution.

Steele looked up, wet-eyed, his pasty face twisted in utter despair. "You don't have a damn clue what that evil devil has done. He's robbed me of my reason to live. Each one of those paintings is more to me than any silly child or worthless human would ever be. I can relate to my masterpieces. I converse with them. They are the only important things in my life." Steele wiped his tear-stained face with the tail of his red poppy-flowered shirt, his hot-teared desperation turning to cold, hard-eyed fury.

"McCoy is your pal, Hartwright. Are you in this together?"

"No, and I'd hardly call Nick a pal," Miles said. "We are colleagues. I don't think you would put a friend in the rotten position he's put me in."

A buzzer sounded. A deep, French-accented voice came over the intercom by the gallery door. "Dixon, it is *Antoine de Guise*. I am at the front gate with my adviser."

Steele worked to get his raw emotions under control and hobbled to the intercom. "Hello, Antoine," his voice rasped. He feigned a cough. "I've come down with a blasted illness, and I'm not fit to meet with anyone today. Very sorry you had to make the trip. I'll be in touch."

"I regret you are ill, Dixon. Another time then. *Au revoir.*"

Steele turned around and glared at Miles, eyes like hot, black stones. "You'd better not breathe one goddamn word about this to anyone."

"You don't plan to report this to the police?" Miles asked.

"Hell no! I take care of my own problems. If I hear you've leaked anything about these works to the media, the police, or anyone, I'll have you eliminated or cut your throat myself. Follow me, Hartwright?"

"That's hardly a subtle threat, Mr. Steele."

"Tell McCoy his days are numbered."

"You tell him. I'm not your thug for hire. My job here is done."

PART II

LONDON, ENGLAND

CHAPTER 34

What's done cannot be undone.

—Shakespeare—

Monday Night, October 22

Kate woke up on an acre-sized bed, cocooned under a quilt, looking up at a wine-red velvet canopy. Across the softly lit bedroom, two tall windows framed the night sky. Lights from the Tower Bridge sparkling on the Thames signaled she was in London. Somehow, she'd escaped the horror town, flown across the ocean, and made it to the Leonardo Hotel. She whispered a thank you to Nick for reserving this posh suite in her name. Upon arriving, exhausted from twenty-two hours of travel, she'd crawled into bed and closed her eyes, shutting out dark thoughts of Raquel's murder, the hunt for Nick, and a treacherous future.

Her watch said 8 p.m. She'd been out cold for about four hours. Guessing it would be around noon in California, she called Sam, got his voicemail as usual, said she'd arrived safely, and sent her love and a big hug.

After a pit stop in the pristine marble bathroom, Kate checked out the elegant lounge, graced with three tall windows and a long dining table in front of a black and white marble fireplace. The posh furnishings looked like French antiques. The framed mirrors and paintings, the oval-backed chairs, and the filigreed tables reflected the most exquisite taste. She felt dizzy and disoriented. *Had she landed in someone else's story, like in one of Daniel Silva's stylish international thrillers?*

To ground herself, she arranged her toiletries in the bathroom, shed her smelly clothes, and put on a flannel nightgown and robe. No point unpacking; the future was too uncertain. She'd justified coming here to determine if she and Nick had any hope of being together. *Would he even show up tonight?*

Her stomach growled, which made her realize that filling her stomach was more important than pondering her precarious romance. She grabbed the room service menu from the antique desk, then heard a discreet knock on the door. Cracking open the door, she was about to shoo the maid away when she saw a cart full of silver-covered dishes emanating savory smells. A bottle of champagne sweated in an ice bucket.

"Your dinner, Madame," said an old gent in a dapper butler outfit.

"I think there's some mistake. I was just about to order dinner. You folks must read minds."

"We try," he said straight-faced. "But in this case, someone ordered dinner for a Dr. Kate O'Dade."

Kate smiled. "That's me." Nick must have done this. She opened the door, and the butler pushed the cart toward the dining table in front of the fireplace.

"Shall I set the table for two, Madame?"

"No, it's just me, thanks." Her stomach cried out for the food.

"I was rather hoping to join you." The butler bowed graciously, then raised his head, and she saw a familiar cocky smile flash across his lined, elderly face.

"Nick? Good lord, is this old relic you?"

He bowed. "At your service, Madame."

She flew into his arms. "I'll spoil your make-up if I kiss you."

"Spoil it," he said and covered her mouth with his.

Breaking apart, she examined his disguise. "My God, your hair! What happened to it?"

He touched a limp, dirty-white strand. "This is a wig. Pardon me while I fix my face and hair." He lifted a travel bag from under the cart and moved to the bathroom with his usual youthful stride.

Kate set the table with the fragile-looking dishes, lit the ornate candelabra in the center, then opened the champagne. When Nick returned, she stared at him wide-eyed, unable to conceal her shock. His face, features, and skin color were back to typical Nick, but his thick mane of curly black hair was gone, brutally sheared to a close-cropped cap of dyed gray hair. She felt like crying. She'd loved his hair, and now he looked like a different man. He was still good-looking in a more severe, military way—with a haircut reminiscent of Julius Caesar.

"I see you don't like my new hairstyle."

"Well . . . it's a dramatic change."

"Sorry, Kate, I had to do it; my hair was too distinctive. You could spot me a mile away, and it was too bushy to conceal easily under wigs or hats."

"I'll get used to it. It'll grow back." She tried to sound lighthearted and accepting, but his need for disguises brought home the reality of their enemies in pursuit. It crossed her mind that losing his hair might weaken him as it did Samson. "Let's eat and pretend we're on vacation instead of dodging bullets."

They heaped their plates with the traditional English roast dinner of beef, Yorkshire pudding, roast potatoes, steamed spinach, and salad. Kate had a glass of champagne, and Nick opened the bottle of burgundy. They avoided talk of the future and updated each other on the events since their last meeting. Kate brought up Inspector Cromwell's surprise visit just as she was preparing to leave for the airport.

"He noticed my suitcase, and I told him I was going to Berkeley to visit Sam."

Nick winced. "That means he knows you're here. He would have checked out your flights. We have to assume he had you followed to this hotel."

"Oh no!" Kate slapped her hand over her mouth. "That didn't occur to me."

"Why would it? This is not your world." He reached for her hand. "No one would have seen me coming here since I was in disguise before walking into the staff entry. Did you learn anything from Cromwell?"

"He said Raquel's death was considered suspicious, but he didn't know the results of the autopsy and toxicology reports."

"What about Steele and his paintings?" Nick downed a hefty swallow of burgundy.

"According to Cromwell, Steele hadn't yet reported any stolen art to the Sheriff's Department."

"I'm not surprised," Nick said. "Check your text messages. Miles Hartwright was covering for me as Steele's adviser in my absence. I asked him to send me any news about Steele to your mobile. After Kate fetched her iPhone from the bedroom, they sat on the settee, looking out the window at the view. She opened her phone.

"There are messages from Miles." She gave Nick her cell.

Kate watched Nick's solemn profile as he scanned the message, then read it aloud.

> *YOU FUCKED ME, MATE! I want to believe it wasn't your intention, just my bad luck. Steele asked me to evaluate several of his masterpieces for a trade he hoped to make with Le Comte Antoine de Guise. I found five of these masterpieces to be expert forgeries and a sixth to be a less good Tom Keating. When I broke the news, Steele went berserk. Called me a liar and fraud, swore he'd take me out—and you as well— if word of these vicious*

lies was made public. Somehow, the news media uncovered the story. The headline read: DIXON STEELE's AWESOME COLLECTION OF FAKES.

"Yahoo!" Kate crowed. "So, you did more than just steal the masterpieces."

"I replaced them with my forgeries," he said. "I've never left anyone empty-handed." He cracked a half smile.

"Thoughtful," Kate said. "How did you do it?"

"As Steele's conservator, I took many of his paintings to my studio for cleaning and restoration. I copied five of them and returned these to Steele as the newly restored originals. The sixth forgery he mentioned was Monet's *Water Lily Pond* done by Tom Keating."

Kate nodded. "I wondered what was in that canvas bag you were carrying. Were the last of the copies to be substituted inside?"

He nodded, unsmiling. "I thought it would take him longer to discover the fakes, and it didn't occur to me that he'd pursue a deal with the count right after Raquel's death. But that scumbag has no heart or shame."

"You wanted Steele to discover the fakes?" she asked.

"Eventually. Poetic justice and humiliation were the points. It just happened sooner than I expected. I didn't foresee Miles's role in it." His voice sounded hollow.

"Shouldn't we be celebrating?" Kate raised her champagne flute.

He glanced at her iPhone. "Miles has more to say."

> *In case you don't know about the investigation of Raquel Steele's death, the police suspect she was brutally raped and murdered. The DEA raided Simon Steele's room and found a million-dollar stash of drugs. Simon is in jail, awaiting indictment. Dixon suffered a major coronary this morning. He's in intensive care—a humiliated, badly injured lion. Watch your back, mate.*

Nick dropped the mobile into his lap, his face contorted in pain.

"What's wrong?" Kate took his hand. "You wanted the scum to suffer and lose everything."

"Right," he snapped, "but the price was too bloody high."

Raquel's crumpled body and twisted neck flashed through Kate's mind. Brutally raped meant she must have suffered horribly before she died. Kate gripped Nick's hand as they looked out at the lights blurred on the water. At least Raquel was spared knowing of their betrayal—one small comfort. But an insidious question wormed its way into Kate's mind. If Raquel had lived, would Nick have chosen to be with her? Then the voice inside her head—*What would you have done*?

There was no romance that night. Nick brooded silently and eventually fell into a fitful sleep on their vast bed. Kate was too wired to sleep, her mind filled with frightening images of Steele surviving and sending his goons after Nick. *What would Nick do? What about her?* They needed a plan. The prospect of Simon's revenge was almost as scary. Inspector Cromwell was another worry. But at least he wasn't a psychopath.

Stop counting calamities, Kate instructed herself. She slipped out of bed and took her briefcase into the lounge, where she began looking through her unsorted mail from the past five days. She stopped at the letter postmarked Rancho Santa Fe and tore it open. It was from Raquel, mailed on the day she died, possibly shortly after their last session.

CHAPTER 35

Guilt: the gift that keeps on giving.
—ERMA BOMBECK—

Monday Night, October 22

As she read the letter, Kate could hear Raquel's distinctive voice—her charming accent, careful diction, and sudden bursts of French.

Ma plus chère Kate,

Forgive me for not being entirely truthful today. I won't be going to a shelter tonight because I am leaving town tomorrow morning, so I will be safe. I have another confession to make. I am the one who left Matisse's La Fenêtre Ouverte *on your doorstep. I did an awful thing and stole this masterpiece from my lover. I am not proud of this double cross, but I am a practical femme française. I have few resources, and I needed a way to make a fortune quickly in case I had to escape and hide on my own. As an international art dealer, I learned how to work the black market and knew I could sell the Matisse for at least a hundred million dollars.*

I believe it is foolish to rely on any man—or anyone—but I have decided to take the scary leap and trust mon amour not to desert me and to share the spoils.

I must apologize. At first, I left the Matisse with you for safekeeping, but now I give it to you as a true gift of gratitude and love, for you have taught me to trust again.

Adieu, chère Kate.

Je t'aime,
Raquel

Kate took in the touching tenderness of Raquel's ending, but the last phrase was like a knife in her heart—*for you have taught me to trust again.* Devastated, she curled up in a ball on the couch and cried, soaking the velvet upholstery with her tears.

Sometime later in the night or early morning, Kate woke up to an anguished cry. She jumped up, disoriented. The light was still on in the lounge.

"No!" Nick's hoarse voice shouted.

She rushed into the bedroom and turned on the bedside lamp. Nick was writhing on the bed, the covers thrown off his naked body. He was muttering incoherently, his skin clammy, his breathing erratic.

Kate sat on the bed and shook him. "Nick, wake up. You're having a nightmare."

His eyes opened, staring, sightless. "Raquel?" he choked out, gasping for air.

"It's Kate. Look at me, Nick." She grasped his cold, clammy hands and tried to pull his torso up. "You need to sit up so you can breathe better. Now, put your feet on the floor." She supported his back as he swung his legs around and sat on the edge of the bed.

"Slow down your breathing," she said calmly. "You're hyperventilating, and you need more carbon dioxide. You've had panic attacks before. You'll be okay."

She kneeled on the plush carpet in front of him. "Breathe in slowly when I say *one*. Then hold and breathe out on *two*. Okay. One, inhale slowly. Hold. Two, exhale. One, inhale slowly. Hold. Two, exhale. You're doing well." His eyes looked glazed. She could feel him trembling, the demons no doubt creating havoc inside his head. "Look at me. Hold your hands over mine. Think of painting. Think of our painting, *The Open Window*. We're sailing on one of those blue and orange boats under a pink and white sky." She could feel his muscles relaxing. His breathing gradually slowed to normal. "Well done," Kate said. "Isn't that what you British always say?"

A few minutes later, she sat in bed next to Nick and held his hand while he was quenching his great thirst with a bottle of stout.

"You're a brilliant doctor, love. Thanks." He smiled at her.

She kissed his cheek. "Was your nightmare about Raquel?"

He nodded. "It's blurry now, but my part in her death remains crystal clear."

Her guilt would remain forever etched in her brain. "Nick, it was Raquel's mission in life to avenge her father. Just like yours. She knew the risks and insisted on taking them. But I understand your guilt. If only I'd acted more quickly and gotten her away from Steele's estate that afternoon."

"She wouldn't have cooperated," Nick said. "She hated Dixon more than I did."

"Do you realize . . . you put hating Steele in the past tense?"

"At the moment, I hate myself more," Nick said.

"Raquel wouldn't want either of us blaming ourselves," she said.

"I am to blame." His voice rose. "You should not blame yourself, but I should. I'm not done with revenge. Raquel's rapist and killer will not get away with it, not on my watch."

His ferocity gave her the shivers.

"You know revenge is a hollow victory," she said. "It just begets more revenge. You may not need to take any action. Steele's bad heart could kill him."

"Nothing will kill that motherfucker," Nick said. "Besides, I'd rather he lived to enjoy his losses, crimes, and humiliation. I doubt Dixon murdered Raquel. He might have raped her, but he's too cunning to kill his wife right after he abused her in front of an audience. Raquel's murder was a crime of intense hatred. Dixon did not hate Raquel, but Simon did, with a sick obsession."

"You believe Simon's the killer?"

"I do, and he's the type who would torture her beforehand to make her suffer."

"Simon's in jail. You can't reach him, Nick."

"Not for long. Papa will bail him out, no matter the price."

"Revenge isn't going to help *me,* Nick. And I'm against you sacrificing yourself for no good outcome. Can't we think of something positive to do in honor of Raquel's memory, something she would appreciate?"

Nick nodded. "I have, love. I plan to give Picasso's *Blue Room* to Raquel's stepsister, her closest relative. That's the most important painting Steele stole from their family."

"You have it?"

"It's in a safe place," Nick said. "*The Blue Room* was among the five copies I substituted for Steele's masterpieces."

"Raquel would be pleased," she said. "It's very generous of you. Can't that be enough?"

"It's not nearly enough," Nick said.

They sat in silence. Nick's determination to pursue Simon struck her as suicidal. How could she divert him from this new dark quest? *Dammit*, she thought. *Was she destined to always play the role of savior with him?* Maybe it would help if he could see Raquel more realistically, and not just as a beautiful, innocent victim.

"I loved Raquel," Kate said, "in the way a therapist can feel deep affection for a client. But she was not perfect."

"I know," Nick said.

"Before I cried myself to sleep tonight, I read a touching letter she wrote to me the day she died. She confessed that she was the one who stole *The Open Window* from your vault at the Steele Museum. She left it on my doorstep for safekeeping. It wasn't Allegra."

"Yes, I know," Nick said. "I wanted it to be Allegra, but when thinking it over more objectively, I realized she just wasn't smart enough to plan and execute that kind of subterfuge. Raquel had the smarts, the skill, and the nerve, and she was the only other person it could have been. That she left the painting with her trusted therapist also made sense."

"In the end, she wanted me to have it," Kate said, "but her original intention was to keep it in reserve as insurance. She was afraid of being left alone with no money."

Nick groaned. "She didn't trust me . . . and rightly so. You shouldn't trust me either."

CHAPTER 36

Let's all pretend to be someone else, and then perhaps we'll find out who we are.

—John le Carré—

Tuesday Morning, October 23

Eddie Cromwell stepped out from behind one of the two Trafalgar Square fountains. He scanned the majestic façade of the National Gallery of Art through a pair of binoculars. A few people were on the steps this morning, but he focused on a familiar figure standing at the bottom—Dr. Kate O'Dade. *Where was bloody McCoy?* They hadn't spotted him going in or out of the Leonardo Hotel, but Eddie suspected he had done both, wearing a convincing disguise. A couple of feet from Eddie, a dark-skinned man and woman sat on the rim of the fountain's pool, their backs to the shooting spray and the gallery.

"Do you see her?" a deep voice asked.

"Yeah." Eddie glanced at Flynn. The PI wore a navy beanie pulled low over his forehead, his ponytail tucked inside. Oversized, cool-dude sunglasses and a rash of black stubble obscured the rest of his face. A black leather jacket, tight jeans, and combat boots completed his tough guy look. "I wouldn't want to meet you on a dark street." Eddie chuckled.

"No worries, my type never picks on old duffers." Flynn grinned.

"Is McCoy with Kate?" Desi asked. A black floppy rain hat and fashionable sunglasses mostly concealed her hair and face. An oversized raincoat covered up her figure. The clear sky and shining sun belied the prediction of rain.

"No, but I'd guess he's somewhere nearby." Eddie packed the binoculars into a briefcase and put on a pair of wire-rimmed spectacles. Wearing a shapeless tweed jacket and a newsboy cap that covered most of his whitened hair, Eddie aimed to pass as an elderly, art-loving academic. He patted his new dingy beard and picked up the battered briefcase.

"You look quite fetching, Grandpa." Desi smiled.

"You too, my dear. I quite like the hat," Eddie said. "I've had a report from Archie. Somehow, the media got wind of the story about Steele's forged masterpieces and ran a devastating exposé. My guess is Miles Hartwright—the chap acting as Steele's adviser—leaked the story so the thug would hesitate to incriminate himself by silencing him. Since Steele has not reported the theft of the originals or that a substitution occurred, the authorities don't suspect McCoy's involvement. So, we can safely assume that McCoy swapped his forgeries for the originals." Eddie paused. "Archie also said Steele had a heart attack and is in hospital."

"Good." Flynn smiled. "Any news about where McCoy hid the masterpieces he stole?"

"Not yet," Eddie said. "Here's some other news—Steele, Simon, and McCoy are the main suspects in Raquel's murder, and Simon's in jail for drug dealing."

Flynn whooped and shot his fist in the air.

"Does any of this affect our plans for today?" Desi asked.

"No," Eddie said. "I'm going to start walking toward the gallery. I'll keep tabs on Kate and see if she hooks up with McCoy somewhere inside. You and Flynn should take over when you see Kate or both coming outside. Expect to see McCoy in a clever disguise. Our main strategy is to hound and rattle him enough so that he's willing to make a deal.

I figure the best way to get his cooperation is to make Kate disappear. Concern about her might be enough to bring him to the table."

"He has to care about her a lot for that to work," Flynn said.

Eddie shrugged. "It's a gamble. Do you have a better idea?"

"Nah," Flynn said. "So, we snatch her in a dark alley like a pair of thugs?"

"I'd prefer you to act the part of a well-mannered detective. Can you do that?"

Flynn laughed. "Piece of cake."

CHAPTER 37

You Can't Go Home Again

—Thomas Wolfe—

Tuesday Morning, October 23

Nick leaned against one of the Corinthian columns fronting the Greek temple façade of the National Gallery. After Kate had gone inside, he turned his gaze to the wide stairway leading up to the entrance. He'd set up this outing as the best way to identify the undercover cop who would be following her. Once identified, there was no better place than his old home to evade a tail.

He'd spotted no one obvious yet—mainly families and a couple of middle-aged ladies. Nick looked anonymous in a charcoal watch cap, wraparound sunglasses, faded jeans, and a nondescript black anorak with an inside pocket that concealed his knife, lock picks, and a different hat. A black turtleneck covered the burn scars on his neck.

The mid-morning air was cool and moist. On the promenade below him, a group of toddlers and mums scattered seeds to a flock of overfed pigeons. More birds kept flying in for a meal, lining up along the balustrade, the sour smell of their poop polluting the air. Memories surfaced from his horrific childhood. As a terrified boy, he recalled running up these stairs to escape the bullies following him from his East End school. Once he made it inside the gallery doors, he'd be safe from the dangers of the outside world. But not today. He'd find no refuge here or anywhere.

Nick eyed a lone young man dressed much like he was. The daft bloke stumbled up the stairs, his gaze glued to the face of his mobile. He couldn't be undercover; this chap drew too much attention to himself. To his right, Nick noticed a young girl talking to a busker in a Yoda costume, who appeared to be sitting in space, levitating about two feet above the ground. Nick smiled at the neat trick, recalling his days out here as a half-starved kid selling quick portrait sketches and copies of Impressionist painters for a bit of cash. He'd gotten a Yoda mask to hide his disfigured face since the scars seemed to scare off both kids and adults. Business improved after that. Soon, he met his first partner in crime—slick, savvy Jackson Chase—who bought his copy of a Pissarro. He flashed on Jackson's rakish smile and the way his canny blue eyes lit up when he wooed a mark. He recalled, with a shiver, the thrill of those days when he was the chosen mark.

A group of five elderly folks was slowly climbing the stairs. The old, bespectacled bloke who looked like an academic caught his eye. Something was off about him; he was talking familiarly to the lady next to him, but a clever agent knew how to blend in. Ah, now he spotted the wrong note. The slight spring in the chap's step seemed too youthful for a stooped old professor with white hair and a beard. After the group walked through the door, Nick followed.

Inside the entrance hall, he replaced his sunglasses with regular tinted glasses that obscured his eyes. He scanned the magnificent octagonal interior—maroon marble columns, dramatic diamond-checkered floor, graceful arches, and light pouring in from the glorious glass dome overhead. The group of old folks seemed to be looking in the gallery store. He nodded at the two Gainsborough portraits on the pale crimson walls on either side of the doorway leading to the exhibition hall. When he was a boy, he used to think of them as Lord Piffle-Whiffle and Lady La-di-da—his museum mum and dad there to welcome him home from school.

At the info desk, Nick indicated he had nothing to check and then skirted the short line to the cloakroom. He passed the restrooms and stopped in front of the door with a baby silhouette. He knocked on the door.

"Anyone in there?" he asked softly.

Kate opened the door, smiling. "About time you showed up."

Nick saw no one looking his way and quickly slipped inside. The deep pink walls and the faint smell of talcum powder sent him back thirty years.

The bell was ringing, the signal that the gallery was closing. Nick scuttled to the warm, rosy-walled sanctuary for mums and poopy babies. He had to slip into this room without being seen, as boys were not allowed in there.

"Glad you made it," Kate said. "Did you spot anyone following me?"

"Maybe. On your way from the hotel, did you happen to notice an old, white-haired chap wearing wire-rimmed spectacles, a tweed jacket, and a newsboy hat?"

"Don't think so, but I was trying not to appear suspicious. Any problems getting our stuff out of the Leonardo and to the new hotel?"

"Nope. I looked like an old bellhop wheeling luggage around. The new place is the Gull's Nest, and I reserved the room in the names of Mr. and Mrs. Nigel Blackman, but you'll remain registered at the Leonardo for the next two days." He pulled out a mobile from his pocket. "Here's a burner phone. Only use this phone to call me, never your iPhone." He had her memorize his number, then she put the burner into her daypack and pulled out her cell.

"Let's sit here for a minute," Kate said. "My nerves are still jangled, and I want to check my messages." He helped her onto the changing table. After listening to her messages, she said, "Damn, nothing from Sam. I hope he's okay."

"Of course, he is." Nick leaned against the table next to her. "He's a cool, young stud who's thinking about hot girls, not his hot mom."

"Right." Kate laughed. "You slept here, didn't you, and this was your bed?" She patted the pink vinyl cover.

"Ah, you remember the story," Nick said. "I wasn't sure you believed me."

"Indeed, I did. Who would or could make up that incredible tale?"

"Someone like me." Nick grinned.

She laughed. "How gullible I was. You played me beautifully, just as you probably did the dear old janitor who took that gutsy orphan boy under his wing."

"Charlie," Nick said, recalling that gruff old gnome, his first fan. He touched Kate's thigh. "We better get moving. Any moment, a mom with a squalling kid will walk in here."

Kate hopped off the table. "What's next?"

"I need to flush out your tail so we can lose him. This gallery is a good place to do that; I know every nook and cranny. While we're at it, you'll see a bit of my grand boyhood home. Got a map?" She pulled one out of her shoulder bag. He pointed to Room 43. "Van Gogh, Pissarro, and Manet are in this room upstairs. Study Van Gogh's *Sunflowers*. I'd like your reaction."

"You'll meet me in front of the painting?"

"I'll be nearby. Wait until I give you a slight nod, then slowly follow me at a distance."

"Then what?" she asked.

"It depends."

Climbing the stairs to the second floor, Nick looked down on the Annenberg Court, a stark, modern exhibition hall. He glimpsed an old gnome and freak-faced kid taking turns pushing the polisher around the gleaming floor. Charlie had been popular and trusted, so pretending to be his grandson allowed Nick to go anywhere in the gallery and make friends with the crew and a few staff. The reminders of Charlie and losing him darkened his mood. He would lose Kate, too. People he got close to usually ended up dead.

He stopped inside what he'd called the Orgy Room, the walls pulsating with naked, writhing bodies. He then proceeded into the octagonal Turner Room, capped by a large glass dome. Turner was one of his first loves, not just for the masterful painting but because his stormy seas and skies depicted Nick's inner world so exquisitely.

In the next, hall-like gallery, Nick spotted Kate standing in a group gathered in front of one of the five most well-known versions of Van Gogh's *Sunflowers*. A gangly curator with a prominent Adam's apple and a melodic voice spoke to the elderly folks Nick had seen climbing up the entry staircase. Nick stood at the edge of the group next to a stout woman who seemed mesmerized by the lecture. Standing next to her was the bloke he suspected was Kate's undercover tail—the stooped, bespectacled professor.

"Most people are drawn to this Van Gogh," said the curator. "The vase of yellow flowers looks so inviting at first, but then . . . can you feel the mood gradually shifting as you gaze into the yellows?" The women nodded, and the men looked perplexed. "*Sunflowers* is a deceptively complex painting. If you look at it long enough, you begin to sense signs of the artist's despair and madness lurking within the expressive shades of yellow. It is a unique and devious work."

Unique and devious for another reason, Nick thought. This work was a brilliant fake; the artist was none other than his father. The scoundrel Dixon Steele had commissioned this project, and Nick recalled his dad copying the original from multiple detailed photographs. He was itching to tell Kate the whole story. She looked genuinely entranced with the painting and the lecture, as were the others—except the old professor, who stared at the curator fixedly, his head cocked as though listening hard. Nick knew a well-acted pretense when he saw one. As if sensing that someone was watching him, the professor glanced in Nick's direction just as Nick turned and crossed the gallery.

His back to the Van Gogh group, Nick stood in front of one of the paintings he most admired—Manet's *The Execution of Maximilian*.

Life-sized, bristling with phallic menace, the black-clad soldiers were sighting down the long barrels of their raised rifles, ready to fire. *Bloody hell!* He'd never noticed this before, but the tall, dark bloke facing the firing squad looked like him.

His skin felt hot and prickly, the hairs rising on the back of his neck—that telltale sensation of being watched by hostile eyes. He didn't need to turn around to know the imposter professor had identified him. The chap was probably one of Cromwell's undercover hounds or even the Chief Inspector himself. The gallery was cool, but Nick was sweating. He pulled out a handkerchief and mopped his brow. His gaze riveted on Manet's painting, Nick felt pulled into the lifelike picture, the tall, dark captive awaiting his death. Nick stood rigid with tension, then the deadly blast of rifles firing sounded in his ears. He recoiled as though shot. *Fuck's sake, am I losing it?*

He glanced over his shoulder and saw the curator and his group moving to the next painting—a Pissarro. Remaining in character, the undercover cop moved with them, but Kate hung in front of the Van Gogh. In a few moments, she turned and saw Nick give her a slight nod. As he began ambling back toward the Turner Room, she waited a minute, then slowly followed.

Once in the Turner room with Kate a few yards behind him, Nick moved faster, retracing his steps through the East Wing and Central Hall. He paused at the staircase and spotted no one following either of them. Instead of going downstairs to the entrance gallery, Nick led the way through the West Wing. Passing through rooms with Renaissance paintings, he strode quickly to the far west Sainsbury Wing, the home of Botticelli and Leonardo da Vinci. Assuming another tail was watching the main entrance, Nick planned to leave the gallery from a different exit. Plunging down the stairs to the first floor, he headed for the Sainsbury Wing exit. When Kate joined him outside, they were breathing hard and facing a double-decker bus near the corner of Pall Mall and Trafalgar Square.

"What was that about?" she asked, gulping air. "Are a pack of demons chasing us?"

"No, just an old devil with white hair."

The sky was darkening. Nick looked up at the gray, bottom-heavy clouds blotting out the sun. A crack of thunder. Dark, ominous clouds churned in the sky. They reminded Nick of Turner's cloud painting. Then he heard more thunder. Any moment, those bloated, gray bastards would drop their heavy load.

"Let's get on this bus," Nick said.

"Where's it going?"

"We'll find out."

CHAPTER 38

There is no den in the wide world to hide a rogue.

—Ralph Waldo Emerson—

Tuesday Afternoon, October 23

Nick and Kate ran out of the downpour into The Rogues, a pub on Glasshouse Street in Piccadilly. They looked quite different from when they got on the bus at the Sainsbury Wing exit. Nick had exchanged his navy watch cap for an olive fisherman's waxed cap and reversed his hoodie to show a muted plaid instead of plain black. Kate had donned a black bucket hat and black-rimmed tinted glasses, then she took out a tightly folded rain cape from her shoulder bag, unpacked it, and draped it over her gray jacket.

The Rogues looked more like an upscale pub than Nick remembered. He often came here as a student at the Royal Academy of Arts. The place still had old plank floors, but the comfortable wine-red leather chairs and booths were new. He nodded to the beloved, familiar Manet masterpiece—*A Bar at the Folies-Bergère*—hanging behind the dark cherrywood bar. The pink-cheeked, buxom barmaid still had that slightly dazed, wistful expression, a dazzle of lights, bottles, and the audience reflected in the mirror behind her. The painting needed a good cleaning, but it still looked like Manet's last major work instead of what it was—a talented student's copy.

Savory cooking smells and the enticing scent of dark ale filled the air. Now, after the noon hour rush, the pub was uncrowded. Nick eyed an elderly couple at a table under one of the windows and three scruffy artist types seated in the corner sketching. The David Bowie album *Heroes* was playing in the background.

Nick requested a table on the empty upper level next to the railing. Seated at a small round table, almost side by side, they had a clear view overlooking the lower level and the wall, with two rows of paintings and drawings a few feet across the open stairwell. To the right, Nick could see three tall windows and the entryway. He'd be able to spot anyone suspicious coming through the door in the unlikely event a tail had managed to follow them. The rain pattered against the windows and the skylight overhead.

"What a charming place," Kate said, scanning the paintings along the stairwell wall. I'd swear that picture over there is a Sisley." She pointed at a small street scene. "And the one next to it looks like a Degas."

Ignoring his hunted status, Nick focused on Kate's delight. "The Sisley is by Tom Keating, England's most beloved forger, and the Degas is a John Myatt fake. Those splendid Renaissance drawings are by Eric Hebborn, England's best forger. Every picture hanging in this place is a forgery, a student's copy, or a pastiche of a well-known artist's work. For example, that famous Manet hanging behind the bar is a copy donated to this place by the copyist."

"Who was that?"

"Nick was the art student's name, I believe," he replied, smiling.

"You?" Kate asked, wide-eyed. "It looks so genuine."

"Thanks. I got three months of free meals and drinks for that student work. This pub is a gallery of rogues—first-rate copies and forgeries collected by the eccentric owner."

Kate grinned. "I love it."

Looking over the menu, Nick said, "Try one of their special craft beers or cocktails. They're named after famous artists or paintings."

Kate chuckled over the oddball names of the drinks and dishes. When a young, curly-haired waiter appeared, Kate ordered a Virgin of the Rocks, a fancy gin drink in honor of Leonardo, and Nick selected a Caravaggio Black Ale.

"Mine will probably be spiked with something deadly," Nick said. "Caravaggio was a great painter and also an accused murderer."

"No one's died from it yet, sir," said the waiter deadpan.

Nick was famished and ordered one of his old standbys—Toad in the Hole, pork sausage inside Yorkshire pudding.

Kate chose the Posh Stargazy because she liked the quirky name. "Salmon and prawns in a creamy parsley sauce with cured bacon and quail eggs. Can I go wrong with that?"

"You won't starve," the waiter stated.

"Now that's reassuring." She smirked.

The waiter flashed her a flirty grin, turned, and bounded down the stairs.

"No waiters talk like that back home," she said.

"Pity, isn't it? No more rhapsodizing about a succulent yet kinky clump of raw kale or the health wonders of lime and basil green juice garnished with a spry sprig of—"

"Stop it!" Kate covered her mouth, muffling her laughter.

A hip-looking lass with tattoos on her arms arrived with their drinks.

Kate sipped her pink-tinged Virgin and resumed studying the paintings.

"Tell me how you got into this rogues' club. You've always managed to avoid this important piece of your history."

Nick took a long pull on his black ale, his gut hurting at the thought of Jackson's diabolical seduction. He couldn't risk telling Kate about his Faustian deal with the devil. Not yet. "I can't focus on the past right now, not with the present smack in my face."

Kate sighed. "Okay, you face reality. I'll try to listen."

He took Kate's hand. "I think you should go back home ASAP. If you're near me, you'll be in danger from various goons—Steele's thugs, Simon, Bulldog Cromwell, and anyone who hears I've snatched the best of Steele's art collection." He flashed on his old partner, Jackson Chase, now known as Charles Hamilton.

"You're in worse danger," she said.

He shrugged. "I'm used to running and hiding. If things get too hot for me, I can disappear to my lair in the Caribbean and use my funds stashed in offshore accounts."

Kate raised her brows. "I'm glad you have a good backup plan, but it does underscore that you're one of those rich crooks on the lam."

"Not so rich, just well-heeled," he said. "That's the naked truth about me, and you're a first-class, respected psychologist who does important work. Living in exile or on the run is no life for you. You have a real home by the sea and a smart son. Where's he going to go at Thanksgiving and Christmas?"

"Dammit, Nick, must you spell it out? None of that seems real now. You are what's real." She looked at their clasped hands, her eyes tearing. "I hate the thought of life without you."

He squeezed her hand. "We'll risk one more night."

Nick tensed at the sound of the front door opening below. He glanced down at the couple coming inside. As the tall, tough-looking bloke closed his wet umbrella, Nick stiffened, the hairs on his neck and arms bristling. He took off his sunglasses and glanced up, his sharp blue gaze seeming to pierce Nick's tinted glasses. Where had he seen those distinctive eyes before? The pair sat at a table next to one of the windows, right in his line of sight. *How the fuck had they managed to follow them?* One of the pair must have been watching the Sainsbury Wing exit. Kate hadn't noticed the threat. She was staring at the dregs of her drink.

She looked at him, her eyes pleading. "Have you considered turning yourself in and returning the paintings?"

"Considered and dismissed," Nick said.

She took a deep breath, the warmth gone from her eyes. "Listen to me, forgers don't usually get much punishment, especially here in England. I studied the British forgers when I was trying to understand you. Fascinating stuff. The charges were dropped against Tom Keating, and the old rogue did a series of popular BBC shows, demonstrating old masters' techniques." She took a long swallow of her drink. "John Myatt was sentenced to one year and got out in four months. A movie is being made about him. Then there's the infamous Eric Hebborn. He bragged about his clever scams, and the authorities didn't even charge him."

"Right, he was murdered," Nick said. "He wrote a book telling where the bodies were buried. His need to brag killed him."

"Bodies?"

"He made the mistake of revealing the locations of many of his fakes—in what collections, museums, auction houses, and private estates. I believe Hebborn was killed because he humiliated a platoon of art world muckety-mucks and collector goons like Dixon Steele. The police have no hard evidence against me, but if I were to confess and expose all the 'experts' and collectors I've fooled with my fakes, I'd likely meet with an unpleasant accident in or out of prison."

"Dear God, I'm going to cry. Tell me you've thought of a clever way out."

Kate looked down at the people below and noticed the new arrivals. A broad-brimmed hat concealed the woman's face, but she immediately recognized the man's distinctive profile.

"That man down there," she whispered. "I know who he is. He's a PI by the name of Francisco Flynn. I ran into him at the gala. He was working undercover as one of the guards. He must be following you."

Nick frowned. "I'd wager he's on Cromwell's undercover team, the woman too."

"This is very bad news. Flynn is one of the best trackers there is."

"Relax." Nick smiled. "No one catches me."

She sighed. "Was Cromwell at the gala, too?"

An image shot up. *"Antoine de Guise,"* he whispered. "The bloody French count."

The waiter arrived at the top of the stairs with a platter of food. They stopped talking, and Nick's mind went into overdrive, concocting and discarding plans. When the young man put his Toad in the Hole before him, his hunger took over. He cut into the sausage. Kate eyed her tiny, speckled quail eggs suspiciously.

"Try to eat. Never take your next meal for granted." Nick ate another piece of sausage along with a scoop of the pudding. Kate took a small bite of her parsley-sauced shrimp and washed it down with a swallow of Virgin of the Rocks.

"Give me your iPhone. I need to text Miles," Nick said. "Then we'll evade surveillance and get to the Gull's Nest."

Kate handed him her phone.

He sent a quick text message, asking for the latest news about Steele and Simon. He leaned forward, voice lowered. "Listen closely. We'll pay the bill and go down the stairs, looking relaxed and unhurried. Near the entrance, within earshot of the phony couple, I will tell you to get us a taxi while I quickly hit the gent's room." Her phone pinged.

"There's a reply from Miles."

Nick took the phone from her and quickly scanned the message. "Miles says Steele is out of intensive care, and Simon is out on bail." Nick kept his racing thoughts to himself. Steele would most likely send his son here to hunt him down, and Simon would stay at his father's mansion in Chelsea. Nick might be able to beat him there.

"There's a strange light in your eyes," Kate said. "What are you thinking?"

"About how to get out of here. The cops will be keeping tabs on me, not you. So, I'll leave through the back entrance. You go to the Ritz Hotel and get a cab, then take it to the Gull's Nest."

She recorded the address and phone number in her cell.

"The cops will soon know what I've done and try to find and follow me. I'll shake them. You've got your passport with you, right?"

"Yes."

"Good. I'll meet you at the new place when I'm sure I've lost the latest tail. It may take me some time. I'll need to stop for supplies. Don't be concerned if I'm late." He quickly reviewed the plan in his mind. It was full of wishful suppositions and potential glitches. Beyond their Gull's Nest bolt hole, the future looked like a maze of pitfalls and traps. "Okay, got it?"

Kate nodded. "What's the plan then?"

He smiled, taking her hand. "We'll hole up in the hotel and manage to find something to do."

CHAPTER 39

*Considering how dangerous everything is,
nothing is really very frightening.*

—Gertrude Stein—

Tuesday Afternoon

The rain had stopped, but dark clouds hung low overhead. Kate walked briskly toward the Ritz Hotel in Piccadilly to get a taxi. A few people in rain gear or carrying umbrellas hurried along the dark maze of streets between the pub and the hotel. She stopped and conferred with an older woman who gestured to a shortcut to the right through an empty courtyard. Kate splashed through puddles and stumbled over cobblestones, wondering if Nick had fooled the two cops and gotten away. She knew this was a safe area with posh galleries, but even ordinary muffled street noises heightened her tension.

Then, out of the gloom, someone from behind grabbed her, his slab-like hand clamping over her mouth. Terrified, unable to breathe, Kate struggled against his iron grip.

"Kate," said a familiar deep voice, "I'm not going to hurt you."

She continued to struggle and frantically clawed at his arm. Then a woman stepped in front of her, took off her floppy rain hat, and shook out her hair.

"Dr. O'Dade, do you recognize me?" She smiled. "I'm Detective

Desi Hawk. We met at your house a couple of days ago. I was with DCI Cromwell."

Kate nodded, still wild-eyed.

"We're the cops, the good guys," she said. "We're not going to hurt you; you have my word. We just need your cooperation. Detective Flynn will let you go if you don't scream or try to run. Understood?"

She gave an abbreviated nod as Flynn loosened his grip, lowered his arm, and stepped next to Detective Hawk. "Remember me?" he grinned. "We met at the Impressionists Exhibition in San Diego."

Kate slapped his face hard. "Cut the bullshit, Flynn. We met long before that."

"Yes, and I remember every thrilling moment, especially your lethal right hook." He rubbed the side of his face, still grinning.

"Why are you following me?"

"I'm doing my job," Flynn said. "I'm sure you've already figured that out. Nick McCoy is a criminal and a fugitive. What the hell are you doing with him?"

"Pardon me," Hawk said. "It seems you two know each other."

"Yes, indeed," Flynn said. "The last time we met, we were on the same side of a murder investigation nine years ago."

"Now, it seems, we're adversaries," replied Kate.

She glanced at each of them. "So, what's this about? Why grab me like a pair of street thugs?"

"We had to meet you privately and away from McCoy," Flynn said.

"Did that require terrorizing me?"

"I'm sorry we scared you." Hawk put her hat back on. "Will you come with us willingly?"

"Why would I?"

"For a talk with DCI Cromwell," Flynn said in a softer tone.

"Forget it. I'm not helping you catch Nick McCoy."

"Listen, Dr. O'Dade, the point would be to help us *save* McCoy. He's in grave danger from Dixon Steele, for one. And Simon Steele has managed to get out on bail. Our team has word that Simon's left the US for London on a private jet. Papa Steele got him a fake passport."

Kate shuddered. Nick would soon find this out and go after the psycho. The sadistic horror of that pervert's bedroom flashed in her mind.

"We could offer McCoy a fair deal and protection," Hawk said. "We thought it might be helpful for you to be the emissary, but only if you decided it was the right thing to do."

Her mind in a whirl, Kate took a deep breath and considered her options. Resisting would do neither one of them any good. But cooperating had a chance of helping Nick. Additionally, she might be able to influence Cromwell. At least he'd appeared civilized and rational.

"I'll go with you, but only to listen," she said. "Where are we going?"

"For a drive first." Flynn flashed his wolf's grin. "No worries. There's nothing to fear."

The rain started up again.

CHAPTER 40

People are very secretive—secret even from themselves.
—John le Carré—

Monday, October 22, San Diego

Archie stepped out of the swank elevator at Jacobs Medical Center in La Jolla. Dixon Steele was recovering in high style on the tenth floor. To get permission to interview Steele from the sheriff, he had to reveal he was part of a hush-hush undercover art crime operation to find Nick McCoy.

Archie saw no hint of the usual hospital room in Steele's luxury corner suite. Two walls of floor-to-ceiling windows met at the corner, and the oversized bed was positioned so that the coddled patient had an expansive view overlooking the UCSD Campus, with a blue strip of ocean showing in the distance. Steele was propped up in bed, watching a football game on the large-screen TV enclosed in a cabinet of exotic dark wood. Archie cleared his throat.

Steele glanced at him, a scowl on his hollow-eyed, sunken face. "Who the hell are you?"

"Detective Hasofer." Archie showed his credentials and said, "I am sorry for your loss."

Steele eyed Archie's meaty paw and scowled. "What the fuck do you want? I've already talked to you jokers. I don't like repetition. Wastes whatever time I've got left."

"Hey, but this is a grand place to waste time in," Archie said, radiating bonhomie. He glanced around the airy space furnished with a modern couch, two comfortable chairs, and a raised bathtub encased in marble so that the patient could see the stunning view out the windows while bathing.

"This place sucks," Steele said, his gaze fixed on a pileup of bulky bodies on the TV screen. "What they called art on the walls almost gave me another heart attack. It's gone."

"Hospitals are the pits," Archie said, "but this place has managed to disguise its real purpose jolly well, don't you think? Look at that hot sunset outside your acres of glass."

Steele snorted. "It looks like a bad, amateur painting. This place is a fake luxury hotel. Get a load of the perfumed air."

Playing along, Archie sniffed. "Yeah, that sickly, floral smell gives it away."

Steele clicked off the TV. "Pull up a chair, Hasofer." He sounded almost cordial.

Archie rolled a chair over to the side of the bed, pleased that he'd broken through the top layer of Steele's prickly armor. He sat down and now had to look up at Steele's ugly mug.

"Are you from Down Under?" Steele's red-rimmed eyes looked down at him.

"Yeah. Tasmania."

"That fits. You remind me of a Tasmanian Devil." He cackled.

Archie grinned. "Ugly as a pig's bum, you mean?"

"Ha! Join the club, mate." Steele showed off his repulsive teeth. "State your business."

"I'm working on finding McCoy and your masterpieces," Archie said. "Your input—"

"Forget it," Steele said. "I didn't report any stolen paintings."

Archie cocked his head. "Why not?"

"I have my reasons," he said. "I can get along fine with Nick's copies. They look the same as the original ones anyway."

Bullshit, Archie thought. He didn't believe in Steele's sudden Zen-like acceptance of the fakes. The old crook didn't want the police to find the genuine paintings because they were probably stolen. Steele likely had his own private hunt for the masterpieces underway. He could also arrange to sell the copies as originals to some greedy collector and make big money off McCoy's brilliant fakes.

"What about McCoy? Don't you want him caught and strung up?"

Steele chuckled. "I'd rather deliver the punishment."

"Any idea where he might be?"

"Nope." Steele reached for the water pitcher on the rolling table projecting over the bed. His face reddened as he tried to lift it.

Archie stood. "I'll do that, mate." As he poured water into the glass on the rolling bed stand, he caught a whiff of Steele's sour breath. "Did you ever suspect what McCoy was up to?" He sat back down.

"Nah." Steele swallowed some water and burped. "He cast a spell, I reckon. Alchemy."

"Con artistry," Archie said. "Wouldn't you like to deep-six the bastard?"

Steele groaned and clapped his hand over his heart, wincing in pain. "Yeah, sure, I want to gouge his eyes out. Trouble is, I also want the fucker back. Got nobody smart to talk to now, nobody with any class or taste. He was like a good son to me." Steele closed his eyes, his pasty bald head sinking into the pillow, his face collapsed like a death mask.

Archie almost felt sorry for the lonely old crook, but the cunning toad was likely playing him. "Why do you suppose McCoy went to so much trouble to bust your balls? He could have just nicked the paintings."

"He owes me, I expect," Steele said. "I've done a lot of bad shit in my life. I've even played the same trick on collectors that Nick played on me. It's fate—an eye for an eye, a fake for a fake." He cackled as though accepting of his just desserts.

Archie didn't buy the act. "Mr. Steele, Nick screwed you in every way that counts. He stole your masterpieces and your beautiful wife. He betrayed your trust. It's enough to make a bloke crazy and blind with rage. You'd hardly be the first chap to strike out at a cheating wife."

"Nice try, Hasofer, but you won't sweet talk me into a confession. I was seriously injured and had to go to the emergency room that evening. So, I've got a medically documented alibi."

A bitten willy. Archie squelched the guffaw rising from his belly. "What do you think happened to your wife?"

"Raquel was a raging lush. So, it's no surprise that she got drunk and fell."

"We've got the medical examiner saying she was raped, beaten, and possibly shoved down the stairs. Let's suppose that's correct. Who would you suspect?"

"Loverboy, of course. Raquel pissed off Nick—she was good at that—and he didn't want to share the spoils. Can't blame him."

"What about Simon? He has no alibi."

"Simon wouldn't have the balls."

"Suppose he did, Mr. Steele; would you want him punished?"

Steele let his bald head sink deeper into the propped pillow and closed his eyes, clearly pained by this subject. Archie, his team, and the sheriff's boys were all waiting impatiently for the DNA report from the semen found in Raquel's rectum and vagina. That should settle which one of the three prime suspects raped her and then, most likely, killed her.

Steele's eyes opened. "Simon's not much, but he's all I've got. I take care of my own."

"I hear you." Archie believed his statement. "That's why you bailed him out of jail, and now he's flown the coop. Do you know where he went?"

"Nope."

"Is he going after McCoy?"

Steele didn't respond and closed his eyes again. He lay still, looking shriveled. Archie had his fill of the old vulture, but he'd make one more attempt to shake the truth out of him.

"Rumors in the Sheriff's Department say that the deaths of your previous wife and son, Samuel, were not an accident." Archie paused. "You got any such suspicions?"

"Fuck off," Steele rasped. "I've had enough of your rutting around like a marsupial pig."

"Just a few more thoughts," Archie said. "You may be a man of steel, but that's not your real name, is it? Dixon Steele sounded stagey to me. Then I remembered that grand old noir movie from the 1950s—*In a Lonely Place.* You took the name of the anti-hero played by Humphrey Bogart." Steele lay still with his eyes closed. "I bet his story spoke to you, didn't it? In that story, the Dixon Steele character was lonely, violent, and suspected of murder."

Steele's eyes flashed open, hot spots of rage, his face turning a muddy puce. "Get the fuck out of here!"

"Your parents were Russian immigrants, and your actual name is Boris Pavlishchev. Your surname means *small*. I understand why you'd want to get rid of that name."

"Get out, or I'm calling security."

"I am security," Archie said. "Maybe it's time folks knew who you are. That Dixon Steele is Boris Pavlishchev, a criminal from a Brooklyn slum, who was arrested for theft, assault, and rape in his youth. I'll pass on your real profile to the sheriff and the world unless you tell me more of the truth about you, Simon, and your accident-prone family."

A discreet knock on the door, then a smiling nurse walked in. "Detective Hasofer, I am sorry to intrude, but Mr. Steele must rest now."

Archie nodded at the nurse and stood. "Better rest up, Mr. Small. I'll be back."

—

Alone in the descending elevator, Archie glanced at his blurry reflection in the polished brass doors. He called Eddie in London, who answered immediately.

"Hey, boss," Archie said, describing his interview with Dixon Steele and impressing Eddie with his exposure of Steele's fictional name.

"Priceless." Eddie chuckled. "Did you get anything useful out of him?"

"Not much. Steele denied killing Raquel and accused McCoy. He wants his golden boy back, and he wants to gouge his eyes out. Said he didn't know where he might have gone."

"McCoy is here," Eddie said. "I spotted him at the National Gallery with Kate. Then I lost him. Luckily, Flynn and Desi picked them up coming out of a side exit and followed them to a pub. I tailed McCoy from the pub and lost him in Harrods. Same old vanishing act. But thanks to Flynn and Desi, we've got Kate."

"Great work, boss." Archie scratched his crotch.

"Did you get anything out of Steele on Simon?"

"No," Archie said, "but I suspect after Simon got bail, he flew to London on Pop's private jet in pursuit of McCoy and the paintings."

"Sounds likely. If Simon's here, we'll find him," Eddie said. "I don't want that garbage stinking up my town. Steele has a house in Chelsea. He could be holing up there." Pause. "Did you get anywhere on the Nick-Jackson Chase connection?"

"Yeah, I tracked down a few more details. Chase was known as a predator and a slick con artist, described as handsome and probably gay. He picked up Nick selling copies and pastiches on the street, saw that his artwork was good enough to sell as originals, and made him his protégé and later his partner. I haven't been able to locate Chase. He appears to have dropped off the planet along with his gallery."

"Things probably got too hot, and he changed his name," Eddie said. "Maybe he opened a different gallery. Have you been able to find out anything about Nick before he hooked up with Chase when he was fourteen?"

"No. The problem is we don't know Nick's real surname or Chase's current name."

"Try checking if any art transport service in your area has sent crated paintings labeled as reproductions to a dealership or gallery in London. Start with the upscale places."

"Right, boss. One more thing. I chatted with Allegra Castlewhite, McCoy's intern. She's tried to reach McCoy on his mobile several times but hasn't gotten a response, and he hasn't contacted her. She was quite pissed about that. When I brought up Steele's stolen masterpieces and that McCoy was a suspect, she got a cagey look in her eyes. I knew she had the hots for McCoy, so I stoked her jealousy, hoping to make her squeal."

Eddie chuckled. "You're a natural."

Archie beamed. "I told her we knew he'd gone to London with his girlfriend. 'What girlfriend?' she screeched. Dr. Kate O'Dade, I told her. Allegra accused me of lying and said Nick would never go for a plain jane like her."

"Well done," Eddie said. "Anything else?"

"Yeah, when I asked what she knew about Steele's missing masterpieces, she said she suspected McCoy had stolen *The Open Window* and left it on Kate's doorstep. That possibility made no sense to her at the time, but now it did, given that Kate was 'his secret whore.' When the two of them met with Nick to evaluate the painting, he'd said it was an expert copy. Allegra was certain he'd lied, saying, 'If he stole one masterpiece, he nicked them all.'"

"Sounds a tad hysterical and vindictive," Eddie said. "Did you believe any of it?"

"Maybe part of it is true, but it was obvious that jealousy drove Allegra's accusations."

"Unrequited lust?"

Archie sighed. "Yeah. It wouldn't be a broken heart. That bitch doesn't have one."

CHAPTER 41

Will you walk into my parlor? said the spider to the fly.
—Mary Howitt—

Tuesday, October 23, London

"Chief Inspector Cromwell will meet with you soon," Flynn said, ushering Kate into a posh, slate-blue Bentley. Kate glared at him as he gave her hand a warm squeeze and shut the door. The rain started up again, beating down on the car's large skylight and streamlined windows. Still rattled, Kate appreciated the cradling effect of her soft leather seat. A pleasing fragrance permeated the interior, not an old or new leather smell, but one that was creamy smooth and rich. The silver and black control panels looked like artwork. She glanced at the freckled young man sitting behind the sculpted-looking steering wheel. The lad wasn't handsome, but he had a winsome Huck Finn look. He gave her a shy smile and said his name was Dylan, Lord Cromwell's driver.

Lord? Kate was surprised. That explained the Bentley, which was hardly a typical cop's car. It fit the patrician Cromwell, who also didn't look like a regular cop.

"Where are we going?" she demanded as the elegant car purred into traffic.

"South to Angler's Mill, Lord Cromwell's fly-fishing retreat on the

River Test. Romsey is the village." Dylan pushed a button, and the door locks clicked.

Kate was irate. "This is crazy. Why would I be taken there? I don't fly fish, for example. But that's the least of it!"

"I don't know, Miss," Dylan said.

"Why did you lock the doors?"

"Uh, instructions. For your safety."

"For Christ's sake, I'm not going to jump out of a moving vehicle. Besides, I've agreed to meeting Cromwell. How far is it to this retreat?"

"Not far," he said.

"Jesus, Dylan, I want to know *exactly* how far."

"Okay. Forty-five minutes in this weather. A half hour if the rain stops."

She glanced at the water streaming down the windows, then rooted around for her phones in her daypack. She had to call Nick and let him know what was happening. Her hand couldn't find either phone. She took out everything. "Shit," she muttered. They weren't there. She couldn't have lost them. *Damn Flynn*. He must have snitched her phones. And her passport as well. After Dylan politely but firmly refused to lend her his phone even to call her son, Kate spent much of the slow progress in the driving rain nerve-wracked and futilely trying to extract more information from the monosyllabic driver. Worn out from her nerves and lack of success with Dylan, she could no longer avoid facing her reactions to Flynn.

She felt the pressure of tears building behind her eyes. *Why did he have to come barging back into her life?* Nine years she'd done without him and used her considerable powers of repression to forget him. Next to facing and solving her father's murder, leaving Flynn had been the hardest thing she'd ever done. Without Flynn's smarts and strength, she could not have faced the truth of her past. He was most certainly a better man than David, her estranged husband, but Sam had hated him. He'd blamed Flynn for keeping his parents apart, even though she was the one responsible. But when faithless David repeatedly promised to do anything, including therapy, to bring their family back together, she eventually yielded. For all his faults, David had been a good father, and Sam had adored him. Since she'd come from a painfully fractured family, she could not put Sam through the same kind of nightmare. And her love affair with Flynn began to erode. They could only spend time together when Sam was with his father. A future of living together was many years away. Now, nine years later, with Sam in college and David dead, they might have had a chance. But it was too late. Her closed fist of a heart had finally let in someone else, ironically another rakish rogue much like Flynn. She wondered if the stunning Desi Hawk was Flynn's latest love. *Probably a better fit than she had been*, Kate thought, with sharp twinges of sadness and regret.

It was almost dark and still pouring when they arrived at Angler's Mill. Kate could see a three-story plain brick structure with a sharply gabled front door and several gabled high windows at the edge of the steeply sloped roof. She expected the interior to be cold and dank, but the great room was warmly lit and dry. A fire blazed in the stone fireplace, its chimney soaring about fifteen feet to a magnificent open-beamed ceiling. Lord Cromwell rose from his seat in front of the fire and strode across the wide-planked floor toward her. He wore an old, bulky cardigan and smiled like an experienced host.

"Welcome to Angler's Mill, Dr. O'Dade," he said in his Basil Rathbone voice. "I trust you had a pleasant trip." He offered his hand.

Pleasant? What planet are you from? She gave his hand a firm shake. "The only pleasant part was the Bentley."

His deep laugh boomed in the cavernous space. "Would you like a drink and then some supper? Dylan is cooking us up a fresh rainbow trout from our river."

Thoughts of a drink fizzed in her mind. If she wanted to win against Cromwell—whatever winning might mean—Kate knew alcohol would dull her wits and loosen her tongue. The trouble was her tight, aching muscles screamed for release. A drink would make her less stiff and formal and allow her to appear more respectful and receptive. This self-important lord was probably addicted to the sound of his own resonant voice.

She accepted a glass of white burgundy.

Kate sat by the fire across from Cromwell, sipped her drink, and reined in powerful urges to demand, "What's your game?" She wanted to cut him down and watch him squirm. Sighing inwardly, she knew that would be stupid. The point was to save Nick and forge an agreement in his favor, not to alienate this adversary who held most of the cards. The fire crackled and popped in the silence between them. Would he try to lure her in with an upper-crust variant of charm? Or would he attempt to intimidate her with his Chief Inspector, Lord of the Manor arrogance? His pensive demeanor didn't fit either scenario. Kate shifted her gaze to the tall, striking oil painting on the wall behind Cromwell and catty-corner to the fireplace. From the vivid reds, oranges, and yellow hues, she guessed it was an abstract interpretation of floating down the River Test in autumn. She was about to ask about the artist when Cromwell interrupted her thoughts.

"I suspect you're wondering why I invited you here."

"Hijacked me, you mean. I believe you're hoping I will help you catch and arrest Nick McCoy, which will lead to recovering the stolen masterpieces."

"Close." Cromwell took a swallow of his scotch. "Can you see why your cooperation might be helpful to McCoy and, therefore, to you?"

"Not entirely," Kate said. "I think you would argue that if you were to catch him in a criminal act, you could arrest him and thereby save him from Dixon Steele's thugs or other crooks who want those paintings and his head. You might also argue that you'd be saving him from further harassment from your team."

"And the FBI," Cromwell said. "There's another point. If you convince him to turn himself in, things could work out more in his favor."

"How?"

"If McCoy returned those masterpieces and revealed the locations of his other forgeries, there's a good chance he would not be convicted. Wouldn't that be better than an escalation of his ghastly life of running from pursuit until he's out of steam, his mind, and money? Sooner or later, he will make a fatal mistake."

Kate's stomach clenched. His description spoke straight to her fears.

"Tell me, Dr. O'Dade, what would you do if Nick chose to stay on the run?"

Kate shifted in her seat and took a big swallow of wine. "I love Nick, but I have a son."

"Ah, yes. Never take a priceless son for granted," he said. "Aren't you supposed to be at Berkeley visiting him?"

"A lie, Inspector, as you well know. I led you right to Nick, didn't I?"

"You've been a big help, yes." He paused, a slight twinkle in his eyes. "One hopes that might continue."

She looked away from his probing gaze and stared at the crackling fire, then expanded her gaze to take in the impressive fireplace constructed of gorgeous river stones. She wanted to lose herself in the shapes and earth-tone colors. A clattering sound came from the kitchen behind the fireplace, and the smell of grilling fish wafted into the great room. Her gaze shifted to the wooden table, laid for dinner in front of a long window overlooking the river.

"I see the positive points of your proposal," Kate said, "but also the negatives. Even though the master forger Eric Hebborn confessed and avoided conviction, that didn't save him. He was murdered. In his book, he identified the collectors, curators, dealers, and auction houses he fooled and humiliated. Many believe one or more of his enraged, mortified victims murdered him."

"That's pure speculation," Cromwell said. "Eric Hebborn's murder has never been solved. Since he got involved with the Mafia, it's more likely he was murdered by them. If you cross the Mafia, you are dead. Hebborn was a monumental smartass and a braggart. Poor devil."

Nick could end up the same way, Kate knew. "Even if I thought Nick's turning himself in was the best way to go, I could not get him to agree."

Cromwell's eyes narrowed. "There are ways, Dr. O'Dade."

She ignored the implicit threat, caught up in worrying that Nick would not just wait around for her and fret. Instead, he'd take some kind of risky action, like going after Simon. "Before we go any further," she said. "I'd like to call Nick."

Cromwell regarded her soberly. "Forgive me, Dr. O'Dade, but I cannot agree to a call."

"Why not?"

"Two reasons. One, I want you to discuss this matter as objectively as possible. Hearing McCoy's voice might stir up emotions that will not help your cause or mine. And two, if he stays worried and suspicious about you, he'll be more inclined to cooperate."

You bastard. "What about letting me call my son. I'm worried about him."

Cromwell sighed. "No calls tonight. Sorry."

"How can you be so heartless?"

Pain flashed in his eyes. "I'm doing my job, which is often not about pleasing people."

Kate calmed her impotent fury with a swallow of wine. She would find another way to reach Cromwell or find a phone in this house. Then she glanced at the stunning painting she'd noticed earlier, losing herself in the pulsating colors.

"That painting is quite wonderful," she said. "Who's the artist?"

Cromwell's long silence amplified the spitting fire.

"My son, Rafe, painted it. He was once a very talented artist."

"Yes, indeed," Kate said. "What does your talented son do now?"

"Nothing," he said in a deadened tone. "He died a year ago in a road accident."

Cromwell's terrible loss and ravaged face touched Kate's heart. She was surprised at this highly personal admission and show of emotion. It seemed out of character for the reserved, upper-class Cromwell.

Dylan's voice called out, "Trout ready in ten minutes."

Kate stood and asked to use the bathroom. Cromwell led her up a narrow staircase. She stumbled a couple of times, the steps spaced higher than average. Then down a murkily lit hall—the old boards creaking under the worn Turkish runner—he ushered her into a charming guest room and gestured toward the door to the bathroom.

"It will be late, dark, and still pouring rain by the time we finish dinner," Cromwell said. "I think it best if we put off further negotiations until the morning when we are both rested. I invite you to spend the night. This is a comfortable room."

Kate stared at Cromwell, feeling she was stepping further into the pages of a British gothic novel. "If I'd rather not stay here, would you let me leave?" she asked.

"Of course. Dylan will take you back to London tonight, but driving will be slow and hazardous. Reports say the storm will get much worse." He regarded Kate with a weary expression. "Do you want to give up on negotiating an agreement that could benefit McCoy?"

Kate did not want to forgo the chance of influencing Cromwell on Nick's behalf. She had confidence in her powers of persuasion, perhaps too much confidence. She was impressed with how smartly he'd cajoled her into accepting his conditions while at the same time leading her to think she was in charge.

"I accept your invitation, Inspector. If I'm to be your houseguest, do call me Kate."

"And I am Eddie, your delighted host." He gave her a slight bow.

"*Enchantée, Monsieur Le Comte*," Kate said prettily, delighted to see Eddie taken aback.

"*Touché, Madam.* So, you saw through my act?"

"No, Nick did. I thought your act was flawless."

He smiled. "Please, no worries. Dylan will drive you back to London tomorrow."

Hearing his footsteps go down the stairs, Kate quickly relieved herself in the small, modernized bathroom. Then she began a quick, furtive search of the other rooms, hoping to find a telephone or something she could use to get the upper hand with Cromwell.

The spacious, open-beamed room at the end of the hall was obviously the master suite. High-quality paintings, prints, and drawings covered the walls. She quickly scanned the surfaces of the two bed stands. No landline or mobile was on either one. She promptly moved to the adjoining small office and, again, found no phones on the desktop. One of the two displayed photographs showed a smiling Eddie with his arm around a blond, good-looking young man. His talented son, Rafe? Each held up the prize catch of a plump, spotted trout, the Test flowing behind them. The second picture showed Eddie with his arm around a pale, refined-looking woman who was probably his wife. Then she saw the file on the left side of the desk labeled "N.M. articles/photos." N.M.—Nick McCoy. She suspected this was left here intentionally and that Cromwell would guess she'd search his room.

Her fingers stiff with tension, she opened the file, flipped through a few pages of notes, and stopped at an old, faded photo taken in front of the National Gallery. Nick appeared as a skinny, scruffy teenager. With his head turned so only a streak of his facial burn scars showed, he was eagerly showing a small painting to a smartly dressed gent, whose long-fingered hand grasped the boy's bony shoulder. The man's refined face, with its seductive smile, gave Kate the chills. He looked predatory.

Kate glanced at her watch. *Hurry.* Eddie would come looking for her at any minute.

She quickly scanned a news article about Nick winning the Drawing Prize at the Royal Academy of Arts. There was a grainy photo of him as a handsome young man holding up a plaque. Another photo caught her eye. It was taken at The Rogues in 1999. Kate recognized Nick's splendid copy of Manet's *A Bar at the Folies Bergère*. A twenty-year-old Nick stood in front of the bar and the painting, his arms around a dark-haired beauty, the pair gazing lustfully at each other. *Who was that girl?* The young woman reminded her of Raquel, clearly Nick's preferred type. Sickened, eyes stinging, she closed the file. How could she have forgotten that con artist Nick had also deceived her?

Fury at Eddie heated her face. Had the wily inspector deliberately left out this file for her to see—possibly to expose her foolish loyalty to a womanizing con man? Another unwelcome thought had lodged in her brain. Cromwell hadn't needed to tell her about his dead son. Had the manipulative bastard shared this tragedy simply to evoke her sympathy to soften her up for tomorrow's kill?

CHAPTER 42

Survival . . . is an infinite capacity for suspicion.
—John le Carré—

Tuesday Afternoon, October 23

Nick took his time, employing his usual tactics to evade any possible tail. He'd told Kate that he would pick up supplies and some new clothes before going to the Gull's Nest. He also did not mention his plan to check out Steele's house in Chelsea in case Simon might be there.

First, he took a taxi to Harrods department store on Brompton Road in the Knightsbridge area. After wandering around for a while to assure himself that he'd lost any tail, he shopped for new clothes in the men's section. He chose a classic charcoal trench coat, a black fedora, jeans, and a pair of Doc Martens. He also purchased a tweed flat cap and stashed his old hoodie, jeans, and trainers in a new backpack.

On his way out of the store, he paused to admire the natty new version of himself in various mirrors, checking for a possible tail behind him. Exiting from the back entrance, he took a taxi to King's Road in the historic district of Chelsea. He had the driver drop him a couple of blocks from Steele's London retreat, a remodeled old chapel that Steele liked to say was his blasphemous "Fuck You" to God. A gangster now owned this former house of worship and stored his growing stash of art booty in a large, temperature-controlled vault in the basement. If

Simon wasn't here, Nick thought this would be an excellent place to temporarily store Steele's masterpieces. The paintings were unsafe with Charles Hamilton, formerly his old partner, known as Jackson Chase. Nick smiled at the thought of Steele's reaction were he to learn of this additional dirty trick.

The rain had calmed to a drizzle as Nick walked briskly past Steele's twenty-million-dollar pile. Recalling the former chapel, Nick saw that Steele's architect had smartly retained St. Mark's circular bell tower structure, the gothic stonework, arched stained-glass windows, and a brick-walled garden. Keeping his eyes peeled for signs of occupancy, Nick noticed lights in a few stained-glass windows. Someone could be living there, and there was no way to see if any cars occupied the separate garage. Nick would have to wait until dark to do a closer and more thorough inspection. Across the street was The World's End Distillery, an ideal place to take shelter and keep watch on Steele's unholy retreat.

Once across the street, Nick stood in front of the pub—senses on full alert—scanning for a tail. Although he spotted no suspicious vehicle or person, he sensed an unseen, tireless tail out there, circling closer and closer.

The World's End Distillery used to be a nondescript pub, but now it was a cozy bar with a thirties-style dining space. It was filling up with well-dressed types like him. Plain wooden tables dotted the checkerboard floor, and Nick zeroed in on one next to a tall window with a bird's-eye view of Steele's chapel. He scanned the walls dotted with WWII paraphernalia, his gaze landing on the sculpted head of a unicorn on the wall behind the bar. Its glassy eyes were staring straight at him as if the mythic creature was another silent stalker. He looked at his watch. It was 5:20 p.m. and would start to get dark at about six. He decided to wait until 7 p.m. to leave. He ordered a Guinness stout and fish and chips from the disapproving, purse-lipped waiter. People came here for the world-famous, slow-cooked ox tongue and steak tartare, not ordinary pub grub.

Nick called Kate on her burner phone. She should be at the Gull's Nest by now and might be worried. No pick-up. He checked his messages but nothing from her. He called her iPhone but got no answer. He left her a voicemail, "Call me ASAP," and wondered what her lack of response meant. Nothing good, he figured. His empty belly started aching.

The light was fast fading from the misty gloom outside. He'd finished his hearty meal and ordered a second Guinness, knowing this was a bad idea. The minutes crawled. He called Kate's cells again but got no responses. Then he called his iPhone, which was connected to a charger that he'd left hidden in the wall of his San Diego loft. He checked it daily in case he'd received any important messages. Nick listened to another insistent message from Allegra. This time she demanded that he return her call, or she would contact the authorities. Christ, would he never be rid of that parasite?

He stared out the window at the dripping London plane trees across the street. *Why didn't Kate answer?* Had she forgotten the hotel's name or address or possibly lost her mobile storing the information? In that case, she'd find a phone and call him. If she'd decided to shop for clothes or something else, that wouldn't have stopped her from answering or calling back. His gut churned as the most likely explanations crept into his mind. She could have been in a bad accident or possibly kidnapped, either by Cromwell's team or Steele's thugs, though he doubted Dixon knew about his relationship with Kate. If someone had snatched her, he expected to hear from her captors soon.

It seemed dark enough now for Nick to examine Steele's unholy chapel. He'd detected no activity there from where he sat. He paid for his meal, went to the loo, changed from the trench coat into the black, hooded anorak and flat cap, and then packed the coat and fedora into his backpack. As he strolled across the street, he noticed the same subdued colored lights shining through the lower-level stained-glass windows. Shielded by large shrubs and trees, he moved stealthily around the high circular wall surrounding the chapel's garden. Hoisting himself over the back wall, Nick crept soundlessly around the structure. He could see through none of the unopenable stained-glass or opaque-glass windows as wire mesh protected all of them. The place was a sealed vault, the interior concealed from curious eyes. A sophisticated alarm system likely protected this fortress, but he was unable to see any outdoor cameras. Fortunately, he hadn't set off anything yet, and the entry door was at the back of the structure, invisible from the street.

He rang the bell, then stepped behind a potted tree. Soon, a muscular guard holding a revolver stepped onto the stone porch. Using his martial arts training, Nick moved quickly and chopped the guard's wrist. He smashed the heel of his hand under the bloke's bulbous nose, blood spurting from his nostrils. Then Nick knocked him out with a paralyzing vagus strike. The guard fell onto the stone entry deck, and Nick picked up the revolver and stuck it into the back of his jeans. He dragged the guard's body behind a clump of bushes, zip-tied his hands behind his back, and gagged him with his neckerchief. Then he waited behind the bushes to see if anyone else came to the open door.

After a few minutes of silence and no voices or footsteps, he moved stealthily to the doorway, stopped to one side, and listened. No sounds. Three minutes later, he slipped through the open door and closed it quietly. He stood in the white marble foyer, head cocked, ears pricked and heard no signs of life. He moved cautiously into a dramatic, circular reception room supported by arches and white pillars. As he stepped into the room, Nick heard a slight rustling sound to his left.

"Welcome, asshole." Simon Steele stepped out from behind a pillar, a revolver pointed at his chest. "I've been expecting you."

CHAPTER 43

Up a lazy river, how happy you can be,
Up a lazy river with me.

—Hoagy Carmichael—

Wednesday, October 24

At the breakfast table, Kate drank Dylan's strong coffee, never more in need of caffeinated courage and sharp wits. After persuading her twitchy body that she was safe in this ancient, creaking mill, she'd managed a restless sleep, fraught with nightmares of being trapped in a dark attic. Her unsettled stomach growled, and the unfamiliar, rustic kitchen made her feel homesick, as did Dylan's cheerful chatter about what a grand, sunny day it would be. She predicted precious little sunshine and a godawful day of mind games with a cunning master. Before she could consider her first move, Eddie strode into the kitchen, greeted her cheerily, and sat down.

"This would be a fine morning to go canoeing, don't you think?" He gave her a cheerful smile as though they were on a relaxing holiday trip.

"Canoeing?" Had she heard him correctly?

"Have you ever canoed before?" Eddie took a sip of coffee.

"Years ago, when my husband and I used to go camping."

"Thought you might like to take a short trip down the river." Eddie glanced out the window overlooking the Test. "A clear day is predicted, and the foliage is gorgeous this time of year. We can talk during the ride." Eddie bit into a scone. "Perhaps the river and scenery will ease the difficulty of our subject matter. I find canoeing on the Test quite salutary."

How quaint, Kate thought, now on full alert—*a sightseeing outing to entertain his adversary.* Under normal circumstances, she would love to see the river, but anything Cromwell suggested made her suspicious. What lay behind this generous host's plan? Was this a means of currying favor to win her over to his side?

"Let's just talk on the drive back to London," Kate suggested.

"I can't have Dylan hearing our conversation," Cromwell replied.

"Why don't you drive?" Kate asked. "Then we'll be alone."

"At your peril, my dear. I'm practically blind in one eye. It's called a lazy eye." He pointed to his right eye. "I have almost zero depth perception. I must be alone, without distractions, to risk driving on motorways. Even so, there's still the chance of a bloody smash-up." He regarded her with a regretful expression.

Thwarted again, Kate felt a rush of heat on her cheeks. He was toying with her. She doubted his lazy eye. If her husband hadn't had the same deficit, Cromwell's claim would've been harder to swallow. She'd never felt safe with David's driving and knew she couldn't manage the Bentley on the wrong side of the street. Not that Eddie would have permitted it.

"If you prefer, we can always sit right here and talk," he offered smoothly.

The sly bastard was appearing to give her a choice, but it was an unpalatable one. The thought of sitting face-to-face with Eddie for any length of time made her squirm. His good probing eye would be reading her every expression, making her feel at once transparent and suffocated—as she did right now. She wouldn't lose much by not seeing his typically unreadable face. His expressive voice was more likely to give away his emotions, and she couldn't see any real risks on a canoe. He'd gain nothing—and lose a potential ally—if he were to drown her in a convenient river accident. Also, it was in her interest to lull him into believing she was cooperating.

"Canoeing it is," Kate said, "but I don't do rapids."

Eddie laughed. "No worries, the River Test has no rapids. It's the smoothest, gentlest chalk stream in England."

His claim was hardly reassuring.

—

Eddie squatted on the dock and gripped the gunnels of his canoe at the stern. He held the boat steady as Kate bent low and stepped toward the bow, paddle in hand. Wearing a borrowed red life jacket and a fly-fishing truck cap like his, she looked confident and steady, seating herself without tipping the boat. Eddie, experienced and heavier, sat on the stern bench, taking the steering position. He told Dylan to pick them up downstream in about an hour at the Church of St. Boniface in Nursling. He would call ten minutes before they'd arrive. Dylan then untethered the boat from the dock, gave it a shove, and wished them a grand trip.

"Paddle on the left," Eddie said to Kate as he began paddling on the right. As they paddled in synchrony, the boat glided forward. Now in the power seat, which had been his aim for this crucial interaction, Eddie determined the course and strokes. In the bow, Kate had control of the speed of paddling, but she was nicely handicapped, being out of practice and a stranger to the river. From years of fly fishing and canoeing, Eddie knew the Test's moods, quirks, and many faces. Its healing waters had the power to ease, if not dispel, his darkest moods.

"Looks like no chance of rain." Kate glanced up at the clear, blue sky.

"Right, according to the forecast," Eddie said, "but this is England. British rain likes to catch us by surprise."

The Test was swollen, the current faster than usual from the recent heavy rains. These signs meant the river might be dangerous close to the shores. The overflow could uproot trees, causing a tangle of submerged roots and branches. If they ran into a half-hidden branch, staying afloat could be challenging. He should keep them moving in the center of the river to avoid an accident, especially when paddling around bends. Whether he took the necessary care would, of course, depend on Kate's responses.

They were gliding through a straight, narrow section of the river, overhung with trees, blazing in vivid shades of red, orange, and gold. Eddie could see Kate's body relax, her guard lowered as she took in the beauty of the scenery. The clear water reflected the dancing leaves and branches like a mirror, creating a magical tunnel of shimmering water and color. Every so often, Eddie spotted ripples in the water, indicating the movement of a trout. Around a bend, the river widened, and through a broad opening in the trees, he pointed out Broadlands, the famous Palladian-style manor, the home of the Earl and Countess Mountbatten.

"Queen Elizabeth and Prince Philip spent their honeymoon here," Eddie said in the genial tone of a good guide, "so did Prince Charles and Princess Diana."

"The mansion looks rather stiff and formal for this charming storybook of a river."

"Royalty and the upper class are supposed to be stiff and formal, much to my regret," he said.

They glided in silence, the only sounds from their paddles dipping rhythmically in the water and the trilling calls of myriad birds. Ahead, a turquoise and orange kingfisher dove for a minnow, and a pair of white swans floated toward them as if they were greeting them.

"Eddie." Kate's sudden, sharp tone took him by surprise. "Please lend me your phone."

Bollocks, this nonsense again. "Sorry, my dear, but I can't permit a call to Nick."

"Why not? What do you accomplish by refusing?"

Eddie sighed. "As you should know, people don't change their stripes unless forced. Intolerable fear, serious loss, failure, or illness can do it, or the need to protect or save someone you love. I believe the only way Nick might give himself up is to protect you."

"That's ridiculous, and you know it. Nick is too smart to fall for a trap like that. What you don't seem to understand is that Nick wants to change his stripes. He came to therapy for the purpose of giving up forging."

"I suppose you think he's done that."

"Yes, I do, and I have excellent bullshit detectors." Her lie sounded convincing.

"I'm sure you did an admirable job, Kate, but Nick shows no signs of becoming a model citizen. Once a con, always a con; that's my experience. Need I remind you, he just pulled off a diabolically clever scam."

"The Dixon Steele scam was about revenge, not forging or stealing to make a fortune," Kate asserted. "If you'd done your job properly and bothered to uncover Nick's childhood history, you'd know that Steele killed Nick's entire family and almost destroyed him in a major fire that burned down his home."

Eddie knew about the fire from Archie, but Steele's critical role was news. She'd succeeded in getting under his skin, and he replied, testily, "Even if revenge was one motive, the facts are that McCoy has stolen the masterpieces, hidden them, and appears to be keeping the lot for his pleasure or to sell."

"The fact is you are a rigid, narrow-minded policeman who can only see people in simplistic terms. You lack insight, Eddie. Your armchair psychology is not only childish but blatantly wrong." Kate dug in her paddle, destabilizing the boat.

"J-stroke, Kate," Cromwell barked, maddened by her insult. "Whether I'm wrong or right doesn't change the fact that my priority is to find those paintings. Do you know where Nick hid them?"

"No, and he's not likely to tell me."

"I believe there is a way you can find out," Eddie said.

"Possibly," Kate said. "But I'm not going to help you unless you help me."

She sounded strong and in charge, but Eddie noticed the jerkiness of her paddling and her stiff limbs. She was off-balance, perhaps not as confident of her position as she pretended. He needed to smash her illusions about Nick. He felt the breeze picking up, a chill in the air. He glanced behind him at the sky darkening to the North. Rain might be coming. Time to step up the pressure.

CHAPTER 44

*Anyone who sees and paints a sky green and
the fields blue ought to be sterilized.*

—ADOLF HITLER—

Wednesday Night, October 24

"Fast, ruthless work, Nikko," Simon said. "Hardly what you'd expect from an art conservator. Why are you here—to shoot the shit with your new girlfriend or me?"

Nick froze. Blood thrummed in his ears. "What the hell are you talking about?"

"Kate, of course." He cocked his head. "Dr. Kate O'Dade."

Nick managed to show no hint of his surprise, wondering how Simon knew Kate or knew that she was with him in London. He swallowed the bile coming up into his throat. "You're full of it, Simon. You don't even know this doctor."

"Now I do." Simon giggled. "She's quite a dish."

"You're bluffing."

"Want to know what she was wearing before we stripped her?"

Nick just glared at him, refusing to take his bait.

Simon sighed. "She wore a navy rain poncho. A black bucket hat, gray slacks, and gray and black Nike's. Want to hear about her underwear?"

"Shut the fuck up." How could he know what she was wearing? Nick's insides were in free fall.

"She's quite cute, especially in her birthday suit." Simon leered as though picturing her naked body. "She won't be so cute after we have a little fun with her. Picture it, Nikko."

Nick blocked the image of that horror. "Prove you have her. Let me see her."

"Not until we do a little business."

Nick guessed what was coming. "What do you want, Simon?"

"What do you think, smartass? The stolen masterpieces plus your heartfelt apology."

"You'll get nothing from me until I can see Kate or speak with her."

"Sorry, can't do either. Kate is out cold." His lips twitched a pseudo smile. "Had to dope her up. She's a wildcat, you know."

"Touch her, and I'll kill you." Nick lunged toward Simon, who quickly stepped back. Then a Slavic-looking brute stepped out from behind an adjacent pillar, his tattooed arms bulging with muscles. His pumpkin head, deep set, cold stone eyes, and minimal chin reminded Nick of Vladimir Putin.

"Igor," Simon said, "disarm the intruder and tie his hands. For fuck's sake, don't underestimate him."

Smelling as vile as he looked, Igor grabbed Nick's backpack, stripped off his anorak containing his phone, lock-picking tools, and wallet, then effectively frisked him. After removing Nick's pocketed Swiss Army knife and Klaus's revolver that was tucked into the waistband of his jeans, Igor quickly zip-tied his hands behind his back.

Nick still doubted that Simon had snatched Kate. *How had he gotten all the necessary information?* Nick started digging, keeping a neutral tone. "How did you know Kate and I were together in London?"

"Dad's a wreck, but he's still got his marbles," Simon said. "He guessed you'd come to London, and when you found out I'd jumped bail, you'd look for me here. Your loyal intern, Allegra, spilled the beans about you and Kate. She heard from a police detective that you and your girlfriend were in London."

"Allegra?" Fear fogged up his mind. "How do you even know her?"

"Pops and I met her briefly at the gala. She's the tart who wore that trashy red dress, remember? Now that chick's a piece of work. You shouldn't have pissed her off, Nikko. She told on you to Dad. He passed the info on to me."

Nick knew Allegra was vengeful and full of spite. He should have foreseen she would find a way to retaliate. "How did you find Kate here?"

"Assuming you weren't a cheapskate, we first checked the upscale hotels and found her registered at the Leonardo. My boys followed her, hoping she'd lead us to you. And sure enough, she did. We snatched her in front of the Ritz."

Nick was dying inside. The snake could be telling the truth for a change. His big mistake was assuming that neither the Steeles nor Allegra knew of his relationship with Kate.

"Where is she, Simon?"

"You'll find out when I get what I want." Simon crossed his arms. "Ready to talk?"

"Fuck you." After finding out where Nick hid the masterpieces, he knew Simon would eliminate them both. Nick stiffened his spine, preparing to withstand their torture.

Igor in the rear, Simon ushered Nick across the circular room furnished with modern Italian couches and chairs in grays and slate colors. None of the lit-up stained-glass windows depicted religious figures. Nick took note of the stained-glass rendering of Botticelli's *Birth of Venus* seductively posed in a giant clam shell and the window showing Caravaggio's erotic *Mary Magdalen in Ecstasy*. Steele's need to mock religion never flagged.

Simon led them down a short circular staircase to a dining area adjacent to a space-age kitchen. Nick glanced up at the stairs leading to a horseshoe landing with an Alexander Calder mobile hanging down through the center from the high ceiling above. They went down more stairs to another level. Every room had windows, but there seemed to be no pane of clear glass in the whole place. No one could see in, but those inside could not see out. Nick felt imprisoned in a claustrophobic, vault-like bell tower.

The fifth level was the basement, with a lap pool and exercise equipment. Crossing this space, Simon stopped in front of a door. He unlocked and opened it, ordering Igor to go wake up Klaus and drag him down here. Nick quickly stepped inside and had the impression of moving deeper into a dungeon where he feared he would find Kate strapped naked on a rack and the walls fitted out with torture equipment.

In the room's low light, Nick saw no sign of Kate or torture devices. He could make out a large, rectangular space furnished in part like an ordinary living room. A long couch ran along the right wall, facing an oblong glass coffee table flanked by two chairs. Over the sofa hung a well-lit Constable landscape. Across the room was a brick fireplace warming the dank, refrigerated air with a roaring blaze. Nick instantly recognized the well-lit paintings hanging on either side of the fireplace. They were the five never-recovered masterpieces stolen from the Paris Museum of Modern Art in 2010. The joyous *Pastoral* by Matisse was in this group, as well as a Cubist Picasso, a Braque landscape, a Léger still life, and a Modigliani portrait. The estimated total value of the works at the time of the theft was a hundred million euros. They were worth much more than that today. Supported on pedestals in the corners were an attenuated Giacometti sculpture and Brâncuși's elegant, abstract *Bird in Space,* carved from white marble.

At the opposite end of the room were two heavy wooden doors. He suspected one led to the storage vault containing Steele's overflow of stolen art. The numerous works likely stored in this vault-like mansion reminded Nick of the Nazis stealing and hiding great quantities of looted art in dwellings and museums all over Europe. The masterpieces hanging in this room would have fallen into the category that the Nazis denounced as Degenerate Art, which included all they considered modern art. Nick thought of the rapacious Nazi collector Hermann

Göring, who stole and hoarded any art that was considered valuable, degenerate or not. He had hated Matisse's wildly colored *Pastoral,* with its orange and blue trunked trees and purple sky, but he understood its value to "inferior races." The egocentric, bombastic, greedy Göring reminded Nick of Dixon Steele, who was also given to self-indulgence and mercurial mood swings. A side glance at psycho Simon gave Nick a deathly chill as he sized him up to be the twenty-first-century version of a sadistic Hitler-Steele youth.

Shifting his attention to the other door, Nick noticed it was open a crack. Kate might be tied up in that room. He hurried across the windowless gallery and shoulder-shoved his way into an empty, black marble bathroom with gold fixtures. Enraged, Nick strode toward Simon, straining to free his hands from the zip ties.

He glared at the grinning psycho. "What have you done with her, Simon?"

Igor and a cleaned-up Klaus lumbered into his prison with the stolen masterpieces.

Simon dropped his sneering tone and said, "By the way, Pops guessed your real identity and why you fucked him over. He asked me to tell you he didn't intend for your father, you, or your family to die in that fire. He just wanted to scare your dad into keeping his mouth shut about the commissioned copies. Your father was supposed to be out of his shop when the fire started. The hired dumb fucks bungled, and the fire got out of control."

Nick wanted Steele to eventually discover that someone had stolen his favorite masterpieces and substituted forgeries and that the culprit had to be Nick. Steele was no fool.

"I appreciate the message." Nick masked his cynical disbelief in Steele's "confession." He supposed it could be partially true. Maybe Steele hadn't *intended* a mass murder, but he'd chosen to hire dopes and knew that fire would spread rapidly in a shop full of accelerants. What was Steele's point in spinning this yarn? To diminish Nick's hatred and fury, soften him up enough so that he'd give back the paintings? Dixon couldn't be that naïve.

Simon cleared his throat. "Now, will you tell me where you hid Pop's masterpieces?"

"Doesn't the greedy bastard have enough priceless booty?"

"Ha! You should know better than that, Nikko. You stole his favorites. You made a fool of him. Pops never forgets or forgives. And he never has enough."

Like you, Nick thought. "Tell me, Simon, now that I'm in your power, did he kill Raquel, or was it you?"

Simon's eyes glittered. "Guess."

"My money is on you," Nick said.

Simon let out a high-pitched laugh. "I had a lot of fun with her first. What a great piece of ass." He glanced at his musclemen. "Igor, Klaus, do your job."

"A pleasure." Klaus backhanded Nick across the face, and Igor hooked his muscular arm around Nick's throat while Klaus punched him in the belly and jaw. Then Igor loosened his armlock and threw Nick on the floor. In the process, Nick's tweed flat cap fell off, exposing his cap of gray hair. Both goons then began brutally kicking him all over his body. After multiple blows, Nick finally grunted in pain.

"Music to my ears," Simon said. "What's with the gray hair? You look like hell. Got anything to say, old man?"

"Nah," Nick said.

"Have a little rest and think about what's to come. First, we'll have our way with Kate, followed by smashing your fingers one by one. If you don't talk, we'll slowly feed you piece by piece to the fire, then warm ourselves while watching you snap, crackle, and pop." He snickered. "Think about the flames, Nikko. Remember the searing pain and the smell of burning flesh."

Nick passed out to the sound of the fire popping like a fusillade of gunshots.

CHAPTER 45

You can't argue with a river.
— DEAN ACHESON —

Thursday Morning, October 25

Kate felt Eddie's penetrating gaze boring into the back of her head, probing for cracks in her loyalty to Nick. She couldn't be certain of Nick's plans, but she believed he would return the paintings to the proper owners and give back the Picasso to Raquel's family. While she'd won points at countering Eddie's positions, she hadn't convinced him of Nick's worthiness.

A fly fisherman waved to them from the left bank, his other hand holding up a gleaming rainbow trout. Distracted, Kate momentarily lost her concentration, disrupting the rhythm. Out of sync with Eddie's strokes, the canoe wobbled and started to turn.

"Pay attention." Eddie's command felt like a slap.

Fuck you. The gloves were off. She straightened the canoe, realizing her lesser skills and lack of practice disadvantaged her and made her reliant on Eddie. No wonder the wily inspector chose canoeing. She should have foreseen the unequal setup.

"You know, Kate," Eddie said, "I believe Nick might well reveal the location of those masterpieces if he thought your welfare was at stake."

Kate squeezed her paddle, imagining it was Eddie's neck. "That sounds like a threat."

A low chuckle. "If you don't do what I say, it's not exactly torture I have in mind. But I can have you arrested for a crime, actually more than one."

"What crime?"

"Besides aiding and abetting a known criminal, you have one of the most valuable stolen masterpieces—*The Open Window*."

Kate was taken aback. "How do you know I have that painting?"

"One of your so-called friends told us you have it and that it probably came from Nick."

"You're referring to that spiteful bitch Allegra."

"Right, her information plus your involvement with McCoy is enough for us to obtain a search warrant. What will we find, Kate?"

She wanted to slap the bastard. "I'm guessing if you happen to find said masterpiece in my house, you'll arrest me."

"Well, my dear, it could go that way, depending—"

"Depending on what? And my name is Kate, not 'my dear.'"

Ignoring her rebuke, Eddie said, "What I do will depend on Nick's cooperation. If he were to reveal his role in how that painting got to you and the location of the other works, then—"

"You won't throw me in the slammer?"

"Possibly not." She could hear the smug grin in his tone.

"For your information, the Matisse did not come from Nick. Raquel Steele gave it to me as a goodbye and thank you gift."

"Come now, a masterpiece worth a hundred million plus? Who's going to believe that?"

"It happens to be the truth," Kate said. "Besides, a Post-Impressionist expert told me it was a first-rate copy." That was true until the same expert took back that assessment.

"None of that matters, Kate. What matters is that Nick believes I will have you arrested on these charges, and your practice and reputation will be ruined. All because of him. What do you think he'll do in that case? Charge to the rescue and cooperate with me? Or keep on running in the delusional hope of saving his precious skin?"

"You surprise me, Eddie. How could you possibly think a notorious crook would sacrifice himself for me? Don't you believe Nick is a sociopath, a con man without a conscience who cannot love or care about anyone but himself?"

"I don't believe Nick is a *typical* sociopath. He may love you in a certain kind of way, the kind he feels toward a captivating painting he wants to appropriate, annex to himself, so to speak—a psychologist might call it a perverted version of self-love."

"A brilliant diagnosis, Dr. Cromwell. What's your point? To demean Nick and mock my profession?"

They stroked in silent, stiff-armed synchrony, gliding on crystal clear water through a tunnel of trees, the red and gold leaves flickering in the stronger breeze. Kate scowled at the surrounding beauty and the storybook setting, which had become more like a Grimm's fairytale. She was on the defensive, letting Eddie get to her. Time to turn the tables. Drop the sparring. Feed his ego. Pretend interest in his ideas, principles, and goals.

"Tell me, Eddie, do you really believe in what you do?"

"I believe in great art; it speaks for all of us," Eddie said in a self-important tone. "Art is our cultural heritage and expresses our most profound feelings and truths." He paused. "I believe great art is demeaned by forgeries sold for illicit profit and stolen by criminals who use it as collateral for gun running and drug dealing. When that happens, I feel called upon to stop those criminals, recover the stolen art, and safeguard our most important cultural treasures. These creations give us our unique identity. Art tells us who we are—the joys, the sorrows, the good, the bad, the beautiful, the ugly."

"I respect your high-minded principles. But I can't believe Nick sells his stunning works to underworld criminals."

"I'm sorry to disillusion you, Kate, but we are quite certain several *stunning* forgeries, which only Nick could have executed, were sold to underworld collectors like Dixon Steele. In addition, we know Nick worked in partnership with the crooked art dealer Jackson Chase from the age of fourteen. That pervert seduced and used talented young boys to copy and forge for him." His deep voice rose, rolling out like thunder. "For years, these ingenious scoundrels flooded the art world with bloody brilliant fakes!"

The boat trembled. Kate felt the possible truth of Eddie's angry accusations. She flashed on the photograph of a scrawny teenaged Nick with the slick gent Jackson Chase, who looked like a predator. Blocking out these disturbing revelations, Kate dug in her paddle and watched the crystalline water slip by the canoe.

"Listen, Eddie, let's get down to it," Kate said. "I'd like to propose a deal—a win-win. You get what you want, and I get what I want."

"Good concept," Eddie said. "Go on."

"I know how to find out from Nick where he's hidden the paintings, and I'll also guarantee he will sell no more forgeries. In return, I ask that you and your team stop pursuing him."

Pause. "You're suggesting I let a criminal go free? I can't . . . Hang on, Dylan is ringing me." To Dylan, he said, "We're a few minutes from meeting you."

There would be no deal with Eddie, Kate thought. As she turned to grab his cell, a surging current buffeted the canoe. "Paddle as hard as you can," Eddie yelled and paddled at her rate to keep the canoe moving straight. Rounding a bend, Eddie's more vigorous paddling on the left moved the boat closer and closer toward the right bank, where the current was faster, the water deeper.

Kate saw the right bank coming up fast. "Fallen tree ahead," she shouted.

"Pivot," Eddie yelled. "Sweep strokes on the left."

Switching sides rapidly, her hands trembly and sweaty, Kate lost hold of her paddle. The canoe smashed into the broken-off tree branch. "Kneel! Lean downstream!" Eddie shouted. In the next moment, the canoe turned on its side and tipped over, dumping them into the cold water, the shell coming down on top of them.

It was pitch-dark underneath the boat. Kate quickly swam under the gunnel, coming up facing the capsized canoe and the shore. Holding on to the boat's top, Kate waited for Eddie to emerge. She was freezing in the ice-cold water. After a few seconds, she called out, "Eddie!" Where was he? Something was wrong.

She remembered from lessons how to flip the boat upright by herself. She managed this with difficulty and then saw Eddie floating face down in the water. "Eddie!" His head must have hit a strut or the canoe's floor, and the blow knocked him out. Either that or he'd had a heart attack or a stroke. As the empty canoe drifted downstream, a chilling thought ripped through her mind. *Let him drown. A dead Eddie would solve her problems. She and Nick would be free. Jesus Christ, what lunatic, horrifying thoughts.* She felt sick.

Kate struggled to turn his body face up. His skin was deathly pale. He did not revive when she slapped his cheek and called his name. She saw no blood or signs of a head injury. She grasped him across his chest and started side-stroking toward the shore. She was a strong swimmer and had seen enough rescues on the beach and in the movies to know what to do. Luckily, it was not very far to the shore. When she reached shallow water, she dragged his heavy, inert body through the debris and up onto the grassy bank and laid him flat on his back.

The light had gone. Dark clouds hung overhead, threatening rain. Kate saw the gothic Church of St. Boniface in the background, but no one was around to help. Where was Dylan? He should be here. She kneeled next to Eddie's chest and leaned close to his mouth, listening for breathing sounds. Nothing. His ice-cold lips brushed against her cheek as she studied his diaphragm. No movement. He looked old, shrunken, and dead. She'd taken CPR lessons as a professional requirement, so she didn't give in to total panic.

She recalled the Fire Department Captain's voice from those practice sessions. "We no longer blow breaths into the victim's mouth. We just do rapid, hard chest compression to get the heart beating and blood to the brain. Start immediately." She leaned forward and began chest compressions, pushing as hard as she could to the rhythm of "Staying Alive," as the captain had suggested. Eddie's chest felt more unyielding than the practice dummy's. After about a minute she felt worn out, and Eddie was showing no response. "Keep pushing for at least two minutes," the captain had said. "It's hard work."

Kate pushed, pushed, pushed, keeping the rhythm but getting weaker and weaker. *Dylan, where the hell are you?* Kate cried out in her head, watching Eddie's gray face for any signs of his coming to life. No flush on his cheeks, no breath or cough. Tears burned her eyes, her chest hurt, she was panting, her breath coming in frantic gasps.

Damn you, Eddie, please wake up! she silently screamed.

CHAPTER 46

Create like a god; command like a king; work like a slave.
—Constantin Brâncuși—

Wednesday Night, October 24

Nick woke up in a sweat, curled on the floor, every inch of his body in sheer agony. He couldn't move his legs or his hands, as both were tied tightly with a rope. After the room stopped rocking and rolling, he forced his screaming body to sit up. Just a few feet in front of him, the fire blazed, the heat scorching his face. He flashed back to his father leaning over him the night of the horrific fire, white-faced, his eyes full of terror. "Wake up, Nicky!"

"Hey, McCoy," an unfamiliar deep voice said. "Your face is a mess."

Nick glanced to the left, a knife-like pain slicing through the mush in his head. A giant of a man with dark skin and hair sat on the floor, leaning against the pedestal supporting Brâncuși's *Bird in Space*, his arms tied behind his back, his ankles bound. *Who is this smartass?* Then Nick spotted the sharp blue eyes, cutting through his fuzzy vision.

"You look familiar," Nick managed to say.

"You saw me as a guard at the Impressionists Exhibition, then today at The Rogues. Detective Hawk and I followed you there from the gallery. Name's Flynn, Private Investigator."

"Damn, then you tracked me here, too?" Nick was sure he'd lost any tails.

"No, it's complicated," Flynn said. "Our boss, DCI Cromwell, lost you at Harrods. After we delivered Kate, Hawk and I came here looking for Simon. We figured he'd hole up here and thought you might show up as well. Got that right, didn't I?" He smirked.

"Then what?" Nick glared, his eyes mere slits in his bruised, swollen face.

"A Hulk lookalike caught me snooping around the yard outside. Hawk didn't get caught. She's out there cutting off the other guard's balls. The Hulk doesn't stand a chance. Our Desi is Wonder Woman in disguise."

This chap was maddening. He spoke in a hip-dude manner as if they were indestructible characters in a video game. Still ablaze, the fire crackled, the vicious heat cooking Nick's bruised and broken skin. Soon he'd be a heap of charred parts. The olfactory memory of his own burned flesh made him gag. He glanced at Matisse's *Pastoral* to the right of the fireplace, but not even the vibrant, carefree painting of naked nymphs frolicking in an idyllic woodland gave him relief. The contrast between art and real life only seemed to intensify his dread and physical pain.

"What did you mean about delivering Kate?" Nick asked. "Did you see her snatched? Simon said his thugs kidnapped her."

"Simon's a pathological liar," Flynn said. "We followed Kate and convinced her to meet with Cromwell. Then we escorted her to his driver waiting at the Ritz."

Hearing this, Nick felt faint with relief. Simon or his hired hands must have witnessed this transaction. That's how the lying snake knew Kate wasn't with him.

"Where's Kate?" Nick asked.

"She's with the Bulldog at his fishing retreat out in the boonies."

A fishing retreat sounded made up, but at least the Bulldog wasn't a killer or a rapist.

"Why the hell did Cromwell run off with Kate?" Nick asked. "What's his point?"

"Isn't it obvious?" Flynn asked. "He wants you in his power and the masterpieces. Same as Simon. You'll get Kate back if he gets the stolen masterpieces."

And my head in a noose, Nick thought. He had to get out of here. He pushed against his restraints, sending sharp pains up his battered arms and legs. He considered how to get bloody Flynn to cooperate enough to plan an escape. *Who was this chap with a major chip on his shoulder and a perpetual snarl on his face?*

"Why are you mixed up in this, Flynn? Can't be you're a closet art lover."

"I don't give a flying fuck about art. It's you I can't stomach. Simon hired me to get dirt on Raquel, his dad's lovely young wife. That's how I came across you, lover boy. I found out you were a notorious forger, a liar, cheat, and phony who seduces and uses women. I told my cop pals about you."

"So, I have you to thank for this latest hunt for my scalp?"

"I take full credit," Flynn said. "Maybe you're not the killer, but I hold you responsible for Raquel Steele's death."

"Yeah? Well, so do I." Nick closed his eyes against this painful accusation. "Sorry to disappoint you, but Simon raped and killed Raquel. He just bragged to me about it."

"That fucking sadist!" Flynn's deep voice boomed. "I always thought Simon was more perverted and vicious than his old man. He's a worse motherfucker than you are, McCoy."

"Thanks for nothing," Nick said. "Stow your opinion of me until we get out of here. Otherwise, nothing matters. Don't expect Simon to let you live—you'll be a witness to my torture and murder. And he'll suspect I told you about his gleeful admission of killing Raquel."

Flynn's insolent expression turned grim. His big body tensed as he strained against his bonds. "I can get out of zip ties and handcuffs, but a rope is a bigger problem. Got anything sharp hidden on you?"

"Nope, they took my army knife."

"Anything in here we can use?" Flynn glanced around the room.

Nick felt the edge of the glass coffee table poking into his back. He turned to study it. The glass was thick, and the rounded edges wouldn't cut anything. Could they break the glass somehow? They'd need a sledgehammer or something heavy. He scanned the wall of stolen paintings, his gaze settling on the marble Brâncuși above Flynn's head.

"Someone's unlocking the door," Flynn whispered. "Get down on the floor and play dead."

Nick's shoulder hit the floor. He quickly curled into the fetal position as Simon strode in. Closing his eyes, he imagined Simon with a sledgehammer in his hand, a ghoulish grin on his pretty-boy face.

"Flynn, you fuck," Simon said. "Why did you turn against me? I was paying you well."

"I was never against you," Flynn said. "It's McCoy I've hunted. I want him skewered just like you do."

"Well, you're in for a treat," Simon said.

"Untie me," Flynn said. "I'm on your side."

"Sorry, I can't do that. Can't trust you now." Simon sounded almost regretful.

He heard heavy footsteps on the marble floor. The guards were coming in, no doubt jacked up by the fun to come. Nick was an expert at managing pain, but could he endure the destruction of his hands? Even if he managed to survive, he'd never be able to paint again.

Simon's voice again. "Igor, prop up Nicky-boy."

Nick smelled Igor's rank odor as he roughly yanked him into a sitting position. He let his head flop forward. Klaus grunted and delivered several hard blows to the sides of Nick's face.

Nick stayed inert, controlling his flinching reflexes.

"Klaus, bring over the bucket of ice water and soak him," Simon said.

Cold water drenched Nick's hair and face. He silently endured the sharp kicks to his upper body as an alarm suddenly rang through the house.

Igor grunted. "Another fuck outside, trying to break in."

Nick heard the goons running out of the basement and then the door banging shut. He opened his eyes.

"They're gone," Flynn said. "That's probably Desi, my partner, outside. I expect she deliberately set off the alarm to draw them out. You okay?"

"I'm alive," Nick groaned, wrenching his injured, angry body into a sitting position.

"You're one tough fucker; I'll give you that," Flynn said. "We gotta do something fast."

"I have an idea," Nick said. "Can you stand, pressing your back against the Brâncuși pedestal, and then slide upward?"

"What's a Brâncuși?"

"The multimillion-dollar sculpture of a bird sitting on the pedestal behind you. In case you care, Brâncuși is considered the patriarch of modern sculpture."

"No shit," Flynn said.

"After standing, try to get the sculpture into your hands and off the pedestal. It should be heavy enough to break the glass. Then we'd have a sharp edge to cut the ropes."

Flynn snorted. "Not a bad idea, but it sounds like a bitch to bring off."

His back against the stone pedestal, Flynn inched his way up to a standing position, sweating and spitting out swear words. Nick urged him on as Flynn inched into an upright position.

"Now lean forward slightly," Nick said, "and raise your hands as high as possible and feel for the sculpture. I think it's thin enough at the bottom that your tied hands can grasp it."

After a few grunts, Flynn said, "Got it."

"Now lift it off the pedestal. Yank it if you must, but don't you *dare* drop it!"

Flynn eased the bird off the pedestal. "It's damn heavy for a bird."

"Now hobble over here. When you get to the table, turn around and lift the bird as high as you can above the corner. When I tell you you're in the right position, drop it hard with as much force as possible. Hopefully, the sculpture will break the glass. Christ, it kills me to sacrifice a Brâncuși."

"I'm doing the dirty deed, not you," Flynn said, shuffling and half-hopping over to the end of the table. He turned so that his back and hands holding the sculpture were facing the corner of the table. Nick had him move slightly to the left.

"Okay, you're positioned correctly," Nick said. "Now drop it. *Hard!*"

The marble bird landed with a crash on the table, and the corner cracked off.

As Nick eyed the ruined sculpture on the floor, its pointed head and flared feet broken off, he felt the damage as though it was another of his injuries. Thinking of Steele's fury consoled him.

Flynn was on his knees, and Nick directed him where he needed to position his hands to effectively rub the rope against the sharp edge of the table. The friction sound was worse than nails on a chalkboard and went on for many long, nerve-wracking minutes. Nick gazed at the door, his ears pricked to hear their captors return. He frequently glanced at Flynn's progress.

"Think I'm almost through," Flynn said. He yanked his hands apart the next moment, quickly rubbed his wrists, then untied his legs.

"Well done, mate," Nick said, sitting on tenterhooks, his pulse racing. *What would Flynn do now?* For a few crucial minutes, they had become an effective team. Would that partnership continue so they could escape this hellhole? He was doubtful. If Flynn still despised him, Nick figured he'd probably save himself and leave his expedient new partner at Simon's mercy.

CHAPTER 47

We live in a world where justice equals vengeance.
—Toni Morrison—

Wednesday Night, October 24

Taking deep, steady breaths, Nick prepared for his cellmate's desertion. Flynn stood and stamped the circulation back into his feet.

"Your turn, buddy," Flynn said as he began freeing Nick from his bonds.

Buddy? Had his enemy's scorn softened? Maybe Flynn saw him as the brains behind their escape. Nick rubbed his wrists and ankles, feeling the welcome sting of rushing blood. His legs buckled as he tried to stand.

Flynn pulled him up. "We've gotta get out of here without being seen."

Nick glanced at Matisse's *Pastoral* on the wall with a strong urge to rescue it. Madness. Reluctantly, he let the prize go and moved his shaky legs toward the door.

"The guards charged out of here and forgot to bolt the door," Flynn said as he turned the handle and pushed the door open. "The fools figured no way we could escape."

"Brilliant!" Nick felt a surge of energy as he strode out of the torture chamber.

With Flynn in the lead, the new comrades silently climbed the first set of circular stairs and stopped near the top. Listened.

All quiet.

"Where's the back exit?" Flynn whispered.

"Second level from the top floor," Nick said, "through the kitchen."

As they crossed the black-walled billiard room and headed toward the set of stairs to the kitchen, Simon stepped out of the dimly lit stairwell. He carried a large can, his revolver in his other hand, now pointed at Flynn. The men stopped.

"How the hell did you get out?" Simon demanded.

"Brâncuși rescued us," Flynn said. "But the bird lost his head. Sorry."

"What? You're losing it, Flynn." He glared at him for a moment. "Okay, change of plans. See this can?" Simon set it on the floor and unscrewed the cap. "It's filled with gasoline."

Simon picked up the can, stepped forward, and tossed a stream on the floor in front of his captives. Some of the deadly accelerant splashed onto Flynn's and Nick's jeans. A sharp, noxious smell polluted the air.

A scream lodged in Nick's throat.

"Nicky-boy, if you don't tell me where the masterpieces are, I'll soak you and Flynn in this stuff and set my lighter to it. Then whoosh, up you'll go in flames." Simon giggled. "I've got a fire extinguisher somewhere if you cooperate." He set the can on the floor in front of him, reached into his pants pocket, and pulled out a gold lighter. Holding it up, he flicked it open and let the flame flicker a couple of moments, his grin even more diabolical in the flickering light. Then he stuffed the lighter back into his pocket.

Flynn made a show of looking behind Simon. "Hey, man, is that your unexpected visitor coming down the stairs?"

As Simon quickly glanced over his shoulder, Flynn and Nick leaped on him. Struggling to disarm him, Flynn chopped his wrist, and the gun fired and fell to the floor. The bullet penetrated the gasoline can, the gas leaking onto the wood-planked floor. When Simon saw it flowing around his shoes, he screamed for Igor and Klaus and tried to back out of the puddle. From behind, Nick hooked his arm around Simon's neck and held him in place, choking him until he passed out. Nick let him fall into the growing puddle of gasoline.

"Where are the guards?" Nick asked.

"Outside. Desi must have subdued them. She's my guardian angel."

Nick squatted, reached into Simon's pants pocket, and pulled out the gold lighter. He stared at it, mesmerized, the stench of gasoline stinging his nostrils.

"Go ahead, light the gas," Flynn said. "Some people are truly evil, and Simon is one of them. He deserves to burn in hell before he gets there."

"That's called murder, Flynn."

"I'd call it justice," Flynn said. "Let me remind you, Simon was gleefully going to set us on fire and burn us to death. He raped and killed Raquel, and I suspect he murdered his mother and brother. Simon is a psychopathic serial killer."

Nick took in the horror of Flynn's accusations. Simon was capable of committing any kind of atrocity. Still, Nick hesitated to ignite the flame. Perhaps he believed in the rule of law after all.

"Don't kid yourself, buddy," Flynn said. "Don't expect the law to punish him. With Steele's fortune and connections behind him, he'll get away with all of it. And go on raping and killing for the next fifty-plus years."

Nick recognized the likelihood of this prediction. Law enforcement had notoriously bungled the investigation of the deaths of his family, and money bought anything in the US.

He glanced down at Simon's pretty-boy face, the snot still running from his nose. Steele's evil spawn now looked innocent and helpless. Nick flicked on the lighter. The flame shot up in front of his eyes. He flashed back to the seminal fire, his frantic father wrapping his burning body in a blanket and shoving him out the door. *Get on the ground,*

Nicky! Roll over and over!" Then he dove back into the inferno to rescue his mother and sisters, but it was too late. They all burned to death at the orders of Dixon Steele, the father of the serial killer sprawled at his feet.

Simon's girlish, long lashes were fluttering. In a moment, they would open, and a pair of soulless black eyes would look up at him. Then what? He'd like to see this scum of the earth suffer, beg, and howl in terror. He lowered the flame of the lighter closer to singeing those fluttering lashes. What would his father do in his place now?

CHAPTER 48

The past is never dead. It's not even past.
—William Faulkner—

Wednesday Night, October 24

Nick charged up the stairs, the gold lighter left behind. He rushed through the dark kitchen and out the back door to a small brick patio. He turned, expecting Flynn to be behind him. But no one was there, nor did he hear any sounds of movement in the kitchen. *What the devil was Flynn doing? Tying up Simon?* Nick couldn't call out to him for fear of alerting Klaus or Igor, who must be somewhere in the garden.

Listening for the sounds of Desi Hawk and the guards, Nick could only hear the soft drips from wet leaves. Otherwise, the garden was eerily dark and quiet, the brick fortress of a house blocking the street noise.

What had gone on out here? Could a lone female detective subdue two armed bruisers? Maybe, with proper martial arts training.

Nick crossed the patio and proceeded to search the garden's maze of narrow stone paths lined with ferns, star jasmine, pittosporums, and trees. The smell of wet foliage, lavender, and mold scented the air. Around a big pittosporum, he tripped over something. Looking down, he could see an oversized pair of black-booted feet. He stooped to examine the body and recognized Igor lying face down with his arms zip-tied behind his back. The Russian guard was out cold, still breathing. Hawk must have overpowered the muscle-bound brute. Nick stood and felt a hard jab in his back.

"Don't move," a woman's voice whispered. "Hands up, there's a gun muzzle in your back."

"Detective Hawk?" he whispered. "I'm Nick McCoy."

"I know who you are. Where's Flynn?"

"I thought he was following me out here to find you," Nick said, "but he must still be inside. Where's Klaus, the other guard?"

"Knocked out and tied up on the other side of this circular structure," she said.

"I'm impressed," Nick said.

Low chuckle. "If you know Krav Maga and have a gun, you don't need size and muscle to be effective."

"And you don't need that gun in my back," Nick said. "We're on the same side, at least for the time being."

"How so?"

"Flynn and I teamed up to escape Simon Steele and his two guards. He told me about you. He called you Desi, Wonder Woman, and his guardian angel. Now, may I lower my hands?"

Pause. "For the time being," she said.

The gun no longer jammed in his back, Nick turned around and faced a dark-skinned, slim figure in a black hooded sweatshirt that obscured her face. His body stiffened. The damp air smelled acrid and stung his nostrils.

"Holy shit, I smell smoke! Flynn and Simon are still inside."

As Nick led the way toward the back entrance, he saw Flynn's tall figure jogging toward them. Darting ahead of Nick, Desi ran toward her partner. Before colliding, both stopped abruptly. Flynn grabbed Desi's upper arms. They exchanged fast, whispered words.

Nick approached. "Is the house on fire?"

"Thought I should complete the job Simon started." Flynn's white teeth flashed.

"Where is he?" Nick asked.

"Where you left him, buddy. In his own piss-puddle of gas."

"Christ, Flynn, you set him on fire?"

"Not exactly," Flynn said. "I started the fire lower down. Heat and fire rise. Get the whole filthy hellhole that way."

"You bloody moron!" Nick shouted. "There's a treasure trove of paintings in the basement."

Nick flashed on Matisse's sublime *Pastoral* catching fire, the canvas splitting, curling, turning to ash. All the other treasures would perish as well. Unable to save his family in his past, Nick lunged toward the door in the blinding compulsion to act. Flynn grabbed him.

"Don't be a fool, McCoy. You can't save the art."

Nick struggled in Flynn's iron grip; the art and his family felt synonymous. He had to save all of them. As his awareness of the present began to return, his legs felt rubbery, his feet leaden. They were standing on the patio's edge as the smell of smoke grew stronger. Nick coughed, his chest so tight that he could hardly breathe.

"We have to get Simon," Desi said. "There's not much time. You get fourteen to seventeen minutes to escape a burning house. We've wasted at least ten minutes."

Flynn stood unmoved. "Simon is a butcher. He raped and murdered Raquel Steele and likely murdered his mother and brother. And he was about to burn up Nick and me. Fuck's sake, Desi, you know that scum will never pay for his crimes."

"Doesn't matter," Desi said. "We're the law. We can't commit murder."

The chapel's brick walls emanated heat like a furnace. Nick was in a cold sweat, his skin clammy. He heard glass breaking. Smoke billowed out of a high window in the left wing. Orange flames shot out and upward. His scars itched and stung, and he felt like they were about to rip open. Every nerve in his body screamed at him to run like hell, but his legs stayed rooted like immovable dead stumps. He flashed on the hellish memories of his mother and sisters upstairs, caught in the fire as his dad rushed through flames to save them while he lay on a stretcher on the ground. He couldn't do a damned thing then, and now he was just as helpless. A hoarse cry caught in his throat.

Desi grabbed Nick's arm. "What room is Simon in?"

"The billiard room at the bottom of the stairs from the kitchen," Nick said. "Luckily, the fire is moving much faster in the left wing."

"I'm going to get him," Desi said.

"No!" Letting go of Nick, Flynn grabbed her wrist. "You can't drag him up a long, steep staircase alone."

"Listen to me," Desi hissed. "If you murder Simon in cold blood, you'll never be able to live with yourself. If you can, you'll become like him—a soulless, heartless shell of a man."

"She's right, Flynn. Let's get—"

"Shut up. I'll be just fine knowing I saved a lot of people from a psycho serial killer."

"If you can't do this for your own conscience, do it for mine," Desi said.

Flynn did not reply. They seemed stuck in a moral conflict with a lovers' quarrel subtext. But the truth in Desi's arguments reached Nick. He stared at the closed kitchen door, concealing the disaster inside, and cursed the day he survived the fire. He cursed Steele, the worthless god above and the triumphant devil below. It would be up to him to rescue— or not—the worst motherfucker on the planet.

"Damn you, Flynn, do it for me," Desi said.

"Why should I?"

Desi grabbed him and kissed him hard on the mouth.

"Hurry it up." Nick stumbled forward.

Desi doused them with cold water from a garden hose she found coiled on the patio. To Nick's surprise, his legs came alive, propelling him back into his worst nightmare.

With Flynn behind him, Nick started down the stairs through a haze of dark smoke. His eyes were smarting, and the harsh fumes and acrid chemical smell scorched his nose and throat. Slapping his wet handkerchief over his nose and mouth, he gasped for air. At the bottom of the stairs, he stood in the intense heat, hypnotized by the flames darting across the billiard room and consuming the art on the walls. He heard his dad yelling as the past came rushing back.

"The shop's on fire!" Strong hands pulling him up. Pain searing one side of his body and face. Fiery tongues licking up the sides of an old tapestry, then leaping to his dad's beautiful sunflower painting on the easel.

"No! No!" His grown-up voice rasped.

"Move!" Flynn shouted. "Simon's just a few steps ahead."

Tears streamed from Nick's eyes; Van Gogh's last words in his head—*The sadness will last forever.*

They found Simon unconscious in the burning pool of gasoline, lifted him up, and rolled him over onto a clear space of floor to extinguish the fire. Sirens sounding in the distance, he and Flynn spewed curses as they reluctantly hauled Simon's scorched body up the stairs.

CHAPTER 49

O, beware, my lord, of jealousy.

—SHAKESPEARE—

Thursday Morning, October 25

The next day, Nick awoke to the nightmare images of swirling smoke and crackling orange flames. His eyes adjusting to the dim light coming through the flowered drapes, he recognized his room at the Gull's Nest. He'd checked in late last night, registering as Mr. and Mrs. Nigel Blackman.

He reached for his mobile on the bed stand and checked his messages. The one from Flynn said Kate was fine, stating that she could meet him late tomorrow. The second message was from Jackson Chase, now known as Charles Hamilton, asking him to come to his gallery this morning to discuss "their business."

Nick scanned the over-decorated room cluttered with antiques and floral wallpaper. The scent of roses from the bouquet on the table perfumed the air. The room contained an alcove with a small kitchenette comprising a couple of dish cabinets, a counter with a microwave, and a small sink with a mini fridge below. In anticipation of Kate's arrival, Nick had purchased basic food and drink supplies, now stored in the fridge. When Kate arrived, he pictured them diving under the flowered quilt, seized by an explosion of pent-up longing and lust.

Then food and drinks would be at hand to provide the necessary fuel for repeats.

On his way to the Gull's Nest from Steele's ruined mansion, he'd picked up their suitcases at the Leonardo and unpacked their toiletries. He had a long wait for Kate and was glad he had plenty to do to fill the hours until she arrived. Since cuts and bruises on his face prevented shaving, he was washed, dressed, and out the door in minutes.

He hailed a taxi and headed for the Hamiltons Gallery in Mayfair. Nick knew choosing Jackson to receive and hide the masterpieces was risky, but he hadn't had time to arrange something more secure. On a previous call, Jackson had reported moving the five paintings to a safer location than his gallery, but he would not reveal where until Nick met with him in person. Nick dreaded the encounter, expecting Jackson to engage him in a tricky negotiation to ensure he would secure the upper hand.

Jackson was not at his gallery when Nick arrived. Instead, he'd left instructions for Nick to meet him at an art storage facility on Mill Mead Road in Tottenham. When he arrived, Nick found an empty, locked warehouse, a repellant reminder of Jackson's deceitfulness and sadistic sense of humor. He suspected this misdirection was just the beginning of a treasure hunt Jackson had arranged to jerk him around. If Nick followed all the false leads, would he find the masterpieces at the end? *Doubtful*, he thought. This hunt would likely end in still yet another game. The bastard loved to seduce and then be chased.

Nick read Jackson's latest text: *Meet me at the National Gallery—the storage facilities.* Jackson signed off with a smiley-faced emoji. Nick had no expectation that the joker would be there.

—

In the evening of the next day, Nick was back at the Gull's Nest, nervously pacing while waiting for Kate to arrive. She had notified him of the approximate time that afternoon. Finally, after what seemed like hours of pacing, Nick heard a discrete knock, then a voice whispered, "It's me." He opened the door, and Kate rushed into his arms.

Saying her name repeatedly, he covered her flushed face with kisses. "Are you all right? How did you get here?"

"Dylan, Cromwell's driver, drove me to the Ritz from Romsey. I took a taxi from there." She leaned back in his arms. "I'm okay physically, but I can see that you're not. Your poor face. What happened?"

"Later. First things first." He pulled her onto the bed.

They spent a long time exhausting themselves, desperate to sustain the other's living, breathing reality. Temporarily sated, Nick brought them snacks and drinks from the kitchenette—chardonnay for Kate and a Guinness for him. Sitting on the bed propped up with pillows, they nibbled crisps and sipped their drinks. Euphoric sex had served as an anesthetic to assuage Nick's body pains. He tingled all over, a warm glow spreading through him. He was reluctant to puncture their bubble by venturing into the trials each experienced during their time apart.

"You go first," he said.

Kate described the encounter with Flynn and Detective Hawk after their late lunch at The Rogues and her agreement—under pressure—to meet with Cromwell at his fly-fishing lodge on the River Test.

"Ah, the beautiful Test; I know it well," Nick said. "Grand place for fly fishing."

"So, I hear," Kate said. "Flynn took my cell and the burner phone, so I couldn't call you. He still has them. On a canoe ride the next morning, Eddie tried to convince me that it would be in both our interests for you to turn yourself in. If you returned the stolen masterpieces and revealed the buyers of the other forgeries, he didn't think you'd be convicted."

"He fed you a fantasy, Kate. That outcome can't be trusted, as I already explained."

"Eddie also threatened to arrest me for aiding a suspected criminal and harboring the stolen Matisse."

"You didn't buy that, did you? It was a devil's ruse to lure me in."

"I wasn't sure," she said. "Then we had an accident on the river; the canoe tipped over, and Eddie was knocked unconscious." She related her attempts to save him with CPR, then downed a gulp of wine.

"Jesus! Did you save the pisser or not?"

"Yes, but at first, I was tempted not to. Eddie finally came to, just as Dylan arrived. We got him to the local hospital and took turns watching over him all night. It pained me to keep you waiting, but I couldn't leave until I was sure he'd be okay. I hope you can understand."

"Do I ever." Nick was laughing. "Don't you get it, love? You're in the driver's seat now. Lord Cromwell, the Chief Inspector of Scotland Yard's famous Art Squad, owes you his life."

Kate's flushed face paled. She set her wine on the bed stand and pressed her hand against her stomach, groaning. "All the stress is catching up with me. It gets me in the gut every time." She got up and rushed to the bathroom. Nick could hear her retching.

"Can I help?" Nick started to rise.

"No, stay away," she yelled.

When the siege passed, she closed the door, and Nick could hear the shower turned on.

"Shall I join you?"

"Not now."

Nick heard annoyance in her tone, as if he were a pest. Guzzling stout, he began to feel queasy. What was wrong with her? Stress, he understood, but she sounded so cold. Nick looked down at his battered, bruised body. Was she sickened by his looks? To cover his scars, he got up, pulled out his gray flannel bathrobe from his suitcase and put it on. A growing suspicion chilled his clammy skin. Her behavior struck him as strange, even guilty. She must have gotten close to Cromwell at his beguiling retreat. *Had she been seduced over to his side?* There was a Chinese saying about the obligation that accompanied saving someone's life. What the hell was it? Something about being responsible for them forever.

CHAPTER 50

There is an old illusion. It is called good and evil.

— Friedrich Nietzsche —

Thursday Night, October 25

Eddie sat with Desi and Flynn, drinking beer around a scarred wooden table at The Spotted Dog, a traditional pub a block from the Gull's Nest.

"It's so late; can't we leave confronting McCoy until morning?" Desi asked.

"No, I'm afraid we can't." Eddie looked around the dim, smoky interior, ensuring that no carousing regulars could overhear them. He was still aware of a dull ache in his concussed head, but after one night in the hospital and a day of rest, he seemed to be seeing and thinking well enough.

A stout chap lifted his shirt and flashed his naked, tattooed belly at Desi. It said NECK DEEP. *Neck deep in what?* he wondered. A young bloke with a gold front tooth gave him a daffy grin. Unlike his hip colleagues, blue-blooded Cromwell knew he looked out of place in this pub full of characters in ripped jeans and slouchy caps, their naked parts sporting tattoos of rock singers and bands he didn't know.

Desi drained her glass. "Well, maybe it's better to face the lovers now when they're half asleep rather than well-rested and more alert in the morning."

"I doubt they're half asleep or will be well-rested in the morning," Flynn said. "What's the plan, anyway? I'm not for railroading or tricking McCoy. I wouldn't be sitting here if it weren't for him and my new best friend, Brâncuși."

"Who's that?" Desi said.

"The patriarch of modern sculpture," Flynn tossed off.

Desi chuckled. "You've sure changed your tune about McCoy and art."

"Yeah, well, the dude saved me from torture and death by fire. Hard to despise your savior. I must admit I misjudged McCoy. He's not the typical con artist. He's surprisingly decent, even principled in certain ways."

Eddie was aware that he and Desi were holding hands under the table. She looked radiant, and Flynn was much less abrasive. His gaze lingered on the rebellious PI.

"I'd like to go over what happened again," Eddie said. "You reported that McCoy did not set the fire. Correct?"

"Yeah," Flynn said. "Simon threatened to set off the puddle of spilled gasoline with his lighter unless McCoy revealed where the paintings were hidden. McCoy and I managed to wrestle the gun away from the prick and knocked him down. Then we beat it out of there."

"I met them outside in the garden," Desi said. "Soon we smelled smoke, and it became clear that a fire was burning inside. We assumed Simon must have started it either accidentally or on purpose."

"Why would he start a fire on purpose?" Cromwell asked.

Flynn shrugged. "Simon is hardly a model of mental health. He thinks he's God, or the Devil, and has infantile rages. He'd assume us mortals would burn up in a fire, but not him."

Eddie raised his brows, unconvinced.

"Before the fire got out of control," Desi said, "Flynn and McCoy returned and rescued Simon from the blaze."

"A decision I deeply regret," Flynn said. "Now that rattlesnake is still alive."

"Pity. Where is Simon now?" Eddie asked.

"The ambulance took him to the Adult Burns Centre at Chelsea and Westminster Hospital," Flynn said.

Eddie gave Flynn a sharp look, finding his report and Desi's backup a little too pat. It sounded rehearsed. "At least this is a better outcome than me having to arrest you or McCoy for murder." Eddie swallowed the last of his beer, his gaze still fixed on Flynn. "You know McCoy better than anyone now. How do you recommend we approach him?"

"Play it straight," Flynn said. "Say what we propose, lay out the alternatives, and give him overnight to think about it."

Desi glanced at Eddie. "Will Kate play along?"

"Maybe, but she's a wild card." He cleared his throat. "I owe that remarkable lady my life. You know what that means, don't you, Flynn? It changes a lot of things. It took a while after I woke up to start making sense of what had happened. My neat world no longer looked so clearly black and white—righteous me versus the bad guys. I've always considered the shades of gray kind of thinking to be the product of weak minds and character. Kate badgered me into seeing a grain of truth in the viewpoint that there are no absolute wrongs or rights. Unfortunately, this makes my job a lot harder." He stared into his empty glass. "I promised Kate I'd offer the fairest deal it was in my power to make."

"Yeah, what's that?" Flynn asked.

"It'll depend on how things go. I just ask you to follow my lead."

Flynn grinned. "Don't I always, boss?"

CHAPTER 51

Life isn't about finding yourself. Life is about creating yourself.
— GEORGE BERNARD SHAW —

Thursday Night, October 25

Nick watched Kate emerge from the bathroom, wrapped in a towel. She did not look in his direction. Her furrowed brow indicated that she was preoccupied. He felt pangs of jealousy, imagining that she was thinking about the asshole Cromwell's health. She pulled out her bathrobe from the suitcase and put it on, then turned and gave him a weak smile.

"Thanks for packing my robe. The cleansing hot water made me feel more human." She slipped into bed next to him. "Let me hear what happened to you. Nothing good by the looks of your bruises. Are you hurting a lot?"

"I'm used to pain." He took her hand and began telling her about his fateful decision to check out Steele's Chelsea retreat and how he found Simon holed up there. In quick brushstrokes, he conveyed the events with Flynn in the gallery dungeon of Steele's chapel, then described their escape and the near-deadly showdown with Simon in the billiard room.

"When Simon lay at my feet, passed out in a pool of gasoline, I had his lighter and really wanted to use it." He bowed his head.

"I wouldn't blame you."

He thought back to those high-wire moments. "I couldn't get myself to do it, even though Simon is the scum of the earth. I thought if I committed cold-blooded murder, I'd become the same kind of monster as Steele and his son."

"I doubt that, but I think you made the right mental health decision."

He reported that the fire must have happened accidentally, omitting Flynn's role. "Flynn and I rescued Simon, who was badly burned but still alive. The poor disfigured lad, he'll suffer for years, and so will his devoted father." He almost smiled. "Then the whole place went up. It started raining, the fire trucks arrived, and I returned here."

"Where's Simon now?" she asked.

"At the local hospital, being treated for multiple first, second, and a few third-degree burns. Simon's pretty-boy face is badly burned, I heard. He'll have hideous scars."

"Now that's poetic justice at its finest." She turned and pulled him to her. "Can you believe we're both still alive?"

This time they showered together, and Nick allowed Kate to see the whole of his scarred and bruised body in the light.

"These scars and bruises sure make you look tough . . . and hot." She ran her hands lightly over the rough terrain of his back, then swatted his butt. "Give us a kiss, laddie."

After their slower, gentler lovemaking, they lay entwined in each other's arms. She asked, "Do you trust me enough now to tell me where Steele's masterpieces are?"

"So, my sweet Delilah, you want the secret of my strength?" He regarded her through narrowed eyes. "They're here in London with an old associate."

"Jackson Chase?" she asked.

Nick shut his eyes, sickened to hear her say this name. "How do you know about Jackson?"

"Cromwell told me. He said Jackson was a shady dealer who preyed on talented boys. He told me you had worked with him since you were fourteen and were likely still partners. He said you would never quit forging. He swears by the old motto: once a con, always a con."

"Jackson and I are *not* still partners. He's supposedly doing me a favor. He owes me many. I assure you, the Steele job, including *The Open Window*, were my last forgeries."

"I believe you, Nick, but I need to know why you stayed with a predatory crook like Chase for so long."

He ground his teeth, feeling cornered. "Survival mainly. You don't know what it's like to scrounge for your next lousy meal. Even after I realized he was cheating me, I agreed to continue working with him as his partner. He made me an offer I couldn't refuse." He stopped, reluctant to reveal any more about his deal with the devil.

"Tell me."

"He promised to make up for the amount he cheated me by paying whatever it cost for plastic surgery to fix my scarred face. He understood the hell it was for me to look like a freak."

She nodded. "I'm glad to hear he did something good for you."

"He also helped me to discover what happened to my family, who started the fire, and why. Being in the art world, he knew about Dixon Steele. When I saw a picture of him in *ARTnews*, I recognized Steele as the bloke my dad was making copies for right before the fire. Jackson helped with other parts of the investigation as well."

"Okay, Jackson wasn't all bad," she said. "But something Cromwell said bothered me. He implied that Jackson was a pederast. Is that true?"

Nick stared at the dark ale in his glass and fought the impulse to run.

"I can't face you and tell you this." He swung his legs over the side of the bed, his back now facing Kate. For several minutes he sat frozen, unable to clear his clogged throat. An image of Jackson's seductive smile flashed in his mind, along with his youthful reaction of excitement and revulsion. He broke out in a cold sweat. His mouth went dry, his breathing fast and shallow.

"Are you having a panic attack?" she asked, touching his shoulder.

"Yes, but I know what to do." He slowed his breathing and began silently counting—one, inhale, two, slowly exhale. One, inhale. Two, slowly exhale. After a few minutes of this, he felt his body relaxing, and his breathing gradually slowed to normal. He stood, went to the bathroom, and doused his face with cold water. In the mirror, he saw the full extent of his bruised face. His mug looked plenty ugly but definitely not as freaky as the burn-scarred face of his youth. The black rings around his eyes and the purple bruises would eventually fade. He returned to the bed, sat beside Kate, and grasped her hand.

She kissed his cheek. "We don't have to talk about Jackson anymore."

Nick's mouth was so dry he couldn't speak. He took two long pulls of stout. "I was afraid, that's all—afraid of hearing myself talk about it and afraid of your reaction." He was in love with a wonderful woman for the first time and, at this moment—on the edge of self-revelation—he started to tremble. What if she couldn't handle the truth about him? He might have to face the unbearable possibility of losing her love. He took another swallow of courage. "I didn't want to tell you . . . Jackson and I became lovers."

He could feel her hand squeezing his. He sat frozen. Her silence seemed to go on forever.

"Thank you, my love, I'm very glad you're telling me now," she said. "Because of Cromwell's remark, I did think sexual abuse might have happened to you. Would it help you to say more about it? You know I don't have a problem with difficult details. However it happened, you were victimized."

Her understanding and lack of judgment felt genuine. He cleared his throat. "Jackson seduced me when we got high together. He didn't exactly force me, but I felt I had to go along to survive. He was doing a lot for me, more than anyone ever had. I wanted to believe he cared about me. I had no one else, and I admired him. I even convinced myself that a con artist was a cool thing to be. He also agreed to try and sell my original work, but that never happened."

"That bastard. I'm so sorry. How disappointing for you."

He bridled. "Don't be sorry for me. Makes me feel like a pathetic, kept boy toy."

"That's not true!" Her voice rose. "I don't see you like that at all. You were a boy who needed love and a father, and Jackson looked like the only way you could get something like both. You were not 'kept' or a 'toy.' It sounds like you worked hard and were the real breadwinner."

He kissed her hand. "Thanks for that, my dearest, silver-tongued shrink."

"It's the truth. What happened is more than understandable." Her voice rang with a preacher's fervor in the small room. "How long were you and Jackson together?"

"About five years, until my second year at the Royal Academy. By then, the faculty and students had accepted me, and my work won prizes. Jackson couldn't handle my having another life. He needed a boy who worshipped him, and that wasn't me anymore. I know he was a self-serving manipulator who groomed me to be a slick con. But his spending the money to fix my face gave me the looks and confidence I needed to succeed at anything. I'm still grateful to him for that."

Kate got up from the bed and shuffled to the window. He stared at her rigid back and then at the flowered wallpaper, feeling raw and overexposed. He'd worked hard to bury those tumultuous years with Jackson.

She turned and got back into bed next to him. "This is very hard for me to ask." She took a deep breath. "Do you prefer men?"

Lying would be the easiest way to drive her away. Lying was what he usually did when he needed to end an affair, or he'd just vanish. But she deserved better treatment. She deserved to hear the truth from him.

"No, I prefer women, and I am not a switch-hitter. I had to get high to have sex with Jackson. Then I always pretended I was somewhere else or that I was fucking a pretty girl."

She touched the back of his neck. "Well, you can fuck this hot chick right now."

He turned around and wrapped her in a crushing embrace, his heart beating like he'd been running a marathon.

CHAPTER 52

Nothing can be accomplished without love.
—Henri Matisse—

Thursday Night, October 25

There was a loud rapping on the door. Nick jumped out of bed and shouted, "Who's there?"

"DCI Cromwell. I'd like a few words, please."

"Kate," Nick whispered. "Did you tell Cromwell where we were?"

"No, and I didn't have his driver drop me off here." She flashed on her missing phones. "Remember, I told you Flynn took my phones, and I'd put the Gull's Nest address on one. He must have figured out my simple-minded passcode." Turning away from his accusative glare, she pulled the flowered quilt to her chin.

"Hey, buddy," Flynn's voice boomed through the door. "Better open up. It's in your best interest to hear out the chief."

Nick said nothing, his gaze fixed on Kate's profile. *How much had she allied with Cromwell?*

She turned, looking him straight in the eyes. "Be reasonable, Nick. We should at least find out what he proposes. Otherwise, we'll be up all night, wondering."

He wished Kate had let the persistent bugger drown. "Hang on," he called out.

After they put on bathrobes, Nick unlocked and opened the door. Cromwell came in first and gave Nick's hand a firm shake. The attractive woman behind him looked to be Desi Hawk. Now that she was out of her hoodie and in the light, Nick could see why Flynn was smitten. Flynn strode in and glanced around the room, then flashed Nick a crooked grin.

"This place is not your style, buddy. All this clutter and spinster aunt, flowered stuff. Doesn't it drive you batshit?"

"It suits me better than Simon's torture chamber. Take a seat." Nick gestured toward the table. He and Kate sat on the blanket chest at the end of the bed.

Cromwell and Hawk pulled out chairs from the small, round table and sat down.

Flynn eyed the roses and asked if he could move them. "They smell like old lady perfume." With Kate's permission, he carried the vase to the kitchenette counter, then came over to where she was sitting and pulled her iPhone, burner phone, and passport out of his jacket pocket. "Sorry, I had to borrow these." He handed her the essential items.

"Thank you, Flynn. I trusted you'd take good care of my stuff." She gave him a warm smile.

Flynn sat next to Desi at the table, and Nick focused his gaze on Cromwell. As an undercover cop, Cromwell had kept away from cameras and public appearances, so Nick had never seen his long-time adversary without a disguise. Now he could detect *Le Comte de Guise* in the gent's natural poise, patrician nose, and penetrating stare. Nick saw nothing of the formidable Chief Inspector of his imagination in this man's refined features. Add that deep, resonant voice, and he had all the characteristics of a Shakespearian actor. From the glint in the sleuth's eyes, it looked like Cromwell assumed he had the upper hand.

"Tell me why you're here, Chief Inspector," Nick said.

Cromwell cleared his throat. "We've found the location of the masterpieces you stole from Dixon Steele. We have Charles Hamilton, a.k.a. Jackson Chase, in custody."

Kate took Nick's hand. "Has Chase implicated Nick?"

Nick felt Cromwell watching for his reaction and held his face in neutral. How the hell did Cromwell find Jackson and the paintings when he could not? Knowing Cromwell was a smooth manipulator, Nick considered the inspector might have Jackson but not the masterpieces. Knowing Jackson, he could be playing games with them both.

"No loyalty among thieves, right, McCoy?" Cromwell asked.

"Mind telling me how you found the paintings?" Nick asked.

"Chase had them secured in a hidden chamber beneath his gallery. We had evidence that one of his assistants was guilty of petty theft and drug dealing. I told the lad that we'd turn a blind eye to his crimes this time if he could reveal the location of Chase's cache of stolen and forged paintings."

Glaring at Cromwell's smug face, Nick kicked himself internally for being taken in by Jackson once again. "So, are you taking me in?"

"No," Cromwell said.

Nick regarded him warily. "Why not?"

"I prefer to offer you a deal."

"Is that so?"

"I see no point in locking up exceptional talent if we can make good use of it. I've always wondered why you chose to work on behalf of the wrong side of the law when you were a first-rate conservator and could have been a successful painter in your own right. But since learning of the significant challenges you've had in your life, I've come to some understanding of your unfortunate choices. Also, I've recently been made aware of your positive efforts and desire to change course." He glanced at Kate.

"Go on," Nick said.

Cromwell leaned forward. "Mr. McCoy, your art expertise, knowledge of art crime, and powers of persuasion amplified by your acting skills make for an impressive skill set. You'd make an ideal art crime consultant and undercover operative, and I'd like to hire you in one or both of those capacities. This would take some time to arrange, but I'll find a way to expedite a position and pay you well. A formal change in your identity would also be part of the deal. Only the people in this room will know that the notorious Phantom, a.k.a. Nick McCoy, is working for Scotland Yard." He turned to Flynn and Desi. "Is there anything either of you would like to add or modify?"

Desi and Flynn looked stunned and said, "No," in unison.

Grinning, Kate was the first to get out a complete sentence. "Thank you, Eddie. I don't see anything wrong with this deal. Do you, Nick?"

Nick shrugged. "What are the strings?"

"I'd require only that you sign a statement agreeing to give up forging and other art crimes unless such activities are in the service of Scotland Yard's Art Squad."

Nick nodded. "Fair enough. And what if I decline your generous offer?"

"Then, I suppose, you'd have to go back to watching your back, dodging, and hiding from your enemies. You'd have Steele's thugs, among others, hounding you. But you'd no longer be a priority with my department. I would file your case in cold storage."

"That's good of you. What about the fact that Jackson Chase has implicated me in stealing Steele's paintings? Aren't you obliged to arrest me?"

Cromwell chuckled. "Chase is a dealmaker, as you well know. He'll take back his finger-pointing if it's in his interests to do so. Besides, I believe Mr. Steele stole those paintings first, so I don't think the fact that you *rescued* them from him could be considered theft. Do you?" He cocked his head, half-smiling.

Nick studied Cromwell. "I'm perplexed as to why you are going out on such a professional limb for me. I fancied you wanted my head on a platter."

"Ask the lovely lady next to you. She put in a word or two. You're a fortunate man."

"Yes, I'm aware of that." He flashed Kate a grin. "To accept your offer, I would need your assurance that Steele's stolen masterpieces are returned to their rightful owners and not to Steele."

"Of course. As soon as we get the five paintings authenticated as the stolen originals, I will ensure that happens." Cromwell took out a small notebook and pen from the inside pocket of his raincoat. "Where do you think they belong?"

"Raquel Steele's father originally owned *The Blue Room* by Picasso," Nick said. "Steele essentially stole it from him. Since Raquel's parents are dead, this painting should go to Raquel's half-sister, who lives in Paris. Her name is Renée Arquette."

Eddie jotted down this information in his notebook.

"Van Gogh's *Sunflowers* belongs to London's National Gallery," Nick said. "*The Card Players* by Cézanne belongs to the Barnes Foundation in Philadelphia, and Matisse's oil sketch for the *Joy of Life* belongs to the San Francisco Museum of Modern Art. These places now exhibit my father's copies of the original paintings, which Steele stole from the well-known collector Stuart J. Whitney. Much later, Whitney unwittingly donated my father's copies to these museums."

Cromwell nodded. "And the fifth painting, Matisse's *Open Window*? I'm guessing the original belongs to the National Gallery of Art in Washington, DC. Is that correct?"

Nick hesitated, glancing at Kate, whose raised eyebrows conveyed puzzled surprise.

"That is correct," he said.

"We were told Kate has the original *Open Window*," Desi said.

"Actually, Kate has a copy," Nick said firmly. "I made two copies. One for Steele as a substitute for the original and one for myself, which I subsequently gave to Kate."

"That's good of you; I think she's earned it," Eddie said, a knowing look in his eyes. Nick sensed he didn't buy this story but was willing to let it go for Kate's sake and to secure the deal.

"What's this lot of art worth?" Flynn asked, looking from Eddie to Nick.

"About five hundred million," Nick said.

Flynn's brows arched. "That's obscene."

"Probably more, I'd guess." Eddie stood. "Well, I believe we're done." He started toward the door, Flynn and Desi behind him. "Please give me your answer in the morning. Call me at this number." He handed Nick his card. "Then, depending on your decision, we'll set up a meeting."

At the door, Eddie turned and said to Nick in a fatherly tone, "As one of my favorite authors would say, it's time to come in from the cold."

Flynn pumped Nick's hand. "Don't blow it, buddy. We make a good team."

—

Kate pushed Nick away when he tried to hug her. "Did you lie to Cromwell or me about *The Open Window*? You assured me it was a genuine Matisse. Raquel thought so, too."

He hesitated. "I lied to you, and Raquel made a mistake. She didn't know I'd made two copies."

"But why lie to me? What was the point of having me believe it was the original?"

"Sorry, love. It was a loyalty test," he said. "Possessing a multimillion-dollar painting, especially that stunning Matisse, can warp people beyond anything you've ever seen. I needed to know what you'd do, whether you'd turn on me somehow. In my world, no one plays fair; no one is trustworthy. Even loyal Raquel, who supposedly loved me and adored you, set up a clever plot to cheat me and use you."

Kate winced. "Well, have I passed your loyalty tests yet?"

"With flying colors." He grinned. "Wouldn't you rather have our *Open Window* be a copy, my copy? Otherwise, I believe you'd feel too guilty to keep it."

She gave him a wicked grin. "That would be true of Good Girl Kate, but she's long gone. It will give me added thrills, knowing it's my favorite forger's last masterpiece."

Nick clasped her hands. "I think you're also entitled to know who I am. McCoy is not my real surname."

"I've assumed that. I figured you adopted the McCoy surname as one of your wiseass jokes."

He chuckled. "Sorry to disappoint, but I never took that name as a joke. I was eleven when I borrowed the McCoy surname from my pretend grandfather, Charlie, the custodian at the National Gallery. I didn't realize then how ironic it would be for a forger to be named McCoy. The purpose of adopting a new surname was to prevent anyone from my past from finding me, especially social services and my abusive, money-grubbing guardians."

Kate nodded. "Okay, so tell me, who is the *real* McCoy?"

He cleared his throat. "Nicholas McDonagh is my real name." He paused. "In Irish, McDonagh means Brown Warrior. Sort of fits, don't you think?"

"Sure does, and you have the battle scars to prove it." Kate leaned against him. "McDonagh sounds more melodic than McCoy. You're in good company, too. It's the name of another self-taught wunderkind—Martin McDonagh, the famous Irish-Anglo playwright."

"Yes, I know," Nick said. "I've done some research. The McDonagh family has produced several generations of accomplished poets, writers, and artists."

"And you're another one of them, you and your father," Kate said.

"It's an odd feeling to think I might belong somewhere other than the forgers' gallery at The Rogues."

"Can you give it up, Nick? Can you give up Nick McCoy?" she asked.

"I never believed in Nick McCoy. He was a charade."

Kate sighed. "You're ducking the question."

He kissed her long and hard, then held her close. "Until I can give you a straight answer, just believe I love you. It's the one truth in this unholy mess."

Then, until sleep overtook them, he did his ardent best to keep Kate distracted from any more discussion of Cromwell's seductive deal.

CHAPTER 53

*I've come to the conclusion that it's not
really possible to help others.*

— Paul Cézanne —

Friday, October 26

Fear jolted Kate awake at 6:10 the next morning. In the silent emptiness of the room, she knew Nick was gone. Moving like a zombie, a profound ache in her belly, she got up and checked his belongings. He'd left his suitcase and only taken some personal items, including his three passports. She stared at the limp roses on the kitchenette counter, the vase in a puddle of shriveled petals. Had Nick chucked Eddie's remarkable offer and returned to life on the lam? Other than Nick's passionate lovemaking, which she interpreted as celebratory, he'd given her no hint of his decision. She checked her cell for messages—one from him.

"Keep a stiff upper lip, love. I have more dragons to slay."

That was it. *What was he talking about?*

When she called Eddie, she told him about Nick's last message. "What did he mean by dragons?"

"Enemies, probably. Do you know what he was wearing and exactly what he took?"

"His black tracksuit is missing. He must be wearing that and his black anorak, and he would be carrying a black backpack. He took his passports and his shaving kit."

"Passports?" Eddie muttered.

"He had three," Kate said. "That's a bad sign, isn't it? Why would he take his passports if he was planning to stay and meet with you?"

"It could be habit," he said. "A chap who's always on the run keeps more than one passport at hand. So, let's just sit tight and wait. I believe he'll make contact in some way."

For most of the day, Kate didn't dare move from the Gull's Nest. She called Eddie every hour, but he never had any new information. Then he stopped taking her calls. She thought to call Sam just to hear his voice, but she couldn't risk his hearing her panic. She had meals sent to her room, not that she ate much of them. Her cell in hand, she paced around her Victorian cage, her gut twisting. An odd comfort was the wild storm carrying on like a maniac outside, mirroring the tempest inside her.

Sometime in the afternoon, her chronic anxiety began turning to anger. How could Nick leave her with that ambiguous message? Why didn't he say he was returning if that was his plan? Damn him—she'd take off his head as soon as he walked in the door. Dear God, if only he'd walk in the door. She started to sob, terrified that the bastard was not coming back. Eddie was right. Once a con, always a con. He'd lied to her about giving up his criminal life. He was still a world-class liar addicted to forging paintings. Her therapy skills, dedication, and her love had not changed or saved him.

The storm had calmed down. Kate put on her raincoat and hat, took the umbrella, and headed for The Spotted Dog, the pub down the street, to drown her sorrow in the most effective, time-honored way.

CHAPTER 54

*There is a crack, a crack, in everything.
That's how the light gets in.*

—LEONARD COHEN—

Saturday, October 27

Kate spent a restless night, tormented by a never-ending nightmare in which she was chasing a black-clad figure through a maze of dark, rain-soaked streets. Her feet slogging through a substance like quicksand, she would fall farther and farther behind until the shadowy figure vanished in the fog. Each time she woke up in a panic and checked her phone for messages. Nothing from Eddie or anyone else.

After two cups of strong coffee and a glazed donut the next morning, she dressed and caught a taxi to Trafalgar Square. Maybe she could find comfort in revisiting the one partially happy day she and Nick had ever spent together. Since he thought of the National Gallery as his boyhood home, he might go back there to say goodbye—a childish hope, she realized. He was probably halfway to his bolt hole in the Caribbean by now. She left Eddie a message about where she was going.

The sun was coming out as she climbed the grand staircase to the gallery's entrance. The brightness lifted her spirits and made her long for the dry heat and blue skies of sunny San Diego. In the imposing entry, she nodded to the two Gainsborough Lord and Lady paintings—Nick's adopted Mum and Dad. She silently asked them, *Have you seen your boy?* Her eyes stinging, Kate quickly took pictures of them, realizing she hadn't thought to take any photos of Nick or the places they visited. She had no visual record of him or their time together. A new sense of loss gutted her. There would come a time when she wouldn't be able to recall his distinctive image.

In the octagonal Turner room, she quickly scanned the group of elderly visitors. Not surprisingly, Nick was not among them. She rushed out of this opulent room and into the gallery featuring Van Gogh's *Sunflowers*, the copy painted by Nick's father. The picture still looked genuine to her. She gave the brilliant work a thumbs up. Bravo, Mr. McDonagh. She took pictures of his sunflowers but was again disturbed by their frantic cheer.

Then Kate sensed a male presence standing next to her. He looked like a student, bespectacled and smelling of damp wool. He eyed her critically as though she was another obnoxious tourist who didn't belong here, snapping photos. As she stuffed her iPhone into her pocket, an overpowering wave of loneliness sent her racing out of the room, down the stairs, and out of the gallery.

Next stop, The Rogues. Kate walked the few blocks to the unique pub, hoping Nick was there. Hope springs eternal, even with cynics and pessimists. The place was uncrowded, and she sat at a downstairs table that gave her a view of Nick's copy of Manet's *A Bar at the Folies-Bergère*. The distinctive craft beers scented the air. She risked an upward glance at their table on the balcony. It was empty, but she could picture the two of them smiling at each other as they chatted about the pictures that enhanced the walls around them. When she spotted Toad in a Hole on the menu, tears flooded her eyes. Coming here alone had been another mistake.

She heard the door opening and glanced toward the entrance, a bud of hope sprouting within her. But the man entering the pub was not Nick. Eddie moved slowly toward her, his mouth set in a grimmer line than usual. She stood up, her cheeks hot, her pulse racing.

"Kate." He took her hands, gave them a gentle squeeze, then sat across from her. "I have news, but it's not good." He signaled the waiter. "What would you like?"

"A Caravaggio," she said.

"Ah, bitter black ale. Two of those," Eddie instructed the waiter.

"Tell me right now," Kate said when the waiter was gone.

"Brace yourself." Pause. "I'm terribly sorry to tell you that Nick was found murdered this morning."

"What!" she cried and clamped her hand over her mouth. *No! Please, you rotten God—No!* she screamed inside her head. "When? What happened?"

"Our Medical Examiner thinks he died between two and four this morning. At least his death was quick. He was shot on Albemarle Street in Mayfair, near the Hamiltons Gallery, owned by the former Jackson Chase."

"Did Jackson do it?"

"Not directly. He's still in custody. But it looks like a professional job, an execution."

"One of Steele's hired goons?"

"Or Jackson's. There are other possibilities."

"Where is he? I want to see him." Kate's eyes burned.

"I don't recommend it," Eddie said. "He's unrecognizable. He was shot in the face."

Kate shut her eyes, bile surging up in her throat. *Not my handsome Nick, No!* She held her cramping stomach and rocked for a few moments. "How did you recognize him?"

"He still had his passports and wallet on him, so it was not a robbery. There were bruises and old burn scars on his back and arms. And we found this under his shirt, tucked in his waistband." He handed her a sealed letter with her name, the hotel's address, and a stamp on the envelope.

She opened the letter with a trembling hand and began reading.

Kate love,

When you receive this letter, I'll be long gone. I am beyond sorry to disappoint you, but I cannot accept Cromwell's generous offer. First, a new identity can be penetrated by those determined to eliminate Nick McCoy. This is child's play for an art crook with Steele's connections. If I'm unmasked and thought to be alive, you and Sam will never be safe. I cannot permit that to happen. Also, I'm not cut out for a cop's life or taking orders. Cromwell was right. Once a con, always a con, even in death. So, my dearest love, this has to be goodbye. I am not the selfish bastard I used to be. I am vanishing this time for only one reason—to keep you and Sam safe.

Kate reread the letter in choked-up silence. No closing. No signature. How fitting—it's as if it was from a phantom. Maybe his explanation should provide some comfort, but it did not. Something about it seemed off. Nothing about his farewell words sounded passionate or anguished. Disappointing, to be sure, but understatement was the British way. How strange to be picking at his prose and character, considering that he'd just been ruthlessly and horrifically murdered. She must be disassociating and not yet feeling the volcanic eruption of rage and grief brewing inside her. She sensed Eddie's keen eyes watching her as she reread the letter. This time, her gaze snagged on the most ambiguous sentence.

"Listen to this, Eddie. Nick quotes you. 'Cromwell was right. Once a con, always a con, even in death.' What the devil does 'even in death' mean?"

Eddie shrugged. "Nick was not a straightforward bloke." He took her hand. "But I believe he was trying to protect you and your son. You and he can live safely now."

His remarks gave her little solace. He sounded out of touch and oddly matter of fact, given the brutality of Nick's murder.

"Kate dear, please come with Dylan and me to Angler's Mill. No canoe trip this time. We'll teach you fly fishing. I've found there's nothing like fly fishing in paradise to ease one's pain."

Kate did not respond, the phrase "even in death" replaying in her mind. Nick meant something by these powerful words. Something tricky. Her mind went blank for a few moments, and then her eyes flew wide open.

"Eddie," she cried. "You cunning old rogue. You helped Nick, didn't you? You conspired with him to fake his death."

Eddie cracked the hint of a smile. "Whatever do you mean?"

"I'm gobsmacked." She grasped his hands. "I hope your devious scheme didn't require knocking off some poor, innocent sod."

He shrugged, his face impassive.

"Unbelievable," Kate said. "Nick McCoy's last masterpiece is performance art—a fake murder— Can it be that you both have finally embraced the art of this century?"

Eddie shuddered. "Please do not associate me with that *au courant* rubbish."

"Too late, *Monsieur Le Comte*. You're a gifted performer, just like tricky Nick."

Nick McCoy né Nicholas McDonagh. Would Kate ever see her fiercely loved phantom man again? Or was she destined only to catch glimpses of him slipping around the dark corners of her mind? Maybe he'd appear in the flesh someday. Somewhere unexpected—in a magical place like through *The Open Window*. Her mind drifted to gliding on crystalline water through a tunnel of trees blazing in vibrant reds and golds. The trout dimpled the surface, the swans welcoming. Then her lips spread in a slow smile. Could she trust her intuition?

"Eddie, I accept your kind invitation. I suppose I might meet some interesting blokes fly fishing on the enchanted River Test."

ACKNOWELDGEMENTS

I wish I had the perfect words to express how thankful I am for all the help so many bighearted people have given me during the writing and publishing of *Artist, Lover, Forger, Thief.* The following expressions of gratitude may be unoriginal, but they are heartfelt.

I've been with my writing group family for over a quarter of my lifetime. At the helm is the gifted author and teacher Lisa Fugard, whose thoughtful critiques and strong encouragement helped all of us to become effective writers. This process took much courage and stamina because it forced us to face our fears and failures and grow the hell up. I am grateful to all of you for your valuable feedback, comradeship, and loyal support: Nancy Tomich, Chuck Weikert, Linnea Dayton, and Mary Frumkin who might have been my twin in another life.

I am hugely thankful to my book group of 25 years, originally a gang of neurotic headshrinkers, until we welcomed a couple of normal women to straighten us out. This group read and reviewed my novel with care and enthusiasm. Again, my thanks to all of you: Wickliffe Blasi, Lynn Corrin, Lauraine Esparza, Brenda Johnson, Charlotte Lewis, Beatrice Netter, and Sally Taylor. How I wish I could also directly thank Felise Levine, my dear friend and office partner of 15 years who died tragically in August 2023.

In addition, I am particularly grateful to Allan Mallinger, Pamela Simons, William Debolt, and soul-sister Martha Graner. They are longtime book loving friends, who have not only read and critiqued this novel, but also the unpublished prequel to *Artist, Lover, Forger, Thief*.

Special thanks go to author Linda Moore, my fellow art crime writer in San Diego who has written the prize-winning novels, *Attribution* and the recently released, *Five Days in Bogotá*. Her knowledgeable and insightful critique greatly improved my story.

To my super smart friends, Joy and Julie Tilton, I owe a ton of thanks for the inspiration to begin writing this book. In their grandparents storage chest, they found an old oil painting, a California landscape glowing through a century of grime. Was it valuable? I'd just begun my art crime research and brought the work to respected art conservator, Sarah Murray, for evaluation. She recognized the style of a famous California Impressionist. My heart started racing. Was the painting authentic or a first-rate fake? I was hooked. While forgery plots swirled in my head, Sarah taught me the techniques of conservation, many of which apply to art forging. Her contribution greatly enhanced the authenticity of my novel.

Four talented editors—Lisa Fugard, Celia Johnson, Susan Pohlman, and copy editor Dolores Jamison—are majorly responsible for whipping my early drafts into polished prose with fully developed characters and a plot that won't let the reader fall asleep. I can't thank you all enough for your brilliant editing and encouragement. And to Susan, I owe the title, *Artist, Lover, Forger, Thief*, an homage to the master of deception, John le Carré.

Even given all the above love and care, my novel might never have seen the light of day without the bold intervention of Joe Marich, an expert book and publishing consultant, and the president of Marich Media. He believed in my book, developed a brilliant marketing plan, and stormed the publishing world to find the right publisher for me. She is Sara Stratton of Redwood Digital Publishing, and I am very thankful to her dedicated team for producing such a top-quality book, strikingly enhanced by the clever cover design of Michelle Manley of Graphique Design Co.

I also want to thank the important friends who have not yet read the book but have kindly listened to me obsess about it and provided helpful input: Marianne Buncher, AnneMarie Mohler, thriller writer Jim Dutton, and Ann Boon, dedicated leader of my other fabulous book club. And not to be forgotten is my wonderful physical therapist, Bob Quintas, who keeps my body from falling apart so my mind can keep being creative. Thanks to Nate McCay's encouragement, I joined Toastmasters to defeat my life-long stage fright in order to confidently speak to audiences about my book.

Del Mar Community Connections (DMCC) deserves my undying support. This unique service organization has not only enriched my life as a board member and volunteer but given me the opportunity to support talented writers with a popular program to discuss their books. I'm especially thankful to Ashley Simpkins, the Executive Director, and Kara Adams, the Programs Director, who have helped me secure the ideal setting for launching my book.

I spent hundreds of spellbound hours researching art theft, forgery, famous forgers, and the dangerous art underworld. Two excellent books on art crime are *Hot Art* by Joshua Knelman and *The Gardner Heist* by Ulrich Boser. For understanding the complex psychology and techniques used by an art forger, I studied the autobiographies of Eric Hebborn and Thomas Keating, both famous British forgers. Of riveting interest was *The Man who Made Vermeers,* Jonathan Lopez's biography of Han van Meegeren, the greatest art forger of all time. To understand the specialized work of an art crime detective, I dove into *Priceless* by Robert Wittman, former head of the FBI Art Crime Team, and *The Rescue Artist* by Edward Dolnick. While there is no one book devoted to the ground-breaking detective work of Don Hrycyk, head of the former LAPD Art Theft Detail, many of his fascinating cases are discussed in *Hot Art.*

This novel could not have been written without the support of my husband, Michael, and my son, Colin. Devoted to their own creative projects, they understood my need to spend great gobs of time alone writing. Remarkably, they seemed able to forgive my hot love affair with art forgery by joining the intrigue. Through contributing their ideas, clever plot twists, and pithy critiques, my family of creative loners became an effective team. Colin has provided a beautiful website design, a unique second book cover for a special edition, and is managing my social media in concert with Content Dog, an expert marketing agency.

Countless drafts of every page of this book have passed under Michael's sharp-eyed scrutiny and received his invaluable criticism. In my constant war with a fiendish computer, I would have died a thousand deaths without Michael's rescue and technical prowess to bring the dragon to heel. Recalling their contributions in my behalf, I am overcome with gratitude and affection for my phenomenal partner and son who have given me so much love when I was unable to give all of mine.

ABOUT THE AUTHOR

Sheila's first foray into writing was her successful non-fiction book, *The Ways We Love*, published by Guilford Press in 2000, that explores how love relationships develop, why they fail, and how couples can regain intimacy. It has been called "groundbreaking," by her colleagues, with one adding that, "This book demonstrates that Sharpe is among the most creative and astute couples therapists of our era." Sharpe has been a therapist for more than 40 years, specializing in treating trauma, couples, and artists. Being a detective of sorts to determine patients' issues and their solutions like she does in *The Ways We Love*, along with her past history as an artist and fascination with art forgery, led to the creation of her new fiction book series, the Kate O'Dade Art Crime Novels, beginning with the thrilling first book in the series, *Artist, Lover, Forger, Thief.*

To learn more about her professional book,
The Ways We Love, find it on Amazon:
amazon.com/Ways-We-Love-Developmental-Approach-dp-1593850190/dp/1593850190

To see the paintings referenced in this book,
visit: **SheilaSharpe.com/copy-of-art-2**

To follow Sheila and stay up-to-date on the next books in her mystery thriller series, visit her website: **SheilaSharpe.com**

Printed in Great Britain
by Amazon